Praise for Anna Todd and the After series

"Todd [is] the biggest literary phenom of her generation."
—*Cosmopolitan*

"I was almost at the point like with *Twilight* that I just stop everything and my sole focus was reading the book . . . Todd, girl, you are a genius!!!"
—*Once Upon a Twilight*

"The Mr. Darcy and Lizzy Bennet of our time . . . If you looked up 'Bad Boy' in the fiction dictionary, next to it would be a picture of Hardin alongside *Beautiful Bastard* and Mr. Darcy."
—*That's Normal*

"The one thing you can count on is to *expect the unexpected.*"
—*Vilma's Book Blog*

"Anna Todd manages to make you scream, cry, laugh, fall in love, and sit in the fetal position . . . Whether you have read the Wattpad version or not, *After* is a can't-miss book—but get ready to feel emotions that you weren't sure a book could bring out of you. And if you have read the Wattpad version, the book is 10x better."
—*Fangirlish*

"A very entertaining read chock-full of drama drama drama . . . This book will have you from the first page."
—*A Bookish Escape*

"I couldn't put this book down! It went with me everywhere so I could get my Hessa fix every spare moment I had. Talk about getting hooked from page one!"
—*Grown Up Fangirl*

BOOKS BY ANNA TODD

After
After We Collided
After We Fell
After Ever Happy
Before

BEFORE

ANNA TODD

G
GALLERY BOOKS
New York London Toronto Sydney New Delhi

G

Gallery Books
An Imprint of Simon & Schuster, Inc.
1230 Avenue of the Americas
New York, NY 10020

The author is represented by Wattpad.

First Gallery Books trade paperback edition December 2015

GALLERY BOOKS and colophon are registered trademarks
of Simon & Schuster, Inc.

For information about special discounts for bulk purchases,
please contact Simon & Schuster Special Sales at 1-866-506-1949
or business@simonandschuster.com.

The Simon & Schuster Speakers Bureau can bring authors
to your live event. For more information or to book an event,
contact the Simon & Schuster Speakers Bureau at 1-866-248-3049
or visit our website at www.simonspeakers.com.

Manufactured in the United States of America

20 19 18 17 16 15 14 13 12 11

Library of Congress Cataloging-in-Publication Data is available.

ISBN 978-1-5011-3070-0
ISBN 978-1-5011-3069-4 (ebook)

To all of my brilliant readers,
who inspire me more than they will ever know

Hessa Playlist:

"Never Say Never" by *The Fray*
"Demons" by *Imagine Dragons*
"Poison & Wine" by *The Civil Wars*
"I'm a Mess" by *Ed Sheeran*
"Robbers" by *The 1975*
"Change Your Ticket" by *One Direction*
"The Hills" by *The Weeknd*
"In My Veins" by *Andrew Bollo*
"Endlessly" by *The Cab*
"Colors" by *Halsey*
"Beautiful Disaster" by *Kelly Clarkson*
"Let Her Go" by *Passenger*
"Say Something" by *A Great Big World, ft. Christina Aguilera*
"All You Ever" by *Hunter Hayes*
"Blood Bank" by *Bon Iver*
"Night Changes" by *One Direction*
"A Drop in the Ocean" by *Ron Pope*
"Heartbreak Warfare" by *John Mayer*
"Beautiful Disaster" by *Jon McLaughlin*
"Through the Dark" by *One Direction*
"Shiver" by *Coldplay*
"All I Want" by *Kodaline*
"Breathe Me" by *Sia*

part one

BEFORE

When he was little, the boy used to dream of who he would grow up to be.

Maybe a policeman, or a teacher. Mummy's friend Vance read books for a job, and that seemed fun. But the boy wasn't sure of his own capabilities—he had no talents. He couldn't sing like the kid in his class Joss; he couldn't add and subtract long numbers like Angela; he could barely speak in front of his classmates, unlike funny, loudmouthed Calvin. The only thing he liked to do was read page after page of his books. He waited for Vance to bring them by: one a week, sometimes more, sometimes less. There were periods when the man wouldn't show and he would grow bored, rereading the same torn pages of his favorites. But he learned to trust that the kind man would always come back, book in hand. The boy grew taller, grew smarter, an inch and a new book every two weeks, it seemed.

His parents were changing with the seasons. His dad grew louder, sloppier, and his mum grew more and more tired, her sobs filling the night, louder and louder. The smell of tobacco and worse began to fill the walls of the small house. As sure as the dishes overflowing the sink was the smell of scotch on his dad's breath. As the months went on, he would sometimes forget what his dad looked like altogether.

Vance came around more, and he barely noticed when his mum's sobs changed in the night. He had made friends at this point. Well, one friend. The friend moved away, and he himself never bothered to make new friends. He felt like he didn't need them. He didn't mind being alone.

The men who came that night changed something deep within the boy. What he saw happen to his mum made him harden, and he grew angrier as his dad became a stranger. Soon after, his dad stopped stumbling into the small, filthy house at all. He was gone, and the boy was relieved. No more scotch, no more broken furniture or holes in the walls. The only thing he left behind was a boy without a dad and a living room full of half-empty packs of cigarettes.

The boy hated the taste the cigarettes left, but loved the way the smoke filled his lungs, stealing his breath. He found himself smoking every single one, and then he bought more. He made friends, if you could call a group of rebels and delinquents who caused more trouble than they were worth friends. He began to stay out late, and the little white lies and harmless pranks the group of angry boys would play began turning into more serious crimes. They turned into something darker, something that they all knew was wrong—the deepest level of wrong—but they thought they were just having fun. They were entitled and couldn't deny the adrenaline rush that came with the power they felt. After each innocence they stole, their veins pulsed with more arrogance, more hunger, fewer boundaries.

This boy was the softest one still among them, but he had lost the conscience that once made him dream of becoming a fireman or a teacher. The relationship to women he was developing wasn't typical. He craved their touch, but shielded himself against any type of emotional connection. This included his mum, to whom he stopped saying even a simple "I love you." He barely saw her anyway. He spent almost all his time running the streets, and the house came to mean nothing to him except for the place where the packages occasionally arrived. An address from Washington state was scribbled under Vance's name on these packages.

Vance had left him, too.

Girls paid attention to the boy. They latched on to him, long nails digging crescents into his arms as he lied to them, kissed them, fucked them. After sex, most of the girls would try to wrap their arms around him. He would brush them off, placing no kisses or soft caresses to their skin. Most of the time he was gone before they caught their breath. He spent his days high, his nights higher. Hanging out in the alley behind the liquor store or in Mark's dad's shop, wasting life away. Breaking into liquor stores, making unforgivable home videos, humiliating naive girls. He had ceased being able to feel any kind of emotion outside of arrogance and anger.

Finally, his mum had had enough. She no longer had the funds or the patience to deal with his destructive behavior. His dad had been offered a university job in the United States. Washington, to be exact. The same state as Vance, the same city, even. The good man and the bad man together in the same place again.

His mum didn't think he could overhear her speaking to his dad about shipping him off there. Apparently the old man had cleaned up some, though the boy wasn't quite sure. He'd never be sure. His dad had a girlfriend, too, a nice woman who the boy was envious of. She got to see the benefits of the new side of him. She got to share sober meals and kind words that he never got the chance to hear.

When he arrived at the university, he moved into a frat house, out of spite against the old man. But although he didn't like the place, moving his boxes into the decent-sized room that would be his, he felt a slight twinge of relief. The room was twice the size that his room in Hampstead had been. It had no holes in the walls; there were no bugs crawling up the sinks in the bathroom. He finally had a place to put all of his books.

At first, he kept to himself, not bothering to make any friends. His crowd came together slowly, and with it he fell into the same dark pattern.

He met the virtual twin of Mark, all the way over in America, making him start to think this was the way the world was just supposed to be. He began to accept that he would always be alone. He was good at hurting people, at causing mischief. He hurt another girl, like the one before, and he felt that same storm coursing up and down his spine, fighting to destroy his life with its wild energy. He began drinking the way his dad did, being the worst type of hypocrite.

He didn't care, though; he was numb and he had friends and they helped him ignore the fact that he didn't have anything real in his life.

Nothing really mattered.

Not even the girls who tried to get through to him.

Natalie

When he met the blue-eyed girl with dark hair, he knew she was there to test him in new ways. She was kind, the gentlest spirit he had met so far . . . and she was infatuated with him.

He took the naive girl from her tidy, unblemished world and swept her into a dustpan, then scattered her across a dark and unforgiving world that was completely unfamiliar to her. His callousness made her an outcast, exiled from her church first, then from her family. The gossip was harsh, the whispers traveling from one judgmental Bible-clutching woman to another. Her family wasn't any better. She had no one, and she made the mistake of trusting him to be more than he was capable of being.

What he did to her was the last straw for his mother. Shipping him to America, to the state of Washington, to be with his would-be father, his treatment of Natalie got him exiled from his London homeland. The loneliness he'd felt all along was finally achieved in real life.

The church is packed today, rows and rows of us, all joined together to worship on a hot July afternoon. Every week, usually the same people, all of whom I can call by their first and last names.

My family lives like royalty here in one of Jesus's smallest venues.

My younger sister, Cecily, is sitting next to me in the very front row, her small hands picking at the chipped wooden pew. Our church has just received a grant to renovate some of the interior, and our youth group has been helping gather the supplies donated by the local community. This week, our task is to obtain paint from locals and paint these pews over. I've been spending my evenings going from one hardware store to another, asking for donations.

As if to underscore the futility I feel about this task, I hear a faint snapping sound and look over to see that Cecily has broken off a small piece of wood from her seat. Her fingernails are painted pink to match the bow in her dark brown hair, but boy, can she be destructive.

"Cecily, we're fixing these next week. Please don't." I gently take her small hands in mine, and she pouts just a little. "You can help paint them to make them beautiful again. You would like that, wouldn't you?" I smile at her. She smiles back, an adorable missing-teeth smile, and nods her head. Her curls move with her, making my mum proud of her work with the iron this morning.

The pastor is almost finished with his sermon, and my parents are holding hands, staring toward the front of the small church. Sweat has been gathering on my neck, rolling in sticky drops down my back as words about sinning and suffering float around my head. It's so hot in here that my mum's makeup has started to shine down her neck and smear black rings around her eyes. This should be the last week without air-conditioning we have to suffer through. Or it better be; even I might feign illness to avoid this sweltering place if it's not.

At the end of service, my mum stands to talk to the pastor's wife. My mum admires that woman a lot—a little too much, if you ask me. Pauline, the first lady of our church, is a tough woman, with little empathy for others, so really I get why my mum would be drawn to her.

I wave to Thomas, the only boy my age who's in the Youth

Group. As he walks by, he and his entire family, following the line of people exiting the church, wave back to me. Ready to get some fresh air, I stand and wipe my hands on my pale blue dress.

"Can you take Cecily to the car?" my dad asks with a knowing smile.

He's going to try to get my mum to stop talking, just like every Sunday. She's one of those women who chat and chat after saying goodbye a minimum of three times.

I didn't take after her in that way. Instead, I strive to take after my dad, whose few words usually hold a lifetime's worth of meaning. And I know my dad loves how much of himself has been passed down to me, from his quiet demeanor, to his dark hair and pale blue eyes (the most obvious traits), to our height. Or lack of height. The pair of us barely stand five and a half feet, though he's ever so slightly taller than me. Cecily will surpass both of us by age ten, my mum teases us.

I nod to my dad and take my sister's hand. She walks quicker than me, the excitement of youth causing her to rush straight through the remainder of the small crowd. I want to pull her back, but she turns back to me with the biggest smile on her face, and I can't bring myself to do anything but run with her. We break into a sprint, rushing down the stairs and onto the lawn. Cecily dodges an elderly couple, and I laugh when she shrieks and barely misses knocking down Tyler Kenton, the meanest boy in our church. The sun is bright and the air is thick in my lungs and I run faster and faster, chasing after her until she tumbles onto the grass. I drop down to my knees to check on her. I lean in and brush the hair back from her face. Little pools of tears are threatening to burst, and her bottom lip is trembling fiercely.

"My dress . . ." She pats her small hands on her white dress, focusing on the grass stains on the fabric. "It's ruined!" She buries her face in her dirty hands, and I reach for them, pulling them down to her lap.

I smile and speak softly. "It's not ruined. It can be washed, darling."

I swipe my thumb across the tear trying to roll down her cheek. She sniffles, not ready to believe me.

"It happens all the time; it's happened to me at least thirty times," I assure her, even though it's a lie.

The corners of her mouth turn upward, and she fights a smile. "Has not." She calls me out for my fib. I wrap my arm around her and pull her up to stand. My eyes glance over her pale arms to make sure I didn't miss anything. All clear. I keep my arm around her as we walk across the churchyard toward the parking lot. My parents are approaching us from that direction, my dad having finally gotten Mum to stop gossiping.

During the drive home, I sit in the backseat with Cecily, drawing little butterflies in her favorite coloring book while my dad talks to my mum about the raccoon problem we've been having in our bins out back. My dad leaves the car running when he parks in the driveway. Cecily gives me a quick kiss on the cheek and climbs out of the backseat. I follow her and hug my mum and get a peck on the cheek from my dad before I step into the driver's seat.

My dad looks down at me. "Be careful now, Junebug. There are a lot of people out today with the sun." He lifts his hand to shade his squinted eyes. It's the sunniest day Hampstead has had in quite a while. We've had the heat, but no sun. I nod and promise my dad that I'll be safe.

I wait until I'm out of the neighborhood to change the radio station. I turn the volume up and sing along to every song on my way to the center of the city. My goal is to get three buckets of paint from all the three shops I'm visiting. I'll be happy with one from each, but my goal is to get three so we have enough to cover everything.

The first shop, Mark's Paint and Supply, is known for being the cheapest in town. Mark, the owner, has a really good reputation in our area, and I'm delighted to meet him. I park in the nearly empty lot; only a classic-style car painted candy-apple red and a minivan are parked in the entire lot. The building is old, made out of wooden planks and unstable drywall. The sign is crooked, the *M* barely legible. When I open the wooden door, it creaks and a bell sounds. A cat jumps down from a cardboard box and lands on its feet in front of me. I pet the fur ball for a moment before making my way to the register.

The inside of the shop is just as untidy as the outside, and what with all the clutter, I can't see the boy behind the register when I first approach. His presence there shocks me a little. He's tall and broad-shouldered; he looks like the kind of boy who's played sports for years.

"Mark . . ." I say, stumbling to remember his last name. Everyone just calls him Mark.

"I'm Mark," a voice behind the athletic-looking boy says. Bending to the side a little, I notice another boy, sitting in a chair behind the desk, dressed in all black. His frame is much leaner than the first, and yet the presence he exudes is somehow larger than the other boy's. His hair is dark, grown down the sides, leaving a swoop of hair across his forehead. His arms have tattoos on them, randomly scattered black ink patches in a sea of tan skin.

It's not really my thing, but instead of being critical of him, all I can think is how everyone has a tan this summer except me.

"He's not, I am," a third voice says. Looking to the other side of the first boy, I find a kid of average height, thin build, with a very tight buzz cut. "I'm Mark *Junior*, though. If you're looking for my old man, he's not here today."

The third boy has a few tattoos as well, though they're more organized than the wild-haired boy's, and he has a piercing in his

eyebrow. I remember asking my family about getting my belly button pierced, and still to this day I have to laugh when I remember
their horrified reactions.

"He's the better of the two Marks," the wild-haired boy in-
tones, his voice deep and slow. He smiles, and two deep, beautiful dimples cut through his cheeks.

I laugh, suspecting this is not even close to the truth. "I
somehow doubt that," I tease. They all laugh along, and Mark Jr.
steps closer, a smile on his lips.

The boy in the chair stands up. He's so tall his presence is
magnified even further. He comes forward and towers over me.
He's attractive; his face is strong. A sharp jawline, dark lashes, full
brows. His nose is slender and his lips are a light pink. I stare at
him and he stares at me.

"Are you looking for my dad for a reason?" Mark asks.

When I don't immediately respond, Mark and the athlete
both look back and forth between me and their friend.

Snapping back to the moment, and a little embarrassed to
be caught staring, I begin my spiel. "I'm here from Hempstead
Baptist and was wondering if you would like to donate paint or
supplies to us. We're remodeling our church and are in need of
donations . . ."

I stop because the charming one with the pink lips is deep
in discussion, whispering with his friends in a voice that is too
low for me to hear. Then they stop, and the boys stare at me all at
once, three smiles in a row.

Mark speaks first. "We can absolutely do that for you," he
says.

His smile reminds me of a feline of sorts. I can't quite put my
finger on why. I smile back and begin to thank him.

He turns to his friend with the giant ship tattooed on his bi-
ceps. "Hardin, how many cans are over there?"

Hardin? What a very strange name; I've never heard it before.

This Hardin's black shirtsleeves barely cover the bottom half of the wooden ship. It's nicely done; the detail and shading are attractively rendered. When I look up at his face, stopping for a beat on his lips, I can feel my cheeks get hot. He's staring right at me, noticing my intense scrutiny of his face. I see Mark and Hardin make eye contact but miss what Mark mouths to him.

"How about a proposition?" Mark says, nodding toward Hardin.

I'm interested in hearing this. This Hardin seems funny—a little off, but I like him so far. "And what's that?" I wrap my finger into the ends of my hair and wait. Hardin is still staring back at me. There's something about him that's guarded. I can sense it from across the small shop. I find myself very curious about this boy who's trying awfully hard to look so tough. I cringe imagining what my parents would think, how they would react to me bringing him to our home. My mum thinks tattoos are evil, but I don't know. They're not entirely my thing, but I feel like they can be a form of self-expression, and there's undoubtedly always beauty in that.

Mark scratches his smooth jaw. "If you go out on two dates with my friend Hardin here, I'll give you ten gallons of paint."

I look over to Hardin, who's eyeing me with a smirk playing at the corners of his lips. Lips that are so pretty. His slightly feminine features make him more attractive than his black clothing or messy hair. I wonder if this is what they're whispering about. Hardin liking me?

While I consider the idea, Mark ups the ante: "Any color. Any finish of your choice. On the house. Ten gallons."

He's a good salesman.

I click my tongue against the roof of my mouth. "One date," I counter.

Hardin laughs; the lump in his throat moves with his laugh, and his dimples crease in his cheeks. Okay, he's very, very hot. I can't believe I didn't notice just how hot he was when I first arrived. I was so focused on getting the paint that I barely noticed how green his eyes are under the fluorescent lights of the paint shop.

"One date works." Hardin shoves his hand into his pocket, and Mark looks at the buzz-cut gentleman.

Feeling quite victorious at the success of my little haggling, I smile and list the colors I need for the pews, the walls, the stairs, all the while pretending that I'm not already anticipating my date with Hardin, the guarded, messy-haired boy who's so innocent and shy that he's willing to trade ten gallons of paint for one date.

Molly

His mum told him stories about dangerous girls when he was a boy. The meaner a girl is to you, the farther she runs from you, the more she likes you. You should pursue her, young boys are taught.

What those pushy boys grow up to find is that most of the time, when a girl doesn't like you, she simply just doesn't like you. The girl grew up without a woman to show her how to be. Her mum dreamed of a fast life, bigger than she herself could offer, and the girl learned how men were supposed to behave by observing the actions of those around her.

As the girl grew up, she quickly caught on to the game and became a master player.

I pull my dress down as I turn the dark corner to enter the alleyway. I hear the mesh fabric rip as I tug it, and I curse at myself for doing this again.

I'd taken the train to downtown hoping to accomplish . . . *something*.

What, I'm not entirely sure, but I'm so, so tired of feeling like this. Emptiness can make you behave in ways you could never imagine, and this is the only way to satisfy the giant fucking hole inside of me. The satisfaction comes and goes as the men ogle me. They feel entitled to my body since I dress in a way that purposely entices them. They are disgusting and entirely wrong, but I play into their lust, encouraging their behavior with a wink of my eye. A shy smile at a lonely man goes a long way.

Needing this attention makes me sick to my stomach. It's more than an ache; it's a scalding white-hot burn inside of me.

As I turn another corner, a black car approaches, and I glance away as the man behind the wheel slows down to look at me. The streets are dark, and this zigzag alley is located behind one of the richest parts of Philadelphia. Shops line the streets, each of them having their own back dock here.

There's too much money and not enough pleasantness in the Main Line.

"You want to go for a ride?" the man asks as his automatic window rolls down with a smooth whir. His face is slightly wrinkled, and his sandy-brown-and-gray hair is neatly parted and combed down on the sides. His smile is charming, and he looks good for his age, but there's a warning that sounds in my mind each and every weekend that I take this walk, follow this zombie routine for some unknowable reason. The faux kindness in his smile is just that, as fake as my "Chanel" bag. His smile comes from money; I know this by now. Men with black cars that are so clean they shine under the moonlight have money but no conscience. Their wives haven't fucked them in weeks—months, even—and they search the streets for the attention they've been deprived of.

But I don't want his money. My parents have that, too much of it.

"I'm not a prostitute, you sick fuck!" I kick my platform boot at his stupid shiny car and notice the gleam of a band on one finger.

His eyes follow mine, and he tucks his hand under the steering wheel. Douchebag.

"Nice try. Go home to your wife—I'm sure whatever excuse you've given her is set to expire."

I begin to walk away, and he says something else to me. The distance catches the sound, carrying it away into the night, no doubt to some dark corner. I don't bother looking back at him.

The road is nearly empty since it's after nine on a Monday night. The lights on the backs of the buildings are dim, the air calm and quiet. I pass behind a restaurant where steam billows from the roof, and the smell of charcoal fills my senses. It smells amazing and reminds me of backyard barbecues we'd have with Curtis's family when I was younger. Back when they felt like a second family.

I blink the thoughts away and return the smile of a middle-aged woman wearing an apron and a chef's hat walking out of the back entrance of a restaurant. The flame from her lighter is bright in the night. She takes a drag from the cigarette in her hand, and I smile again.

"Be careful out here, girl," her raspy voice warns.

"Always am," I reply with a smile and a wave of my hand. She shakes her head and puts the cigarette back to her lips. The smoke fills the cold air, and the red fire at the end of the cigarette makes a crackling noise in the night's silence before she tosses it to the concrete and loudly stomps on it.

I continue walking, and the air grows colder. Another car passes, and I move to the side of the alley. The car is black . . . I look again and realize it's the same shiny black as the last one. A chill runs cold down my back as it slows, tires crunching on the trash covering the alley.

I walk faster, choosing to step behind a Dumpster to gain as much distance from the stranger as possible. My feet pick up the pace and I walk a little farther.

I don't know why I'm so paranoid tonight; I do this nearly every weekend. I dress in a hideous smock, kiss my dad on the cheek, and ask him for train fare. He frowns and tells me that I spend too much time alone and that I have to move on in the world before life passes me by. If moving on were so simple, I wouldn't be doing this quick change into this dress or shoving the smock into my purse to put back on during the ride home.

Move on. As if it were so simple.

"Molly, you're only seventeen; you have to get back to real life before you've missed too much of the best years of your life," he tells me each time.

If these are the best years of my life, I don't see much point in living any longer than this.

I always nod, agreeing with him with a smile while silently wishing he would stop comparing his loss to mine. The difference is, my mom wanted to leave.

Tonight feels different somehow, maybe because the same man is now stopping next to me for the second time in twenty minutes.

I break into a run, letting my fear carry me down the pothole-filled street to the busier road up ahead. A cab honks at me when I stumble into the street and jump back to the sidewalk, trying to catch my breath.

I need to go home. Now. My chest catches fire, and I struggle to breathe in the cold air. I step back onto the sidewalk and look in every direction.

"Molly? Molly Samuels, is that you?" a woman's voice shouts from behind me.

I turn around and see the familiar face of the last person I want to run into. I fight the need to bolt in the other direction when my eyes meet hers. She has a brown grocery bag in each hand as she walks toward me.

"What are you doing out here, and this late?" Mrs. Garrett asks as a chunk of hair falls down over her cheek.

"Just walking." I try to push my dress down my thighs before she looks again.

"Alone?"

"You're alone, too," I say, my tone more than defensive.

She sighs and shuffles the grocery bags to one arm. "Come on, get in the car." She starts toward the brown van parked on the corner.

With the click of a button, the passenger-side door unlocks, and I step inside hesitantly. I would rather be inside this car with her and her judgment than out on the street with the guy in the black car who doesn't seem to take no for an answer.

My temporary savior gets into the driver's side and looks straight ahead for a minute before turning to me. "You know you can't act out like this for the rest of your life." Her statement ends in a strong tone, but her hands are shaking on the wheel.

"I'm not—"

"Don't act like nothing has happened." Her response lets me know that she isn't in the mood to dance around social niceties. "You're dressed completely different than you used to, certainly different than your father would probably approve of. Your hair is pink—nowhere near its natural blond. You're out here at night, walking alone. I'm not the only one who noticed you, you know. John, who goes to my church, saw you the other night. He told us in front of everyone."

"I—"

She waves her hand at my protest. "I'm not finished. Your dad told me you aren't even going to Ohio State now, in spite of all those years of you and Curtis preparing to go together."

The name coming from her lips slices through me, breaking away at some hard shell I've gotten used to inhabiting. The thick nothingness I've been guarding myself with. Her son's face covers my mind, and his voice fills my ears.

"Stop," I manage to say through my pain.

"No, Molly," Mrs. Garrett says.

When I look over at her, she's flustered, like she has bottles upon bottles of emotions inside of her that have been shaken over the last six months and now are within an inch of exploding.

"He was my *son*," she says. "So don't you sit here and act like you have more of a reason to be hurt than me. I lost a child—my only child—and now I'm sitting here watching you, sweet Molly, who I've watched grow up, get lost, too—and I'm not going to be quiet anymore. You need to get your butt into college, get out of this town just like you and Curtis planned on. Get on with *life*. It's what we all have to do. And if I can do it, hard as it is, you sure as hell can, too."

When Mrs. Garrett stops talking, I feel like she's spent the last two minutes tying my stomach into knots. She has always been a quiet woman—her husband has always done most of the talking—but in the span of five minutes she's become less fragile somehow. Her usually soft voice has taken on a new tone of determination, and she impresses me. Makes me feel heartbroken, too, at the fact that I've let my life turn into this ghoulish existence.

But I was driving that car.

I agreed to drive Curtis's small truck the night before I got my license. We were excited, and his smile was persuasive. I loved him with every thread of my body, and when he died, I came unstitched. He was my calmness, my reassurance that I wouldn't end up like my mother, a woman who lived and breathed to be more than someone's wife in a big house, in a rich neighborhood. She spent her days painting and dancing in our big house, singing songs and promising me that we would make it out of the cookie-cutter town.

"We won't die here—I'll convince your father someday," she always said.

She only held up half of the deal and left in the middle of the night two years ago. She couldn't cope with the shame that apparently came from being a mother and a wife. Most women would have trouble finding shame in that, but not my mom. She wanted all the attention on her—she needed people to know her name. She blamed me when they didn't, even though she tried to deny the fact. She was always ashamed of me; she constantly reminded me of what I did to her body. She told me—many times—how her body looked so good before I came around. She acted as if I chose to be placed there, inside this selfish woman's womb. One time she showed me the marks I made on her stomach, and I cringed right alongside her at the sight of her shredded skin.

Despite me hindering her lifestyle, she promised me the world. She told me about bigger, brighter cities with giant billboards that she wished she was pretty enough to be on.

And early one morning, having listened to her tell me about the world she wanted the night before, I watched her through the staircase's thick metal banister as she dragged her suitcase across the carpet toward the front door. She cursed and flipped her hair off her shoulders. Dressed like she was going to a job interview, she had full makeup, blow-dried hair—she must have used half a can of hairspray to get it to look that way. She was excited and confident as she touched her hair to adjust it slightly.

Just before she walked out the door, she looked around her beautifully decorated living room, and her face filled with the biggest smile I had ever seen on her. Then she closed the door, and I could imagine her happily leaning against it outside, still smiling like she was going to paradise.

I didn't cry as I tiptoed down the stairs, trying to memorize how she looked and acted. I wanted to remember every interaction, every talk, every hug we shared. I realized even then that my life was changing again. I watched through the living room window as she got into a cab. I just stared at the driveway. I guess I always knew she wasn't reliable. My father might be afraid to leave the town he grew up in, where he has an amazing job, but he's fucking reliable.

Mrs. Garrett touches the tips of my pink hair with a cautious finger. "Dipping your head in pink food coloring won't change anything that happened."

I smile at her choice of words and say the first thing that comes to mind. "I didn't dye my hair because I watched your son bleed out in front of me," I snap, remembering the way the deep pink dye resembled blood as I rinsed it down the drain.

I push her hand away, and, yeah, my words are harsh, *but who the fuck is she to judge me?*

As she takes in what I said, I'm sure she's picturing Curtis's mangled body, the one I sat with for two hours before anyone came to help us. I tried to rip his seat belt from the driver's seat, to no avail. The way the metal bent when we hit the rail made it impossible to move my arms. I tried, though, and I screamed as the jagged metal tore into my skin. My love wasn't moving, he wasn't making a sound, and I screamed at him, at the car, at the entire universe as I struggled to save us.

A universe that betrayed me and went dark as his face paled and his arms went slack. I thank it now, grateful that my body shut off just after he died and I wasn't forced to sit and watch the thing that was no longer him, watch and hope that he would somehow come back to life.

With a soft sigh, Mrs. Garrett starts the car and pulls out. "I understand your pain, Molly . . . if anyone understands, it's me. I've been trying to find a way to continue with my life, too, but you're ruining yours over something you had no control over."

I'm baffled and try to focus by running one hand over the plastic of the car door. "No control? I was driving the car." The sound of twisted metal colliding with a tree and then a metal barrier floods my ears, and I feel my hands shaking on my lap. "I was in control of his life, and I killed him."

He was life, the very definition of it. He was bright and warm and loved everything. Curtis could find joy in the most stupid, most simple things. I wasn't like him. I was more cynical, especially after my mom left. But he listened to me every time my anger fueled a mistake. On his birthday he helped my dad clean up my mom's painting room after I'd trashed it by splattering black paint across the precious paintings she'd left for us. He didn't ask me why I wished her dead on more than one occasion.

He never judged me, and he held me together in a way that I couldn't do myself. I always thought he would be the reason I made it through college or made any friends in a new city. I was never good at hiding what I thought of people, so it wasn't the easiest thing in the world for me to make friends. He always told me it was fine, I was fine the way I was, that I was just too painfully honest and he would have to be the one who took the role of liar in our relationship. He would pretend to like the pretentious, sweater-tied-around-their waists rich kids at our school. He was always the nice one, the one who everyone loved. I was his plus-one. We were together so much that everyone began to accept me and my attitude. He made up for it, I suppose, with his charm. He was my excuse to the world, because apparently he saw something in me. He was the only person who would ever accept me and love me, but then he left me, too. It was my fault, just like I'm sure my mom left because she was tired of that town, of my dad's normalcy, and of her blond daughter with the bow in her hair.

The last ounce of my need to pretend to be normal was gone as the sink turned pink and my blond disappeared.

"I have a friend with some clout out west in Washington."

I had almost forgotten where I was, my mind reliving every shitty experience in my life in less than ten minutes.

"I could ask him if he could pull some strings and get you into a good school there. It's pretty out there. Refreshing, green. It's late in the year now, but I will try it if you're willing," she offers.

Washington? What the hell is in Washington?

I consider her offer, mulling over whether or not I even *want* to go to college anymore. And as that question spins through me, I realize that I *do* want to get out of this God-awful town, so maybe I should agree. I used to think about other cities when I was younger. My mom talked about Los Angeles and how the weather made for a perfect day every single day. She talked of New York and the way the streets are full of people. She told me about the glamorous cities she wanted to live in. If she could handle those cities, I have to be able to handle Washington.

But it's far, across the entire country. My dad would be alone here . . . though maybe that would be good for him. He barely has any friends anymore because he's always so worried about me, trying to get me to be happy. He's given up even attempting to worry about his own life. Maybe me going away to college would help him. Maybe it would restore some sense of normalcy.

It's possible that I could make friends, too. My pink hair might not be so intimidating to people in a town with some sophistication. My revealing clothing might not be so threatening to the girls my age in another city.

I could start over and make Mrs. Garrett proud.

I could give Curtis something to be proud of, too.

Washington could be just what the witch doctor ordered.

And so sitting in this woman's car, this kind mother to the boy I loved and lost, I vow, right now, that I'm going to do better.

I won't take trains to shady parts of town in Washington.

I won't wallow in the past.

I won't give up on myself.

I'll only do things that will help my future—and I won't give a shit what anyone says along the way.

Melissa

He underestimated the girl when he first met her. He didn't know anything about her then, and still to this day he doesn't really know much. He met her brother first and spent nights getting drunk with him, getting to know him and learning just what a terrible person the guy was. Her brother was a snake, slithering through the campus like it was his personal hunting ground, picking and choosing his prey.

But through constant observation he saw that this snake had one weakness: his sister, who was a force, tall with jet-black hair and tan skin. As he grew to hate the snake, he noticed just how tender this weakness was, how he would hover over the girl like there was nothing else on earth of importance—other than his own devious desires, of course. And convincing himself that the snake was getting out of hand, that he was spreading his filth like a proud pestilence that had to be stopped, the boy formed a plan.

This filth had to be knocked down, and his sister was nothing but a causality of war.

The house is so empty for a Friday night. My dad is at a banquet for his promotion at the hospital, and all of my friends are at another party. Neither option sounds appealing.

The party would be okay if it weren't at the fraternity house my brother always hangs out at. I can't even enjoy myself there because he's so protective of me. It's so frustrating.

The banquet may be a better option, but only marginally. My

dad, the most prestigious doctor in this town, is a better doctor than parent . . . but he tries. His time is precious and expensive, and I can't compete with sick people whose medical bills bought this massive house I'm currently sitting around complaining in.

Feeling a little guilty, I grab my phone to text my dad that I'm coming after all. Then, noticing it's past nine, with the banquet having started at eight, I realize I'll just be an interruption and give my dad's young girlfriend more of a reason to complain about me. Tasha is only three years older than me and has been seeing my dad for over a year now. I would be a little more understanding if I hadn't gone to high school with her and didn't remember how bitchy she was. Or if she didn't act like she doesn't remember me even though I know damn well she does.

No matter how rude she is to me, I don't complain to my dad about her. She makes him happy. She smiles when he looks at her. She laughs at his corny jokes. I know she doesn't care about him the way she should, but I've seen my dad transform into a better version of himself since she came into his office with a broken finger and perky boobs. My dad took the divorce much harder than did my mom, who quickly revealed that she was moving back to Mexico to live with my grandparents until she got on her own feet.

I don't know who she thinks she's fooling. She was awarded enough money in the settlement to afford a lifetime's worth of glass slippers.

Instead of bothering Tasha and my dad, I text Dan. He's been dating a girl I went to high school with. She, unlike me, is still *in* high school. My brother is protective and loyal to a fault, but he's a total pig. Let me repeat: a *total* pig. I try my best to stay out of his dating games. His friends are pigs too, usually younger and even worse than him. He likes to surround himself with people who are just as shitty as him, so he can feel better about himself. He wants to be the king of the rats, I suppose.

Dan responds rapidly, I'll pick you up in twenty.

I send back a smiley face and jump out of my bed to get ready. My bare face and gray WCU T-shirt won't do. I should look better than that. Still, I have to be somewhat careful with my out-fit choice if I don't want to hear my brother bitch all night.

I rummage through my closet, searching through the sea of black and sequins. I have too many dresses. My mom always gave me her dresses after she wore them once. My dad liked to try to make her happy with shiny dresses and a red sports car, but somehow her happiness never arrived. When she was leaving, she gave me the option of moving back to Mexico with her. But, funny as it might sound, I just couldn't give up swimming or my swim team. It's more important to me than anything else here in Washington. It was the only thing—outside of my dad and Dan—that I would miss. Dan considered moving back, but he didn't want to leave me here. Or *couldn't*, given the constant eye he keeps on me.

After trying on two dresses and then throwing them back into my closet, I pull out a jumpsuit I haven't worn yet. It's all black except for some small print on the thick shoulder straps. It's tight enough to show off my butt, casual enough to wear to the party, and covers enough of my body for my brother to keep his mouth closed.

Just as I finish getting ready, Dan's obnoxious horn blows outside, and I grab my purse and rush down the stairs. If I don't hurry, the neighbors will complain about the noise again. I quickly set the security code and bolt out the door, and when I reach Dan's Audi, I realize he's brought a couple of his dudebro friends along.

"Logan, let her in the front," Dan says.

I've been around Logan a handful of times, and he's always been nice to me. He hit on me once at some party. When I stood up from the couch I was on, and he realized that I'm at least four

inches taller than him, he said we would make great friends. I
laughed in agreement, impressed by his gentle teasing. Since
then, he's become my favorite of my brother's band of idiots.

"It's fine. I'll just get in the back," I say when Logan unbuck-
les his seat belt. I climb into the backseat to find a guy with dark,
wavy hair hiding his face. It's swept to the side in a weird emo
way, but it matches perfectly with the piercings in his eyebrow
and lip. He doesn't look up from his phone when I sit down or
when I say hi.

"Ignore him," Dan says, meeting my eyes in the rearview
mirror.

Rolling my eyes, I pull out my own phone. Might as well entertain myself during the drive.

At the frat house, there's nowhere to park. Dan offers to drop
me at the house so I don't have to walk. I pop out, but after I
close my door, I hear the other door close too. Looking up, I see
the guy from the backseat walking toward the house.

"Fucker!" Dan yells to him.

The stranger lifts his hand into the air, middle finger raised.

"I'm pretty sure he'd rather you walk with them," I tell him,
following him up the lawn. A group of girls stare at him as we
walk by; one of them whispers something to another and they all
look at me.

"You got a problem?" I ask them, meeting their dolled-up,
desperate faces. All three of them shake their heads in a way that
says they didn't expect me to call them out.

Well, they were wrong. I don't react kindly to prissy blonds
who talk about other people to make themselves feel important.

"They probably just pissed their pants," the wavy-haired guy
says to me. His voice is deep, so deep, and I swear I heard an English accent. He slows down his pace but doesn't turn around to
look at me. His arms are covered in tattoos. I can't make out what
any of them are, but I can see that they're all black ink, no color

at all. It fits him, with his black jeans and matching T-shirt. His boots make a muffled stomp against the soft grass.

I try to keep up with him, but his strides are too wide. He's tall, a few inches on me.

"I hope they did," I tell him, and look at the girls one more time. They've moved on now, staring and pointing at a drunken girl in a small dress who's stumbling by them.

He doesn't say another word to me as we walk inside the house. He doesn't look back at me when he walks into the kitchen or when he screws the top off of a bottle of whiskey and takes a swig. I'm curious about him now, so when Dan and Logan walk into the living room, I decide to get the dirt on the tattooed stranger. I grab a wine cooler from a bucket on the counter and walk over to my brother. He's sitting on the couch, beer in hand. He smells like weed already, and his eyes are bloodshot when they meet mine.

"Who was the guy in the backseat?" I ask him.

His expression changes. "Who, Hardin?"

He's not happy that I asked. And *Hardin*? What kind of name is that?

"*Stay away* from him, Mel," Dan warns me. "I mean it."

I roll my eyes and decide this is not something worth fighting my brother over. He never approves of any of my boyfriends, and yet he tried to set me up with his best friend, Jace—by far the most disgusting of his friends. Clearly my brother's standards are as inconstant as the highs and lows of his weed and alcohol intake.

When my brother pats an empty cushion next to him, I sit quietly and people-watch for a bit. The music gets louder, the crowd more and more into their drinks, their moods, the vibe.

A few minutes later, when Logan asks my brother if he wants to smoke again, I look around the house for Hardin. I don't think I'll get used to that name.

But there he is in the kitchen, standing alone against the counter. The bottle of whiskey is significantly less full than it was when I last saw him—say, fifteen minutes ago.

So he's a party boy, then. Good.

I get up from the couch quickly, too quickly, and as Dan grabs for my arm, I realize I better come up with a reason for leaving the room. If I tell him that I'm going to find Hardin, I know he'll follow me.

"Where're you going?" he asks.

"To pee," I lie. I hate that he always invites me to these parties but acts like he's my dad when it comes to me leaving his side.

He stares at me, studying my eyes as if he can tell that I'm lying, but I turn away. I feel his eyes on me as I cross the living room, so I walk toward the staircase. The only bathrooms in this massive house are all upstairs, which of course makes no sense, but that's frat houses for you.

I take the stairs slowly, and when I reach the top, I look back at my brother, then turn around and run smack into a black wall.

Only it's not a wall—it's Hardin's chest.

"Shit, sorry!" I exclaim, wiping at the splatter of wetness on his shirt from my wine cooler. "At least it won't stain," I tease.

His eyes are bright green and so intense that I have to look away.

"Haha," he says, monotone.

Rude. "My brother told me to stay away from you," I blurt out without thinking. His stare is so intense it's driving me crazy to keep eye contact, but I don't want to back down from him. I get the feeling he's used to that. I get the feeling that's how you lose with this one.

He raises the brow that has a ring in it. "Did he, now?"

Yep, definitely an English accent. I want to comment on it, but

I know how annoying it is when people point out how you talk. I get it all the time.

I nod, and the Brit opens his mouth to speak again. "And why is that?"

I don't know . . . but I want to.

"You must be pretty bad if Dan doesn't like you," I joke.

He doesn't laugh.

My shoulders are tense now; Hardin's energy has captured me already.

"If we're taking character judgments from him, we're all fucked," he says.

My instinct is to fight him, to tell him that my brother isn't that bad, just misunderstood. I should defend him against this insult.

But then I remember the day when the entire family of Dan's last girlfriend showed up to the house, the poor pregnant girl hiding behind her angry father. My dad wrote a check, and the lot of them disappeared with my niece or nephew, never to be heard from again. Something inside me knows there's something darker inside my brother, but I refuse to acknowledge it.

With my mom so far away and my dad so far up Tasha's butt, he's all I have.

I laugh. "I'm sure you're so much better."

Hardin lifts his tattooed hand up and pushes his hair off his forehead. "Nope, I'm worse."

Looking directly into my brown eyes, I somehow know he's serious. I can feel the warning behind his words, but when he offers me the half-empty bottle of whiskey, I take a swig.

The whiskey burns as bright as his eyes . . .

And I have the feeling that Hardin is made of gasoline.

Steph

When he first met the flame-haired girl whose arms were covered in tattoos, he saw something dark in her. He felt something competitive in the way she stared at her friend with hair lighter than her own. She compared everything they did, and he saw that desperation for attention that she held inside of her. She reminded him of a maiden named Roussette from a fairy tale he'd read when he was a child. The red-haired princess was jealous of her younger sisters when they married princes, even though she'd wed an admiral herself. It wasn't good enough, though; he wasn't good enough unless he made her better than her sisters. The girl hated the idea of losing anything, even things she claimed were not hers. She couldn't stand being second-best, and she hungered to be the one people paid attention to. She couldn't stand the idea of someone else getting what she felt she deserved, and she believed that what she deserved was nothing less than everything under the sun.

My dad is home late from work again. He's been late every night, and I was supposed to be able to use his car to pick up my prom dress this week. All of my friends got their dresses a month ago, and I'm starting to panic. If I don't have a dress for prom, I will lose my fucking mind. I'm so frustrated, and it's complete bullshit that my dad is late again and my mom is too busy watching my niece to listen to my justified complaints.

Everything revolves around my sister and her baby. People

always talk that bullshit about the youngest being the baby of the family. It sounds nice, but I grew up with nothing but hand-me-downs and last-minute birthday parties where no one showed up except my immediate family. I'm the reject of the family, the weird one who's become a ghost in her own home. And I'm not even sure why.

The last time my mom said more than two words to me was when I stained the sink upstairs red with cheap hair dye. She was frantic because my timing was perfect: the night before my sister Olivia's baby shower. I may have accidently spilled a little on the bath mat, and it's possible that I used my parents' embroidered towels to cover my shoulders while I let the fire-engine-red dye soak into my strands.

But I hadn't *dared* ruin Olivia's shirt from when she was my age, you see.

That's another thing I hate to hear: *"When Olivia was seventeen, she was the student council president,"* or *"When Olivia was seventeen, she had straight A's and a popular boyfriend who she married right after high school."*

I'm so tired of being compared to my sister—she was the golden child, and there's nothing I can do to even win silver, it feels like. I can't wait to leave for college. Due to my parents' constant pressure, I'm going to Washington Central, where Olivia graduated with honors.

They never cared about that college until my sister went there, and I'll never live up to the comparisons to her, but I'm done trying and it's easier just to say yes to going there and blow this place.

As soon as my dad's Jeep pulls into the driveway, I grab my purse, check the mirror one last time, and rush down the stairs, where I nearly run into my mom—not that she even notices my fishnet tights or red leather top. She just mumbles something while looking at her e-reader. That's all she ever does.

The front door opens, and my sister walks into the living room with my dad. Sierra, my baby niece, is asleep in my sister's arms.

"I'm so tired," Olivia announces to the room as she strolls through it.

Quickly, my mom appears, closing the case of her tablet and setting it absentmindedly on the mantel of the fireplace. Of course, for Olivia she can take a break from her precious screen.

"Stephanie can drive you home, honey," my dad offers on my behalf.

"Dad, I have to get my prom dress, and they close in thirty minutes!" I toss my bag across my shoulder and reach for his keys.

"Olivia and Sierra can ride with you."

My sister interrupts. "I won't mind. Just let me use the bathroom for a second."

Her soft brown hair moves when she talks. She's wearing khakis and a short-sleeve shirt with bright flowers printed on it. My dad smiles like his eldest daughter is the most thoughtful and considerate girl alive.

It's *super* annoying.

"Fine," I huff. "But this is the last day they'll hold it for me, so if I can't go to prom, it's your fault." I glare at my sister. Olivia nods, and I push past my dad to get outside. "I'll be in the car."

I start the car and wait for Olivia. Five minutes pass. Ten minutes pass. I send two texts and she doesn't respond. I know she read them from the little indicator on my phone. Yet she's still inside the house. I'm guessing her and my mom are on their fourth goodbye hug. My mom does that when we go to my grandma's house, too, requiring multiple hugs to satisfy her need for affection. Twelve minutes go by, and I finally leave the car to return to the house.

Just as I begin to close the car door, my sister walks outside with a languid pace and an oblivious smile on her face. She still has to buckle Sierra into her car seat.

"Olivia, we have to go," I say, to rush her along.

She sighs and mutters a half-hearted apology.

IT'S 8:03 WHEN I PARK in front of the dark shop. The sign on the door is turned around to CLOSED and the lights are off.

And now I can't get my dress. Today was the last day, and this was after my second extension. I begged for extra time, but I was told repeatedly that this was my last day. This sucks so bad.

"I'm sorry, Stephanie," Olivia says as I lay my head on the steering wheel.

I turn my head to the side and scowl at her. "This is your fault."

"It's not my fault," she says, with the nerve to look surprised. "Dad wanted to take me shopping to get some new shoes for Sierra. She outgrows them so fast—"

New baby shoes? Are you freaking serious? I missed my prom dress because her baby needed new shoes—the child doesn't even walk!

"Why couldn't Dad just take you home directly? You would have been back way sooner," I say, raising my head, and my voice.

"I wasn't tired then . . . I don't know." She shrugs her shoulders like my time means nothing to her. Like this isn't a big deal.

"This is such bullshit!" I shake my head and put my hands over my face.

"Don't talk like that in front of the baby!" my sister whisper-yells.

I groan and back out of the parking space. We're both silent the entire way home. Olivia doesn't feel as if she's done anything wrong, and I'm too mad to talk to her right now. I'm so tired of her stealing everything from me—and on top of that, Sierra keeps crying as if she's trying to split my brain in half.

I hate my life.

When we get to Olivia's house, she thanks me for dropping her off. I don't want to step foot into her new house, so I'm glad she doesn't ask me in. A house that I'm pretty sure my parents helped her and Roger buy. Her husband is quiet; he doesn't say much around my family. Olivia probably tells him not to. I'm sure everyone gets the warning label read to them before they have to have any exposure to me.

I don't really want to go inside, but I have to pee and it's another fifteen minutes back to my parents'. Walking into Olivia's house, I immediately notice that it smells *heavily* of cinnamon. Olivia burns those candle-oil things in every room.

Roger is sitting on the couch with a remote in one hand and a computer on his lap. When he notices us entering the room, he smiles up at his wife and then politely asks me how I've been. I say I'm the same as before, though I can't remember the last time I actually saw him.

After a few minutes of awkward small talk, Olivia tells us that she's going to put the baby to bed. She walks upstairs with a stuffed teddy bear in one hand and a bottle in the other. Roger barely glances at me as I walk by, looking at all of their stupid family pictures on the mantel above the fake fireplace. Roger stands up and walks into the kitchen—trying to avoid further conversation with me, no doubt.

In the last picture, their perfect little family poses in all matching white and black in a small wooden frame. Heading toward the kitchen, I find, hanging on the hallway wall in a big metal frame, a picture of Olivia and Roger on their wedding day. She's so perfect in the picture: perfect hair, perfect makeup, and her dress is beautiful. A soft, silky white dress that touches the floor in a regal way. She looks like a princess, like she was made for that dress.

Her dress is the exact opposite of my would-be prom dress. The dress I was supposed to pick up tonight is made from black cotton and tulle. The bodice is tight, lined with lacy tulle along the edges of the star-shaped skirt. It's a dress that, thanks to Olivia, I'll never have. I find myself wishing I had a bucket of black paint to ruin her stupid, perfect dress. I look to the next photo on the wall and stop at a picture of Roger, his arms wrapped around Olivia's pregnant stomach.

She ruined my prom dress. I'll ruin her wedding dress.

When I walk into the kitchen, Roger is standing in front of the fridge, his face buried inside and hidden by the doors. I tap my hand against the stone counter to get his attention. The moment he turns around, I tug on the hem of my shirt, exposing a nice amount of my cleavage to him. He inhales and then lets out a little cough.

I smile. I bet my sister hasn't fucked her husband since she popped out his baby.

"Sorry." I wrap my hair around my finger as Roger's eyes try not to run down my legs, taking in my fishnet hose.

"Hi," I say, and keep walking toward him.

My heart is racing and I don't know what the fuck I'm doing, but I'm pissed off at my sister and I'm fucking tired of her getting everything and I'm thinking of how everything is always about perfect Olivia and nothing is ever mine and so she shouldn't have anything that's hers either. Especially not a cute and loyal puppy of a husband.

"W-what are you doing, Stephanie?" Roger asks me, his face much paler than it was just seconds ago.

"Nothing. Just talking." I grab the waistline of my skirt and pull it up further, to the middle of my stomach, showing my lace panties to him, and when Roger backs away, his back hits the wooden cabinets, slamming one of the doors shut.

"What's wrong?" I ask with a laugh. My stomach is in a knot and I feel like I'm going to pass out any freaking second, but I feel amazing and powerful at the same time. Adrenaline, it must be. I love it. I want more of it. I step even closer and reach for the zipper on the front of my shirt.

Roger covers his face. "Stop it, Stephanie."

Fuck this, he's actually a loyal puppy like I thought. Knowing this adds to the burn of my jealousy.

"Come on, Roger, don't be such a—"

"Stephanie! What the hell are you doing?" Olivia's voice fills the kitchen.

I look over to the doorway to see her leaning there. She changed into pajamas, flannel ones with blue lining. She's pissed.

After a few seconds, she turns to her husband. "Roger?"

"I don't know, babe, she just came in here and started trying to take her clothes off." He tosses his hands up in the air in a frantic plea for his wife to see how crazy her slutty sister is.

She turns in my direction, glaring a hole through me. "Get out, Stephanie."

"You didn't even ask me if it wasn't true," I tell her, getting pretty pissed off about that fact. I toss my purse over my shoulder and pull my skirt back down to cover my body.

"I know you," she says matter-of-factly.

She knows me? She doesn't know me at all, actually. If she did, she would know better than to be such a selfish cunt.

"And . . . ?" I look at Roger, and he inches back like I'm a snake. Like he can judge me? If he wasn't afraid to get caught, I guarantee he would have me bent over their shiny granite counter.

"Well, did you try to come on to my husband or not?" Olivia's mouth is trembling; she's holding back tears. I should deny it, flip the script on both of them and blame him. He's pathetic enough that she would believe me. I can cry on demand, too, and if I wanted to, I could convince her of anything.

Oh, please.

"You're such a spoiled bitch!" she yells at me, and Roger crosses the kitchen and wraps his arm around her shoulders.

I'm a spoiled bitch? Is she serious? She gets everything she fucking wants, and it's bullshit. I'm sick of being the runner-up to her. She's lucky I didn't do something worse. I could have hurt him, or her, in a far more serious way. Even some of the thoughts I'm having now are surprising me . . . and I like it.

"Get out, Stephanie." Olivia shakes her head as her husband rubs her trembling hands.

I do just that. I won't have to put up with any more of this shit soon.

I'm going to college soon.

And once I'm there, I'm going to *run* that fucking campus.

part two

DURING

Hardin

He was misguided, moving through life with minimum expectations of himself. He was getting too used to life in that foreign place—even believing that his accent was slightly washing away with each night he spent away from home. He nailed his life down into a robotic loop of the same actions, same reactions, same consequences. The women were blending together, their names becoming an endless loop of Sarahs and Lauras and Jane Does.

He wasn't sure how his life could continue this way, day in and day out.

And then the first week of the next year, he met her. She was strategically placed at Washington Central by someone or something more powerful than him—to taunt him. He—or it—knew who he was, the kind of person he was known for being, and he had an agenda. He was set to steal another innocence, to ruin another girl's life. *It won't be so bad this time,* he figured. He wouldn't go to the same extremes as before. This was different, more juvenile. This was all just in fun.

And it was, until the wind caught her hair and it whipped around her face. Until the gray of her eyes haunted his sleep and the pink of her lips drove him mad. He was falling hard for her—at first it was so fast that he wasn't sure if he was actually feeling it or imagining it. But he felt it . . . he felt it rip through him like the roar of a lion. He began to rely on her for his every breath, every thought.

One night in the middle of it all, the snow falling, blanketing the concrete, he sat alone in the parking lot. His hands were gripping the steering wheel of his old Ford Capri, and he could barely see straight, let alone think straight.

How could he have done this? How did it go so far so fast? He wasn't sure, but he knew, he felt it deep down inside of himself, that he shouldn't have done it, and he knew that he would regret it. He was regretting it already.

She was supposed to be an easy target. A beautiful girl with an innocent smile and odd-colored eyes that weren't supposed to hold depth or meaning behind them. He wasn't supposed to fall in love with her, and she wasn't supposed to make him want to be a better person.

He thought that he was fine before.

He was getting by just fine before—before he made the beautiful mistake of allowing her to become his entire world. He loved her, though, he loved her so much that he was terrified of losing her—for losing her meant losing himself, and he knew he wouldn't be able to bear such a loss after going his entire life without something to lose.

As his fingers gripped harder and his knuckles turned white against the black steering wheel, his thoughts became more jumbled. He became more irrational and desperate, and he realized in that moment, with the silence of the empty lot drowning his fears, that he would do anything—absolutely anything—to keep her forever.

He had her, lost her, and had her again over the months that followed. He just couldn't quite get it. He loved her. His love for her burned brighter than any star, and he would highlight passages from ten thousand of her favorite novels to show her that. She gave him everything, and he watched her fall in love with him, hoping he would stop letting her down. Her faith in him made him want to be good for her. He wanted to prove her right and everyone else wrong. She made him feel a type of hope that he had never felt before. He didn't even know it existed.

Her presence made him feel at ease; the fire in his heart was cooled and he was becoming addicted to her. He craved her until he had her, and once he took her, neither of them could stop. Her body became his safety, her mind his home. The more he loved her, the more he was hurting her. He couldn't stay away, and through their struggles and growth, she became the normalcy he'd craved his entire life.

His relationship with his dad continued to grow slowly into something close to familiar. A few family dinners, and he had begun to chip away at the hatred he felt toward the man. He was seeing himself differently, and that helped him see the wrongs of his father in a different light. And that's when he needed her to anchor him, as his life changed again and his family shifted. He was growing to care for a houseful of strangers in a way that he swore he never would.

It wasn't easy for him to fight against twenty years of destructive patterns and base animal reactions.

He had to fight each day against the liquor calling to his blood, against the anger he was trying to let go of . . . but didn't know how to. He vowed that he would fight for her—and he did. He lost a few battles, but never lost sight of winning the war. She taught him laughter and taught him love—and he has expressed this time after time to her, but he will never stop.

one

The last few days of summer break are always the best. Everyone is fucking frantic, living out their last-minute summer plans and wishes. The parties get more crowded, the girls get more wild . . . but even so, I can't fucking wait for the semester to start. Not because I'm some idiotic freshman, excited for the wondrous world of university. No, I'm anxious because if I play my cards right, I'll be graduating in the spring, a full year ahead of time.

Not bad for a delinquent no one assumed would even attend university, much less graduate early.

My mum was so terrified for my future that she sent me half-way across the damn world to the grand state of Washington to live near my father. She used the bullshit excuse that she wanted me to "reconnect" with him, but I wasn't fooled. I knew she simply couldn't and didn't want to put up with my shit anymore, so off to America, like some colonial Puritan of old.

"Are you almost done?" Pink hair and swollen lips look up at me from between my legs. I had nearly forgotten she was here.

"Yeah." I wrap my hands around her shoulders and close my eyes, letting the physical pleasure she's giving me take over. A distraction, that's what she is. They all are.

The pressure in my spine builds, and I don't bother to pretend that I enjoy her company for more than sexual pleasure as I release into her warm mouth.

Seconds later, she's wiping at her lips with the back of her hand and getting to her feet.

"You know . . ." Molly reaches for her purse and pulls out a tube of dark lipstick. "You could at least pretend to be interested, asshole." Her lips pucker, and she wipes a finger across the excess crayon painted onto her mouth.

"I am." I clear my throat. "Pretending, that is."

She rolls her eyes and raises her middle finger to me. I'm interested—sexually, at least. She's a good enough fuck, and she's okay company sometimes. We are a lot alike, her and I. Both rejects of our families. I don't know too much about her past, but I know enough to know that some bad shit has happened to her to make her run all the way to Washington from some rich-bitch town in Pennsylvania.

"Dick," she mutters, pushing the cap back on her makeup. She looks better with naturally pink lips, lips that are swollen from having my cock in her mouth.

Molly is an acquaintance of mine. Well, a friend with benefits, I would say. Our "friendship" isn't exclusive, not in the least, and we both have full freedom to do whatever, or whoever, the fuck we want. She hates me half the time, but I'm okay with that. It's mutual.

The rest of our friends give us shit about it, but it works. I'm bored and she's here. She gives good head and she doesn't stay around long after. Perfect situation for me. Her, too, it seems.

"You'll be here tonight, for the party?" she asks.

I stand, too, pulling my boxers and jeans up my legs. "I live here, don't I?" I raise a brow at her.

I hate it here, and daily I find myself wondering just how the fuck I ended up in a fraternity in the first place.

My shitbag sperm donor. That's how. Ken Scott is a grade-A fuckup, the worst type. Alcoholic fuckhead who destroyed my entire childhood, only to magically turn his life around and move in with some lady and her son, a loser only two years younger than me.

His do-over, I suppose. Ken Scott gets a fucking do-over, and I get to be in a stupid-ass fraternity at the college he's basically in charge of. On top of this, he practically begged me to move in with him, as if he thought I would actually live under his roof, under his control. When I refused, I had assumed he would get me an apartment, but of course he didn't. So here I am, in this stupid house instead. It really pissed him off that I chose this shithole rather than his clean, pristine palace.

The stupid-ass fraternity does have its perks, I guess. A massive house with parties almost every night, a constant stream of endless pussy. And the best part of all: no one fucks with me.

None of the pissant frat boys seem to mind the fact that I don't do shit to actually represent the house. I don't wear their stupid sweatshirts or plaster their stupid bumper stickers on my car. I don't participate in any of the volunteer shit, and I sure as hell don't go around yelling the name of the shit. They do some okay shit for the community, but they don't actually give a fuck about the community, and none of that matters.

When I glance around the room, I realize I'm alone. Molly must have left without me even noticing.

I get up and open the window to air the place out before it gets used again tonight. All of these empty rooms in the house work in my favor since I can't stand to have people in my own. It's too personal or something, I don't know, but I don't like it, and everyone has learned one way or another not to come in here. Molly and whichever other girls come around know we're bound for these empty rooms and not mine.

As I approach my door, I see Logan stumbling down the hall, a short, curly-haired girl under his arm. She isn't quiet about what she wants to do to him, and I'm not quiet about my disgust.

"Get a damn room!" I shout to them.

She giggles and he flips me off and I close and dead-bolt the door. That's the pattern around here. Everyone sort of ignores me or simply tells me in one way or another to fuck off. I'm okay with that. I'd much rather sit here, in my room, alone, waiting for the next artificial high.

My fingers trace over the dusty shelves of my bookcase. I can't decide which novel I feel like living right now . . . Hemingway, maybe? He can give me a good dose of cynical. The middle Brontë sister? I could use a dysfunctional bullshit love story right now. I grab *Wuthering Heights* and kick my boots off before lying down in my bed.

I don't know what it is about this novel that brings me to read and reread it so many damn times, but I always find myself skimming the pages of the dark tale. It's fucked up, really—two people coming together, then falling part. Destroying themselves and everyone around them because they were too selfish and stubborn to get their shit together.

But to me that's the best type of fucking story. I want to feel something while I'm reading, and sappy, roses-and-sunshine novels make me want to vomit on their pages and burn away the evidence afterward.

"Fuck, yes!" I hear a female voice screech through the paper-thin walls.

"Shut the fuck up!" I pound my fist against the old wood, grabbing my pillow and pushing it against my ears.

One more fucking year. One more year of bullshit courses and easy exams. One more year of boring parties full of people who care way too much what everyone thinks about them. One more goddamn year of keeping to myself and I can get my ass back to London, where I belong.

two

To this day, he can still remember the way vanilla filled the small dorm room the first time he was alone with her. Her hair was soaked, she had a towel wrapped around her curvy body, and it was the first time he paid attention to the way her chest flushed when she was mad. He would see her mad again, so damn mad, more times than he could count, but he would never, ever, forget the way she tried to be polite to him at first. He took her politeness as pride. *Another stubborn girl who pretends to be a woman,* he thought. The strange girl kept on being as patient as she could. For no reason at all. She didn't owe him anything, she still doesn't, and he can only hope to see her mad at him again and again, for the rest of his life.

He grasps for the memories of those days now, as he sits alone, trapped by his own mistakes. These memories of his anger, of her anger, are a few of the only things that kept him afloat after she left him.

The first day of the fall semester is always the absolute best for people-watching. So many fucking idiots running around like chickens with their heads cut off, so many girls dressed in their favorite outfits in a desperate attempt to gain attention from men.

It's the same cycle every year at every college across the globe. Washington Central University just happens to be where I'm condemned to attend. I like it enough; it's easy, and my professors cut me a lot of slack. Despite my lack of giving an actual fuck, I'm pretty decent academically. If I "applied myself more," I could be even better, but I don't have the time or the energy to waste obsessing over grades or plans or anything that could be obsessed over. I'm not as stupid as the professors always assume I'll be. I can miss an entire week of class and still ace an exam. I've learned that as long as I can do that, they'll leave me be.

The front of the Student Union is the prime location for the show. Sitting here watching all the parents in tears has to be my favorite part. It's amusing to me because my mum couldn't seem to get rid of me quick enough, and some of the parents here act like their damn arms are getting cut off when their children— *adult* children, might I remind you—are off to college. They should be happy, not sobbing like annoying children, that their kids are actually doing something with their lives. If they took a walk around my old neighborhood, they would kiss the ground of Washington Central University for giving their child a chance in the world.

A woman with huge fake tits and bleached hair hugs her puny, plaid-shirt-wearing son, and I'm full on grinning as he starts to cry into his mum's shoulder. Fucking pussy. His dad is standing back, away from the pathetic sight, checking his expensive watch, waiting for his son and wife to stop their blubbering.

I can't imagine how that would feel, having my parents obsess over me. My mum cared enough, when she wasn't working from sunup to sundown, leaving me to fend for myself as she made up for my shitbag father's lack of common sense. She tried to make up for it the best she could, but one can only do so much when so much has already been lost. And I fought her help. Every step of the way. I wouldn't accept it then and still won't accept it now. Not from her, not from anyone.

"Hey, man." Nate sits down across from me at the picnic table and pulls a cigarette from his pocket. "What's the plan for the night?" he asks as his fingers flick over the lighter.

I shrug and pull my phone from my pocket to check the time. "I don't know; we're meeting Steph in her room."

As he smokes, Nate annoys me into agreeing to walk to Steph's dorm from the Student Union. It's not a far walk, fifteen minutes or so, but I'd much rather drive than push through the masses of eager pupils decked out in their college best.

By the time we reach the dorms, Nate is going on about the party this weekend. It's always the same every single weekend. *What's there to be excited about?*

Everything is always the same for me. Same group of friends, same amount of sex, same parties, same old shit, different day.

I'm about to barge into the room when Nate reminds me, "We should knock. Remember how pissed she was last time?"

I laugh to myself. Yeah, I do remember that day. It was last semester, and I walked into Steph's dorm room without knocking. I found her on her knees in front of some asshole. I call him an asshole because . . . well, because he was wearing flip-flops. A man-child in flip-flops is automatically an asshole in my book. He was embarrassed, and Steph was pissed. As he snuck out, she threw just about every item she owned in the direction of my head.

It made my entire week to see her so horrified. To this day, I give her shit about it.

I finally stop laughing at the memory when I hear her yell for us to come inside.

And when I do, I'm greeted by the sight of a blond guy in a cardigan standing in the middle of Steph's room. Steph is standing between Nate and me, looking at the newcomers with amusement dancing in her eyes. It takes me a moment to notice a tense-looking woman and younger girl with them. The woman is hot . . . my eyes take her body in: tall frame, long blond hair, decent tits.

"Hey, you Steph's roomie?" Nate says, and I finally get a good look at the girl.

She's decent enough: pouty lips, long blond hair. That's about all I can tell, because the chick is wearing clothes that are three times her size. I notice the way her skirt literally touches the floor, and cringe inwardly. Just from a glance, I can tell college is not going to be fun for this girl.

Case in point: she's staring down at her feet, nervous as hell. What's wrong with her?

"Um . . . yes. My name is Tessa," she mumbles. Her voice is quiet, obnoxiously so.

I look over at Steph, who smiles a slick smile and sits down on her bed, never taking her eyes off the girl.

Nate responds with a smile, always the friendlier of the two of us. "I'm Nate. Don't look so nervous."

I don't see the point in small talk, especially with this little mouse. She's staring at Nate wide-eyed, and he reaches out to touch her shoulder.

"You'll love it here," he adds.

He's full of shit.

Steph's roommate looks terrified as her eyes rake over the band posters hanging on the wall. This girl couldn't have been a worse match for her. She's quiet, timid, scared of the world, apparently. She's lucky I'm feeling nice today; otherwise I would have made her even more uncomfortable.

"I'm ready, guys," Steph says, popping up from the bed. She pushes her purse thing up onto her shoulder and walks toward the door. The blond boy—likely her roommate's brother—is staring at me, and I glare in his direction.

"See you around, Tessa." Nate waves goodbye to the girl, and I notice her staring at me. Her eyes move from my eyebrow ring to the loop in my lip and back and forth between both of my arms. Then I notice the woman and that dude are doing the same thing.

What? You all've never seen tattoos before? I want to ask, but I get the feeling her mum isn't as nice as the rack she sports, so I may as well behave. For now.

The moment we step into the hallway, we hear the woman shriek, "You're getting a new dorm!"

Steph bursts into laughter, and Nate and I join in as we walk down the hall.

three

The next morning I don't feel like going to my first class, so I head to Steph's room instead. She's probably still asleep, but I'm bored and her dorm is closer to my next class than anyone else's in the crew. I text her and tell her I'm on way, but I don't wait for her reply.

The hallway of the old building is nearly empty, only a few frantic stragglers rushing by with their arms full of books. I knock, so as not to give Miss Prim a heart attack, and, hearing no reply, let myself in with the key Steph has given me.

To keep myself from falling asleep on Steph's shitty mattress, I flip through the basic cable channels. Just as some stuffy "doctor" is giving marriage advice to two idiots, the door opens and Steph's roommate rushes in. She's wrapped in a wet towel, and her long, soaked hair is stuck to her face in an almost comical way. As her eyes widen with surprise, I turn the TV off and stare at the specimen before me.

"Um . . . Where is Steph?" she practically squeaks. She stares down at the floor, back to me, to the floor again.

I smile at her embarrassment and stay silent.

"Did you hear me? I asked you where Steph is." Her voice is softer now, more polite.

My smile grows. "I don't know."

She's squirming, and I suspect that with how hard she's gripping the edges of her towel, she'll shred the material. I turn the TV back on and sit up.

"Okay? Well, could you like . . . leave or something, so I can get dressed?"

Well, I'm not going to leave. Not when I just found the only comfortable position on this bed.

I roll over and cover my face with my hands to humor her. "Don't flatter yourself—it's not like I am going to look at you."

She's awfully full of herself to think that I would sit and stare at her.

Well . . . okay, I probably would, especially given that the towel she's wearing is hugging her body in a damn nice way.

I hear her shuffling around, the sound of a bra fastening, and her breathing heavily. She's nervous still, and I would love to see her face as she tries to put her clothes on as fast as she can. I would uncover my eyes just to annoy her, but I'm in a decent mood. Plus, I'm only going to see this girl a few times, so may as well keep it somewhat civil.

"Are you done yet?" I roll my eyes under my hands.

"Could you be any more disrespectful? I did nothing to you. *What is your problem?*" she yells.

The fuck? I hadn't expected such a smartass mouth on such an innocent-looking girl. She's trying hard to be patient with me, and I'm trying hard to make her explode. I can't help but laugh.

As I stare at Steph's pissed-off roommate, it feels odd laughing this way, this hard, but her expression is just fucking priceless. She's *so* pissed.

The door shoots open, and Steph enters, dressed in last night's clothes. "Sorry I'm late. I have a hell of a hangover," she whines.

I roll my eyes again. Of course she has a hangover . . . when doesn't she?

"Sorry, Tess, I forgot to tell you Hardin would be coming by." She shrugs her shoulders. Like she gives a fuck.

"Your boyfriend is rude," the blond girl snaps.

That does it for me, and I laugh again. Steph looks at me, brow raised at how much I'm laughing.

"Hardin Scott is *not* my boyfriend!" she exclaims—maybe a little too emphatically—and starts choking on laughter along with me.

We've fucked around before, but never dated.

I don't date.

"What did you say to her?" Steph turns to me and puts her hands on her hips in a failed attempt to scold me. Then she turns to the girl. "Hardin has a . . . a unique way of conversing."

Conversing? I'm not attempting to talk to either of them. I shrug my shoulders and go back to finding some mindless shit to watch.

"There's a party tonight—you should come with us, Tessa," I hear Steph say. Yeah, right, like this chick is going to go to a party? I pull my lip ring between my teeth to stop from laughing again. I stare straight ahead at the TV.

"Parties aren't really my thing. Plus I have to go get some things for my desk and walls."

"C'mon . . . it's just one party! You're in college now—just one party won't hurt," Steph practically pleads, trying to convince her. "Wait, how are you getting to the store? I thought you didn't have a car?"

"I was going to take the bus. And besides, I can't go to a party—I don't even know anyone," she responds. I laugh again. "I was going to read and Skype with Noah."

Because going to a store is so much fun. I bet she shops at fucking Target; she seems like the type. And her Skype date . . . I bet she's going to show an ankle to her poor excuse of a boyfriend.

"You don't want to take the bus on a Saturday! They're way too packed. Hardin can drop you on the way to his place . . . right, Hardin?" Steph glances at me.

I won't be dropping anyone off anywhere.

"And you'll know me at the party," Steph continues. "Just come . . . please?"

"I don't know . . . and no, I don't want Hardin to drive me to the store," the obnoxious girl whines. I shift over and smile at the two of them; it's all I can do, since they're both annoying the shit out of me.

"Oh no! I was really looking forward to hanging out with you," I say. "Come on, Steph, you know this girl isn't going to show at the party." I take a moment to look at the way her white T-shirt is tight across her chest and hips. She should dress this way instead of that long-ass skirt she was wearing the other day. Her khaki shorts are still too long, but you can't win 'em all.

"Actually, yeah, I'll come," the girl says—Tessa was her name, I think. Yeah, it was. I hear shrieking and squealing, and it's my cue to leave when the girls start hugging and shit.

"Yay! We'll have so much fun!" Steph promises the girl as I leave the room.

I DRIVE FARTHER on to campus and sit through the rest of my classes for the day. Afterward, I get a text from Nate to meet him and Tristan at Blind Bob's and head that way. I turn the music up in my car and roll the window down. When I was a teen, I used to think people were fucking show-offs when they blasted music from their car windows, but now I get it. Sometimes I just want to drown out the world around me, and music and reading are the only things that do that for me. Everyone has their thing, and these are mine.

When I need silence, the noise helps.

Better than a fifth of Jack, I suppose. My mum, crying on the phone in the middle of the night, would say so.

"What took so long?" Tristan takes a bite from a hamburger; half the toppings fall onto the plate in front of him.

"Traffic was a bitch." I slide into the booth next to Nate. Our usual server nods at me, and moments later she appears at the table with a glass of water.

"Still sober, yeah?" Nate questions; his eyes carefully avoid my glass as he takes a drink of his beer.

"Yep. Still sober." I finish half the glass of water, trying not to think about the way an ice-cold beer would taste on my tongue.

"Good for you, man. I know everyone gives you shit about it, but I think it's pretty fucking awesome, the self-control you have."

At Nate's praise, I shift awkwardly.

Tristan laughs, wiping a napkin across his chin. "Self-control? I heard Molly screaming your name just last night."

"Well, sober with *drinking*. No, no, of course not chicks." Nate laughs along, pushing his shoulder into mine, and I'm thankful for the change in tone. It was getting too personal for my liking.

Nate ends up convincing me to let him drive my car. He only had one beer, and I don't feel like driving really, so I agree to let him if he drives me to pick up Steph and her roommate.

"She's been blowing up my phone, says you won't answer her," Nate says as we pull out of the parking lot.

I roll my eyes. "I told her an hour ago that I would give them a ride." Steph can be really fucking annoying.

"I just told her we're on our way. I'm glad that Tessa girl is coming with her," he says, and rolls down the driver's-side window.

"Why?"

"Because she seems nice and should definitely get out more. Steph said she thinks her boyfriend is her only friend or something."

"Boyfriend? You mean Mother Theresa has a boyfriend?" I scoff. Wait, the blond guy in the dorm? They look like siblings, not boyfriend and girlfriend. Is that who she's Skyping with? Definitely a fully clothed video, then—with an added blazer, probably, for protection.

"Yeah, he was there with her, that preppy dude."

"Go figure." I laugh and turn up the music. Tess and her stuck-up Gap-model boyfriend would hate this music. I turn it up even louder.

When we pull into the parking lot of Steph's dorm, my phone buzzes. It's Molly's name, so I hit ignore.

"Ladies." Nate greets the girls as they walk up to the car. Steph is dressed in a fishnet dress, and her tagalong is wearing what looks like a maroon sack. I don't get it. I saw the outline of her body in that towel—why does she wear this hideous shit?

"You do know that we're going to a party, not a church—right, Theresa?" I say as she climbs into the car.

"Please don't call me Theresa. I prefer Tessa," she says succinctly. Snobbily.

I knew her name would be Theresa. I've read enough novels to put that together. I seem to have struck a chord with this one.

"Sure thing, Theresa," I taunt her. As we drive, I glance in the mirror a few times to look at her. She doesn't appear annoyed when she doesn't know my eyes are on her. The house is close; we only have to sit through a few minutes of awkward silence until we arrive. Nate parks in front of the house behind a line of cars.

She huffs and rolls her eyes. "It's so big—how many people will be here?" Theresa asks. Doesn't the full lawn give that away?

"A full house. Hurry up," I tell her, shutting the car door. She just sits there, in shock, I think, and I walk up the yard.

four

He knew from early on, from their first encounter to the first time she used that smart mouth against him, that he felt something different when it came to her. He wasn't sure . . . no, he had no fucking idea that the fire inside of her would weaken, then be extinguished by his habit of making mistake after mistake, but often he finds himself sitting alone, reliving the days when she was on fire. When her voice and her actions were filled with so much passion that the air between them would fill with smoke. He should have known that that much passion would lead to destruction, to the burning of her soul, and make every ounce of her spirit disintegrate, taking the girl he loved, the girl that he couldn't and still can't breathe without, and he would have to watch her drift away, with the last few clouds of gray smoke.

I walk through the crowded party, pushing my way through a group of wasted assholes playing some sort of drinking game to occupy their time while trying desperately to fit in. Their bloodshot eyes and stupid grins make me nauseous as I pass them. One by one they give me the same "he's an asshole" look, while tossing plastic balls into beer-filled cups and cheering as if they've won some sort of medal for being completely brainwashed into drinking the cheapest beer from shared cups.

When I get to the crowded hallway, I spot Steph and her tag-along. The blond girl looks clueless, completely out of place in the swarm of moving bodies. A drink is pushed into her hand, and she smiles politely, despite the fact that she doesn't want it. I can tell by the look in her eyes. She takes it, though, bringing the red cup to her mouth.

Another follower. Surprise, surprise.

"Helloooo, Earth to Hardin!" Molly's voice cuts through the noise. I glance down at her, noting the annoyed expression on her face while she rests her hand on her hip. Her eyes are on Tessa and Steph.

"What were you staring at?" she asks, voice tight.

"Nothing. Mind your damn business." I continue on, up the stairs and toward my room. Behind me I hear tacky and excessive jewelry clanging in the most annoying way. I turn back to Molly and her puppy-dog eyes. "Are you following me for a reason?"

She flips her pink hair from her shoulder. "I'm bored," she complains.

"And . . . ?" I pull my phone from my back pocket and pretend to be doing anything but listening to her.

Molly runs her hand down my arm. "Entertain me, asshole."

I look her up and down, enjoying the way her tiny dress shows off all the things I've already seen. Her nails push into my skin, and her smile grows.

"Come on, Hardin, when was the last time you got off?"

She has no shame. I like it.

"Well, considering you blew me two days ago . . ."

Her lips are on mine before I can get another word out. I pull back, she pushes forward.

Ah, may as well. She's not half bad, and there are worse things I could be doing with my time. Like Steph, hanging out with Goody Theresa all night. That would put anyone to sleep.

Molly leads me to the farthest bedroom on the right; she already knows better than to try to go into my room. No one comes into my room. The door closes behind her, and she's on me within seconds. Her mouth is hot, her lips painted with sticky gloss.

The act of touching, be it with Molly or someone else, gives me an escape. Doesn't make much sense to me, but when my mind is turned off for a while, it's easier. It's a rush, the only time I really feel much of anything.

Molly leads me to the bed, an empty one without so much as a sheet on the damned thing. These small details don't make a difference when you don't feel any of it. Molly lays her small body on mine, grinding herself against my leg. I wrap her pink hair around my fist, pulling her mouth off of mine

"No," I warn her. She groans, whining like she usually does when I remind her not to kiss me.

"You're such an asshole," she complains, but shifts to straddle my waist.

The door clicks open, and she stops moving her hips. Turning around, she sits up, and I lean up on my elbows.

"Can I help you?" Molly's tone is harsh with impatience and need.

And of course—*of course*—standing in the doorway is Tessa, Steph's roommate, with a look on her face that tells me she's more embarrassed than Molly and I put together.

"Oh . . . no. Sorry," she stammers. "No, sorry, I was looking for a bathroom; someone spilled a drink on me." She frowns down at her soiled dress as if it was evidence. This girl spends a lot of time looking down, it seems.

"Okay? So go find a bathroom," Molly mocks with a flip of her hand. "Go find a bathroom."

Tessa leaves the room immediately and closes the door.

Still, as Molly starts in on my neck, I can see the shadow of Tessa's feet under the doorway. Is she listening to us? How fucking weird. A few seconds later she disappears and Molly reaches her hand down between my legs.

"God, that girl irritates me," she complains.

For someone who isn't very well liked herself, Molly sure has a lot of people who "irritate" her.

"Should I have asked her to join us?" I shrug my shoulders, and Molly grimaces.

"Ew. No way. Bianca or Steph, maybe, but that Tessa dud, no way. She's not even hot, and she's twice my size nearly."

"You're a bitch, you know that?" I shake my head at her. Tessa, plain and all, has a nice body—the kind of body that men love, the kind of body that I would devour in a heartbeat if she could learn to tame that attitude of hers.

"Whatever. It's just her tits that you like." Molly's mouth latches on to my neck.

"I *don't* like her," I say, feeling the need to defend myself.

"Well, obviously you don't like her." Molly draws back to look at my eyes. She smiles like we're in on a secret together or something. "That doesn't mean you wouldn't fuck her."

Her mouth catches my jaw, nipping at the skin there. Her hands grip me, one over my cock, and she continues to move her small body over mine.

"No more talking." I reach down between her parted thighs and run my fingers over her. She groans against my neck, and I focus on the pleasure she's providing me. Molly is more like me than she would ever admit. She, too, finds her days bleak and unexciting. She, too, uses sensation to escape her own head. I don't know much about her really, and she'll never share, but I can tell it was rough.

Molly's body shakes as I pump my fingers into her, knowing by now how to get her off quickly. Just as she moans, I catch the sound of "Lou," but she quickly recovers and says my name.

Lou? What the fuck? I try not to laugh at the thought of her talking about Logan, saying his nickname while I pleasure her. She knows better than to think he would give her the time of day.

He's nice enough to her—simply because he's a nice guy—but the guy has standards.

If I cared, I would call her out on it, but I simply don't give a fuck. I use her and she uses me—we both know this. My mind wanders to the party downstairs. I wonder how many times Steph's roommate has cried so far. She's quite the emotional one, with her ranting and sassy attitude that belies a frailty.

Molly's hands tug at my jeans, unfastening the button, and I close my eyes as her warm lips wrap around my cock.

Afterward, she doesn't say a word, and neither do I, when she wipes her fingers across her swollen lips. Molly stands, pulling her dress down to cover her body as much as the scrap can, and she leaves the room.

I lie there, on a bed that isn't mine, and stare at the ceiling for a few minutes more before wandering out into the hallway. The party is still going; the floors are getting messier and messier by the minute. A group of three drunk girls holding hands walks by.

"You guys are my best friends," the shortest of the three says.

One of them is wearing a blue sweater, her eyes bloodshot as she stumbles down the hall, nearly tripping over her feet. "I love you both!" she replies, her eyes filling with tears.

Drunk girls are there, crying and being "best friends" with everyone . . .

Logan appears at the end of the hall, a crooked smile on his face and a drink in each hand. He offers me one, but I shake my head.

"Yours is water," he says, holding the red cup between us.

I grab it, bringing it to my nose to smell the liquid. "Erm, thanks." I take a drink of the cold water and ignore the way Logan is silently judging me for drinking water.

"The house is packed, man," he says to me, clearing his throat with a grimace. "This cheap vodka burns like a bitch."

I don't say anything, I just let my eyes roam around the hall as we walk toward the stairs.

"Oh, hey, I saw that Tessa chick go into your room," he says from behind me. I turn to face him.

"What?"

"She went in there, with Steph. Steph's sick, puking in the bathroom."

"Why would they go into my room?" I raise my voice. I could have sworn I locked it. No one goes into my room. Sick or not. They especially don't go in there to throw up on my things.

He shrugs. "Don't know. Just warning you."

Logan disappears into the crowd as I head toward my room. Steph knows better than to go into my room—why didn't she warn her little tagalong?

I enter in a huff, and sure enough, standing next to my book-shelf is Tessa. I immediately notice that her hand is on my oldest copy of *Wuthering Heights*. The worn pages show its use to me.

"Why the hell are you in my room?" I say to her. She doesn't even flinch. She gently closes the book in her hands.

"I asked you what the hell you are doing in my room?" I repeat, just as harsh as the first time. I cross the room take the book from her and toss it back onto the shelf where it belongs. She still hasn't answered me; she's standing there, near my bed, with wide eyes and a closed mouth.

"Nate told me to bring Steph in here . . ." she whispers. She waves her hand in the direction of my bed. Steph is passed out on the mattress, and I'm not happy about that one bit. "She drank too much, and Nate said—"

I've heard enough.

"I heard you the first time," I calmly interrupt her.

"You're a part of this fraternity?" she asks, her voice curious and a tad bit judgmental. Not that I'm in any way surprised by this. I'm used to being judged, especially around rich kids with haughty attitudes. I don't think this girl is rich, though. Her dress looks like it came from a consignment store instead of a department store, which surprises me, for some reason.

"Yeah, so?" I step toward the nosy girl, and she backs away, hitting the bookcase in the process. "Does that surprise you, Theresa?"

"Stop calling me Theresa," she snaps at me.

Feisty.

"That's your name, isn't it?"

Sighing, she turns away from me. I glance over at my bed as she attempts to leave the room.

"She can't stay in here," I say to her. No way is Steph sleeping in my bed all night.

"Why not? I thought you guys were friends?"

How sweet . . . how naive.

"We are, but no one stays in my room." I cross my arms over my chest and get a good look at her. Her eyes are following the tattoos inked onto my arms. I like the way she's looking at me, trying to figure me out. It's exciting, even—to be examined in this way . . . she's intrigued, and it's obvious.

She seems to snap out of her staring fit.

"Ohh . . . I see." She snorts. "So only girls who make out with you can come into your room?"

I can't help but smile at the little feisty freshman. Long blond hair and killer curves hidden underneath that hideous outfit . . . but something about this girl irritates me on a deeper level than Steph does, or even Molly. I can't put my finger on it, but she's getting under my skin pretty quickly and I need to put a stop to that.

"That wasn't my room. But if you're trying to say you want to make out with me, sorry, you're not my type."

I smile and watch her face twist into embarrassment and anger.

"You are . . . you are . . ."

I feel uncomfortable as she fights to find the insulting words.

"Well . . . then *you* take her to another room, and I'll find a way back to the dorms."

Me? She's so sure of herself it's pissing me off more and more by the second.

She wouldn't actually leave Steph in here. Would she? She opens the door and walks through it.

Damn, she has more balls than I thought. I'm slightly impressed. *Annoyed*—but impressed.

"Good night, Theresa!" I yell to her as she slams my bedroom door.

I take a visual sweep of the room, seeing what else has might have been disturbed. The mirror on my wall catches my attention, mainly because the man standing in it is barely recognizable. I don't know who I've become in the last few years.

But more surprisingly, I don't understand where the stupid smile now on my face has come from.

I'm used to bickering with obnoxious people during these parties. Why did I enjoy this so much more than usual? Is it because of this new girl? She's not my usual prey, but she's fun to toy with.

The noise from downstairs fills my room, and with Steph in my bed, I have nothing to do. I will have to get Nate to carry her out of here—and drop her in the hallway, if need be. Surely she's slept in worse places. I find myself thinking about Tessa and her attitude. The way she stubbornly placed her hand on her hip and wouldn't back down from me.

I walk out into the hallway and convince some frat newbie to move Steph's body to an empty room down the hall. I watch a moment to make sure he doesn't stay in there with her, and when he pops out of the room, I head back toward my own.

Passing the bathroom, I hear a frantic voice through the door. It's that Tessa girl—I know her voice immediately.

"Yeah . . . no . . . I went to a stupid party with my roommate, and now I'm stuck at a frat house with nowhere to sleep and no way to get back to my room."

She's full-on crying now. I should just walk away from the door. I don't have the energy or remote interest in dealing with a crying, overly sensitive girl.

"But she . . ."

I can't make out her words between her sobs. I press my ear to the door.

"That isn't the point, Noah," I hear her say.

I try to open the door. I'm not even sure why I do, so it's probably fortunate that it's locked.

"Just a minute," she says loudly, losing patience.

I knock again.

"I said just a minute!"

She yanks the door open, and her eyes grow wide when she sees me. I look away as she storms past me. I reach for her arm, gently stopping her.

"Don't touch me!" she yells, and jerks away.

"Have you been crying?" I ask, even though I already know the answer.

"Just leave me alone, Hardin," she says, no conviction in her tone. She sounds so exhausted. *Who was she talking to on the phone? Her boyfriend?*

I open my mouth to tease her, but she holds a finger up. "Hardin, please. I'm begging you, if you have one decent bone in your body, you will leave me be. Just save whatever mean comment you're going to say for tomorrow. Please." Her blue-gray eyes are shining with tears, and the rude remark I had planned suddenly lost its spark.

"There's a room down the hall you can sleep in. It's where I put Steph," I tell her. She stares at me like I've grown three heads.

"Okay," she simply says after a moment.

"It's the third door on the left." I walk toward my room. I feel an overwhelming urge to get away from this girl, and fast.

"Good night, Theresa," I say, and step into my room. I close the door and lean against the back of it.

I feel dizzy. I don't feel right. Logan better not have tricked me and slipped some shit in my water.

I walk to the bookshelf and grab *Wuthering Heights,* opening to the middle of the novel. Catherine is the most infuriating female character I've ever read, and I cannot for the life of me understand why Heathcliff puts up with her shit.

He's an asshole, too, but she's the worst.

IT TAKES ME A WHILE to fall asleep, but when I do, I find myself dreaming about Catherine, or rather a young blond version of her, stumbling into college. But the sound of my mother's screams wakes me, and I bolt upright, sweat soaking through my shirt, and turn on the light.

When will this shit end? It's been years and it won't go away.

After a few more fitful hours of staring at the ceiling and walls and trying to convince myself I must've slept in all that time, I take a shower and walk down to the kitchen. Grabbing a trash bag, I decide to help clean up, for once. Maybe if I do some nice shit for people, I'll get a full night's sleep sometime.

In the kitchen, I find Tessa, still here, laughing and leaning against the counter.

"What's so funny?" I ask, sweeping a bunch of empty cups off the counter and into my bag.

"Nothing . . . does Nate live here, too?" she asks me.

I ignore her.

Her soft voice gains some volume: "Does he? The sooner you tell me if Nate lives here, the sooner I can leave."

"Now you have my attention." I take a step toward her to

clean a pile of soaking paper towels off the counter. I smile at the annoyed girl. "But no, he doesn't live here. Does he seem like a frat boy to you?"

"No, but neither do you," she scoffs.

I don't respond. Damn it, this house is a fucking disaster.

"Is there a bus that runs close to here?" She taps her foot against the floor like a child, and I roll my eyes.

"Yep, about a block away."

"Could you tell me where it is?"

"Sure. It's about a block away."

Something about her quick annoyance makes me smile.

She turns on her flat shoes and walks away in a hurry. I laugh to myself and ignore the way Logan is smirking at me from across the kitchen. I walk toward him but change my direction as I watch Tessa approach Steph.

"We aren't taking the bus. One of those assholes will take us back to our room. He was probably just giving you a hard time," I hear Steph say. She enters the kitchen, looking like Hurricane Katrina. Her dark makeup is smeared around her eyes. I glance at Tessa, who is barely wearing any, and note the difference. "Hardin, you ready to take us back now? My head is pounding."

"Yeah, sure, just give me a minute." I drop the bag of trash onto the floor and laugh to myself when I hear Tessa scoff. It's so easy to get under this girl's skin.

Tessa and Steph meet me by my car, and I can't help but choose one of my favorite metal songs, "War Pigs," during the drive back to campus. I roll all the windows down and enjoy the breeze.

"Can you roll those up?" Tessa asks from the backseat.

I glance in the rearview mirror and pull my lip ring between my teeth to keep from laughing at the way her blond hair is whipping around her face. I pretend not to hear her and turn the volume up on the stereo.

When the joyride is done and they're climbing out of the car, I say, "I'll come by later, Steph." I can see her panties through her outfit, but I'm pretty sure that's the point of her wearing fishnet stockings.

"Bye, Theresa." I smile, and she rolls her eyes. I find myself laughing as I drive away.

five

He woke up one night, months after he'd met her. He rolled over to find her cradled against him, her legs wrapped around his. He had never felt anything like this before, his pain felt so diminished but his heart and mind so electric at the same time—and he had no experience of anything of this sort. He wanted to wake her, he wanted to confess his sins to his angel that night, but she woke at the exact moment he was going to ask for forgiveness . . . and he didn't have the strength.

He was a coward and a liar and he knew it. He could only hope that she would have mercy on him. Her eyes fluttered and searched for him, and he felt a crushing weight on him. He couldn't ruin who she thought he was, but he was terrified of their future, for he learned as a child that every lie made in the dark becomes an evil truth in the light.

The sounds of laughing and a dog barking wake me from my three-hour sleep. I never get much sleep anyway, but I would appreciate a little peace in the hallways, considering it's a Monday morning and I have class in . . . I reach for my phone and check the time.

8:43.

Fuck.

I have less than thirty minutes to get to my Literature class— and why the hell is there a dog in the house, anyway?

Grabbing last night's black jeans from the floor, I pull them on, stumbling slightly and cursing at the tight fabric. My legs are

just too damn long to wear baggy jeans without looking like fucking Gumby. I tossed my keys onto the floor last night, so I'm sub-
jected to the ordeal of rummaging through the clutter of shit to
find them. Black T-shirts, dirty black jeans, and filthy socks crowd
the floor.

I make my way through the house, ignoring the telltale signs
of last night's party. Logan waves to me, bags under his eyes and
an energy drink in his hand.

"I feel like shit, man," he groans, trying to smile. He's always
smiling, and I catch myself wondering what that would feel like.
To be happy all the time like he is. Even this hungover. I never
managed it.

"You've got the right idea, not drinking." He walks over to the
fridge. He pulls out a half gallon of milk and drinks it straight
from the container.

"Nice." I shake my head at him, and he smiles, then drinks
some more. The kitchen starts to fill up with other members of
the fraternity, and since I'm not in their clique, I grab a piece of
pizza from the detritus of last night's drunken decision to order
ten pizzas at 4 a.m.

As I'm leaving the room, I hear Neil asking everyone if they
want to go to some restaurant tonight before the party. I didn't
expect them to invite me . . . they never do. It's not that I would
ever be caught dead hanging out with a bunch of dumb-ass frat
boys with too much gel in their hair outside of a party or two.

My mum's always giving me a hard time about "making
friends," but she doesn't get it. It's not that fucking easy, or remotely entertaining. Why would I put myself out there to get the
approval of people I can't stand, just to feel slightly more important in life? I don't need friends. I have a small group of people I
can slightly tolerate, and that's more than enough for me.

By the time I get to campus, the parking lot is almost full and
I have to cut off some douchebag in a Beamer to take his spot.

The professor is already blabbing when I enter the lecture room. Looking around the space, I search for an empty seat and notice the girl in the front row. Her long blond hair is *mildly* recognizable; it's the long skirt touching the floor that confirms it. Tessa, Steph's prudish roommate.

Sitting next to Landon Gibson. Of course she is. This should be fun: Tessa trapped in a classroom with me, an empty seat next to her. This has quickly become the highlight of my day.

As I get closer, she looks back at me and her eyes go wide. She turns around quickly, and I move quickly to sit next to her. Just like I knew she would, she ignores me. She's wearing a blue button-up shirt that has to be at least two sizes too big, and her hair is pinned back away from her face.

Just as I approach them, my phone vibrates in my pocket.

A text from my sperm donor: Karen's making a nice dinner, you should come by.

Has he lost his damn mind? I look over at Landon, who happens to be Karen's perfect son, all fresh in his polo shirt.

Hell no, I'm not going. Like I would ever, ever go to his shiny new house for dinner with his girlfriend and Landon. Perfect little Landon, who loves sports and kisses everyone's ass to be the nicest, most respectful boy in the land.

Bleh.

I wait for dear "brother" Landon to say something to me, but he doesn't. So much for my dad's promise of "blending our family." *Fucker.*

"I think this will be my favorite class," Tessa says to him once the professor has dismissed us.

Weirdly, it may be my favorite, too, even though I'm sitting in the class for fun, really. I got away with classifying it as an elective even though I've taken it before.

She turns to me when she realizes that I'm following them. "What do you want, Hardin?"

It's already working.

I smile at her, an innocent smile, as if I'm not trying to get under her skin. "Nothing. Nothing. I'm just so glad we have a class together." My tone is mocking, and she rewards my sarcasm with an eye roll. I continue to stare her way the entire duration of the class, getting a rush each time she huffs or fidgets uncomfortably. She's so easy to rile up—I love it. The hour is over before I would like it to be, and Tessa starts packing her bag up before the professor dismisses us. Not so fast.

I jump to my feet, ready to follow her and Landon out of the building. I'm not ready for my fun to end just yet. When we reach the hallway, Landon turns to Tessa. She looks nervous having both of us standing in front of her.

"I'll see you later, Tessa," Landon says without a word to me.

"You would find the lamest kid in class to befriend," I tease her as he disappears into the crowd of freshmen trying to find their way around campus.

I picture Landon's mum and my dad holding hands in a cheery, "look at how much we love each other" way. His mum's hand holding that of my father, Ken Scott, aka Father of the Fucking Year, makes me cringe. I can't remember a single time when he held *my* mum's hand like that.

"Don't say that about him; he's a sweet guy. Unlike you," she snaps.

I turn to her, surprised by her vehement loyalty to him. Does she know him already? Does he know her? Does she like him? *Why the fuck would I care?*

Pushing the questions far from my mind, I have an electric urge to push her buttons more. "You're becoming more feisty with each chat we have, Theresa."

She begins to walk faster to get away from me, so I speed up to match her pace.

"If you call me Theresa one more time . . ." Her full lips purse together, and she attempts a glare at me. But her eyes warm mid-glare, shifting from gray into a pale blue and the tension slips from my shoulders. I feel it, something creeping up my spine as my body starts to relax.

I shake it off, this weird feeling. She's still staring. I changed my mind; I thought I liked how she stared at me before, trying to decipher me, but now I can feel her judgment crawling over my skin. Now she's looking at my inked arms the way my gran does. I don't need her questioning me and my fucking choices.

"Stop staring at me!" I demand, and walk away. I turn the corner and feel breathless. It reminds me of those nights when I'd smoke just way too many cigarettes. *I don't smoke anymore, I don't do that anymore,* I have to remind myself, and lean against the brick wall and catch my breath.

She's odd, that blond girl with too much attitude.

THE ENTIRE WEEK was shit. Party after party, noise after noise. All the sounds of misery.

At most I've slept a total of twenty hours in the past week, and I'm exhausted today. I can barely see straight through my throbbing headache, and I can't find my keys this morning. I'm irritated as fuck and in a fighting mood.

While I'm turning my room upside down, there's a knock at the door. I consider ignoring it, but the knock comes again, this time louder.

When I answer, a girl in a WCU jersey is standing in my doorway, her eyes red and her cheeks flushed.

"Can I come in?" she asks, her hands shaking.

"No. Sorry." I close the door in her face. Seconds later another knock. Damn it. I don't know who the chick is, but she needs to find another door to knock on. She continues tapping away at my door, and I yank it open.

Neil, one of the biggest of the douchebags in the fraternity, is standing there. His blond hair is ruffled, messy, and he smells like beer and pussy.

"What the fuck do you want?" I ask him, and walk back into the room, tossing a pair of jeans at him.

"Have you s-seen Cady?" His tone is off, his words slurred.

"Who?"

"The girl I was with last night? Have you seen her?"

I think back to the red eyes of the girl in the jersey, the way she was wandering the halls, and I shake my head. I thought she was high at first, and maybe she was, but it never does well to assume.

"She left and she's not coming back. Leave her alone." I grab a book from my shelf and throw it at him.

Groaning, he calls me a dick and leaves.

I'm still pissed as I drive back to campus, and I continue my newly found pattern of annoying Steph's roommate.

"I'm excited for this class. I've heard really good things about it," Landon tells her as I walk up behind them. They must be closer friends than I thought. Her voice is quiet when she responds to him, and he smiles at her. Her smile is warm, so warm that I look away for a moment.

Do they like each other? She has a mannequin boyfriend. He has a girlfriend, as far as I know. They must have broken up, by the way he's looking at Tessa.

Halfway through class, Landon leaves and Tessa literally moves her chair farther away from me.

"Monday we begin our weeklong discussion of Jane Austen's *Pride and Prejudice,*" Professor Something-or-other announces to the class. I glance over at Tessa, and she's smiling. Not just smiling—she's grinning from ear to ear.

Of course she is. Chicks love *Pride and Prejudice.* They can't get enough of Darcy and his pride-turned-charm bullshit.

I watch Tessa gather her things: a massive planner and every textbook this campus carries. I'm trying to pretend to stall, but really, even doing that is difficult, considering just how long it takes her to pick everything back up and put it neatly into her bag.

Following her outside, I say, "Let me guess: you are just madly in love with Mr. Darcy."

I have to tease her over this. *Have to.*

"Every woman who has read the novel is," she responds, her tongue sticking out a little at the end and her eyes focused anywhere other than my face. I follow her still and watch her look both ways before she crosses the street at the intersection.

"Of course you do." I laugh, pausing a moment before I realize she's gotten most of the way across the street without me. Damn, she walks fast.

"I'm sure you aren't able to comprehend Mr. Darcy's appeal." Tessa tries to insult me as I catch up, but I just laugh again.

"A man who is rude and intolerable being made into a romantic hero? It's ridiculous. If Elizabeth had any sense, she would have told him to fuck off from the beginning."

Miss Priss turns to face me, and to my surprise I hear the soft sound of a giggle. As in, the innocent and unintentional giggles that have seemingly disappeared from the world today. She covers her mouth the moment the sound hits the air, but I heard it. I heard it, as if it had pierced through me.

"So you do agree that Elizabeth is an idiot?" I press.

"No, she is one of the strongest, most complex characters ever written."

She defends Elizabeth Bennet in a way that most eighteen-year-olds would never be able to, with a Tom Hanks movie thrown in there to boot. I find myself laughing, genuinely laughing, and she joins in. Her laugh is soft, like cotton.

What the fuck did I just . . .

I immediately stop laughing and I look away from her. This is too damn weird.

She's weird. And obnoxious.

"I'll see you around, Theresa." I dismiss her and walk the other way.

Soft like cotton? Her giggle *pierced through me?* What the fuck was that?

I push that bullshit to the back of my mind and walk to my car. Tonight there's another party, as always, and I'll get my mind away from this shit by burying myself in a tight, wet—

My phone vibrating in my pocket distracts me from my perverted thoughts. Pulling it out, I see Jace's name pop up on the screen, and I quickly answer.

He's been gone for a while, and I'll be glad to have him back. Everyone has that one person they hang out with who makes them feel better about themselves. For me, that's Jace. He's an asshole—grade-A fucking dickhead, ask anyone—but he's entertaining and he always makes for a good time.

six

The closer he got to her, the more of her he needed to explore. When he found himself wondering what she thought of when she woke up in the morning, or how long she takes to get ready, he knew she was becoming something more than a passerby in his life. Suddenly, she was more than the game he was playing with her. In his own sick way, he was glad that he could use the game as an excuse to spend more time with her. He had leverage and a reason to find out everything there was to know about her without his friends getting suspicious. He had validation for wanting to spend as many hours with her as he could.

In order to win, he had to, right?

Why does she have to come again?" Molly asks the small group as she takes a drag of her cigarette.

"Because she is Steph's roommate, and Steph likes her for some heretofore unexplained reason, so she's bringing the kid along," Nate explains.

"She's a total bitch, though. Super fucking obnoxious." I groan, rubbing my head. She irritates me even when she's not around. Molly must like my reaction, because she leans into me. I move away before she touches me, pretending that I didn't realize her intention.

I spent the afternoon fucking her, burying my cock inside of her and thinking of someone else. I could feel the soft curves of her hip, the full breasts. I could hear her voice saying my name. I wrapped my hands in pink hair I imagined blond and came hard into the condom. Molly was so proud of herself for finally getting me off without her mouth.

If only she knew.

"She's hot, though," Nate adds.

Has *everyone* noticed how hot Tessa is by now?

"Hot? No, she's not," I lie through my teeth.

A tan hand swipes over neatly gelled hair. "She's definitely hot, dude," Zed says with surprising certainty. "I would fuck her in a heartbeat."

"You wish. She's a total prude, obviously. I mean, who's a virgin in college?" Molly mocks Tessa.

Nate laughs. "Right—when did you become friends with her and she told you that?"

Molly scowls at him. "Me? I wouldn't talk to her, but Steph has to, and she overheard something about it when 'Princess' was talking to her boyfriend, it seems."

"Maybe that's why she's such a bitch, because she hasn't been fucked properly," I say, and move a few inches away from Molly, hoping she won't follow.

"I may need to do that, then," Zed says, trying to make everyone laugh. He fails.

"Yeah, right. You couldn't even if you tried," I taunt him.

"And you could? I would have a better chance than you!" he counters.

He can't be serious. Does he not remember his precious Samantha?

"What did I miss?" Jace sits down on the concrete and pulls a joint from his pocket.

"Steph has a total snob for a roommate, and Zed and Hardin here are arguing over who could fuck her first," Molly informs him with a growl.

Does Zed actually think she would fuck him? I look around

the group, annoyed that everyone is thinking about her that way. If her body is as pure as they say, I can just imagine what the smallest touch would do to her. I would have her twitching beneath me, begging me for more. Zed could never make her come the way I could.

But would she let him try? If the playing field were completely equal, would Tessa choose him over me?

"You know . . . we could make this much more interesting. You up for it?" I turn to Zed.

Zed smiles. "Depends."

"Hmm . . . Okay, so let's see who can hook up with her first."

What's the point of this? I ask myself the moment I say the words.

And another part of me replies, *It could be fun. At least it will give me something to do and a reason to annoy her further.*

"I don't know . . ." Zed's voice is full of doubt. I figured he would be all for beating me at something, given our past and the unspoken grudge he holds against me.

"Come on, don't be a pussy. It won't be that hard. We'll get Steph to make sure she comes to the next party, get her to be friendly with us," I explain to them. "She's young and naive—it'll be simple."

I've done this sort of thing before—different stakes and different prey, but a game all the same.

"This is stupid. Who gives a shit who can take some random girl's virginity?" Molly huffs, whining like usual.

"If you're so convinced you can do it, I'll give you a week." Jace chokes on the smoke in his lungs and passes the joint to Molly.

"A week? Dude, she's super bitchy and we already don't get along. I think I'll need longer than that." They don't know how stubborn this chick is. She's rude and fucking pushy.

"How long? Two weeks? Look, if you get it within a month,

I'll give you five hundred," Zed says, leaning back against the concrete.

"Five hundred dollars?" Molly gapes. Her fury is amusing. She's an attention whore, through and through, and she hates Tessa for stealing the limelight from her.

"And I'll add three. Eight hundred. You think you can do it?" Jace asks with bloodshot eyes.

"Yeah, of course I can do it. I just hope she doesn't get all psycho and clingy," I say, deciding whether or not to brag about the times I've won games like this in the past. I decide against it. I'm impressed by how easy it is for my signature smirk to come back, the one that Mark, my old friend from Hampstead, always called "the seal." It's the look I get when I know I'm going to win something, or someone. Here I am, smirking at Zed, plotting in my mind as the group waits for someone to take me down a few pegs.

"Doubt it." Nate laughs, lighting another cigarette.

"She isn't going to go for you. She doesn't seem that stupid." Zed glares at me.

Jace laughs, looking directly at me. "Yeah, so we need proof when you hit it."

Proof? That shouldn't be too hard. I can be creative.

"What about a video? I could use some new material." Jace leans back, still eyeing me.

"No, no. That's too risky," I argue. I've been down that road before and want to steer fucking clear of it from now on. "Trust me, you'll get your proof without all that." I look directly at Zed and pull out that smirk again. "I've never fucked a virgin. This should be fun."

I smile a fake smile and bring my fingers to my lip ring like I'm trying to hide it.

Molly interjects, "Wait, how exactly are you two idiots going to get this show on the road? It doesn't make sense: all of a sudden you're both just trying to fuck her?" She flips her hair in annoyance. "At least be fucking smart about it," she gripes, and holds her hand out to borrow Nate's lighter.

"Good point," Jace says. "How about a game?"

"A game?" Zed looks intrigued.

"Like Truth or Dare. We could ask her questions about sex, confirm she's a virgin so you two aren't wasting your time to begin with." Jace waves his hand between Zed and me.

"Truth or Dare? You've gotta be shitting me," I groan. No one plays that bullshit anymore.

"Stupid idea." Nate shakes his head, mock disappointment playing on his face.

No one outside of sixth grade would ever want to play Truth or Dare.

"Actually, it's a good idea. Less obvious," Steph adds. "She's so clueless, she'll think it's something people do in college for fun. It's just edgy enough to seem dangerous to her, and just juvenile enough for her to understand."

As I look around the group, everyone is nodding and laughing. These idiots.

I shrug, giving in to their idea, but only because I don't have a better one.

"Truth or Dare, it is." Jace finalizes it.

THE PARTY IS CROWDED, even more than the one last week, and I'm sober, like always. I stayed in my room as the music got louder and louder, then decided to come down.

As I'm wandering around the living room to find Nate, I stop walking when I see Tessa sitting on the couch. Well, at least I *think* it's Tessa? She's dressed differently from before. Way differently. The intriguing blue-gray eyes stand out more when they're lined with makeup, and her clothes are snug on her curvy body.

She's fucking hot. I wouldn't let her know that, but goddamn, she's fucking hot.

"You look . . . different." I can't stop looking at her as she gets to her feet. Her hips—damn, those fucking hips should have my fingertips imprinted on their skin.

"Your clothes actually fit you tonight." The sound comes out as a laugh, but I didn't mean for my comment to be a joke.

She rolls her eyes at me and pulls the top of her shirt up to cover her incredible cleavage.

"It's a surprise to see you here," I say to her, still checking her out.

She sighs. "I'm a bit surprised myself that I ended up here again." She walks away from me without a warning, and I hesitate for a moment, considering whether I should follow her. I know the plan, and now that she's dressed like this, I'm even more ready to get the ball rolling on this shit. I decide not to follow her, not yet. I let her get lost in the crowd for a bit.

A few minutes later, I'm leaning against the counter in the kitchen, when Molly approaches me. "Are you ready for this bull-shit or what?" she asks.

She's irritated and jealous of the new center of attention. I get it. She's used to getting attention from the opposite sex; it's how she feels needed.

I understand that more than anyone.

"Are you?" I raise a brow to her.

She rolls her heavily lined eyes at me. "I'll have Steph find her and bring her to the living room, since you obviously aren't going to be of any help."

By the time I sit down, water cup in hand, Tessa is joining the group. I feel uneasy but excited for some reason as the game be-gins. I try not to think of Natalie or Melissa or any of the others. It's not their fault they were born into this society right along with the scum of it, myself included.

"Let's play Truth or Dare," Zed starts, and our small group of tattooed friends gather around the couch. Molly is passing around a bottle of vodka, and I look away from it, drinking my water as if it was burning my throat in that familiar way.

Steph; Nate; his roommate, Tristan; Zed; and Molly take turns drinking from the bottle. Tessa watches them but doesn't have any. I don't take her for an addict like me. Maybe she just doesn't like to drink. Even in college, at a party.

"You should play, too, Tessa." Molly smiles at her. I know that smile. It's no good. I still can't believe we're going through with this childish bullshit game.

"No, I'd rather not." Tessa picks at her fingernails, and I glance at Zed. He looks a little worried. Perhaps he's intimidated by the way she keeps glancing at me instead of him.

"To actually play, she would have to stop being a prude for five minutes," I goad her. The group laughs—all except Steph, who's putting on a good show. She's not fooling me; I know her ass better than that.

I watch Tessa struggle with the peer pressure, ready to give in, then I lean into Zed. "This will be easy. You may as well pay me now," I tell him.

Maybe this game was a good idea after all.

During the first few turns, Zed chugs a beer, Molly shows off her nipple piercings. I get a kick out of watching Tessa's eyes bulge and her cheeks turn a deep red as she watches Molly. I can't help but imagine Tessa's full tits, perky and soft, decorated with small barbells.

"Truth or dare, Theresa?" Nate asks, getting this show on the road. Finally.

"Truth?" She sounds unsure. I don't miss that she didn't correct Nate when he called her Theresa, whereas every time I do it, she acts as if she wants to chop my balls off and feed them to her lapdog of a boyfriend.

"Of course," I taunt. She glares at me as Nate rubs his hands together while trying to pretend like we all haven't already agreed upon what he's supposed to ask.

"Okay. Are you . . . a virgin?" Nate finally asks.

Tessa's eyes go wide, wider than usual, and she makes a light choking noise in the back of her throat. She's shocked, horrified, and offended that a stranger would ask her such a personal question. A blush runs down her neck to her chest. Her hands fidget, and I get the feeling she's trying to decide whether to curse his ass out or run from the room.

"Well?" I ask, all the while picturing her naked body under mine. Her voice, soft and subtle, would be making noises that no man has ever heard before. The thought is beyond fucking intriguing, but also fucked up, since I can't speak to the girl without getting assaulted by her snobbish attitude.

At last, this innocent girl gives a quick, silent nod.

Every one of us is thinking about our game and how this sweet, innocent, and crumpling naive girl just became the main piece.

Tessa's a virgin—she's just admitted it to the lot of us. I knew this to be true before she admitted it. I could tell by the way she shivered from our conversations alone. Thinking about being the first one to have her, to show her what she's been missing out on, makes my cock twitch. I imagine what's under her outfit. Her soft skin, full tits, her nipples hardening under my touch. Now the game has begun, and my blood is pumping. I'm anxious to be inside of her.

She plays with her hair from across the circle, and I imagine that blond hair wrapped around my fist, me pulling her closer to me as I fuck her from behind. I would slap her round ass, hoping to leave a mark there. She would be moaning my name through her pink, swollen lips. My name will sound so good coming from her mouth. I adjust my pants and watch Tessa again.

She licks her lips, and I internally groan.

I wonder how many cocks she's had down her throat? I wonder if she's ever tasted a man's come before, and as the conversation continues, I learn that she has done next to nothing when it comes to sex, and I intend to show her every last fucking detail of what she's missed.

seven

There are so many mistakes to be made in life, and he made them all. Every ounce of respect he held for her seemed to disappear beneath the confusion of his mind. He loved her and cherished her more than his own breath, but he failed and failed and failed to show it. To remember it when it counted. He toyed with her, played immature games, and didn't show her his truth. This truth that he had hidden away, locked away tightly and guarded by his upbringing, by the fact that he couldn't remember the number of times he was hugged and cherished as a child. He wasn't trying to make excuses, he was only used to doing so. He always blamed everyone else, never took credit for what he did or said. It was easier that way.

But eventually, he learned his lesson.

"Dare." I roll my eyes at the childish game. Like anyone thought I would choose otherwise.

I stare at Tessa, watching Mother Theresa fumble at the challenge of coming up with a good dare. "I . . . hmm. I dare you to . . ." She comes up short. Everyone is waiting, anticipating her question as she plays into our scheme.

"To what?" I push her to hurry along with this shit.

This girl, who doesn't even know how much trouble she's in with this pack of jackals . . . she still sits in silence, looking around the group in a dramatic panic. It's only a party game, but I can tell she's an overachiever, even when it comes to something this stupid. It's entertaining to watch her worry over something so small. She has a habit of chewing on her bottom lip, the same way I play with my ring. Briefly I imagine her with a ring through her lip. She would look so fucking hot.

"Take your shirt off and keep it off the entire game!" Molly says for Tessa.

And Tessa's cheeks flush. A pattern.

"How juvenile." I lift my black T-shirt up over my head and catch Tessa's eyes on my body. She's staring, hard, so hard that she doesn't even notice me catching her. Steph nudges her with her elbow, and she looks away, cheeks red and eyes downcast.

I'm officially winning this. Zed has no chance.

The game continues, and I sit here half dressed and watch Tessa try and keep her eyes off of me. I can't read her—I can't tell if she's disgusted by my tattoos or intrigued by them. Her jaw keeps twitching; she's trying her best to sit still.

Interesting.

"Tessa, truth or dare?" Tristan asks.

I lean back on my palms. "Why even ask? We know she'll say truth—"

"Dare," the stubborn girl says, surprising me with the challenge in her voice. It's a defiant sound, different than I would have thought possible just a few moments ago.

"Hmm . . . Tessa, I dare you to . . . take a shot of vodka." Tristan smiles.

"I don't drink." She sticks her chin out in refusal.

I figured as much, but I'm pleased by this revelation. Everyone around this place can't wait for their next high; it's refreshing to have someone who doesn't rely on that.

"That's the point of the dare," Tristan counters.

"Look, if you don't want to do it . . ." Nate starts to tell her.

"She's such a pussy," Molly says into my ear.

Pussy? Because she doesn't want to drink?

"Fine, one shot," she says. And like that, Little Miss Oh-I-Don't-Do-X-Y-or-Z caves easily.

Honestly, I'm a little disappointed. Not sure why, but I thought there was something different about her. I thought she wasn't like the rest of us, desperate to get the attention of our peers.

I was wrong about her, obviously.

"Same dare," Zed says to her, and takes a large swig before handing vodka over. I'm annoyed by them drinking from the same bottle; it's disgusting, really.

As the game goes on, drink after drink, she winces and wipes the burning liquid from her lips. Her eyes are red now, her cheeks matching. She looks lost and off balance, even when sitting down.

She lifts the bottle to her lips again, and I find my hand grasping it, pulling it from her. She doesn't try to stop me—does she sense that she's had enough to drink?

Does she see this as her first taste at freedom? Such a sheltered girl, out here in the big bad world of people who drink to numb themselves from whatever issues their shitty parents passed on to them. Maybe hers, like mine, is neglect. Was this girl neglected, too? I move my eyes to the neatly pressed collar of her shirt. Nope, she sure as hell wasn't neglected. It's possible that her low self-esteem is just a phase. She wants to break free of her controlling mummy and daddy and show herself that she can be a wild girl, too. She's fully capable of hanging out with the bad kids and drinking herself sick.

The other possibility is that the lot of us are just that good at dragging people down.

"I think you've had enough," I say, and go to hand the bottle off to Nate. But Tessa quickly grabs it at the last second and takes another drink. The trace of a smirk covers her full lips as she licks them clean. I watch her throat as she swallows in a defiant gulp, and want to push her lips open and drink the liquor from her mouth.

I shake the thought away. Molly glances at me, swirling her finger in the air to say that I'm crazy.

Maybe I am.

"I can't believe you've never been drunk before, Tessa. It's fun, right?" Zed asks her.

She giggles and I roll my eyes.

"Hardin, truth or dare?" Molly asks.

"Dare." Did she have to ask? Maybe I should have done what Tessa did, just to prove a point.

"I dare you to kiss Tessa." Molly's painted lips turn into a smile, and I hear Tessa gasp.

She speaks before I can get a word in. "No, I have a boy-friend."

"So? It's just a dare. Just do it," Molly says, picking at her nails.

"No." Tessa's voice rises. "I'm not kissing anyone." She stands and walks to the other side of the room. I take a drink of my water and watch her disappear out the front door. She was look-ing at me all night, staring at my shirtless chest, yet she was so disgusted by the thought of kissing me that she would throw a fit and run away?

Or is it possible that a kiss could mean more to her than just conceding to a dare?

"There she goes, ladies and gentlemen!" Nate laughs, leaning into me. The beer in his cup tips over the top and splashes onto the carpet in front of him. He doesn't bother to clean it up. These floors have seen worse.

"You better run after her or you'll lose," Steph says in a mock-ing voice as I slip my shirt back on.

Man, she's always so pissy lately, I wonder what her prob-lem is.

"Which of you fuckers is gonna chase her?" Nate asks. I look around the crowded room. She's nowhere in sight. Zed is watching me, gauging my reaction to her little tantrum. I keep my face neutral, not expressing the slightest bit of interest as I scan the room again. There's no way I'm letting him be the one to get to her first. She's pissed because they dared her to kiss me. This stupid-ass game wasn't my idea anyway, and now it's already back-fired. I fucking told them it was a bad idea. When Logan distracts Zed, I lean up to check the kitchen. I spot Tessa and move to get up off the floor.

"Where are you going?" Molly wraps her hand around my arm as I stand.

"Erm, to get some more water." I look down into my nearly full cup, not giving a shit if she notices my ruse.

I glance around the room, passing through the crowd while searching for Tessa's blond hair. When I enter the kitchen, she's standing at the counter, a bottle of Jack in her hands. She lifts the bottle, and I can feel the familiar ache of need in the back of my throat.

I'm appalled that this girl would fall into such a dangerous pattern so immediately. The way her eyes are clamped shut and the gagging sounds she makes when she finishes . . . It burns and makes her half sick, yet she still takes another swig. Will she crave it? Will it make her forget things, numbing her mind to memories, like it used to do for me? Does the girl even *have* memories that she would need to be numb to? By the looks of it, she might.

I watch her still, as she turns the faucet on, searching for a glass. She opens the cabinet and glances toward the doorway. I step back, out of view.

What am I doing in here? Following her around and watching her sudden attachment to the amnesia of liquor?

I quickly turn away and go back to my group. Molly is taunt-ing Logan about his date last night and Nate is lighting a cigarette when I sit back down on the dirty floor.

"Let's get out of here. I'm bored and I can tell you are too." Molly's breath is hot on my neck as she wraps her arms around my shoulders. I shrug her off and shake my head. She latches on again.

"I'm going upstairs," I tell her. Her arms feel like steel, pulling me down.

"Good idea." She presses her lips against my neck.

From the combination of her overdrinking and my quick movement, she falls back onto the carpet when she tries to wrap her arms around me, and I get to my feet.

"Yikes. That was tough to watch," Logan teases her. She flips him off and turns to me.

"Seriously, Hardin?" she growls.

"Seriously, Molly." I turn away from her and head up the stairs.

As I reach the top of the staircase, my phone rings in my front pocket. Ken's name flashes on the screen, and I press ignore. I'm not in the mood to deal with him. I'm usually not. I just want to be alone, away from all this music and all these voices. I want my shitty excuse for a father to stop trying to "connect" with me. I want to be lost in the world of a novel where the characters have much worse problems than me and make me feel slightly more normal than I am.

But when I near my room, I see the door is open, cracked just enough for me to know something is off. I always lock that damn door; did I forget?

Inside, Tessa is sitting on my bed, one of my books in her hand. My phone buzzes again. My anger passes from Ken to her. She thinks she can just do whatever the fuck she wants? She can come into my room, more than once, without my permission?

Why is she in here? I warned her before. What's her problem?

I walk toward her. "What part of 'No One Comes into My Room' did you not understand?"

She squares her shoulders out of surprise. "S-sorry. I . . ." Her voice falters and her eyes grow wide, not with fear . . . with anger. She's trying that thing again, the one where she's really patient with me.

I gesture toward the door. "Get out."

"You don't have to be such a jerk!" she yells at me.

"You're in my room." The volume of my voice matches hers as I remind her, "Again, after I told you not to be. So get out!"

"Why don't you like me?" she says. I can see she's trying to be tough, but her tone has deflated, and her big eyes have made my pulse quicken.

eight

The question, so bold and raw, surprised him, and made him realize he was standing at the edge of a cliff. With one blow of the wind, he would tumble over.

Why would she ask this? Isn't it obvious why I don't like her? She's annoying as hell. She . . .

Well . . .

She's judgmental. She's constantly judging me and giving me shit about my attitude when I start shit with her. And she . . .

She's not that bad, I guess.

"Why are you asking me this?" I ask, trying to keep my voice calm.

She's glaring at me. I return the favor and glare just as hard. She thinks she can intimidate me? She's in my room, asking me stupid questions, looking at me like that . . .

"I don't know . . . because I've been nothing but nice to you and you've been nothing but rude to me. And here I actually thought at one point we could be friends."

Her bloodshot eyes are strong, holding so much that I don't know about her. Or care about.

Friends? Is she actually fucking serious? I don't have friends. I don't need friends.

"Us? Friends?" I force a laugh. "Isn't it obvious why we can't be friends?"

"Not to me," she says plainly, and at first I almost think it's a joke. But the conviction in her voice tells me that she's actually serious. This girl is absolutely mad. She thinks someone like me could be friends with someone like her? Doesn't she know that I can barely stand people in general, let alone my own group of "friends"?

How shall I begin the list of reasons why this would never work?

"Well, for starters, you're too uptight—you probably grew up in some perfect little model home that looks like every other house on the block," I begin, thinking of the black mold covering the ceiling in my childhood bedroom. "Your parents probably bought you everything you ever asked for, and you never had to want for anything. With your stupid pleated skirts . . ." I look at the outfit she's wearing now, ignoring the way the material rests on her full hips. "I mean, honestly, who dresses like that at eighteen?"

Her mouth falls open and she steps toward me. I back away without thinking. I can tell by the stormy gray of her eyes that I'm in for it.

"You know nothing about me, you condescending jerk! My life is nothing like that! My alcoholic dad left us when I was ten, and my mother worked her ass off to make sure I could go to college. I got my own job as soon as I turned sixteen to help with bills, and I happen to *like* my clothes—" She waves her hands toward her outfit, shouting now, so frustrated that her small hands are shaking. "Sorry if I don't dress like a slut like all the girls around you! For someone who tries too hard to stand out and be different, you sure are judgmental about people who are different from *you!*"

And with that, she turns away from me to face the door.

Is she telling the truth? Is this perfect girl actually caught up in the unfortunate cycle of kids having to grow up too fast? If so, why is she smiling every time I see her?

Judgmental? She's calling me judgmental after labeling girls who dress a certain way sluts? She's staring at me now, waiting for my reaction, but I don't have one. I'm rendered speechless by this fiery, *judgmental,* intriguing woman.

"You know what? I don't want to be friends with you anyway," she says before my brain pulls out of its stupor.

Tessa reaches for the door handle, and I think back to Seth, my first friend in my life. His family had no money either, but when one of his rich grandparents he didn't know died, he got a pretty penny. His ratty shoes were traded in for white ones with lights on the bottom. I thought they were so cool. I asked my mum for a pair once for my birthday. She gave me a sad smile, and on the morning of my birthday, she handed me a shoe box. I was so excited to tear the thing open, expecting those damn light-up shoes. Inside the box was a pair of shoes, all right, but with none of those pretty lights on the bottom. I could tell the gift made her sad, but I didn't quite understand why until the months went by and I started to see Seth less and less, until one day, the only time I got to see him was when he walked past my house with his new friends, all wearing light-up shoes.

He was my first and last friend, and my life has been much more simple without friendship.

"Where are you going?" I ask Tessa, a girl who thought we could be friends. She pauses, confused. Just like I am.

"To the bus stop so I can go back to my room and never, ever come back here again. I am *done* trying to be friends with any of you."

I feel like a complete shit. On the one hand, having her hate me will be better in the long run, but on the other . . . well, I want her to like me enough to fuck me.

She can hate me after I win the Bet.

"It's too late to take the bus alone," I say. Looking the way she does and the fact that she's been drinking liquor all night, it would be a really fucking bad idea for her to go to the bus stop by herself.

She spins around to face me, and I realize for the first time there are tears in her eyes. "You're not seriously trying to act like you care if something happened to me?" Tessa laughs, shaking her head.

"I'm not saying I do . . . I'm just warning you. It's a bad idea," I tell her. I glance at my bookshelf, comparing her to Catherine, the main female character in the book she was reading when I walked in. She's a lot like her: moody and with too much to prove. Elizabeth Bennet is the same, always opening her mouth with some emphatic point to make. I like it. College girls these days just seem to have lost the spunk. They only want to please men, not themselves—and where's the fun in that?

"Well, Hardin, I don't have any other options. Everyone is drunk—including myself." She starts to cry all over again.

I soften a little. Why is she crying? She's always crying, it seems.

I try to cheer her up the only way I know how . . . with sarcasm. "Do you always cry at parties?"

"Apparently, whenever you're at them. And since these are the only ones I've ever been to . . ."

Tessa opens my door, but as she goes to leave, she stumbles and grips the edge of my dresser.

"Theresa . . ." My voice is soft, softer than I knew it could be. "You okay?" I ask.

She nods. She looks confused, pissed, and stunning; mostly pissed, though.

Do I care if she's okay? She's sick and drunk, and there's no way in hell I'm going to try and score points against Zed tonight. I don't want to, and that would be cheating, anyway; she's far too drunk.

"Why don't you just sit down for a few minutes, then you

can go to the bus stop," I suggest. Maybe I'll win some points for being the nice guy.

"I thought no one was allowed in your room." Her voice is soft and full of curiosity as she sits on my floor. If she knew all the shit that has been on that floor, she wouldn't be sitting there, I'm sure.

I find myself smiling, and the moment I realize what I'm doing, I stop immediately. I make myself clear. She nods and hic-cups, looking as if she's going to puke any second. "If you throw up in my room . . ." I warn.

She'll be cleaning that shit up, that's for sure.

"I think I just need some water," Tessa tells me.

I hand her my cup. "Here."

Her hand pushes against the cup as she rolls her eyes in an-noyance. "I said water, not beer."

"It *is* water. I don't drink."

She snorts. "Hilarious. You're not going to sit here and babysit, are you?"

Hell yes, I am. I'm not going to leave her alone in here to fuck with my shit or throw up all over my books.

"You bring out the worst in me." Her comment surprises me out of my silence.

"That's harsh," I snap at her. I bring out the worst in her? She doesn't even know me. I continue: "And yes, I am going to sit here and babysit you. You're drunk for the first time in your life, and you have a habit of touching my things when I'm not around."

I sit down on my bed as she cautiously takes a drink of my water. Thought so. The room is probably beginning to spin for her. Poor girl. I watch her carefully as she gulps down the water. The way her eyes close and she licks her lips when she's finished, the way she breathes too heavily. I stare at her without her notic-ing and try my damnedest not to overthink why I'm staring at her in the first place.

There's just so damn much that I don't know about her, so many things I want to know.

She seems so readable from the outside. She's blond, beautiful in a simple way, and I can tell by the old-fashioned way she speaks that she spends hours and hours with her face buried in a book. Yet her temper and the giant chip on her shoulder make me wonder what's underneath all that.

"Can I ask you a question?" I speak without thinking. I try and smile at her, but I get the feeling that I look like a fucking creep.

Her brows push together. "S-s-s-s-sure," she says, drawing out her answer.

What the hell am I going to ask her? I had kind of assumed she would tell me to go to hell.

I go for the easiest question I can think of. "What do you want to do after college?" I know that I should've asked something more personal, something to help me win this game with Zed.

Tessa seems to ponder the question, tapping her finger against her chin before she answers. "Well, I want to be an author or a publisher, whichever comes first."

I could see that, easily.

I don't tell her that I plan to do the exact same thing. Instead, I stare blankly ahead after rolling my eyes.

"Are those your books?" Tessa waves toward my bookshelves.

"They are," I mumble.

"Which is your favorite?"

Fucking Christ, she's nosy.

"I don't play favorites," I lie. She's getting too personal, and she's been in here awhile. Her knowing my favorite books won't help me get what I want.

I need to turn this around, make it less personal. I need to annoy her. "Does Mr. Rogers know you're at a party again?"

My smirk complements her scowl. Mission accomplished.

"Mr. Rogers?"

"Your boyfriend," I explain. "He's the biggest tool I have *ever* seen."

"Don't talk about him like that. He is . . . he is . . . nice."

I can't help but laugh at the way she fumbles for a compliment about her loafer-wearing boyfriend.

She waves a finger at me. "You could only dream of being as nice as he is."

"*Nice*? That's the first word that comes to your mind when talking about your boyfriend? Nice is your 'nice' way of calling him boring." I laugh.

"You don't know him," she insists with admittedly impressive fearlessness.

"Well, I know that he's boring. I could tell by his cardigan and *loafers*." I'm laughing now, really laughing, and my stomach tightens. I can't help it. When I look up at her pissed-off expression, I laugh harder, imagining the human Ken doll whining over a hole in his cashmere sweater.

"He doesn't wear loafers." Tessa covers her mouth to hide her need to laugh. I get it. I would laugh, too. She takes another drink of my water and I keep going.

"Well, he's been dating you for two years and hasn't fucked you yet. I would say he's a square."

As my words hit the air, Tessa spits water back into the cup.

"What the hell did you just say?"

"You heard me, Theresa." I smile at her, fueling her anger.

"You're an asshole, Hardin."

Man, I love how fiery she gets when—

Cold water splashes against my face.

I gasp, surprised by her audacity. I thought we were having fun, throwing rude comments back and forth. I was purposely aggravating her, and it seemed that she was enjoying getting riled up just as much as I enjoyed riling her.

By the disgusted expression on her face, it occurs to me that maybe she doesn't.

Why the hell did I even bring up her boyfriend in the first place? I'm a damn idiot. She was fine, sitting in my room, laughing with me, and I had to ruin it.

Tessa leaves my room quickly as I wipe the water from my face and step into my doorway, watching as she takes the staircase two steps at a time.

Back in my room, the quiet hum of my ceiling fan is my only company. I sit down on my bed, and for the first time since I moved into the house, I wish I wasn't alone in this room.

nine

The moment her lips touched his for the first time, he felt it. He felt a shift somewhere deep inside, somewhere hidden and covered in dust. It was completely untouched since he could remember, likely forever. She awakened him, brought him light and laughter and longing and he knew from the moment her mouth found his, he would never be the same.

Tessa just threw water in my face and left my room in a storm of huffs and puffs and eye rolls. Yet here I am, following her down the stairs after only a few minutes of sitting in my room, whining to myself like a little child throwing a fit over his favorite toy breaking.

Only Tessa isn't my favorite toy; she's too shiny, too new for my dirty hands to play with.

I was only trying to lighten her mood, to cheer her up, but I obviously failed. I should have known that bringing up the subject of her lame-ass boyfriend would be a trigger for her temper.

She's so annoying. She feels entitled and she's moody. Overly sensitive, she is, and she pisses me the fuck off. Who throws a drink, water . . . but still . . . into someone's face like that? For someone who thinks so highly of themselves, she sure does behave like a petulant child.

When I get to the bottom of the stairs, Tessa's in the kitchen, taking a drink from a bottle of liquor. She's looking around the room for someone, and as I watch her my phone goes off in my pocket, another text from Ken: Karen's making dinner tonight if you want to stop by. There's something I want to talk to you about. You haven't responded to my other texts, so I figured one at 3:00 am would at least get to you when you were awake.

Something he wants to talk to me about? I have better things to do, like show Zed who's really the king here. I look back to where Tessa's standing, and notice that Zed's joined her.

Of course that creep is by her side the moment I'm not around.

Tessa's still drinking; she shouldn't be drinking this much. She's going to feel like absolute shit tomorrow. Of course, this is how Zed plans to get her.

"Look how cute they are." I hear a voice, and glancing over, I find Steph next to me, a wine cooler in her hand. Her red hair is messy, falling down around her face.

I look back to Zed and Tessa, this time paying more attention to the way she sighs while staring directly into his eyes. She seems comfortable; her shoulders are relaxed and her eyes are soft. Nothing like how she is around me. She doesn't know Zed any better than she knows me, so why the difference? Is it because, unlike me, he leans against the countertop with his eyes focused only on her eyes? He doesn't let her chest distract him. He leans into her as she smiles at him. He's going the good-cop-to-my-bad-cop route, it would seem.

Damn, he's better than I'd imagined.

Tessa looks toward the door, and Steph jumps back, pulling my arm. I nudge her off.

Steph's eyes are bloodshot, her pupils tiny black dots in a sea of red. "Don't tell her I'm here. I'm sick of babysitting her," she says, and rolls her eyes. Steph doesn't even try to place nice when Tessa's not around. Grade-A bitch.

A drunk blonde in a skintight dress passes by, winking at me. I remember her . . . I think?

"You brought her here," I remind Steph, keeping my voice light. I'm not interested in this at all. Not even sure why I brought it up, really.

"So? I'm bored with her for tonight, and she's for you two to play with, remember?" She shrugs and walks away from me.

Well . . .

"You're going to lose if you just stand around like a creep!" Steph shouts as reaches the front door and takes the hand of that weird dude she was complaining about just last week.

I'm going to lose?

Please. No chance.

But I'm also not going to stand here in this doorway like a damn creep.

I walk back into the living room and find a seat on the couch. I'll wait for her to come to me. She's going to get bored with Zed and his stupid conversation about science and plants, saving the world one flower at a time, all that bullshit. I suppose he believes it, maybe, but with that guy you can never really tell either way. More likely he knows on some subconscious level that only plants can stand to be around him.

In due course, Tessa finds her way into the living room, Zed latched on to her side like a damn lost puppy. She doesn't even notice that I'm in the same room as she sits down on the floor with my crew, only a few feet away.

I feel a squeeze on my bicep and turn just as the blonde from a moment ago wraps her arms around my stomach, holding me tight.

"Hardinnnn . . ." she says with such a drunk lilt that I suddenly can't tell if she's trying to molest me or just keep the room from spinning. "It's good to see you again. Be even better to feel you . . ."

I push her back a little, trying to disengage. But alcohol has made her a persistent octopus, and she grabs me again. Finally, I shift over near one of the frat "brothers" whose name I can never remember, and wrap one of her arms around his shoulder. Sure enough, the rest of her follows suit and she slurs "S-Steeeve, long time no see . . ." as I sneak off, my annoyance with the night rising with each step my boots make across the stained carpet.

"Do the buses run all night?" I hear Tessa ask, clearly gone past buzzed and straight into drunk now. Her voice is thicker. I watch her lips, the bottom one popping out more than the top. She's speaking slowly, teetering on the line of slurring her words.

I force myself to stop listening to her and walk back into the kitchen. She's not my problem—I have no reason to care if she's drunk or not. Less than ten seconds later, I turn the corner and go back into the living room, my feet stopping in front of where Tessa sits on the floor.

When she sees me, this snotty girl rolls her eyes. She seems to do this a hell of a lot.

Not to Zed, though. Never to Zed.

"You and Zed, then?" I raise a brow at her, and she stumbles as she gets to her feet. How much did she drink? Her eyes are clear as they meet mine; I can't tell.

I reach out for her arm as she pushes past. "Let go of me, Hardin!" Her arms fly into the air, and I try not to laugh at her dramatics. Her eyes move around the room like she's looking for something to throw at me. "I'm just trying to find out about the bus."

She pushes past me, her shoulder bumping into mine, and I gently grab hold of her arm to steady her.

"Chill out . . . it's three a.m. There is no bus." I let go of her arm and watch realization hit her. "Your newfound alcoholic life-style has you stuck here again."

The humor in this is undeniable. She's so adamant about hating this scene—yet here she is again, staying the night.

She stares blankly at me, all big eyes and pouty lips, and I take a moment to pour salt onto her wounded ego.

"Unless you want to go home with Zed . . ." I nod toward the living room, and she scowls.

Without a word, she walks off.

What's the point of this? Me following her around, trying to get a rise out of her? There's no point, and really it's a waste of my time. She seems to play the game just as well as I do.

When I get back to my room, I grab a book from the shelf and pull my shirt up and over my head, tossing it onto the floor and then adding my jeans to the mess. I open the novel to a random page and begin to read:

> *What use were anger and protestations against her silly credulity? We parted that night—hostile; but next day beheld me on the road to Wuthering Heights, by the side of my wilful young mistress's pony. I couldn't bear to witness her sorrow: to see her pale, dejected countenance, and heavy eyes: and I yielded, in the faint hope that Linton himself might prove, by his reception of us, how little of the tale was founded on fact.*

A blond Catherine sat there, at the edge of the moors, with her hair tied back in a bow as red as the blood running through his veins. She wasn't thinking; she was lost. She turned to him, her voice ringing through the air between them. "Hardin?"

Catherine's voice is loud, so loud it's breaking through my sleep. Am I dreaming?

"*Hardin! Hardin, please open the door!*"

I jump up out of my bed, confused and panicked as the knob on my door jingles. Fists pound against the door.

"Hardin!" the voice screams again.

Is that . . . ?

I unlock the door and yank it open. Tessa's standing there, her face flushed in horror and her eyes wild with fear. The hair on my neck stands, and I go into instant defense mode.

"Tess?" I wipe my eyes to gain some clarity, trying to dispel the dream, get a focus on what's going on.

"Hardin, please can I come in? This guy . . ." Tessa looks back down the hallway, so I step out to see what's she's so scared of.

Neil is walking toward us, his eyes bloodshot and his shirt stained. He's disgusting. And when he stumbles into the wall, I see just how drunk he is.

Why is she running from him? Did he . . .

Neil's eyes meet mine, and he stops immediately. If he knows what's good for him, he will turn the fuck around and walk away. If not, Tessa and all these people in the hallway—people who didn't seem to want to help her—might be in for a show.

I look back at her quickly, to make sure he didn't do anything to cause me to have to hide his body when the police come.

"Do you know him?" she asks, her voice cracking.

I feel my hands shaking at my sides.

"Yeah, get inside." I lead her into my room and I sit down on my bed. Her gray eyes watch me intensely, and I rub my eyes again. "Are you okay?" I ask.

She looks okay—nervous, maybe, but she's not crying. This is a good sign . . . I think?

"Yeah," she says softly. "Yes. I'm sorry for coming here and waking you up. I just didn't know what—" Tessa's words come out fast and shaky.

She's saying sorry for waking me up?

I run my hand over my hair, pushing it back from my forehead. "Don't worry about it." I notice the way her hands, like mine, are shaking, and I ask the question that's been raking at my mind since I opened the door. "Did he touch you?"

Murderous ideas float through my mind. No one would miss Neil, that's for sure.

"No," she starts, then hesitates. "He tried, though. I was stupid enough to lock myself in a room with a drunk stranger, so I suppose it's my fault."

Her fault? *What the fuck?*

"It's not your fault that he did that. You aren't used to this type of . . . situation." I try to keep my voice calm and not frighten her further. I've seen this happen to a lot of girls in my life. From my own mum, to drunk girls at parties. I had to save Molly's drunk ass from Neil just last year. I thought he would have learned his lesson when I broke his nose and dislocated his shoulder, but I guess not. He obviously needs a refresher course. Logan will help, just like last time.

Tessa walks toward me, and I pat the empty spot next to me on the bed. She sits down and places her hands in her lap. Her vulnerable expression suddenly makes me realize that I'm wearing nothing but black boxers. I want to put something else on, but I don't want to draw her attention to the fact, and I don't want her to feel more uncomfortable since she came in here for escape, for peace.

"I have no plans on getting used to it. This really is the last time I'm coming here—or to any parties, for that matter. I don't know why I even tried. And that guy . . . he was just so . . ."

She shivers, and tears start falling down her cheeks.

"Don't cry, Tess," I whisper, and bring my hand to her cheek. My thumb catches the wet tears as they fall, and she sniffles. It's such an innocent, vulnerable sound that I try to look away from her, but can't.

"I hadn't noticed how gray your eyes are," I confess.

I haven't paid much attention to details beyond her breasts and her susceptibility to my games until now. I was too busy, too shallow.

But then I stop myself. No, I'm a liar. I've been paying attention to the tiniest things about this girl since the moment I saw her.

My hand still rests on her cheek, and she's still staring at me, full lips parted. I bring my metal lip ring between my teeth and tug on it the way I always do. Her eyes are glued to my mouth, and just as I pull my hand away, she leans closer, pressing her mouth against mine.

I take a sharp breath, caught completely off guard. What is she doing? What the fuck am I doing?

But I don't stop. Can't stop. I'm running my tongue along her soft lips; I'm swallowing her small gasps as I cup her cheeks between my hands. She's sighing into my mouth, as if she's relieved to be kissing me. Her skin is hot, her mouth is gentle and nervous, and I move my hands to her hips.

When I taste the vodka on her tongue, I pull back.

"Tess . . ." I breathe into her mouth. She sighs, and I swipe my tongue across her lips, parting them again. I gasp, trying to clear my mind. How did we get to this?

I feel cool, the opposite of the fire inside of me. It feels good. It's a relief from the constant burn. I've never felt this sense of calm before; it's threatening.

My mind is no longer in charge; the feel of her mouth on mine has taken over all sense. I pull her closer, tightening my grip on her hips, and lie back on the mattress. She climbs up onto my torso and rests her hands on my chest. Her tongue teases mine, never leaving my mouth. She's so good at this. Fuck, is she good at this.

Her hair falls down onto my skin, and I pull my mouth away from hers. The whimper that leaves her lips when I do this makes me instantly hard. She wants me. Her hands are moving up and down my chest now, testing her limits, I can tell.

I won't let this go too far. Not tonight. She's been drinking, and that's not my thing. I want her—hell, I want to fuck her over and over again. I will feel her, all of her. But not tonight. She's a virgin, but how far has she gone with her boyfriend? Has he had her like this, on top of him when he's wearing only boxers, rocking her hips over his, teasing him like this? Is this how she really is with him, only to seem all prim and prude to the outside world?

Has his tongue traced along the soft skin of her neck? By the way she's gasping under the touch of my tongue against her skin, I would say no. She moans, and I hold her hair as I kiss her neck. I move my mouth lower, gently nipping at her collarbones, and she moans again, saying my name under her breath.

I bring her mouth to mine, and she continues to rock against me. I know she can feel how hard I am, how badly I want her.

"Hardin . . . stop," she moans, her tongue still running gently over mine. "Hardin!" she repeats. I pull back and look at her. Her lips are swollen, sinfully pink, and her eyes are wild.

"We can't," she says. Her fingers leave my skin, and the dull burn turns to ice.

I knew it wouldn't last; it was just a . . . a heat-of-the-moment type thing. It was a moment I wanted to keep going, but everything must end, in the end. I pull myself up onto my elbows, and she rolls off of me, to the other side of the bed.

"I'm sorry, I'm sorry." Her voice is low, raspy, and she sure as hell doesn't sound sorry by the heavy breaths falling from her lips and the way her eyes can't seem to look away from my mouth.

Looking at her, I think about this book I read where the women in the town vow to stop saying sorry in their everyday lives. It was quite interesting the way they realized 90 percent of the *sorry*s they were giving were for things they weren't responsible for. If Tessa lived in that town, she would fit right in.

"Sorry for what?" I say as calmly as possible, and stand up to dig through the messy drawer full of black T-shirts. As I pull one on, I see her looking at me, down to my boxers. And she blushes.

"For kissing you . . ."

Why would she apologize for kissing me? If she doesn't want to do anything with me, I don't want her to, but I didn't give her any signals that I didn't want the same thing.

"It was just a kiss—I kiss people all the time." I purposely keep my voice neutral, since I don't want to make her feel worse. She already regrets this and is ready to run for the hills any second. I know it, and if she does, I have to chase her. I can't strike out this early in the game when I've already made progress. I've had her hands on me, I've tasted her tongue. I've already had her panting, wanting more. I have the upper hand over Zed now, and I can't let that slip. She's going to make a way bigger deal out of this than need be. If I comfort her now, she's much more likely to trust me, and that trust will lead to me having another chance to get even further next time.

She stares at the floor. Again. She's already so full of regret that she can't even look at me? I don't like how this feels.

She can't regret it already; if she doesn't get past this, I'm fucked and Zed is going to win.

"Can we not make a big deal of it, then?" Tessa asks.

"Trust me, I don't want anyone to know about this either. Now stop talking about it."

She winces at my words, and I wish I could take them back. I'm terrible at this shit.

"So you're back to your old self, I see?" Her eyes are sharpening now, preparing for a battle. I want to snap at her, but I keep my mouth shut.

She doesn't know a damn thing about me. It pisses me off that she thinks after a few encounters with me she's some sort of Hardin Scott fucking expert. She thinks she's so much better than me, and she's terrified that people might find out she kissed me because . . . well, I'm me and she's Little Miss Perfect. I can't keep my mouth shut.

"I was never anyone else," I tell her. "Don't think because you kissed me, basically against my will, we have some sort of bond now."

I can feel my words slam into her like a goddamn battering ram, and she gets to her feet. Her fury is clear in her wide eyes. A modern-day Joan of Arc, getting ready to burn *me* at the stake.

"You could have stopped me," she seethes. Her hands ball into tights fists that she must think are made of fire.

My mouth reacts before I can think of anything to say: "Hardly."

Tessa sighs and brings her hands to cover her face. I look away. She's so emotional, and that's not even the strange part. The act of being emotional is normal, I suppose, but she's just so open to it. I'm not her friend or her family, and here she is throwing her emotions around like I've known her my whole life. She's not afraid to show me how she feels; she doesn't seem to mind being exposed like this.

Theresa Young is such a maddening mystery to me. She's so open and fragile, yet guarded and sharp like glass. I can't figure her out. It's pretty damn strange. The ease she seems to feel about allowing me to see her this way is slightly endearing, but it's still strange.

"You can stay in here tonight since you don't have anywhere else to go," I quietly offer.

Tessa shakes her head, her hands on her full hips, and she scowls at me. I want to tell her that maybe I'm sorry for being harsh to her, maybe I sometimes say shit that I shouldn't, but why use energy on a stranger? She doesn't know me, and she never will.

"No, thanks."

When she disappears down the hallway, I grip the doorframe and silently wish her a good night's sleep, knowing that I won't get one.

"Tessa," I quietly call after her, unsure if I actually want her to hear.

ten

He was always stubborn from the beginning. She pushed buttons he didn't know he had and made him think of the world in a different way. He never expected anything to come from this game of his and he never knew how each glance from her, each smile she awarded him with, was changing him. He grew protective of her from early on, and he didn't recognize when his protection turned to control. He tried to fight it, but he wasn't strong enough until it was too late.

It's been twenty minutes since she stormed off, and I can't find her anywhere. Why can't she be like Molly or any of the other girls I've hooked up with, and come running back? How is it that she's so strong-willed?

Knowing her—the little bit that I do know about this girl— leads me to believe she's going to shatter every preconceived thought I had about girls in general.

Fucking yay. This will be fun.

"She left, dude." Logan walks into the kitchen with a bottle of vodka in his hands.

Left? She wouldn't actually leave. She doesn't even know how to get back to campus, and her ancient phone won't be any help if she's lost.

"No way." I shake my head and reach for an empty cup. When I turn the faucet on, Nate is looking at me with one brow raised and a stupid grin on his face.

"What, fucker?" I ask him, chugging the water.

"Nothing, man." He laughs and shares a shitty look with Logan.

"Am I missing something here?" My hand waves between the two of them.

"Nope." Logan puts his hand on my shoulder, and I move away. "Why are you looking for her, exactly?"

"Why do you think?" I say quickly, unsure whether I'm lying to them or snapping back into the Bet. Yes, I'm still into the game, but at this moment, I just want to know where the fuck she went.

"Right." Nate nudges Logan like me and my mates used to nudge each other when we were in grade school. "Well, she's gone, anyway. I saw her walk out the front door."

"And you just let her?"

"Let her? Why would I care if she walked outside and left? You shouldn't care either . . . I thought," Nate says, his eyes meeting Logan's.

"Where's Zed?" I ask them. Hopefully the question will make them think I'm more worried about him getting a leg up on me than anything else.

They both shake their heads and shrug their shoulders, then go back to shooting the shit together like they've already lost interest in all of this.

As I walk away from them, my hands ball into fists. Maybe she called a friend to pick her up? Does the girl even have any friends? She seems like the judgmental type that no one would actually want to be friends with. Like me, in that way. Except she's slightly more likable. Slightly.

I'm sure she isn't stupid enough to try to walk three miles back to her dorm.

Stupid enough? No.

Stubborn enough? Hell fucking yes she is.

I walk through the halls upstairs one more time to be sure

she actually left the house. My room is empty; I was hoping she would be annoying and break into my room again. I was kind of hoping I would catch her sitting on my bed with one of my books in her hands.

But no, of course she had to be ridiculously difficult and leave the house. Alone.

Alone.

Fucking hell, she's walking the damn streets alone.

What kind of . . . Goddamnit, she pisses me off. Could we have chosen a more difficult girl for the Bet? Not bloody likely.

"Nate!" I shout his name over the music as I rush down the stairs.

"What? You in a hurry?" he says to me, a slow smirk rising to his face. I slow down as I reach the bottom.

"Nah, I just . . ." I push my hair back from my forehead. "I'm looking for that brunette—the one wearing a black tank top, huge tits." I hold my hands out in front of my chest to mimic having this made-up woman's body.

Nate's eyes lower and he smiles. I can barely see the words inked into the inside of his bottom lip when he says, "Oh, I get it."

He winks and Logan laughs.

"Well, I'm going to go find her . . ." I turn away from them quickly. I can hear their faint shit talking as I walk away. I leave the house without looking back and get into my car. The streets are empty. Completely fucking empty, and she's nowhere to be found.

After a few more circles around the block, I decide to just head to her dorm. She has to be there by now. Has to be.

When I get to the dorm, I realize I've been out for about two hours already. At her room, the door opens without any hesitation and I find Steph and Tristan lying on her bed. Her shirt is off, her hands roaming his shirtless body. She removes her mouth from his and sits up.

"Can I help you?" Steph licks her lips, smearing the last bit of lipstick down across her mouth.

"Where's Theresa?" I ask them. Tristan reaches for his shirt, and Steph grabs it from him, tossing it onto the floor. "Well?" I push.

"Not here. We passed her on the way." Steph latches her mouth on to Tristan's neck, and I gag.

"Passed her? You saw her walking and you didn't pick her up?" I bend down and grab Tristan's shirt, tossing it to him, covering both of their faces with it. Tristan moves from the bed, and I back away toward the door.

"Steph told me not to stop," he says while getting dressed.

"What the fuck?" I turn to her.

She chuckles. "She's fine. She could use some walking."

"Hey." Tristan nudges her, a disapproving look clear on his face.

Steph rolls her eyes.

"Get dressed, both of you, and leave. She should be here soon," I say to them.

"This is my room. I'm not leaving," Steph says.

"Come on." I scramble for a reason for her to leave. "I need some alone time with her."

She laughs. "For what? To fuck her?"

"To work toward that, yes."

"Let's just go to my place. Nate probably won't be there," Tristan says, and tucks Steph's hair behind her ear. She smiles, nodding in agreement.

Once the room is empty, I sit down on Tessa's bed. As I'm trying to decide whether or not to look through her stuff out of curiosity, the door opens. There she stands in the doorway, looking a few inches taller, her hands in tight fists. Her eyes are wide; she's bursting at the seams with carefully held-back irritation. When I smile at her, she tears up.

"You've got to be kidding me!" Her voice is high and loud as she throws her hands into the air.

"Where were you?" I calmly ask her, my tone the opposite of the fire quickly growing inside of her. "I drove around trying to find you for almost two hours."

"What? Why?" she asks me, her expression a mixture of exasperation and confusion. Her cheeks are pink from the cool fall air, and her hair is windblown, not the neatly curled mop I'm used to seeing on her.

I struggle to say something to explain it all, but only come up with "I don't think it's a good idea for you to be walking around at night, alone."

She bursts into laughter. Laughter, of all things. What is wrong with her? Her laugh is wild, completely opposite to her controlled smiles and faked laughs. She looks half mad.

"Get out, Hardin—just get out!" she says as her laughter grows softer.

"Theresa, I'm—"

But a pounding at the door interrupts me.

"Theresa! Theresa Young, you open this door!" a woman's voice shrieks through the air.

"Oh my God, Hardin, get in the closet," Tessa whispers, grabbing my arm and yanking me from the bed.

"I'm *not* hiding in the closet. You're *eighteen*," I argue. Tessa rushes over to the mirror, closely inspecting her face and smoothing down her wild hair. She hurries to the other side of the room with a tube of toothpaste in her hand, squeezes a dollop from it, and rubs it onto her tongue. It's like I'm watching a teenage girl get caught sneaking out of her mummy's house. She's frantic as she walks to the door. Her hand shakes when she turns the brass knob.

"Hey. What are you guys doing here?" Tessa asks her mum as

she walks through the door. Her mother commands the room for the brief moment before another person joins us.

It's the guy from before. Noah.

I can see that Tessa's mum is coming straight toward me, but I'm too focused on the boy. Tessa's boyfriend, the infamous Noah. His blond hair is a few shades lighter than Tessa's, and his cardigan is smooth, resting over his neatly pressed khaki pants. It's kind of amazing that at this early point in the morning he so resembles a freshly minted preppy action figure, still in the packaging.

But why is he here? Are they that serious?

Did he call her mum like some sort of morality police?

Her mother takes a deep breath and then lets it all out. "So this is why you haven't been answering your phone? Because you have this . . ."—she waves her hands around in the same way her daughter does—"this . . . tattooed . . . *troublemaker* in your room at six a.m.!"

Tattooed troublemaker? What is with these women and their primary school insults?

Tessa squares her shoulders, and I watch as her back straightens, ready for a fight.

Well, now I know where Tessa gets her judgmental bullshit. Also where she got her frame, curves, and fire. She's shooting daggers at her mum, but the woman doesn't seem to notice the way her daughter's fingers are digging crescents into her palm. Or the way the skin on her neck has turned slightly pink. She doesn't seem to notice. Neither does Mr. Rogers.

This irritates me—that Tessa is being chastised for behaving like a normal college freshman. If anything, she's much tamer than anyone else I know. Her mum should be proud of her.

"Is this what you do in college, young lady? You stay up all night and bring boys back to your room?" the woman fumes. "Poor

Noah was worried sick about you, and we drive all this way to find you running around with these strangers."

Strangers? The way Noah's backing up slowly toward the door without noticing it as the woman's voice grows louder . . . I get the feeling he's even more brainwashed than Tessa-dearest.

I can't help it; I speak up before Tessa gets a chance to reply. "Actually, I just got here. And she wasn't doing anything wrong."

Tessa gapes at me like I'm insane to go up against her mum. For her part, her mother can't seem to believe it either. And their disbelief makes me laugh inside; these people have no idea what I'm capable of.

"Excuse me? I certainly was not speaking to you. I don't know what someone like you is doing hanging around my daughter anyway."

The douche in the corner stays silent, as he should.

"Mother . . ." Tessa says, attempting to be as threatening as possible. She looks at me briefly, her eyes are harder than usual. I can't tell if it's from embarrassment or anger that there's such fire coming out.

Her mum isn't fazed. "Theresa, you're out of control." She speaks through her teeth. "I can smell the liquor on you from here, and I can only assume that this is the influence of your lovely roommate and *him*," she says, looking directly at me. *Pointing* at me.

If she knew me, she would put that finger right back down.

"I'm eighteen, Mother," Tessa begins, but she already sounds defeated. "I've never drunk before, and I didn't do anything wrong. I'm just doing what every other college student is doing. I'm sorry that my cell-phone battery died, and that you drove all the way here, but I'm fine."

Tessa sits on the edge of her chair. I don't like how uncomfortable they make her. She's like a stranger to me as she sits, timidly waiting for the next blow from the bitch.

I don't move. Even when the hurricane in this woman's eyes focuses back on me.

"Young man, could you leave us for a minute?"

She's not really asking. And her "young man" might sound polite, but really she's just trying that bitchy thing where she talks down to me while seeming reasonable. I grew up around rich kids; I know that move.

I look over at Theresa, making sure she understands that I won't leave unless she's okay to face her mum and boyfriend alone. She nods, but I can see the confusion in her gray eyes.

I go, as requested, my chest burning.

eleven

When he began to see her in his dreams, it terrified him. She was now swallowing him whole, taking every ounce of him and running off with it. It terrified him to think about the things she could do to him once she was in. He didn't want to allow it, but he didn't have the strength to fight it. He had always thought of himself as strong. He ruled everything, until she came in and took his crown.

I wait and wait for Tessa's dorm room door to open and for her mum and her minion to leave. Minute after minute goes by, and I begin to question my sanity.

Why am I waiting for her? What will I even say to her when her visitors leave? Will she want to talk to me at all? Maybe she will if I apologize for letting her kiss me. That may solve all of the problems here.

Finally, the door opens and her mum walks out, casting an imperious eye down at me where I lean against a neighbor's door. On her heels is Tessa, her hand snugly wrapped around Noah's.

I get to my feet, not quite sure what to say, but feeling the need to say, to do, *something*.

"We're going to go into town," Tessa tells me, and what can I do but nod and let them go on their way?

I can't stop looking at Tessa's hand in her boyfriend's. She flushes and pulls away as her mum gives me the fakest smile I've ever seen.

"I really don't like that guy," I hear Mr. Rogers say.

"Me either," Tessa quietly responds.

Which is for the best. Because I don't really like her either.

WHEN I GET TO MY CAR, my phone's vibrating in the cup holder. I reach for it and answer when I see Molly's name across the screen. She says one word—"hairpulling"—and hangs up.

Five minutes later, I walk into Molly's apartment without knocking, and her roommate glares at me, smoke pouring from her mouth. The whites of her eyes flicker beneath heavy mascara, and she takes another hit of her cigarette. "She's in her room."

Molly's lying in her bed, her head propped up on a mound of pillows and her bare legs spread wide open. Her room is small, the light blue walls covered in photos from fashion magazines. Mostly black-and-white pictures that she's clipped and taped up. Her bed is positioned against the wall farthest from the door, and her room has no windows. I would hate to be trapped in a room with no windows. No wonder she's never here.

She gestures for me to join her on the bed; her pink hair is wild, tied on top of her head in a nest. "Well, well, well, look who it is," she taunts when I sit next to her. Lifting her skirt up farther, she exposes black panties. She runs her hands down her thighs, circling them around their lacy edges.

"You called me," I remind her.

"And you came," she chirps, reciting the line in a sarcastic and proud voice.

"Don't get too excited. I was bored and you made yourself available." Shrugging my shoulders, I look over at her. Her brows are furrowed, and she's pretending to be offended.

"This is true." She laughs, and I shake my head at her shameless behavior.

Molly's hand is cold when she wraps it around my arm and

pulls me closer to her. The scars on her wrist shine in the half-light from the lamp on her side table.

Molly's lips press to my neck, and I try not to picture Tessa's full lips. Molly climbs down my body, her hands reaching for the buttons on my jeans. She pops them open quickly and drags my pants and boxers down my legs. I lift up, helping her undress me while trying to convince myself that I want this. This is fun. This is what people like me do for fun. People like me and Molly, fucked-up people. I have my issues, and she has her own—ones she fortunately hasn't ever tried to tell me about, ones I don't give enough fucks about to even consider asking her about. I know she's like me. That's all I need to know.

Her tongue licks at the head of my cock, teasing me. I don't do teasing, so I reach for a handful of her pink hair, guiding her mouth to take all of me. She gags slightly, and I release her. I know she likes it rough—in fact, rougher than I'm willing to go with her, ever.

Tessa's hair thick in my fist, I pull tighter. Her mouth is so wet, so warm. Her tongue moves over me with more aggression than I would have imagined. Her hands glide down my thighs; her nails are longer than I remember.

"Hardin," she moans, and takes another lick, drawing me between her lips. Her voice is high-pitched and feels off.

"Fuck, Tessa."

The moment the words come out, Tessa's full lips deflate.

Molly immediately tenses and pulls away from me. "Really?"

I clear my throat. "What?"

She rolls her eyes. "I heard you."

"You didn't hear anything, and even if you did, don't act like you haven't called me Log—"

"Shut up." She holds up a hand and waves it dramatically. "Do you want me to finish?" And just like that, her tone's changed back to playful, and I realize she's looking at me with this weird sympathetic expression, like she needs to feel sorry for me or some shit.

The idea infuriates me. She's just as lonely and fucked up as I am . . . Who is she to feel bad for me?

"No." I pull my pants back up, and when I stand up and push my phone into my pocket, she still has that look. My anger means nothing to her.

"I'm not walking you out," she says with a laugh, back to her normal nihilism for a moment. But then she adds, "Be careful with this shit. Girls like her don't ever end up with fuckups like you."

Her eyes grow even sadder for me, and I feel like puking all over her black rug. I know she's not even trying to insult me—she's being real and honest, but I don't need her advice.

I don't want to "end up with" Tessa. I want to fuck her and win. That's all.

Without another word, I walk out and drive back to my house.

twelve

The pounding at the door won't stop. The man behind the door calls my name, and I try to be as quiet as I can when I open the closet door and hide inside. I close the door and wait, covering my ears as the pounding gets louder.

"Get out here now!" his voice booms.

My father is drunk again; he's drunk every night now.

With one final hit, his fist snaps the wood on the door, and the cracking of the wood sends a shiver down my spine. I hate that I'm afraid of him—I shouldn't be. I'm twelve and I'm pretty tall for my age. I should be able to defend myself.

Why am I afraid? Because I'm so pathetic.

His voice mixes with the other men's voices . . . are they here again? I'm not sure. They shouldn't be because he is, but maybe he wouldn't protect us anyway.

The closet door opens, and I scoot back against the wall until I have nowhere left to hide.

I wake with a shout, screaming into the empty, lonely space. I've stayed in this room for nearly three days straight now, and not one person has called, not one person has knocked on my door. I've gotten a lot of work done, though. I don't want to run into her. I don't want to see Zed or the rest of them. They haven't called on me either.

That's what happens when you're invisible: no one gives a fuck about you, and you have no one to give a fuck about.

I reach for the dirty black shirt on the floor next to my bed and wipe it across my sweat-soaked face. My hair is damp and my vision is blurry, mixing the past and the present, keeping my lack of a future out of this mess for now.

I suppose I wouldn't say "lack of." I'll be one of those men who work too much, fuck too much, and come home to an empty house every night. I'll be successful financially and I'll buy a house even bigger than Ken's and never invite him over, just like Don Draper. Just to prove a point.

I'm not sure what that point will be, but I have one somewhere in there. Somewhere.

I'm getting the fuck out of this bed today.

WHEN I GET TO CAMPUS, I seek out Tessa immediately. It's been a little while since I've seen her. I wonder if Zed has seen her . . . Has he won a few points while I've been in solitude? It's mid-morning, so she'd be getting out of Literature. Unless she's cut class . . .

As if. I get to the building just as class is ending and in time to see her exit the classroom. She's done something different to her hair. Just cut it, I think? It looks nice, mostly the same, but the change is just enough for me to notice. I wonder if anyone else has noticed . . . but when I see her sidekick Landon walking out after her, I realize that *of course* he did.

I walk up behind the pair of them and say, "You've cut your hair, Theresa."

I've surprised her, but she turns around and quickly greets me—"Hey, Hardin"—before she starts walking faster. Her flat shoes make a squeaking sound as they slide across the floor tiles. What is she in such a hurry for . . . ?

And then I get it: she doesn't want her angelic friend here to know that she kissed me. That she practically threw herself on me.

Her discomfort is like a challenge I can't ignore.

"How was your weekend?" I ask with a big grin.

In response, she grabs Landon's arm and pulls him closer to her, walking even faster away from me. "Good. Well, I'll see you around!" Tessa yells over her shoulder.

She pulls them outside through the main door, and I let them go, my urgency to see her dissipating.

I walk around the streets of the campus, slowly making my way to my car. Actually going to classes seems too difficult right now.

After a few minutes, I find Zed sitting on a bench outside the science building, a cigarette between his lips.

He looks up at me, smoke blowing from his mouth. "Hey."

"Hey." I don't know if I should sit down or walk away.

"Have you made any progress with the girl?" he asks.

"Yes, a little," I lie. "You?"

I wait impatiently as he takes another drag. "Nah. I'm feeling a little weird about it. Aren't you?"

"Nah," I say, repeating the word he uses too much. It's always "nah" to this and "nah" to that, like nothing's ever quite good enough to demand his attention and it's all too lowly for him to have to utter a real word for.

Zed shrugs, and I decide to find Tessa now while he's here being a pussy and smoking too many cigarettes. I hate the smell of cigarettes—reminds me of my mum's house. Growing up, I could barely breathe through the thick clouds, and I can almost feel the sticky yellow streaks of tar covering the faded wallpaper of the living room.

To occupy a little time, I stop and get a coffee but end up gulping the thing down in less than two minutes. As my throat burns from the heat, I wonder why I'm so anxious.

After getting up with no aim in sight, I decide to go to Steph's building, but take my time on the way there and look at all the people milling about campus. Couples walking together and brainiacs in clusters discussing something excitedly, a bunch of preppy jocks throwing a ball around. It's just too much.

As I'm walking down the dorm hallway, I spot Steph's red hair.

"Hardin! You looking for me?" she asks with her hand raised.

"Not exactly." I glance across the hallway, toward the door of her room.

"Ohhh, got it." She laughs and adjusts her cleavage. "Well, I'll go find something to do so you can have some time with her." As she walks away, back toward the exit, she turns when she reaches the end of the hallway and shouts, "You're welcome, asshole!"

"I'm not thanking you," I mumble quietly, and knock on her door.

I hear some papers ruffling around and a book close. Tessa takes six steps to the door, and I blow a deep breath into my T-shirt to check my breath.

Did I actually just . . .

"Steph isn't back yet," Tessa says as soon as she opens the door. Surprisingly, she doesn't look at me once before she walks to her bed—and doesn't slam the door in my face. A decent start.

"I can wait." I sit down on Steph's bed and look over at Tessa's side of the room.

"Suit yourself," she replies with a groan and childishly pulls her blanket over her head. I laugh and watch her still body, wondering what's going through her mind. Is this like some method of reverse peekaboo that's supposed to make me disappear or something?

I tap my fingers against Steph's headboard, hoping to annoy Tessa enough to talk to me. No luck, but when a few minutes later an alarm starts beeping, she reaches one arm from beneath the blanket and turns it off.

Is she going somewhere? With who?

"Going somewhere?" I ask Tessa.

"No." She sits up, the blanket falling and revealing her face, filled with attitude. "I was taking a twenty-minute nap."

"You set an alarm to make sure your nap is only twenty minutes?" I laugh, mentally wishing I could get more sleep than every once in a while.

"Yeah, I do. So what's it to you, anyway?"

I watch as she lays her textbooks out in order of her class schedule. I shouldn't catch on to the fact that that's what she's doing, but I do. I apparently know a lot about her somehow. She takes a small binder and rests it next to the neat stack of books. She's fucking obsessive.

"Are you OCD or something?" I ask her, kind of amazed.

"No, not everyone's crazy because they just like things a certain way. There's nothing wrong with being organized."

She's so condescending. She's actually a very unpleasant girl, despite how sweet she appears. I laugh at the idea that she must think she's so perfect and polished but she actually has one of the worst tempers I've seen and she judges people like it's her job.

I walk closer to her, trying to think of a new way to get under her skin. She's so easily annoyed, it won't have to be anything serious. I quickly scan her neat room, taking in the perfectly made bed covered in neat stacks of paper and textbooks. Gotcha.

I grab a stack of papers from her bed the same moment her eyes rest on mine. She looks down, trying to think of a way to negotiate with me. She reaches for them, but I tease her, lifting them too high for her to grab. Debating how far I should go with this, I take in her heaving breaths, the way her chest is rising and her lip is quivering in anger. It kind of turns me on, and I want to go just a little further. Not far enough to actually piss her off, just to annoy her enough that I have to charm my way back in. I toss the papers into the air and watch the white pages float around the room before falling into a scattered mess on her floor. Her mouth falls open, and her cheeks flush with anger.

"Pick those up!" she snaps.

I smirk at her, wondering if she actually thinks I would comply with her command. Maybe if she agreed to wrap her lips around my cock. Upping the ante, I grab another stack of papers and scatter them to the floor.

"Hardin, stop!" Her voice cracks through the air, threatening me.

I repeat the action, and then she surprises me by charging forward and shoving me away from her bed.

"You mean, someone doesn't like their stuff being messed with?" I tease her, laughing at her expense. She's *so* angry now, much angrier than a normal person would be over something so stupid.

"No! I don't!" she shouts, and shoves me again.

I thrive off her anger. Her energy is breathing life into me. I'm just as pissed off as she is—and I need to have her. Now.

I take a quick step toward her, grabbing her wrists and cornering her against the wall. She stares at me, not even close to backing down, and I can see the way her eyes change from frustration to hunger for me. If I know anything about women, it's when they are turned on, and Tessa is most definitely turned on. She gets off on this passionate anger, the same way that I do. She stares into my eyes before her gaze quickly darts to my mouth, and that's when I'm positive that she wants this to happen. She fucking wants me. She may not like me, but she's attracted to me. *It's mutual,* I want to tell her. I stare back, wanting to tell her that I don't like her either, that this thing between us is just pure lust. That we are on the same wavelength here. That it's all animal hunger—a very high level of lust, but lust all the same.

"Hardin, please," she whispers.

Her voice is low, wanting me to go away and to kiss her at the same time. I know this because I want to run as far as I can from this girl, but here I stand, too, my eyes on her mouth. Her chest is rising and falling fast. I reach up, just needing to touch her, and the moment my fingers graze her skin, she sighs. She's staring at me, waiting. I release her wrist but use my other hand to take both of her wrists. Her tongue peeks out, covering her bottom lip, and I lose it. The noise is so faint, so weak, that I don't even think she realizes she made it. I heard it, though. I heard it, and I'm broken by it.

I press my body against hers, pinning her gently to the wall. She groans into my mouth, and her arms reach up and wrap around my shoulders. Her tongue follows mine, moving perfectly in sync with my claiming lips. I grip the tops of her thighs and lift her up to me. As I hold her against me, my heart is beating so fucking fast and I'm so turned on by her that I don't know how I will ever stop this. Tessa's body clings to mine still, and her mouth doesn't stop taking mine as I walk us back to her bed.

Tessa pulls at my hair and drives me fucking wild. I feel like every inch of my body has been scattered across this small room; then, when she moans, her breath coming out in rapid uncontrollable huffs, I sit back on her bed, bringing her with me. I move her to sit on my lap, keeping my hands on her full hips. I know my fingers are digging into her skin, a sign of my body trying to comprehend what's happening. I've done this before, many fucking times, so why can't I keep up with this? I can't keep up with her.

"Fuck," I mutter, feeling my cock straining against my jeans.

I move my hands from her waist and tug at the bottom of her shirt; she moans, and I pull my mouth away from hers to remove her shirt. My eyes trace down from her eyes to her full and swollen lips, to her chest. Her tits are covered by a black bra: no lace, no sparkles, nothing special. Just worn black fabric. So innocent and plain and normal I find it oddly appealing. I bite down on my lip, trying to have some control over myself and not rip her bra from her soft body. Her tits are full, swollen and bursting out of the material. There's a freckle there, just under her neckline, and I want to kiss it. I want to cover her entire body with my mouth and taste her release on my tongue as I make her come.

"You're so sexy, Tess," I breathe into her mouth. She gasps, and I swallow the incredible sound.

My control continues to diminish as she rocks harder against my body. I wrap my arms around her back to bring her even closer to me—

Tessa jumps off my lap and reaches for her shirt. The trance we were in is broken as she pulls her T-shirt over her head and down to cover her body, and it's only then that I hear the sound of the door opening.

How did she hear it—was she not as into it as I was? No way I would have stopped, even if her schoolmarm mum and Mr. Rogers had been coming through that door.

But instead it's Steph, standing there faking a shocked expression. I've seen this look before, and it immediately makes me wonder if Zed paid her to come back and interrupt us.

I hope Tessa doesn't genuinely like her or believe her to be her friend. Steph's personality is faker than her Kool-Aid–dyed hair.

"What the hell did I miss?" Steph asks, her hands on her hips.

"Nothing much," I respond, getting to my feet. Steph winks at me as Tessa stares at the wall, avoiding eye contact.

I leave the room without looking back.

I can't say anything or else I'll explode.

My chest is killing me, my heart is beating loudly, and I feel like a maniac.

In a trance, I get back to the house, to my room, and immediately decide to take the longest shower I've ever taken to try and forget the way this strange, sheltered girl makes me feel. This is getting fucking messy. It wasn't supposed to be messy. I wasn't supposed to crave her mouth and her mind equally. I wasn't supposed to think about how tight she would feel around me as I rock into her soft body. I'm not supposed to get off, imagining my hand is hers.

I was supposed to get what I wanted, win the Bet, and move along with my damn life.

After however long, the water starts to run cold and I finally step out onto the cold tile. When I open the cabinet for a towel, the bottle of brown liquor hidden inside by who-knows-who smiles at me, reminding me of its control over me. I've gone this long without that draw to the cabinet—why am I focusing on it now? I half expected one of the guys in the house to finish it off by now, but had also secretly wished no one would.

I have this nasty need to control everything in my life. So far, since I've been sober, I've done a damn good job of being fully aware and in control of my thoughts and my actions; but Tessa's gray eyes won't stop looking at me, and her brilliant mind won't stop begging me to unlock more of her secrets.

The bottle calls for me, and I slam the cabinet closed.

I still have control.

I won't let Tessa or that fucking bottle control me.

I won't.

I stare up at the ceiling when I finally make it to my bed, and I just know it's going to be a long night.

IT'S DARK, SO DARK in this closet. I'm tired of hiding in here, but there's nowhere else to go. My mum's screams won't be drowned out, and no matter how many times I search downstairs for her, I can't find her. I hear her, but don't see her. I saw them, though, the men. I saw them and I heard their voices echoing through the walls of this small house and into my head.

The closet door opens, and I curl back, hoping not to be seen but slightly wanting them to just end the sounds of my mum screaming.

A hand reaches through the small space, and I look around for something to defend myself with other than a coat hanger.

"Hardin?" a soft voice calls through the dark.

The hanging clothes part in the middle, and she steps in, looking directly at me.

Tessa.

She's here? How?

"Don't be scared, Hardin."

She sits down next to me, her body so warm and unafraid. She has a flower pushed behind her ear, and she's reaching for my hands. Her small fingernails are crusted with dirt, and she smells like a flower shop or a greenhouse.

My mum's screams have stopped, and my heart slows from a panic to a cool rhythm as she wraps her small hand around mine.

BY THE TIME I get to campus, the caffeine has surged through my body, sharpening my sight and helping me forget the fucked-up dream that I had.

Why was she there? Why would I dream about Tessa? It wasn't even Tessa as she is now; it was a version of young Tessa, her cheeks rounded and her eyes bright and comforting with premature womanliness. It was odd—so fucking weird, really—and I didn't like it one bit.

I loved the sleep, though. I loved being able to sleep for once in my fucking life, and today I feel . . . well . . . rested? Hell, calmer, at least.

Inside the literature hall, I take a seat in the front row, next to two empty ones. I gaze toward the front of the room, waiting for class to start. I'm fighting the urge to watch the door, to wait for her.

When I finally look back a few minutes later, Tessa and Landon enter the room. She's smiling, focusing only on him. She's developed a friendship with the kid that has gone beyond what I saw coming.

I wasn't surprised when they hit it off . . . but I didn't think Landon's friendship would be more of a threat than Zed's competition for the Bet.

thirteen

Today will be our last day on *Pride and Prejudice*," the professor tells us. "I hope you've all enjoyed it, and since you've all read the ending, it feels fitting to base today's discussion on Austen's use of foreshadowing. Let me ask: As a reader, did you expect Elizabeth and Darcy to become a couple in the end?"

Tessa's hand shoots up instantly, and I lean back in my seat. She never fails to be a know-it-all. Just like Landon . . . the perfect little American couple.

"Miss Young." The professor calls on her, and I watch her face light up. She really gets off on making other people happy or pleased by her. I could use this to my advantage, for sure.

I shut off my inner monologue and patiently await her rant on good ol' *P&P*. If she's as bright as I think she is, this should be interesting.

"Well, the first time I read the novel, I was on the edge of my seat about whether they would end up together. "

Yeah, I would bet they would end up together, just like I'm betting that Tessa and perfect Landon will have the perfect relationship.

"Even now—and I have read it at least ten times—I still feel anxious during the beginning of their relationship. Mr. Darcy is so cruel and says hateful things about Elizabeth and her family that I never know if she'll be able to forgive him, let alone love him." The smile on Tessa's face is bright when she finishes, and her hands neatly fold together on top of her book. She waits expectantly for the professor to pat her on the head and tell her what a wonderful little pupil she is. Landon looks at her, expecting her to glow like a rainbow and spray out colorful glitter from her fingertips.

I'm going to throw a wrench into that.

Speak, Hardin.

My voice nudges at the back of my throat. All it will take is a few words. My mum's reminder: "Just breathe, Hardin. You can talk in front of others." She would always tell me not to worry. "A lot of people have social anxiety, Hardin. It's nothing to be ashamed of."

But me, I don't have social anxiety. I just don't like people.

"That's a load." My voice is loud, filling up the silent room.

"Mr. Scott? Would you like to add something?" the professor asks, clearly surprised by my participation.

"Sure." I lean forward in my seat. Tessa's face is a blank mask; she's shocked but hiding it well. "I said that's a load. Women want what they can't have. Mr. Darcy's rude attitude is what drew Elizabeth to him, so it was obvious they would end up together."

That said, I look down and start to pick at the torn, pink skin surrounding my fingernails.

"That isn't true, about women wanting what they can't have," Tessa bursts out. I look over at her as smoothly as I'm able. "Mr. Darcy was only mean to Elizabeth because he was too proud to admit he was attracted to her. Once he stopped his hateful act, she saw that he really loved her." And to punctuate her passionate words, she slaps one shaking hand against her desk, hard.

I glance around to the roomful of eyes blinking back at us. My friend Dan's sister is sitting in the front row, smiling widely at me.

I can feel the eyes of my fellow students probing at my skin. I need to say something back. I need to speak. "I don't know what kind of guys you normally go for, but I think that if Darcy loved

her, he wouldn't have been mean to her," I say. Just like I'm sure
your current boyfriend and your future boyfriend, Landon there,
wouldn't be. They wouldn't challenge her. "The only reason he
even ended up asking for her hand in marriage was because she
wouldn't stop throwing herself at him."

Did Elizabeth throw herself at Darcy? No, the exact opposite.

Does Tessa throw herself at me? No, again, the exact opposite.

But I couldn't let her win like that.

"She did not throw herself at him! He manipulated her into
thinking he was kind and took advantage of her weakness!"

"He 'manipulated' her? Try again, she is . . ." I pause, my jumbled thoughts messing up my speech. "I mean, she was so bored
with her boring life that she had to find excitement somewhere—
so she certainly *was* throwing herself at him!"

I pause, kind of shocked that I *shouted* these words at her,
that my bruised hands are gripping the corner of the old desk.

"Well, maybe if he wasn't such a manwhore, he could have
stopped it after the first time instead of showing up in her room!"

By the time she's finished, the snickers, gapes, and laughter
indicate that everyone in the room has definitely caught on to our
little show. LIVE READING should have been written on a sign and
hung in the hall outside the room.

Manwhore?

I may have slept my way across this campus, made more mistakes than she has, and forgotten half of them, but at least I'm not
a prissy, judgmental snob. Imagine if I called her the female version of what she called me?

"Okay, lively discussion," the professor says, looking panicked, likely worried that human emotion has spoiled his perfectly
planned lesson. "I think that's probably enough on that topic for
today . . ."

Tessa grabs her bag, clutches it to her chest, and rushes toward the exit. Landon stays in his seat, always unsure what to do

in any type of stressful situation. Maybe because his life has been so perfect. His mum probably made him freshly baked muffins sprinkled with love every morning before school.

I fed myself stale Cheerios and had to smell the inside of the carton to check if the milk was expired or not. There's no syllabus or menu for what Tessa and I seem to be doing.

I bolt out of the room myself. Tessa doesn't get to flee from every conflict she creates. I can tell she's used to that, always having her way.

"You don't get to run this time, Theresa!" I call to her.

Everyone in the hallway looks in my direction, but she keeps moving and I have to run to catch up to her. Just as she turns to go outside, I grab hold of her arm to stop her. She jerks away and my light grip relaxes.

"Why do you always touch me like that? *Grab my arm again, and I will slap you!*" Her tone is furious and her voice is so loud.

I reach for her arm again. She doesn't flinch.

"What do you want, Hardin? To tell me how desperate I am? To laugh at me for letting you get to me again? I am so sick of this game with you—" She's stomping her foot along with her words, and her hands are swirling in the air like always. It amuses me the way she talks with her hands.

She's still going on and on. I honestly couldn't tell you what she's saying. She's just so mad, so infuriated with me, that she's lost her damn mind. When she's around Landon, she's all smiles and comfort. With me, she's rage and electricity. Her eyes are shining—with anger or sadness, I'm not sure, but at least I know that I still elicit an emotional response from her.

"I really do bring out the worst in you, don't I?" My fingers fidget with a small burn hole along the bottom hem of my black T-shirt. "I'm not trying to play games with you."

Seeing the crowd gathering, I run my hands over my head. Why does everything always get so *dramatic* with her?

Tessa rubs her temples with her fingertips. "Then what are you doing? Because your mood swings give me a headache."

I reach for her arms, grasping them gently to get her attention. She doesn't resist, so I lead her into a small alleyway between two buildings, scowling at the people nearby to back off. I don't want anyone to hear our conversation, anyone to pressure her to put on her "perfect girl" face.

I look down at her, admiring her stillness. She appears so calm, so neutral, even given the proximity of our bodies. I see a chink in her armor when her eyes meet mine, and she gulps, her lips shaking.

"Tess, I . . . I don't know what I'm doing. You kissed me first, remember?" I say. It doesn't matter if I've thought about the way her lips tasted on mine every day since. She made the first move, and that will always be a winning argument for me.

"Yeah . . . I was drunk, remember?" Her eyes stare down, ashamed. "And you kissed me first yesterday." She's never going to admit that she wanted me. There will always be an excuse for her. I'm growing more and more annoyed by her denial. I felt the way she blossomed underneath my kiss.

She may hate me, but her body doesn't.

"Yeah . . . you didn't stop me." I pause for a beat, watching the curiosity build in her eyes. "It must be exhausting,"

"What must be exhausting?" she asks, her chin tilted up in the most defiant way.

"Acting like you don't want me when I know you do." I purposely step closer, making her back touch the wall behind her.

She's so still, like her body's come to the realization of what she wants already.

But then her mind overtakes her again and she blurts out, "*What?* I do *not* want you. I have a boyfriend." She's reaching far to pretend to speak with a calm voice.

I smile a little. "A boyfriend that you're bored with. Admit it,

Tess. Not to me, but to yourself. You're bored with him." I draw each word out as slowly as possible, my face moving closer and closer to hers. Her eyes are drawn to my mouth; of course they are. She's weighing her options. She must be remembering the way I kiss her, because she touches her lips gently. She's caught here, with me. Her desire and burning sexual curiosity for me won't let her walk away, not this time.

"Has he ever made you feel the way I do?" I lay this last line on thick, genuinely curious if he has.

"W-what? Of course he has," she tries to insist.

I'm not buying it. She sounded more sincere talking about a classic novel than about her lovely boyfriend's ability to please her.

"No . . . He hasn't. I can tell that you've never been touched . . . *really* touched."

Her lips are parted now, I can practically hear her heart thumping out of her chest. I wonder how I look through her eyes. Can she see that her shaky breaths and plump lips are making me crazy? Is there something in my eyes that tells her I really want to wrap her hair around my fist, turn her head to me, and kiss her?

Her body knows, her body knows.

"That's none of your business."

She must not be able to tell. Once you wear a mask for as long as she has, it's nearly impossible to take it off. Either that, or she's the one who feels invisible.

"You have no idea how good I can make you feel." I step closer. *Let me convince you, let me show you,* I want to beg her.

Her back touches the wall again, and she looks around for some way to gain distance from me. She's breathing hard now, clearly affected by me. Finally.

"Really, you don't have to admit it. I can tell."

She gasps—a seemingly innocent sound, but I know better. I know she wants more; her mind and body yearn for it.

"Your pulse has quickened, hasn't it? Your mouth is dry, you have that feeling . . . down *there*. Don't you, Theresa?" I imagine her naked body sprawled out for me, my finger tracing over the wetness soaking from her pussy.

She sucks in a sharp breath and tries to look away from me, but fails miserably. "You're wrong." She knows I'm right.

"I'm never wrong." I smile. She hesitates, tucking a stray lock of hair behind her ear. "Not about this."

Tessa takes a breath, and I know I'm in for it. "Why do you keep saying I throw myself at you if you're the one cornering me now?"

"Because you made the first move on me. Don't get me wrong." I laugh. "I was as surprised as you were."

"I was drunk and had a long night—as you already know. I was confused because you were being nice to me . . . well, your version of being nice." *My version of being nice?* I'm usually nice to her. Exceptionally nice now that I have a reason to be. The Bet plays at the corners of my mind, and I remember to tread a little lighter than I typically would.

Tessa moves past me and sits down on the concrete curb. I look around to see if anyone is watching us, but no one seems to notice us at all.

"I'm not that mean to you," I say, though I'm starting to wonder if she really thinks this.

"Yeah, you are. You go out of your way to be mean to me. Not just me, but everyone. It just seems like you are extra hard on me, though."

Mean? I'm no meaner to her than I am to a kitten. I've been easy on her.

"That's just not true. I'm no meaner to you than I am to the rest of the general population," I joke. She doesn't find me funny in the least. If she could, she would send me flying with the flick of her wrist.

Tessa jumps to her feet. "I don't know why I keep wasting my time!"

She's going to leave. I don't want her to leave, do I?

No. I don't. I'm not the best with apologies, especially when I don't feel they're needed, but I have to stop being a bitch about this and just say sorry. She's easily calmed by an apology, as I've quickly learned.

"Hey, I'm sorry. Just come back over here," I say, using the persuasive tone I know girls like. She stands up, and I sit down on the curb close to where she was sitting.

"Sit." I pat the ground next to me. She huffs a little and sits down. She crosses her legs and sighs. I'm surprised by the calm that I feel when I'm granted her forgiveness.

"You're sitting awfully far away," I tease her. She tosses me an eye roll. "You don't trust me?" I know the answer to this.

Of course she doesn't, but she wants to. I want her to trust me more than I care to admit.

"No, of course I don't. Why would I?" Her words are fast, sharp.

I inch back. I don't trust *her* either, but she doesn't need to be so quick about her answers. She obviously has some type of draw to me; otherwise we wouldn't be having this conversation. She has to feel some fraction of it to be here.

"Can we just agree to either stay away from each other or be friends? I don't have it in me to keep fighting with you." I don't feel like we fight a lot; we just talk more than either of us expected. I fight with her less than I fight with Ken and talk to her more. That's saying something.

We've both gotten used to it. It would be strange to think of not seeing Tessa again. I've gotten used to her sassy mouth and the way her eyes give away how angry she gets with me. Her fire is contagious. It's becoming an addiction for me, as if I need another high calling my name.

"I don't want to stay away from you," I admit. I hate that I have to be on my best behavior with her: one small slipup, and she runs. I would like to think that we've grown a little closer today, that maybe she wouldn't be so quick to leave. I'm expected to tell her how I feel, to be more open than I'm comfortable with, and I barely get anything in return. It's like I'm married without the benefits of sex and dinner every night.

"I mean . . . I don't think we can stay away from each other, with one of my best friends being your roommate and all. So I suppose we should try to be friends." I have a game to win here, and she's not being the easiest pawn.

"Okay, so friends?" she asks, her voice mimicking someone making a business deal. I could offer to split half of my winnings with her. A beautiful start to a blooming friendship that would make.

Friends? Friends who fuck, maybe? Fucking friends.

"Friends." I push my hand between us for her to shake.

My smile is cunning, full-on charming. She catches on and shakes her head at me. She senses a little bit of my danger, but not enough to keep her away.

"*Not* friends with benefits," she insists, but then is betrayed when she blushes. I didn't realize how attractive her innocence could be, really.

I reach up to play with the metal ring above my eye. "What makes you say that?"

"Like you don't know. Steph already told me."

"What, about me and her?" She was okay, sort of interesting to be around. She has her issues like the rest of us, but she carries them on her back, hiding them from the world, unlike Molly and myself. I wonder what the redhead told Tessa about our time together. I feel like she probably exaggerated when she told the tale of our escapades. Steph always wanted more than I could give her, and she fed on competition, not knowing when to take no for an answer.

"You and her, and you and every other girl," she chokes out.

"Well, me and Steph . . . that was fun." I smile at Tessa and she looks away.

"And yeah, I have girls that I fuck. But why would that concern you, friend?"

Admittedly, I imagine Tessa as one of those girls, spread out beneath me, her mouth open in pleasure. She closes her eyes and takes a breath. I imagine stealing her breath as she comes from my fingers and my mouth at the same time. I'm sure she's never had someone teasing her clit with their tongue while slowly sliding—

"It doesn't," Tessa says, interrupting my thoughts. "I just don't want you to think that I will be one of those girls." She shoves me, but that only manages to intensify the fantasy going on in my mind.

"Aww . . . Are you jealous, Theresa?"

She shoves me again. "No, absolutely not. I feel sorry for the girls." Tessa shakes her head and I laugh. She wouldn't feel sorry for anyone—she would only feel pleasure, intense amounts of pleasure that she can't even imagine.

"Oh, you shouldn't." I can't stop thinking about her naked body. I need to see what she's hiding under those baggy clothes. She wouldn't know what to do with herself if I got my hands on her. "They enjoy it, trust me."

"Okay, okay. I get it. Can we please just change the subject?" Tessa closes her eyes again and tilts her head back. She groans before she says, "So, will you try to be nicer to me?"

"Sure. Will you try not to be so uptight and bitchy all the time?" I tease.

"I'm not bitchy; you're just obnoxious."

We both laugh as she finishes her statement. Her laugh is soft, floating around me. I feel fluffy, in a weird but nice way.

Fluffy? Really, Hardin?

I need to get my shit together and put this Friendship Train on the right track.

I lean a little closer to my new friend. "Look at us, two friends."

Tessa shrinks back and stands up. Her hands wipe at her skirt, and I backtrack, thinking about taking that skirt off. "That skirt really is dreadful, Tess. If we're going to be friends, you need to not wear it anymore." It's not that bad, but it's certainly not good.

Tessa's eyes flash with embarrassment, and I smile to ease it. I didn't mean it as an insult. I was only teasing her. Really, if she wants to wear unflattering clothing, more power to her. I wear the same few pairs of black jeans and stained T-shirts.

Tessa's phone begins to vibrate, and she pulls it out of her bag. "I need to get back and study," she announces.

I glance at the ancient clunk of plastic in her hand. Is that a Nokia?

"You set an alarm to study?" I ask her, pondering the fact that she must have the last flip phone in existence. It's like she's *trying* to be outdated or something.

She shrugs. "I set an alarm for a lot of things; it's just something I do."

This behavior makes her shy, as if she should be embarrassed that she does such a thing. Why would she think that? Someone in her life must make her feel like she needs to justify her strange behavior. Her mum, I'm sure. Well, I'm sort of doing it now, too, but that woman seems anal as hell. Tessa's mum probably had an alarm set for Tessa to piss, as controlling as the woman seems.

"Well, set an alarm for us to do something fun tomorrow after class," I say.

I want to spend time with her. I need to.

She looks at me, her eyebrows pushing together in confusion. "I don't think my idea of fun is the same as yours."

She's not wrong. My idea of fun is definitely different from hers. Her idea of fun would be to study together, piles of notes and heavy textbooks spread out on the bed between us. An academic cock blocking.

My idea of fun is much different. My idea of fun is sitting on the bed, my back against a headboard while Tessa wraps her mouth around my cock. I would love to add a cold glass of whiskey, one ice cube floating in the dark liquid, clicking against the glass as she draws me deeper into her mouth.

I'm not supposed to be drinking, though, so I suppose I'll take the blow job sans the whiskey.

Instead of telling her all this, I say, "Well, we'll only sacrifice a *few* cats, burn down a *few* buildings . . ."

Tessa giggles, and I can't help but smile back at her. But I'm distracted a little when this couple walks by us, holding hands as they laugh at some lame joke the guy's made. I didn't exactly catch what they were saying, but I know it's lame because they're wearing matching striped socks. Subtly shoving their relationship into innocent passerbys' faces. It's bullshit, really. Tessa doesn't even seem to notice them; she's staring down at the concrete.

"Really, though, you could use some fun, and since we are new friends, we should do something fun."

Before Tessa can refuse me, I turn my back to her and start off. "Good, I'm glad you're aboard. See you tomorrow."

When I cross the street, I look back to see her sitting on the curb. She didn't try to refuse me, she agreed to see me tomorrow, and now I don't know what the fuck I'm going to do, because I had planned on her denying me a few times before I had to actually plan a date thing with her.

When I get to my car, I try to think of what to do with Tessa. I don't go out, ever, aside from parties at other people's places. Other than that, I'm on campus or in my room, alone.

I start the car and keep trying to think of something to do. A movie? What type of movie does Tessa like? Something from a Nicholas Sparks novel, I'm sure. I could sneak my arm around her. I could buy her popcorn or overpriced chocolate to impress her. The problem with seeing a movie is that we can't talk during it. Someone would complain, and I would end up getting into some trouble.

Dating rituals were so much less complicated in the past. If we lived in an Austen novel, I would court her and take her on chaperoned dates where we would walk through the woods, and if I felt brave, I would brush her gloved hand with mine. She would blush and put a finger to her full lips, looking to our chaperone with a warning in her gray eyes.

Modern dating is much different, and now, if I felt brave, I would reach down and tease her nipples through her top and she would move my hand to the warmth between her thighs. No chaperone, no rules.

I'm interrupted in my planning by my phone ringing.

Does Tessa have my number? Speaking of that, I need to get her number from Steph.

When it's Ken's name that flashes on my phone screen, I cringe but I answer this time. I suppose I should reward his persistence.

"Yeah?" I say, turning onto the highway. I tuck my phone between my cheek and shoulder. The only problem with my beautiful 1970 Ford Capri is that it doesn't connect to Bluetooth.

"Um, Hardin, hey," he stutters.

He's confused by me answering. He calls me sometimes, and I'm convinced that he sees it as a good deed on his part. He calls to "check in on me" because he knows I won't answer, and it makes him look good to make an effort with his insubordinate son. His new girlfriend probably praises him, hugging him tightly as she reassures him. "He'll come around one day," she probably promises him. "He's just angry right now."

She would be angry if she had him for an excuse of a dad, too.

"Hey." I press the speaker button and rest my phone in the cup holder.

"How are you, son?" he asks, immediately pressing on my nerves.

"Fine."

He clears his throat. "That's good to hear. I wanted to invite you over to dinner tomorrow night. Karen's making a chicken, and we would really love to have you over."

He wants me to come over for dinner? Why on earth would he think I would come to his house to eat chicken with his new family and talk about how much we all just love each other's company. No fucking thanks.

"I have plans tomorrow," I tell him. I'm not lying this time.

"Oh. Well, you could come by after your plans. Karen's making dessert, too."

"My commitment is for all night," I tell him. I wonder what the weather will be like tomorrow. The clouds are gray, as always in this shitty state. The sun must hate it so much here—that's why it's always raining and dreary.

"Is it supposed to rain tomorrow?" I ask Ken. It's easier than looking up the weather forecast myself.

"No, it's supposed to warm up overnight and the rain's gone until next week," he says.

If I had a normal relationship with the man who helped create me, I could ask him for suggestions about what to do on my date. I don't, though. I can't.

All I know to ask this man about are what forms the university needs filled out when. We have nothing in common and are as far as can be from a place where I would ever ask him for dating advice.

Maybe Vance has some ideas? I'd rather ask him than anyone else, I guess.

"I have to go," I say into the phone, then hang up on Ken and look up Vance in my phone.

He answers after one ring. "Hardin, what's up?"

"Do you have any recommendations on where to take someone?" I ask him. My voice sounds odd as I rush the words.

"As in a dead body?" He laughs into the phone. I smile. He's a jackass.

"No, not this time." I reach for a way to ask for his help without mentioning Tessa. "Like to hang out with someone."

"A date, then?" he assumes.

"No, not exactly. But something like that."

I don't know what to call this meeting with Tessa. It's not a date. We're friends.

Friends until I fuck her, I remind myself.

She's just so prudish. She wears ill-fitting clothing and barely curses. Where could I take her to get her to lighten up? I try to think of my favorite memory since I moved to Washington.

The stream off of Highway 75 is fun. If the weather's nice, this could work. The water is pretty shallow, and you can see the rocks under the water. Would Tessa swim in semi-clean stream water? Probably not, but I can try.

"Well, I've always found nature walks a surefire bet," Vance says.

And just like that, I'm reminded of the Bet for the first time in a few hours.

fourteen

The first time he was alone with her, he knew something was stirring inside of him. He thought he could fight it, that maybe he was softening a little, and not only for her, but everyone in his life . . . he was sure. He had spent his whole life alone, and he had mastered the craft of avoiding any form of intimacy beyond sex. He didn't need friends, and he didn't have a functional family to teach him how to interact with people. He liked that hard part of himself—it kept his life simple. He felt suffocated during his first encounter with her, but as time passed and he began to feel something more, something that could change everything, he vowed to keep the status quo.

He was used to structured solitude, and she was wreaking havoc on that.

The morning is here, and I barely fucking slept last night. It wasn't even the shitty nightmares that kept me awake; it was Tessa.

She was there when I closed my eyes, and not in the way I'd have liked her to be. Instead of being naked, making soft noises as I thrust into her, she was furious and bored during the trip to the stream I've decided we're taking. In one creepy movielike scene that my sleepless, stalkerish mind made up, she stubbed her toe and complained the entire afternoon. In another, she was bored out of her mind and wanted her lame boyfriend to drive all the way to campus to get her. When he arrived, it was like he was *all cardigan*. A giant cardigan monster that was both scary and lame.

It's frustrating the amount of time I've wasted thinking about this girl. None of this is going to matter in a month or so. If this "date" goes well, I'm hoping to win the Bet in less than two weeks . . . Hell, if I can charm her enough, maybe at the stream . . .

My phone alarm rings from across the room, and I climb out of bed to shut it off.

Today's the day. My head is already throbbing, and I'm annoyed by the pressure I feel to make the time I spend with her work in my favor. I should probably take a shower. As I'm getting dressed, I briefly wonder what she's doing right now . . . is she as stressed as I am? I can imagine so; she's so uptight all the time, and she's probably had me literally penciled into her planner-binder since the moment I offered to attempt this friendship thing.

After my shower, I rummage through my drawer to find a clean black T-shirt. The one I find is wrinkly, but it'll do. Outside, as I start my car, I hear a crush beneath my foot and find an empty water bottle under my gas pedal. In my half-sleep state, the sound is so irritating that I get back out and find a place to throw it away.

I really wish I could sleep better.

Getting to campus a little early, I accidentally leave my textbooks, some notes, and my black jumper in the backseat. I don't realize it until I'm halfway to class, but there's no way I'm going all the way back.

In Literature, Tessa's and Landon's seats are empty when I take mine, and a little part of me feels pretty damn smug about it. She's later than I am, and I somehow know that will irritate her. Well, you have to find joy in the simple things.

I spend my time looking back and forth between the door and the list of my missed calls and texts from Molly, Jace, and this one weird girl whose name I forget. When Tessa and Landon finally do walk through the door, they're gabbing away, and *she* looks happy and well rested. No purple shadows under *her* eyes, no sign of a restless night on *her* end.

"Are you ready for our date today?" I ask as Tessa's hip grazes my desk. The curve of that hip is very appealing. The curve on the front of women's thighs, on the side of the hips, is one of my favorite parts of a female body—it's just so sexy.

"It's not a date," Tessa says to me, then turns to Landon and adds, "we're hanging out as friends."

"Same thing." I look at her and take note of her choice of outfit. She's wearing jeans, tight enough for me to make out the shape of her thighs and ass. *Damn.*

Tessa effectively avoids me for the entirety of the class. I don't look her way either.

After class, I don't catch what Landon says to her—the fucker talks too low—but I hear her reply to him, "Oh, we're just trying to get along, since my roommate is his good friend."

Just trying to get along, huh?

I take a few steps closer to the Nerdacula and his nerdy-hot girlfriend. Landon's fucking polo shirt is tucked into his gray dress slacks. Does this man even know he's supposed to be a broke college student? Oh, wait—he's not broke. He lives in a nice big house a short drive from here with the man who is technically my father, while my mum lives back in England in a craphole. And what I call home is an old fraternity house full of sloppy wannabe cool guys who do nothing related to helping this wonderful community the way their charter purports that they do. Tessa's boyfriend would probably be in a frat. Blond hair, blue eyes, loafers, cardigans. It would be a match made in heaven, really.

Well, if he learned to drink way, way too much . . .

Landon makes eye contact with me and doesn't try to muffle his words. "I know, you're really a great friend. I'm just not sure Hardin deserves your kindness."

Really? And what do I deserve, Landon? A nice new daddy who doesn't love liquor more than his only biological son?

"Don't you have something else to do besides bad-mouth me? Get lost, man," I say, as kindly as I can manage. If I said what I was really thinking, Tessa would cancel our hangout for sure.

Landon doesn't respond to me; he only frowns at Tessa, again saying something too low for me to hear. As he walks away, she turns to me.

"Hey, you don't have to be cruel to him—you guys are practically brothers." She all but spits out fire.

Practically brothers? What kind of fucked-up world does this chick live in where Landon and I are anything close to brothers? We are two strangers who happen to have a third stranger in common.

"What did you just say?" I ask her through bared teeth.

Just because my piss-poor father moved Landon and his mummy into a mansion filled with chocolate-chip cookies—wait . . . how does Tessa know that?

I push my fingers through my hair.

"You know, your dad and his mom?" she answers, looking very confused. She nods to herself and frowns as if she just let out a secret.

I look to where Landon disappeared to see if I can chase his ass down. "That is none of your business."

Why does he think he has the right to discuss my family's business? "I don't know why the asshole even told you that. I'm going to have to shut him up, it seems."

I crack my knuckles and ignore the stinging of tearing skin on my eternally busted fingers.

She glares at me. "You leave him alone, Hardin." A real convincing Warrior Queen, this one. "He didn't even want to tell me, but I got it out of him."

So she knows about my family now? Why is that fair? She

doesn't need to know anything about me. This is going too far. The whole thing is.

"So where are we going today?" she asks.

She's getting too close to me now; her nosiness has gone to a personal level, and I'm not fucking okay with that. She probably probed him for answers to other questions about me, too. Why I don't live with Ken and his new family, why I never talk to my dad—she probably even asked what I was like as a child, and Landon probably spilled all that he'd heard about me. She's already judging me, I can tell.

"We aren't going anywhere; this was a bad idea," I tell her, and just leave her ass standing there.

She doesn't need to get any closer than she already is. She's too intrusive, too judgmental. I don't want anything to do with this shit anymore. I need to stay the fuck away from this girl.

By the time I get to my car, my head is pounding and my palms are sweaty. Why did he do that? Why would Landon tell her about my family? That must mean she knows everything. Or at least the positive things that Landon would tell her: that my father's the chancellor of the college, that he was third in his class at university, that he loves sports.

What she doesn't know is that he was a drunk—the worst fucking kind—because precious Landon doesn't really know that side of him.

I wonder if he does in fact know anything at all about the man, anything real? Has he been totally conned by my dear old dad?

I would love to be the one to break the news to him over his mum's coconut cake.

Suddenly I feel claustrophobic and roll the car window down to get some air. The handle sticks, and I yank on the metal rod, annoyed that this beautiful car is so fucking ancient. I catch my breath after about thirty seconds and finally pull out of my parking space. If Tessa had followed me, I don't know what I would have done.

I'm in my room for less than ten minutes when I get a text from Molly: Zeds w/ Virgin Barbie in dorm. Better hurry loverboy.

What? How do you know? I reply, wondering why I'm getting Tessa tips from Molly, of all people . . .

Is she fucking with me?

I don't kiss and tell.

I can practically hear her mocking tone through the screen as I push my feet back into my black boots. The insides are so worn out that I'm waiting to bust through to the street when I walk around in them, but I've had them for years and can't seem to find anything else as comfortable.

I know that I've gotten everything I'm going to get out of Molly, so before I pull onto the street, I text Steph, Is Tessa with Zed?

Her reply is instantaneous. *Nope not here ☺*

I immediately know she's lying, and press my foot harder on the gas.

fifteen

When I open the door, Tessa is on Steph's bed with Zed, with her own bed empty. A small bed, with Zed. And with Steph and Tristan, too, and Tessa's only sitting, nothing more, but still. She's with Zed. On a bed. On a bed with Zed.

It sounds like the worst Dr. Seuss rhyme ever.

And it has me seeing red.

"Jeez, man, you could at least knock for once," Steph says, trying to play stupid. She knew damn well I would come straight here. She wanted me to—that's why she told Molly, I'm sure of it. I'm just surprised Molly told me, though. Steph meets my eyes and laughs. "I could have been naked or something!"

Could've been? *Has* been, her wild eyes tell me. Yeah, I've seen her completely naked, and so I know that her boobs aren't half as big as those padded bras she wears make them seem. Still, she does have one of the nicest asses I've ever touched . . .

I walk farther into the room, and remark, "Nothing I haven't seen before."

Tessa and Tristan both look like someone took a morning piss in their Cheerios.

"Oh, shut up." Steph laughs, loving getting the attention she's always craving.

"What are you guys up to?" I ask, sitting down opposite them all on Tessa's bed. At least Zed didn't make it to *her* bed. I suppose that's some consolation . . . somehow.

Zed smiles from across the tiny room. *Why the fuck is he smiling?*

"We were actually going to go to the movies," he says. "Tessa, you should come."

Tessa looks at me, then at him. She seems nervous. *She's going to say yes!*

"Actually," I interject before they can finalize anything, "Tessa and I have plans."

I look directly at Zed, giving him a warning. He blinks slowly, challenging me. Tristan is silent when I look at him, not wanting anything to do with our drama. He's actually not too bad, except he's dating such a witch.

"What?" Zed and Steph both say.

"Yeah, I was just coming to get her."

But Tessa is sitting still, making no move to leave with me.

"You ready or what?" I say nonchalantly.

She looks so conflicted, like she's fighting against herself. Just as I'm ready to make a move to convince her, she nods and gets up from the bed.

"Well, see you all later!" My voice is too loud, and I push Tessa out the door so quickly it's like I'm on speed or something.

Outside, Tessa follows me, taking quick strides to catch up. Her legs are pretty long. Her thighs are a little thick. I can't stop thinking about holding on to them as I take her while she bends over the hood of my car. I try not to think about her when she's so close. I can feel my cock aching, begging me to think about how soft she would be, how much I'd just like to squeeze her . . .

I break out of my thoughts when I realize we've reached my car and I've pulled the passenger door open for Tessa on automatic. However, looking at her, I see she's not moving to get in, for some reason. Rather, her arms are crossed in front of her chest, pushing her tits up.

I'm sure she's trying to convey anger, but right now this is just hot.

"Well, I'll remember not to ever open a door for you again . . ." I say, giving her a sarcastic eye.

She shakes her head at me, and I know she's about to spit fire. "What the hell was that? I know full well you didn't come here to get me—you just got done telling me that you didn't want to hang out with me!"

She's yelling now. I look around the parking lot, and it's not empty. She doesn't seem to notice the people close by. Tessa doesn't strike me as the public-argument type, even though we've fought twice together in public.

She drives me so fucking crazy.

"Yes, I did come to get you. Now, get in the car." I gesture for her to climb inside. I cleaned it and everything—she better get inside.

"No! If you don't admit that you didn't come here to see me, I'll go back in there and go to the movies with Zed," she says defiantly.

What's her problem? She says *I'm* rude, and look how she speaks to me? Judgmental hypocrite, she is.

What the fuck do I say to that?

Should I tell her that Molly told me? Hell, no—Pinkie will never tell me shit again. And why would Tessa threaten me with hanging out with Zed? Does she somehow know about the Bet? Is she in on it with Steph?

I barely know anything about her, and I can see something in her is a little off. I bet Steph told her.

"Admit it, Hardin, or I am gone," she says.

I can't tell if she's taunting me or not. She looks genuinely annoyed, and her nostrils keep flaring—it's quite comical. I'll take this ego hit.

"Okay, fine. I admit it. Now, get in the damned car. I won't ask again." I want to win the Bet, but she's becoming a messy project, and I'm not putting much more effort into this before I hand the trophy over to another classmate. I walk to the driver's side of my car, leaving the passenger door open for her if she wants to get in.

And no surprise, she does.

I'm annoyed as fuck as I pull out of the parking lot. I'd opted out of this hangout—I got out of it—and now I'm here with her anyway. My head hurts, and my mind seems to be fighting against itself. Part of me wants to scream and roll all the windows down so I can choke on my own breath, but the other half feels a calm creeping through, slowly, but a calm filled with stillness. I turn the music up to shut my head off; that usually does the trick: a few screaming men singing about death and their own depression over repeating bridges—with thunderous drum solos adding to the rage.

Tessa doesn't seem to agree with Slipknot and reaches for my radio dial. Which takes a lot of fucking nerve.

"Don't touch my radio."

"If you're going to be a jerk the whole time, I don't want to hang out with you," Tessa threatens. She pushes her back against the leather seat to make a dramatic point.

"I'm not. Just don't touch my radio."

I can barely breathe, and the noise is drowning out my panic. When I look over at her, she's staring at the radio with an intense look of rage on her face. That breaks my mood and makes me want to laugh, though it's probably not the best time for that.

"Why do you care if I go to the movies with Zed, anyway? Steph and Tristan were going, too," Tessa says, sticking her chin out to underscore her point.

Oh, like a double date? Hello . . .

"I just don't think Zed has the best intentions." I don't know what else to say, so I stare at the road.

After a thick moment of silence, Tessa begins to laugh. *What the hell is wrong with her?*

"Oh, and you do? At least Zed is nice to me."

She's still laughing. Zed is nice to her? *Nice?*

He's betting against your virginity, sweetheart is something I can't say, though.

Because I guess I am, too.

I stay quiet, and Tessa keeps her guard up. "Can you *please* turn it down?" she yells over the music.

I nod. I may as well get her in a little better of a mood.

"That music is terrible," she complains. I knew she wouldn't like it; I can tell by looking at her that she listens to a certain type of music. Opposite of mine.

I tap my fingers on the steering wheel and watch as Tessa absentmindedly does the same to her thighs.

"No, it's not. Though I would love to know your opinion on what *is* good music."

I smile at the thought of her CD player as a teen: 'N Sync, Jessica Simpson, and doubtless some of the horrendous girl groups Mother England spits out on the regular fills the entire thing.

"Well, I like Bon Iver, and the Fray," she says after contemplating the matter for a few seconds.

"Of course you do." One Christian-based band and one über-hipster band. Not remotely surprising.

Okay, sure, both make decent music—they just aren't my thing. Not enough pain for me.

"What's wrong with them? They're insanely talented, and their music is wonderful." She's passionate with her answer. When my eyes meet hers, she turns away and stares out the window.

"Yeah . . . they *are* talented. Talented at putting people to sleep."

Tessa reaches her hand out and playfully smacks my arm. It's a strange thing I see couples doing all the time, but no one has ever done it to me.

"Well, I love them." She smiles proudly. She seems to be having a decent time. "Where are we going?"

"To one of my favorite places." I don't give her an exact answer. She's too nosy for her own good.

"Which is where?" She continues to push, like I knew she would. She's too anal not to.

"You really have to know everything that's going on in advance, don't you?" I say, turning the tables on her.

"Yeah . . . I like to—" She begins to explain herself.

"Control everything?"

She's silent.

I decide to let it go for now. I don't want to push her too far. "Well, I'm not telling you until we get there . . . which will be only about five minutes from now."

As we continue, Tessa looks around, confused. I can see her struggling to not ask me again. She's trying to relax, and that makes this easier for me. After a couple of minutes, I notice she's staring at the backseat.

"See something that you like back there?" I tease, and she shakes her head. A lock of her long hair falls down her shoulder, and she pushes it back. Her hair looks so soft. I wonder if she's a natural blonde, and remembering what her mum looks like, I'd say she definitely is.

"What kind of car is this?" she asks, staring down at her cloth shoe.

"Ford Capri—a classic," I tell her. I love my car more than my own self, and I'm proud as fuck to have it. Tessa engages lightly in the conversation as I tell her about the restored engine and newly quieted exhaust. She smiles and nods along, and even though I can tell she's lost, it's oddly nice to talk to an actual human.

After a few minutes, I glance down at her again, and she's staring straight into me. I feel a pressure building on the back of my neck, creeping down my spine.

Too close. She's getting too close. *It's a game, Hardin. Treat her as a piece of it.*

"I don't like to be stared at." I try to keep a straight face.

She's so curious, and I'm realizing I'm liking it more than I should.

sixteen

I drive down one last narrow road and park toward the end of the small gravel patch nestled between a group of massive trees. I love it out here; no one ever comes here, and that's perfect for me. Especially on a nice, rare day like today when it's not raining in the Olympic Peninsula. The dead sky is one thing I've been used to since growing up in Hampstead; the sun is a rare sighting most fall days.

Tessa glances around the area, then her eyebrows draw together.

"Don't worry, I didn't bring you out here to kill you," I say, attempting to evoke a laugh from her as we get out of the car.

She stares toward the field of yellow wildflowers, and her shoulders slightly relax. *What is she thinking?*

"What are we going to do here?" she asks me.

"Well, first, a bit of walking."

Tessa sighs and follows me down the dirt that used to be a grass path. She looks miserable already. What was *I* thinking? "Not too much walking."

She doesn't trust me, and she seems to be in a bad mood today. Go figure. When is she not? I focus my attention on the cloud of dust that my boots make when they hit the dry, dusty trail. Tessa's steps are nearly silent, and she's incredibly slow.

"Well, if we hurry, we may make it before sundown," I tease her when we reach a tree with an old, abandoned bicycle tied to it. It's the halfway marker, and the walk is about a mile. Not too bad. Tessa slows down, but her face when we reach the water is worth every wasted moment. She gasps a little, as if this simple stream in the middle of the woods is magical. Her lips lift and her eyes go wide.

Does she even like swimming? I probably should have asked her.

I stay quiet and let her take in her surroundings before asking her anything. Now that we're alone together, I can't think of shit to talk about. Maybe I should just get into the water? Tessa's standing in the same spot she was the last time I looked at her. She's pushing the dirt around with her shoe to avoid looking at me.

Fuck this awkward shit. I'm getting into the water.

I pull my T-shirt over my head and listen for the inevitable whimpering sound to come from Tessa. She doesn't say much, but she's very animated when it comes to matching a sound track to her expressions. With a smile usually comes a sigh, with annoyance comes huffing, and with arousal comes her panting.

"Wait, why are you undressing?" she inquires. I don't think she's aware of just how hard she's staring at my bare chest. She clears her throat and asks, "You're going to swim? In that?"

She points to the water with a look of disgust. Of course Little Miss Priss doesn't want to get her clothes and hair wet.

"Yeah, and you are, too. I do it all the time." I pop open the button on my jeans, and Tessa continues to complain.

Still, she watches me undress while doing so.

"I am not swimming in that."

This water is clearer than most lakes I've ever seen, actually. Which is exactly why I can't stand stuck-up, snobby girls who are afraid to get dirt under their manicured nails.

"And why is that? It's clean enough that you can see the bottom." I point toward the sparkling water. I thought she would be more impressed than she is. The idea that I never know what she's thinking unnerves me.

"So . . . there are probably fish and God knows what in there!" she shrieks.

Fish? Really? That's what this strange girl is worried about?

"Besides, you didn't tell me we were going swimming, so I have nothing to swim in."

"You're telling me you're the kind of girl who doesn't wear underwear?" I smile at her, desperate to see her in such attire. "Yeah, so go in your bra and panties." There's no way in hell she's going for that. I can see the anger building behind those gray eyes, and I can't wait to hear her reply.

"I am not swimming in my underwear, you creep." Tessa sits down on the grass a few feet above the bank. "I'll just watch."

She smiles and crosses her legs.

She's staring at my body again. This time she's looking at the outline of my cock in my boxers. Her cheeks are flushed, and she's trying hard to look away, pretending to be focused on the bundle of grass blades in her hand.

"You're no fun. *And* you're missing out," I call to her as I jump into the cold water.

Fuucckk, this water is colder than I thought. I swim out toward the opposite bank, where the sun hits the water all day and the temperature changes drastically.

"The water is warm, Tess!" I call to her.

She looks up from the pile of grass blades she's building to distract herself. She's bored out of her fucking mind, and I don't have the first idea how to change that. She won't even get into the water with me—what am I supposed to do?

"This is one beyond-boring friendship so far . . ."

Tessa rolls her eyes and lifts her head back to the sun.

"At least take your shoes off and put your feet in. It feels amazing, and pretty soon it will be too cold to swim in."

Tessa agrees and pulls off her shoes, placing them neatly beside her. Those shoes she wears are odd—they look like scraps of cloth taped to a piece of floppy cardboard. They can't possibly be comfortable. She rolls her jeans up her legs and pulls her bottom lip between her teeth as she pushes her feet into the water.

I wait for her to complain, but a wide smile fills her face. "It's nice, isn't it?" I ask her.

She looks away, tilting her head farther into the sun.

"So just come in." I dip my head back into the water and soak my hair, trying to convince her.

When I lift back up, Tessa is shaking her head. She still won't get into the water. *Christ, this woman is difficult.* I splash water at her, and she shrieks, scooting back up the grass. I've never been at this place with someone else; it's a little weird having company out here.

How can I get her to come in? The entire day will be a huge waste of time if she doesn't get into the water. I need to negotiate with her. But what would she want in return?

She doesn't seem like the compromising type . . .

"If you come into the water, I'll answer one of your always-intrusive questions. Any question that you want, but only one." I say my idea out loud the moment it comes into my mind. She's so nosy, this will thrill her.

"This offer expires in one minute." I have to give her a time limit or she'll surely take all damn day. I dip under the water and hold my breath as I swim about twenty feet. Tessa is probably scowling above the surface. The thought makes me laugh, and I nearly choke on the water.

"Tessa"—I wish she would just stop thinking so damn much—"stop overthinking everything, and just jump in."

She looks down at her outfit. "I don't have anything to wear. If I jump in in my clothes, I'll have to walk back to the car and ride back soaked."

"Wear my shirt." With my offer, she frowns and looks at the

piece of clothing in question lying close by on the grass. "Go on, just wear my shirt. It will be long enough for you to wear in the water and you can keep your bra and panties on . . . if you wish," I add. I would very much enjoy it if she *didn't* wear her bra or panties, but it's up to her, of course.

Tessa looks around again, taking in the water and my half-naked body before she reaches down and plucks my shirt from the ground. I win.

"Fine." She's such a bratty little thing. She rests her hand on her hip and continues her negotiation. "But turn around and don't look at me while I'm changing—I mean it!"

The little roaring kitten is back. I laugh, and she does this weird little thing with her hips, moving them back and forth as she pushes my black shirt between her thighs to hold while she lifts her shirt up over her head. I quickly turn around. I'm a gentleman—really, I am.

"Hurry the hell up or I'll turn around," I impatiently remark after silently counting to thirty. I sneak a look at her while she's bending down to set her jeans perfectly in line with her shoes. She's a complete psychopath, lining her shoes up like that. For a few seconds I wonder how she'd react if I tossed her shoes into the calm water. She'd be so pissed. I bite back a smile and finally look at her body. Her legs are tan—that's the first thing I notice. My T-shirt fits her body perfectly. Fuck, because of the size of her tits, the shirt barely touches the top of her thighs. I pull my lip ring between my teeth and enjoy the view in front of me.

"Um . . . come into the water, yeah?" I try to clear my throat and stop staring at the top of her thighs. "Just jump in!"

"I am! I am!"

"Get a little running start."

"Okay."

Tessa takes a deep breath before galloping toward the water in an awkwardly stiff run. She squeals and covers her face when she reaches the edge and stops one step before she would actually go over the edge.

"Oh, come on! You were off to such a good start!" My laughter fills the air between us, and I look at Tessa again. She's staring at me, smiling and laughing in the sunlight, and it confuses me. What are we doing here? Laughing at each other at a stream? What is this? One of those Nicholas Sparks movies where the couple's fighting is so cute that the trailer for the film spreads like wildfire on the internet? Bored women thinking they have some literary hero to come save them. It's bullshit, and they always, always end up with a shitty husband who doesn't and will never care about them or their family more than himself.

"I can't!"

She looks pretty frantic. Is she actually scared of the water? Good Lord. "Are you afraid?" I ask her.

"No . . . I don't know. Sort of."

I walk through the water to get closer to her. I stub my toe on a large rock at the bottom of the stream.

"Sit on the edge and I'll help you in," I offer. I reach for her as she scoots closer. She tries to hide her panties by clamping her legs together, and I appreciate the effort. The last thing I need is a distraction.

My hands grip her thighs, and my cock immediately responds.

Fuck her for having such soft, beckoning thighs that I'm dying to get my face between.

"Ready?" I take a breath and move my hands to her waist. Her hips mold to my hands, and I have to forcefully hold on to my last bit of self-control. My hands are itching to squeeze her hips, bend her over, and take her here.

What's my problem? I'm never this much of a horny frat boy. Is it her innocence and sinful body, or is it the competitive drive to win her body, to beat Zed?

Her skin is warm as she sinks into the water, and I let go of her. The water hits just below her chest. She sprawls her hands out in front of her and feels out the water. Her skin is covered in tiny goose bumps accentuated by the sunlight.

"Don't just stand there." *I need you to move so I don't just stand here and stare at you all fucking day.*

She seems to ignore me, but she does move out farther into the stream. As she pushes through the clear water, the T-shirt lifts up from the water as if trying to take flight. Before I can look away, Tessa shoves the wet fabric down, smoothing it underwater the best she can.

"You could just take it off," I say. I sure as hell wouldn't complain.

Tessa scrunches up her nose and slices her hand through the water—she fucking *splashed* me? It's annoying how funny this is to me.

"Did you just splash me?"

Tessa giggles and smacks her hands across the settling water.

I shake the liquid from my hair and lunge at her. I grasp her waist, tugging her under the water. Her small hand reaches up and plugs her nostrils. She still holds her nose?

I laugh, hard. "I can't decide which is more amusing: the fact that you are actually having a good time or the fact that you have to plug your nose underwater." I can barely talk from laughing so hard.

Tessa moves toward me, the look of a woman on a mission clear in her eyes. Her arms lift above her head, and she attempts to push my head under the water. It's a comical attempt. At best. While I tried to ignore the way my T-shirt floated up around her body, now I don't budge, and she laughs at herself and my stomach cramps from joining in. Her laughter is soft; it reminds me of the yellow wildflowers I saw at the beginning of our date-thing.

"I believe you owe me an answer to a question," she pushes.

I knew she wouldn't forget, but I assumed she'd wait a little longer before asking.

"Sure, but only one."

She's probably going to ask something stupid, like "Did your tattoos hurt?" I stare at the grassy bank of the stream and wait for her intrusion.

Her voice breaks through the silence. "Who do you love the most in the world?"

What the fuck?

What kind of question is that? How fucking strange. I don't want to answer it. I don't even *have* an answer. Now I'm growing even more suspicious of her and Landon's conversations about me. *Love?* Who do I love the most in the world?

Who do I love most? Well, I love my mum, I guess. I haven't said the words to her in years, but she's still my mum. That's about it, except for myself. I love myself the most. I don't think that "I love myself the most" would qualify as an answer, however.

Nevertheless: "Myself," I answer truthfully. I wasn't one to have any girlfriends as a puberty-stricken teen, so I never even had to fake any *I love you's* before I or anyone else my age actually knew what the word meant. I dive under the water to disappear for a few seconds while Tessa's brain tallies up her assumptions about me.

"That can't be true," she says the very second I feel the fresh air hit my skin. "What about your parents?" And like that, she crosses the line. Tessa Young has no fucking boundaries when it comes to her invasive personal questions. Her eyes are soft, her lips parted as she waits for me to respond. I hate the way her eyes look when they're full of pity.

Stop it, Theresa.

"Do not speak of my parents again, got it?"

"I'm sorry, I was just curious. You said you would answer a

question." Her voice is quiet. "I really am sorry, Hardin. I won't mention them again," she apologizes.

I'm not sure if I believe her. She's up to something, I can feel it. She's too intuitive and way too pushy. I don't even know her, and she sure as hell doesn't know me. Why does she keep thinking that she can ask such personal shit?

This afternoon is going to go one of two ways: with her and I fighting until she rushes into her dorm room in a pissed-off panic, or with me charming her, making her want to be around me.

I decide to keep it civil. I would rather not spend the drive back in awkward silence. I push my hands out toward her and lock my arms around her waist. Her body is light in the water when I lift her into the air and toss her to the side. She shrieks, and her arms flap around in the air like a bird. She pops up out of the water, her hair soaked and her eyes wild.

She's happy.

This could have gone one of two ways, and somehow I made her happy.

"You're going to pay for that!" she calls out cheerily, and wades toward me. She may actually believe that she has a chance at retaliation. Tessa moves even closer to me, water trickling down her face. Her skin is wet and shining, and why is she still moving closer?

I gasp when Tessa's thighs wrap around my waist and she lifts her body to line up to mine. I'm supposed to be in charge here.

She tenses and loosens her legs. "Sorry."

No, no.

I grip them, coercing her to put them back around my body. She feels so good pressed up against me, so warm. When she wraps her small arms around my neck, a twinge of panic flickers at the bottom of my spine. I look at her and try to read her mind. It's impossible.

"What are you doing to me, Tess?" I wonder while slowly grazing her trembling bottom lip with my thumb. Her hot breath comes out in low, deep puffs. The taste of her mouth is still fresh in my memory. I want another taste, need it.

"I don't know . . ."

She doesn't know. I don't know either. Neither of us has a grip on this, and it could escalate quickly.

I want it to.

Does this girl have any idea how sexy she is? Does she know that the shape of her mouth alone is enough to make me imagine very, very dirty things involving her? Picturing Tessa on her knees in front of me, her full lips open wide, tongue wet and eager to take me, to please me. I want to press my cock against her lips and tease the fuck out of her. I can drive her body insane, the way she's doing to mine. Her lips are a light pink shade, and the curve of her top lip is dramatic, like the lips drawn on a cartoon character. A sexy one, though, like Jessica Rabbit.

Fuck, I'm losing my damn mind over her. This can't be a good thing.

I guess it's fortunate that I have no qualms about being bad.

"These lips . . . the things you could do with them." I pause, remembering the way her mouth sucked at mine in my room and again in hers. "Do you want me to stop?" I stare at her, looking for any signs of nervousness. Her thighs tighten around my body, and I take that as a no, but give her a few seconds to respond before I make my move.

She wiggles even closer, pressing her body against mine under the water.

"We can't just be friends—you know that, don't you?"

At my words, she inhales a quick breath as I lean into her, pressing my lips softly against the line of her jaw near her chin. Her eyelids flutter closed, and I move my lips across her jawline, traversing her wet skin with affection. When my mouth touches the spot on her neck, just below her ear, a moan rises from her, surprising me. "Oh, Hardin."

The words send a shock through me. Her voice is so thick, so needy. For me. She's putty in my arms, and my heart is racing at the idea of molding her pleasure around me. She's never been fucked, though I'm sure she's at least gotten herself off before.

I want to hear her moan my name again, just like I need to taste her mouth again.

"I want to make you moan my name, Tessa, over and over again. Please let me." My own voice is unfamiliar as I beg her.

It's silent except for her heavy breathing and the low swish of the water moving around our bodies in a calm wave. She nods.

"Say it, Tessa," I continue. I pull her earlobe between my teeth and gently bite down on her skin. She whimpers and rocks against me as she nods furiously.

A nod won't do, Theresa. You want this, so tell me. "I need you to say it, baby, out loud, so I know you really want me to." My hands move to her stomach and under my shirt covering her body.

"I want to . . ." Tessa's declaration is rushed, desperate. I smile against the warm skin on her neck, and she sighs. Those three words are invitation enough for me. I hold on to her body, and she tenses—nervous that I may drop her, I assume. I begin to walk out of the water with Tessa attached to me. Her thighs are open, and she's pressing against my hardening cock with every step I take.

I let go of her as we reach the bank, and she whines, literally whines. The sound sends my blood straight to my groin. I climb up the bank and turn around to help her out of the water. She reaches for me; her eyes are set on my bare chest. I watch as her eyes shift to the tattoo on my stomach, the dead tree inked into my skin. She probably hates my tattoos, coming from whatever prissy little town she came from. Her God-fearing mum probably taught her that people with tattoos are evil and will eat her soul or some shit.

Tessa's probably used to seeing her clean-skinned, perfectly groomed boyfriend's chest. I watch closely as she continues to stare, attempting to decipher my ink. Her boyfriend has no tattoos, I'm sure of it. He probably doesn't even have a single scar on his skin, or in his mind.

I move away from her, and she stands still, waiting for instruction.

I find myself unsure what to do with her. She's still staring at my skin . . . Why is she still staring at my skin? More importantly, why does it bother me so much? I got my tattoos for me, not for some judgmental chick.

Why the fuck am I justifying myself right now? I never give a shit what women think of me; I only think about fucking them and how they come undone from my touch, in a mutually distracting kind of way.

Stop thinking, Hardin. I'm just like her, overthinking everything. What is she doing to me?

I cut to the chase: "Do you want it to be here? Or in my room?"

Should I fuck her here? I could lay her on the grass, spread those thighs, and have her crying my name out as I draw circles on her clit with my tongue.

Tessa shrugs as I adjust my boxers. "Here," she decides.

"Eager?" I ask her. I can feel the pull of her body to mine and wonder if she's feeling it, too. I know she's turned on by me, that's obvious, but does she feel this overwhelming call to touch me, the way I do for her?

"Come here," I order. She obliges with flushed cheeks and slow steps toward me. *Faster . . .* I want to rush her.

I don't have the patience to play teasing games now—I need

to feel her. I need her to feel me. I'm going to fuck her, here on the grass. I'm going to lay her down and touch every inch of her sinfully gorgeous body. My black shirt is soaked, completely molded to her body like a latex glove. It needs to go.

I tug at the bottom of the shirt and bring it up over her head. It's not an easy task, removing the wet fabric; it seems to want to stay on her, the way that I do.

The first part of our day was catered to her way of doing things and giving her a nice, simple day with me. The second part will go my way. I'm not used to making conversation or being asked about who I love most in the world. What I am used to is using a soft body to give pleasure to mine.

seventeen

He was about to win. He was ready to win.
And then he realized he wasn't ready for *her* at all.

I spread the wet T-shirt over the grass as a makeshift blanket for her to lie down on. My fingers are shaking.

"Lie down," I instruct, and help her onto the ground with me. I lie on my side next to her and prop myself up on my elbow to get a good look at her. Her body is exposed to me, her full breasts on display; her slightly tanned skin is literally glistening in the sun. She's a juicy, bright red apple, waiting for me to take a bite. I've seen many, many women much more naked than this, but fuck if Tessa isn't in a league of her own. As I'm admiring the curve of her hips all the way up to her perky tits, two small hands attempt to interrupt my visual tour. I sit up; the grass is soft beneath me, one good thing about the damn rain here.

I wrap my fingers around her wrists and push them down to her sides. "Don't ever cover up," I tell her. Her eyes meet mine, and I add, "Not for me."

"It's just . . ." Her cheeks flare, and she looks away. I don't let her finish her ridiculous statement.

"No, you will not cover up—you have nothing to be ashamed of, Tess." She doesn't look convinced. Who fucked up her confidence? "I mean it, look at you."

"You've been with so many girls . . ." Of course she would bring this up. Why does she care if I've been with other girls; we aren't in a relationship and never will be. None of the girls I've been with were like Tessa; a few of them were similar, but I don't typically go for the innocent, never-been-fucked-before girls. I like my women already experienced enough to fuck me like they know what they're doing. I'm no one's teacher, especially not in the art of sex.

Aside from Natalie, I'm reminded by that annoying little voice in the back of my head. Natalie, the sweet church girl with an ass too big not to be admired and hair black as oil. She was so inexperienced she couldn't even get the condom on my dick. Attending Sunday school every week since she came out of the womb hadn't taught her that.

"None like you," I say when I look back down at her. She seems nervous, so deliciously new, and I want to be buried inside of her.

"Do you have a condom?" Tessa's voice drops in volume when she says "condom." Has she ever even seen one? Natalie had only in the dark.

Why the fuck am I thinking about Natalie right now?

I can fuck Tessa now and win this entire thing. I can sink into her pure body and take what I came here for. She's staring at me now. Expecting. She thinks I'm the guy who takes chicks out here to fuck them in the woods. Especially the ones who have never had sex before.

"A condom?" I laugh, deciding right in that moment that fucking just isn't happening here. "I'm not going to have sex with you," I say even though I want to.

"Oh," Tessa says in an ashamed voice.

"Where are you going to—"

Why would she assume we should leave because I won't fuck her?

"Oh . . . No, Tess, I didn't mean it like that. I just meant that you've never done anything . . . like at all, so I'm not going to have sex with you." I try to detect if she believes me, then add, "Today." A little of the redness on her flushed cheeks dissolves.

"There are many other things I want to do to you first." And there sure as hell are. I'm going to make her beg for me. I need her body to surrender to my touch. Every inch of her will belong to me in this moment. I have her lying here, body exposed and ready, and I'm going to make the best of it, for her.

I climb on top of her, and she shakes a little when drops of water fall from my hair onto her face. I smile, watching her close her eyes, expecting more drops.

"I can't believe no one has fucked you before." I mean every word. I want to push my covered body onto hers so she gets a small idea of what it would be like if I was going to fuck her today. I prop myself up on my elbow and place my hand on Tessa's neck, gently running only my fingertips between her ample breasts. They look so soft, big enough that I could fuck them, more than a handful, but they keep themselves supported, creating a perfect set of perky tits. Her nipples are hard pebbles waiting for my mouth to suck on them. If I stop here to admire them with my touch, I'll never keep my dick to myself. Thank God she's wearing a bra.

My fingers trail down her stomach, the soft, modest curve of her stomach. Gooseflesh covers her skin, and she sighs. I dip into her panties, briefly rubbing my thumb against the lining. My fingers drift over her pussy, searching through her wetness to find her clit.

"Does that feel good?" I ask, and take the bud between my thumb and forefinger.

She doesn't respond. She's wet and swollen; her body is surrendering itself to me with only a touch. I've only just begun showing her how I can make her feel. I lean my head down and skim my lips across hers.

"Does it feel better than when you do it?" I ask. I release her clit and run a single finger down her slit. I wonder what gets her off when she's alone. Does she come from rubbing her clit or fingering herself? I get the feeling she's more of a clit girl, straight to the point.

"Does it?" I ask again.

"Wh-what?"

"When you touch yourself. Does it feel like this?"

She still doesn't answer . . . Why would she not just tell me?

It's hot, so fucking hot, to picture her lying on her dorm bed, legs spread and her small fingers teasing herself. She'd have to keep quiet because her roommate is asleep, but she would work herself to orgasm and cover her own mouth with one hand. Sometimes, when she comes hard, she may even bite down on her full lip and swallow her own gasps as she returns to reality. I need to know how she does it, but she's still staring at me like I've grown an extra head. All I did was ask her about how she masturbates.

Oh.

It dawns on me that Little Miss Priss has never made herself come.

"Wait . . . you've never done that either, have you?" I ask. I continue to tease her, enjoying the pool of her arousal coating my finger. "You're so responsive to me, so wet."

She moans. The sound is fucking exquisite. I pay attention to her clit again and gently pinch before rolling it between my wet fingers.

"What? Was . . . that?" Tessa's voice is nothing but a warm whisper, all resistance dissolved at my touch. I repeat the pleasurable pinch and roll while rubbing in small circles with my thumb. Tessa's panting now, her legs are stiffening, and I know she's close. So close. I can't wait to watch her lose herself for me. I can't believe she's never felt the pure euphoria that comes with sex. Fuck, she's been missing out.

Her back arches off the grass, lifting her tits closer to my face. Just one lick wouldn't hurt.

Yes, it would. I would be distracted. I kiss her again, this time in earnest, claiming her and giving her exactly what she needs. I'm providing her with something she's never felt before.

She's inching out of ordinary reality, and I'm the cause of it. My touch. Me.

I push my free hand into her bra, cupping a perfect breast. I massage it, letting her feel more than one sensation at a time. Her legs are shaking now.

"That's right, Tessa, come for me," I encourage her. Her lying on the grass, her teeth sunk into her bottom lip, flushed cheeks, and her eyes . . . those eyes are fucking wild.

"Look at me, baby," I beg, nipping at the flesh overflowing from her bra.

"Hardin," she moans, her voice thick like paste, refusing to let me look away. She's so sexy, so erotic, without even the slightest attempt at being so.

"Hardin . . ." She pulls me closer as she utters my name. She's breathing so hard, trying to regain her composure.

"I'll give you a minute to recover," I say as I slowly draw my hand out of her panties. A slick trail of her orgasm is glistening on her stomach where my hand rests. She sighs, and I move my hand to my boxers to wipe them clean.

I'm so fucking hard right now I can barely see straight. She's still lying here, her face looking like she just had the time of her life. She would like more, I know she would. Lord knows I would give it to her in a fucking heartbeat. Every part of me wants to slide inside of her. I want to hear her gasps and feel her tightness around me.

Not today. I can't today. I stand to my feet and grab my jeans and shoes from the bank.

I can feel Tessa's eyes on me as I get dressed again. "We're leaving already?" Her voice is quiet, laced with uncertainty.

Does she want me to make her come again? Greedy now that she knows how incredible her body can feel.

"Yeah . . . You wanted to stay longer?"

"I just thought . . . I don't know. I thought maybe you would want something . . ."

She looks humiliated. Why would she? Is she already regretting that she allowed me to make her come?

I should've known she would.

Tessa shifts her body, covering herself from me. She's already trying to rush away from me. Wait, she said she thought I might want something . . .

"Oh, no. I'm okay."

I would fucking love to have your warm tongue teasing the head of my cock right now, but it's not part of this plan.

But instead of that, I add, "Not now," to be sure she knows I'm going to thoroughly enjoy it when it does happen. Tessa nods and pulls her jeans over her legs and her shirt over her head.

Watching her get dressed messes with my head. I want to stroll over and undress her again. She shifts on her heels like she's uncomfortable between her thighs. She shouldn't be sore; I didn't enter her at all. She's probably not used to having a puddle of her own come there. The thought makes me laugh and turns me on so damn much at the same time.

"IS SOMETHING WRONG?" I ask Tessa in the car as I pull onto the gravel road. The sun has gone down slightly, and the air is growing wet. Rain is coming soon.

"I don't know. Why are you being so weird now?"

Weird? How?

"I'm not, you are."

"No, you haven't said a word to me since . . . you know." She's too shy to be specific.

I say it for her. "Since I gave you your first orgasm?"

"Um, yeah. Since that, you haven't said anything. You just

got dressed and we left. It makes me feel like you're using me or something."

Using her? For what?

Oh, I *am* using her. Goddamnit.

But she doesn't know that. It's only her insecurity making her think that way.

"What? Of course I'm not using you. To use someone, I would have to be getting something out of it." I half laugh.

When I look over at her, she isn't laughing. Her eyes are red, and a single tear falls down her cheek. Fuck.

She's crying?

"Are you crying? What did I say?" I don't understand her. Why is she so emotional, and why does it make me feel so guilty? She takes everything I say and twists it into something rude. She thinks so little of me, and I can't really blame her. She's so sensitive.

"I didn't mean it like that—I'm sorry. I'm not used to whatever is supposed to happen after messing around with someone, plus I wasn't going to just drop you off at your room and have us go our separate ways. I thought maybe we could get some dinner or something? I'm sure you're starving." I squeeze her thigh with my hand. She smiles at me, and the ache in my chest calms tremendously.

"So what type of food do you like?" I ask her. I don't know where to take her. I've never gone out to eat alone with a woman before. Sad, I know, but most of my time with women takes place elsewhere.

Tessa wraps her tangled hair around her hand to pull it up. I think I may like her hair up . . . it'll give me a better view of her face. "Well, I like anything, really, as long as I know what it is— and it doesn't involve ketchup."

"You don't like ketchup? Aren't all Americans supposed to be wild for the stuff?" What an odd girl she is.

"I have no idea, but it's disgusting."

She's so sure and proud and unwavering in her hatred of ketchup. It's comical.

She laughs with me. "Let's just stick with a plain diner, then?"

When the car grows too silent, I ask, "So what do you plan on doing after college?"

Shit, I already asked her this. I'm fucking terrible at conversation.

"I'm going to move to Seattle immediately, and I hope to work at a publishing house or be a writer. I know it's silly." She looks down at her hands. It's not silly; I have the same dream. "But you already asked me that before, remember?"

"No, it's not silly. I know someone over at Vance Publishing; it's a bit of a drive, but maybe you should apply there for an internship. I could talk to the boss." Vance would kill to have someone as bright as Tessa around that place.

"What? You'd do that for me?" She's astounded. I can hear it in her voice.

"Yeah, it's not a big deal." I shrug my shoulders. I hate the attention I'm getting right now. I can just feel Tessa gushing from the other seat. It's not a big deal, getting someone an internship at Vance. I would help anyone. Really, I would.

"Wow, thank you. Really. I need to get a job or an internship soon anyway, and working at a publishing house would literally be a dream come true!" She claps her hands. Literally claps them together, like a child who's just won a giant bear at the fair. It makes me want to smile.

AS I PARK, Tessa looks a little unsure about the diner, and I watch her eyes take in the outdated appearance.

"The food here is amazing," I promise her, and climb out of the car. The diner is nearly empty when we sit down. A stubby older woman brings our menus, and I try to look anywhere but at Tessa.

She starts a conversation with me after we order our meals. She tries to pry into my childhood, but I don't allow it.

"My dad drank a lot; he left when I was younger," she blurts out suddenly.

I don't say anything, I just frown at my plate and try not to picture her as a little girl, hiding from her version of my fucked-up dad.

I stay inside my head during the drive back, focusing my attention on using my fingers to draw small shapes on Tessa's leg.

"Did you have a nice time?" Tessa asks when we get to campus. Her question is full of expectation.

A nice time was certainly had. I would like to have *another* nice time with her, making her moan my name as I finger-fuck her over and over.

But instead of all that I say, "Yeah, I did, actually . . . Listen, I would walk you to your room, but I don't want to play twenty questions with Steph . . ."

I shift in my seat to look at her. She's disappointed even though she's trying really hard to keep that fake smile on her face.

"It's fine. I'll just see you tomorrow," she says with regret.

I can tell she doesn't want to go, and the thought pleases me. She stares at me, waiting for me to say something. I don't speak, but I reach up and grab a loose strand of her hair and tuck it behind her ear. I don't have much to say, but I want to feel her again. I want to feel this overwhelming calm she brings with her when she touches me. She turns her cheek so it's resting in my palm, and she looks like a younger version of herself, open and waiting for me. I tug at her arms, asking her to come closer. I need her closer. She obliges and climbs over the center console and straddles my lap. My body is warm from the afternoon sun, and Tessa's hands are greedily tracing the ink on my stomach over my thin shirt. Each touch of her fingertips sends another steady flicker through me.

I tease her tongue with mine, taking everything she'll give me. I wrap my arms around her back, pulling her as close to me as possible. It's still not enough. I need more of her. I can't get enough of this girl. My hands travel up her warm stomach, and we're interrupted by the most obnoxious ring tone.

"Another alarm?" I ask her as she digs into her purse. The screen on her ancient phone is small, but big enough for me to see a name flashing across the screen: NOAH.

Her precious little high school boyfriend is calling her while she's in my car with her tongue down my throat. She presses ignore and smiles up at me. Really? Guess she's not as innocent as I thought. A good orgasm seemed to pluck out her morals, one moan at a time.

It dawns on me that she'll never tell him any of what happened today. Not a word. She's going to kiss me, get out of my car, and go call her preppy little boyfriend the moment she gets into her room. She's going to tell him she loves him. He'll say it back, and she'll smile the way she did when I kissed her.

She licks her lips and leans across the center console to kiss me again.

No, no.

"I think I better go." I sigh and stare out the windshield.

"Hardin, I ignored the call," she says, defensive. "I'm going to talk to him about all this. I just don't know how or when—but it will be soon, though, I promise."

Well, I was wrong about her morals disappearing, but this is worse than I thought. She spent one afternoon with me, and now she's going to break up with her childhood lover boy in hopes that I'll be his replacement?

No, no.

No.

The air in the car is thickening, clogging my throat, as Tessa waits for my response.

"Talk to him about what?" I ask, knowing I shouldn't feed this puppy more than I already have.

"All of this." Her hand waves around the car, stirring up the thick air, and I'm convinced I'm going to fucking choke on it. What was I thinking doing this shit with her? I should've just fucked her, no cute little lunch debate over ketchup, no talks about our future plans. As women always do, she now wants to be a part of my life. She's her own brand of crazy if she thinks this could actually happen. "Us," she adds.

She's using words like *us,* and it's fucking terrifying. "*Us?* You're not trying to tell me you're going to break up with him . . . for *me,* are you?" She feels heavier on my lap now, a solid reminder of why virgins aren't my thing. Even Natalie wasn't a first-timer; she had given her virginity to a boy from her church while "experimenting."

"You don't . . . want me to?" Tessa frowns in confusion.

Christ, this is going downhill fast.

"No, why would you? I mean, yeah, if you want to dump him, go for it, but don't do it on my behalf."

"I just . . . I thought—"

"I already told you that I don't date, Theresa."

She flinches, hurt by my words. This is messier than I thought it would be. Part of me wants to tell her I don't mean to be a dick, that it's ingrained into every fiber of me to be this way, it's not my fault. Or hers. Except it *is* my fault—it's my fault that I just don't have the slightest bit of whatever it is that makes people want to pair off and live happily ever after whilst frolicking through wildflower patches. I'm simply not capable.

"You're disgusting." She climbs off of my lap and quickly gathers her phone and bag. Her absence on my lap nags at me. So does the deep gray storm that has brewed in her eyes. "Stay away from me from now on—I mean it!" she shouts and runs off.

Natalie's voice saying the exact same words to me, eyes full of tears, blasts through the speakers in my mind. Tessa's eyes are glossy, but she's holding it together for her pride. We're alike in this way; the enormous, irrational amount of pride we both have could be dangerous.

Tessa opens the car door and climbs out without even looking back at me. She does her best to slam the door and hurries across the parking lot. I immediately pull out and turn the dial up on my stereo. I need the noise to silence the hurricane gathering in my mind. My hands are itching, my mind racing.

Natalie, Theresa, Natalie, Theresa.

Natalie standing on the porch at my mum's house in Hampstead, a book bag covered in floral print clutched to her chest and her bloodshot eyes full of thick tears.

"Please, Hardin," she cried. "I have nowhere to go." She was begging. A puff of smoke clouded in the cold air in front of her as she spoke. I couldn't bring myself to let her in. I just couldn't. I had heard that her family and church had exiled her, kicking her out of both of her lifelong sanctuaries. She looked so young in that moment; her blue eyes were shining through the darkness as she waited, hoping I would change my mind.

I wouldn't, though, I fucking couldn't. I couldn't let her stay at my house. My mum was barely home, and that would leave her with me all the time. What could I do for her? I didn't want to have anything to do with her, and even if I had, I couldn't really do shit to help her. My dad was a drunk who would wake her as he stumbled into the musty house, its walls stained with cigarette smoke the odor of which had permanently seeped into the upholstered furniture. Where would she sleep if he suddenly came back? He'd been gone for a few years, but my childish mind believed that he could return. I was a damn fool.

Now he *is* in fact back, and he has a nice little family in a big house, and I hate how often this thought crosses my mind. I've already moved to another country to live close to him, and now he's become embedded in my thoughts what feels like all fucking day.

A honking noise pulls me back to the present, and I quickly jerk the steering wheel, causing a minivan to honk at me again. My eyes aren't focused; the world outside the windshield is a blur.

Blinking a few times, I reach for the volume dial on the stereo. I need to pull off to the side of the road. My chest is aching, a steady, thick pounding of muscle inside of me. My bones are rattling from the force of it. I can feel beads of sweat, tears maybe, soaking my skin. Embarrassed, I wipe at them.

"Fuck!" I shout into the thick air. I need air. My throat feels like it's closing as I throw open the door. The cool fall air tunnels through, calming my breathing.

Natalie's face is fresh in my mind. Tessa joins her, and the girls are laughing at me, snorting and teasing me. They're mocking the way they have this power over me. Tessa's knowing smile brightens, and Natalie fades out. What the fuck is happening to me? I need to stay away from Tessa, no matter what stupid bet I made or how stupid I'll look when Zed wins.

Zed.

He's always a factor. I can't stand the thought of him having her. His body, beads of sweat on his skin as he presses his body against hers.

I close my eyes and rest my burning cheek against the cool steering wheel. What a goddamn mess I got myself into.

WHEN I NEXT GO TO CLASS, Tessa isn't sitting in her seat. It's empty, along with Landon's. I sit down and pull out my phone. One text from Logan inviting me to a drink during lunch hour. I decline and push my phone back into the pocket of my black jeans. They're a little snug, but it works. My legs are too long to wear loose-fitting pants without looking like a clown. I do have a pen stain—or perhaps it's some sort of makeup that won't wash out—on the sleeve of my white T-shirt. I didn't want to do laundry, and some of the shit women put on their faces has to be bio-hazardous at best.

I'm distracted from the disgusting truth about my hygiene when Tessa comes through the door. I stare straight at her, willing her eyes to meet mine as she walks toward the front row. I'm surprised that she didn't pick a new seat. I do believe her hatred toward me is that strong right now.

"Tess?" I whisper across the small space between our seats. She ignores me, but I noticed her shoulders flinch when I said her name.

"Tess?" She swallows, and her chest is moving at an unnaturally slow pace. The tension is clear between us; I can feel it buzzing, radiating from us.

"Do not speak to me, Hardin." She squares her shoulders to let me know she means business.

"Oh, come on." I try to cajole her with a smile, but she's not having it.

She licks her lips and says, "I mean it, Hardin, leave me alone."

"Fine, have it your way." If she wants to be difficult, I can be difficult, too. Oh, I'm the fucking king of difficult.

Landon comes into the conversation looking like an anxious little puppy. "You okay?" he asks Tessa.

"Yeah, I'm fine." She nods and shifts so more of her back is facing me.

THE WEEK PASSES with sleepless nights and irresistible calls from dusty bottles under the sink. It's becoming harder and harder to ignore their siren song. By Friday I'm fucking exhausted. I look and feel like shit. When I get to Literature, Landon is sitting at his desk, and his eyes meet mine immediately.

"I need to talk to you," he insists. I glance around to see who else he could possibly be talking to. No way it's me, but Tessa only now walks through the door, so maybe?

"Yes, you," he says, looking more annoyed than before.

I sit down in my seat, ignoring him. I cross my legs under the desk and lean my back against the hard plastic chair.

"I wanted to extend an invite for dinner in a few days. Our parents have something to tell you." He must pick up on his own stupidity, because he corrects himself: "My mom and your dad."

Our parents? Is he fucking demented?

"Don't ever say some shit like that again, you prick."

In a move to stand up, Landon pushes his hands against the top of his desk. I fucking dare him.

"Leave him alone, Hardin!" Tessa yells, and grabs hold of my arms to keep me from hurling myself at Landon. She really doesn't know how to mind her own damn business. I drop my arms. *Fuck this.* Why did she have to walk up and join us?

"You need to mind your own business, Theresa."

Tessa leans into her bestie and whispers something to him. *Bestie* is such a stupid word, but I bet these two dweebs use it.

"He's just an asshole. That pretty much sums it up," Landon announces with his most charming grin.

Tessa's giggling peeves me in the deepest way.

She turns to Landon. "I have some good news!" *Ugh.* She's putting on a show for me, probably thinking I'm too oblivious to catch on to her juvenile antics.

"Really? What's that?"

"Noah's coming to visit today, and he'll be here all weekend!"

The slow burn of jealousy is making its way through me, stopping to fray each edge of me on its way. With every clap of Tessa's hands, I can feel my smoldering gaze heating her skin, and each watt of brightness that grows in her smile makes my hands twitch on my desk more and more vehemently.

"Really? That's great news!" Landon sucks up to Tessa, and neither of them pays any attention to me when I pretend to gag.

eighteen

As he got to know the girl, his fears began to grow. He had never had much competition when it came to affections of women. His short-lived rendezvous were never challenged by other men.

That was, until the perfect boy with golden hair came waltzing in, with a book full of her secrets. He knew the boy had watched the girl grow up, been alongside her most of the way and probably knew her better than anyone else. He was easy to hate, but in the end he realized he wasn't the competition after all.

While I walk down the hallway of Tessa's dorm building, I try to shake the thoughts out of my head. I can't help but picture Tessa naked, underneath her boy toy's body. His cardigan tied around his shoulders as he fucks her.

If the thought didn't make me nauseous, I would find this image hilarious.

I knock at Tessa's door once before I turn the handle and walk in. It's not locked, which makes it obvious that she and her boyfriend aren't planning anything too wild. She and Noah are sitting on the bed in the dark, and Tessa jumps a little when she sees me, making a space between them.

"What are you doing here?" Tessa raises her voice the moment she realizes who it is that has just arrived. "You can't just barge in here!"

I give the adorable couple a smile.

"I'm meeting Steph." I sit down on the edge of Steph's bed, knowing that I'm lying. Through my teeth. I turn to Noah, wanting to gauge his annoyance level. Is he easygoing, or uptight like Tessa? Tessa's probably going to piss herself the moment I say his name. "Hey, Noah, nice to see you again." I think about shaking his hand. I'm sure he's used to it at the country club he's a member of.

"She's with Tristan, probably already at your house." She really pushes those words as if she's trying to tell me to leave.

Not yet, Blondie.

"Oh?" I play with Tessa's nerves. "Are you two coming to the party?" That would make it much more fun. I can imagine the boy fitting in well at the frat house—bro-dudes with matching blond hair would have him doing a keg stand within minutes of his arrival. His pure soul would be tainted, and Theresa would have to find herself another blond Abercrombie model. Tough life.

"No . . . we aren't. We're trying to watch a movie," Tessa answers me. Noah moves his hand in the dark, and I cringe as he rests it on Tessa's. I can see her discomfort even in the darkness.

"That's too bad. I better go . . ." I turn on my boot, and some of the pressure disappears from my chest. "Oh, and . . . Noah." I put a pause between my words and watch Tessa squirm. "That's a nice cardigan you're wearing."

Tessa looks relieved when she realizes that I'm not going to cause a scene.

"Thanks. It's from the Gap," he answers me, oblivious that I'm making fun of him.

"I can see that. You two have fun," I say as I leave the room. My chest burns as I close the door. He's a tool.

nineteen

Just as his life was beginning to make a little sense, it was shaken again. He thought he was in complete control of himself, of her, of everything. He was resisting the sweet temptation of the bitter liquor. He didn't crave it the way he had until he found himself on the phone with his father, getting a play-by-play of the man's new—and better—life.

When he hung up the phone, he had no other option.

He was completely alone with his only friend. The bottle of scotch was nearly empty; it mirored him in that way.

When I get to the Scott house, I park right in the middle of the driveway. I hate this fucking beautiful house. It sits high on a perfectly green lawn. Ken and Karen pay a pretty penny to have their yard groomed; no doubt they pay a pretty penny to have themselves groomed as well. Ken's new soon-to-be wife loves living here, I'm sure. She probably loves spending his money on grooming herself, too.

I'm fucking livid.

I'm pissed off and not drunk enough to deal with this kind of bullshit. What fucking piece-of-shit father tells his only son he's getting married to another woman when you're just now getting to know his ass? This is exactly why I didn't want anything to fucking do with him. I'm pissed that I only had a quarter of a bottle of liquor in my cabinet. My head is pounding, my throat is dry, and I'm craving the burn of scotch. Ken Scott has fine bottles of scotch gifted to him from colleagues in sweater vests who have just returned from their vacations in Scotland. My shitty father is getting remarried, and he says it like this: "Karen and I are to be wed. Soon, very soon."

To be wed? What the fuck kind of stilted-ass expression is that? And during a fucking telephone conversation?

"We are to be wed," I repeat as I take his porch stairs in two long strides. The man has so much fucking topiary it makes me feel like I'm lost in the fucking Wonka Jungle, or Wonka Factory thing. Hell, whatever it is, it's hideous.

First and foremost, I need more scotch.

"I'm all out!" I exclaim, my voice leaping out into the darkness.

I'm in a pickle here. I'm drunk, but not as drunk as I want to be. I need more liquor. Ken has more liquor. He always has.

I knock on the door, and no one answers. The man's house is too damn big. Stupid brick showy model home.

"Hello?" I shout into the abyss of a dark yard, with loud crickets shouting back at me. The neighbors all have their porch lights on, and every house has an SUV parked in front, the bumpers littered with WCU bumper stickers. All of the overpaid, highbrow scholars live on this street. I pull my gray beanie down over my hair, hoping it makes me look even more dangerous to the neighbors than usual.

Landon opens the door before I even realize that I'm pounding my fist against the wood. My knuckles are barely healed; the skin never really has a chance to heal before I rip it open time after time.

"Hardin?" His voice is low, like I've woken him up.

"No," I say, passing him in the foyer. I walk straight to the kitchen and raise my voice so he can hear me as he follows. My eyes stop for a beat on their couch; its frilly, floral-vomit-covered mass bothers me. "It's someone else who looks identical to him, only this model thinks you're an even bigger prick than the other one does."

I open a cabinet in the kitchen to begin my search. My sperm donor—that is to say, Ken—since becoming sober has thrown out most of his liquor, but I know he kept at least one rare bottle of scotch. Maybe it's a reminder, maybe it's a temptation, but he cherishes it—fucking treasures it, even. I've heard him talk more about that stupid bottle, and with more pleasure, than he talks about his own son since I've been here. He always keeps it in a different spot; I don't know if he hides it from himself or if he uses it as a constant marker of his sobriety. Either way, it's mine now.

"They aren't here. My mom and Ken went out of town for the weekend." Landon explains what I already know.

I stay quiet, not wanting to converse with my soon-to-be stepbrother. The thought makes me gag. I'm not meant to have family, no siblings looking out for me or vice versa. I'm meant to be alone and take care of myself.

I keep searching, now moving into Ken and Karen's bedroom. The room is enormous, big enough for three king-size beds like the four-poster they have in the center of the room. Their dresser, nightstands, and bed are all a dark cherrywood, the same as Ken's desk in his office.

Anal-compulsive asshat.

The room is hideous and it looks like shit, so I hope Ken and Karen are happy in here with their matching furniture and pristine life. I pull the string in the closet to turn on the light and brush my hand across the shelves. After feeling around some dust and a box, my fingers hit glass. Jackpot.

I carefully bring the bottle down and wipe the thin layer of dust that's gathered since Ken's last public showing. Immediately I twist the top off, feeling deep satisfaction as the plastic tears, ruining the perfect seal.

The scotch is hot on my tongue, and it tingles a small cut on the inside of my cheek. I savor the thick, slow burn of the smooth liquor. Ken Scott has always loved his scotch, and he's a true aficionado of the beverage. The taste is incredible—so smooth, yet with such a rich flavor. I personally think scotch is just a tad pretentious and was disappointed to find out that it's the only whiskey that comes from Scotland. Showy bastards. Still, I love the taste—one trait I got from Ken's short list of actual contributions to my existence.

Half of the bottle is gone now, my head is spinning, and I think I should finish it off. Why not? My dad doesn't deserve it; he doesn't even drink anymore. When he chose to stop holding hands with the devil, he lost the right to possess such an exquisite bottle.

Besides, he already has enough precious, perfect things. Like his new son, for example, who right now seems to think he can stop me from my mission to make his new daddy feel as shitty as I feel. Ken has a perfect soon-to-be wife who keeps his pantry and stomach full. *She* doesn't have to work an eight-hour shift, then turn around and run off to another job. She doesn't have to line up the bills on their kitchen table that's missing a leg, and choose the one she's not going to have the money to pay this month. The times I talk to him he seems to think we were fine back in Hampstead, and I blame a fraction of that illusion on my mum, whose pride was bigger than her brain.

His house is clean, and even his fridge is clean—no fingerprints are visible on the stainless steel. I lick my fingers and drag them down the metal.

Landon scoffs, cursing from behind me. "Did you drink that entire bottle?" he asks. His eyes are wide as he stares at the bottle swinging in my hand.

"No, there's still half left. Want some?" I ask him.

He backs away into the dining room, his hands raised, and I follow him. "No."

Perfect son who doesn't drink. How sweet.

"I thought you weren't drinking anymore?" he says. I turn to him, holding on to a big cabinet filled with expensive, shiny sets of dishes in order to keep myself from falling down. What the fuck does he know about my drinking?

My fingers dig into the wood. "Why would you say that?"

He realizes that he wasn't supposed to say anything like that in front of the poor damaged child, and his eyes widen. "I just meant . . ." He attempts to bullshit me.

"Stop." I hold up the hand with the bottle, and he steps backward into the living room from the dining room. He's not going to stop fucking talking. He's going to push and push—I don't have any control over him, over anything that's happening right now. My shitty dad is getting fucking married, I'm drunk and pissed off, and this motherfucker doesn't know when to stop pushing me.

My fingers wrap around the corners of the china cabinet next to me.

He doesn't know when to stop. "Your dad said—"

And now it's my turn to *push*: before he can finish his sentence, I push the cabinet over. I use extra force, dropping the bottle in the process. Landon yells something, but I can't hear him over the sound of shattering china.

"Get out! You need to leave!" Landon shouts. I bend down and grab the bottle from the mess of broken glass, splintered wood, and slices and fragments of white-and-blue dishes. I cut the tip of my finger and lick away the blood while making sure the scotch bottle is properly closed.

"Tessa would be so impressed by this!" I hear his voice as I pull open the back door.

Tessa? I want to ask him what the fuck Tessa has to do with any of this, but I don't want to give him the satisfaction of knowing he can use her as leverage over me. For whatever reason, he thinks tossing her name out there will make me come down and give a fuck, and I won't let him think he's right. I ignore him even though I don't want to, and walk out onto the back deck.

The air is warm but calm; the beginning of fall is here and the summer nights will soon start to turn chilly, and then chilly will turn into freezing. The next time I fuck up, I'm moving somewhere warm.

"Tessa would be so impressed," I say aloud, mocking Landon's voice. He was trying to be a smartass, letting me know that she wouldn't approve of my mess-making and temper tantrum.

"Tessa, Tessa, Tessa!" I shout into the darkness.

Even this yard is perfect. It's nearly as big as an American football field and lined with tall trees, keeping the property in perfect shade during the day and a black sheet of darkness at night.

MY HEAD IS SPINNING and the silence isn't helping. I take another swig.

A few minutes later, the creak of the screen door has me leaping to my feet. Tessa is standing in the doorway in front of Landon. She walks toward me, and with every step, the bottle in my hand feels heavier. Her light eyes are pinned on mine.

Is she real? Her blond hair is so shiny under the patio lights. She's glowing. Frowning, but radiant.

Is she really there? I think so . . . unless this bottle is laced with some hallucinogen, she must be.

"How did you get here?" I ask her. I follow her eyes to Landon and freeze. That fucker.

"Landon, he . . ." she begins.

"You fucking called her?"

Landon ignores me, walks through the doorway, and closes the screen door behind him.

Tessa points a finger at me. "You leave him alone, Hardin. He's worried about you," she says, defending her friend.

The perfect brother has the perfect friend.

She's generally soft-spoken, but not when she's mad. Her eyes are so pretty, too perfect for such a soft face. I can't keep staring at her; she's giving me a headache. I have to guess what she's thinking, and I've had a long enough night already. I sit down at the patio table and gesture for her to take a seat across from me.

When she sits down, I take another drink and she stares, pure judgment in her eyes. I slam the heavy bottle down on the glass table and she jumps out of her seat. She should leave; she shouldn't be here. Landon should never have called her and told her to come here. Why would she come, anyway? Her boyfriend is in town this weekend, and I'm sure he's penciled in for cuddle time.

The thought makes me cringe. Landon had no fucking right calling her to come here.

"Aww, aren't you two something. You're both so predictable. Poor Hardin is upset, so you gang up on me and try to make me feel bad for breaking some shitty china." I smile at her, letting her know I'm playing the villain tonight.

"I thought you didn't drink," she says,

It's more a question than a statement. She's trying to figure out just who I am. I confuse her, and she hates it.

"I don't. Until now, I guess. Don't try to patronize me; you're no better than me." I point a finger at her, using her old scolding technique.

She doesn't look fazed by my move. I take another drink.

"I never said I was better than you. I just want to know what made you start drinking now?"

I'll never understand what makes this girl think she can ask people whatever the hell she wants. Boundaries? She has none.

"What does it matter to you? Where's your boyfriend?" I burn the question into her. She looks away, unable to keep up with my stare.

"He's back in my room. I just want to help you, Hardin." Tessa's hand reaches for mine, and I flinch away before she can touch me.

What is she doing? This must be some sick joke. Landon must have told her to come here and be all gentle, tame-the-lion bullshit. She wouldn't touch me for no reason.

"Help me." I laugh. "If you want to help me, then leave." I wave the bottle and my hand toward the door.

"Why won't you just tell me what's going on?" she pushes. I knew she would. Her hair is down, resting over her shoulders in waves. She's wearing casual clothes, looking younger than ever. Her eyes release mine, and she looks down at her hands on her lap.

Out of habit, I pull the hat off of my head and run my hand through my hair. I can smell the scotch seeping from my pores, and I can hear Tessa's heavy breaths coming out in long draws. I match my breathing to hers and then wonder what the fuck I'm doing.

I would rather get her talking than sit here in tense silence. "My father decided to tell me just now that he is marrying Karen—and the wedding's next month. He should have told me long ago, and not over the phone. I'm sure perfect little Landon's known for a while."

Tessa's eyes dart to me, and she looks a little surprised that I just spoke to her so candidly.

I hadn't planned to go into that much detail.

I blame the scotch.

"I'm sure he had his reasons not to tell you," she says, defending him. Of course she does. Ken Scott is like her: polished and pretty and always the good guy.

"You don't know him; he doesn't give a shit about me. You know how many times I've talked to him in the last year? Maybe ten! All he cares about is his big house, his new soon-to-be wife, and his new, perfect son." I take a drink from the bottle and wipe my lips with the back of my hand. "You should see the dump that my mum lives in in England. She says she likes it there, but I know she doesn't. It's smaller than my dad's bedroom here! My mum practically forced me to come here for university, to be closer to him—and we see how that worked out!"

"How old were you when he left?" Tessa asks. I can't tell if she's being nosy, pitying me, or just wondering.

I hesitate before answering. "Ten. But even before he left, he was never around. He was at a different bar every night. Now he's Mr. Perfect and he has all this shit . . ." I gesture toward the house. Pots of bright flowers line the ledge of the deck, adding to the scenery.

"I'm sorry that he left you guys, but—"

"No, I don't need your pity." I stop her there. She's always making excuse after excuse for everyone around her. It's fucking frustrating. She doesn't know my father, she didn't have to put up with his shit until she didn't anymore, but then missed it when he was gone.

"It's not pity. I'm just trying to . . ."

Judge me?

"Trying to what?" I push her to respond.

"Help you. Be here for you."

It sounds nice when she says it. Too bad she doesn't know anything about me. She doesn't know who she's trying to help. She needs to understand that I'm not fixable and she's wasting her time here. She needs to leave and never speak to me again.

"You are so pathetic. Don't you see that I don't want you here?

I don't want you to be here for me. Just because I messed around with you doesn't mean I want anything to do with you. Yet here you are, leaving your nice boyfriend—who can actually stand to be around you—to come here and try to 'help' me. That, Theresa, is the definition of pathetic," I say, watching her gray eyes turn to stone.

"You don't mean that." She doesn't know me, though she can read me well.

I deliver the final blow. "I do, though. Go home." I lift the bottle in victory and open my mouth. Suddenly the bottle is snatched from my grip and tossed across the yard.

"What the hell?" I shout at her. Is she mad? Tossing a valuable bottle of scotch across a lawn like that? I look back and forth between her figure striding to the patio door and the bottle, then follow her after grabbing the bottle and leaving it on the side of the deck, near the table. I have to catch my balance, but I manage to step in front of her.

"Where are you going?" I look down at her, stopping her from entering the house. The porch light catches her eyelashes in a way that makes it look like they're brushing her cheekbones. I stare at her as she stares at her feet.

"I'm going to help Landon clean up the mess you made, and then I'm going home." Her voice is full of conviction and leaves no room for arguing. Except that I'm a master of the art of finding a small space, a crevice, no matter how tiny, to argue my way into.

"Why would you help him?" He betrayed me by calling her in the first place, and now she's leaving me to help him?

"Because he, unlike you"—her voice is low, steady, and strong—"deserves someone to help him," she says.

I feel the impact of her words sinking into my chest as she stares into my eyes, challenging me.

She's right. He's the guy everyone wants to be around. He doesn't break shit and throw a fit when he gets bad news. He deserves her time and attention, just like he deserves to walk into that big house and be welcomed warmly and go into his own room. He deserves a home-cooked meal; he shouldn't have to eat takeout in an empty room inside a house full of strangers who all secretly hate him.

She's right about that, and that's why I let her walk past me and back into the house without another word.

The way she looked at me as she walked by is burning through my mind, playing on repeat over and over. I pull out my phone and scroll through a few pictures I've taken of her. One while walking to the stream . . . her hair was so blond under the sun and her skin was glowing. She was quiet—nervous, maybe— but she looks peaceful in the photo. She really is beautiful. Why would she want to help me? What all did Landon tell her about my drinking?

I pull my beanie back on, and after a few minutes I can't help but go inside. My eyes are burning and my head is pounding as I open the door.

"Tessa, can I talk to you, please?" I immediately ask. Landon is crouched over, dropping broken pieces of china into a plastic bin. Tessa nods, and I stare at her face. Then my eyes move far-ther down her body, stopping at her bloody finger, which she's holding under the sink faucet.

I cross the kitchen in only a few steps. "Are you okay? What happened?"

"It's nothing, just a little glass," she says. The cut looks small, but I can't get a good look at it. I reach for her hand and pull it from the water. The cut is about half an inch long and a quar-ter inch deep. She'll be okay; she just needs a bandage. Her hand feels so light in mine, so warm, and I feel my breathing slow as I hold her. I drop her hand and she lets out a deep breath.

"Where are the Band-Aids?" I ask Landon.

"Bathroom." He's annoyed with me. I can tell by his tone. I

find the small box of bandages easily in the cabinet. I grab the antibacterial cream from the bottom shelf and return to the kitchen.

I take Tessa's hand in mine for the second time and squeeze the cream onto the tip of her finger. She's watching me carefully . . . unsure what to think, maybe? Band-Aids remind me of my mum and that fucked-up night a long time ago, and I blink away the memory as I wrap the bandage around Tessa's finger.

"Can I talk to you, please?" I ask Tessa for the second time. She nods, and I wrap my fingers around her wrist, leading her to the back patio again. We have more privacy there; Landon won't be listening in.

When we reach the table, I let go of Tessa's wrist and pull the chair out for her. It's the least I can do, I suppose. My hand feels cold, and the blood is no longer pumping behind my ears. I feel calm and cool.

I grab another chair and drag it across the concrete side of the patio. When I sit down across from her, my knees almost touch hers.

"What could you possibly want to talk about, Hardin?" Tessa asks, sounding completely uninterested.

I pull the hat from my head and toss it onto the table between us. My fingers find my hair. I feel like a complete bastard for being such an asshole a few minutes ago. I want her to know that I'm not her charity case, her broken little doll, but now that I'm coming down from my adrenaline high, I'm starting to see what a complete dick I am.

"I'm sorry," I say quietly. The words settle in the static between us, and she stays silent. "Did you hear me?"

"Yeah, I heard you!" she barks at me. Her chin is lifted in the most defiant way. She's pissed.

She's pissed? *I'm* fucking pissed. She came here, meddled in my family drama, and then doesn't accept my apology?

I reach down for the bottle and open the top. She glares at me as the liquor slides down my throat. "You're so damned difficult to deal with."

"*I'm* difficult? You have to be kidding me! What do you expect me to do, Hardin? You're cruel to me—so cruel." Her lips tremble and her eyes begin to water. She tries to square her shoulders, but they slump; she's more than upset over this.

I whisper my response. "I don't mean to be."

"Yes, you do, and you know it. You do it purposefully. I've never been treated this poorly by anyone in my entire life." That can't be true. I'm not even that mean to her; she hasn't dealt with shit in her life if this is the worst she's been treated.

"Then why do you keep coming around? Why not just give up?" I ask her. If I'm that bad, why doesn't she just quit trying to be with me?

I ignore the part of my brain that's questioning how I would feel if she stopped trying.

"If I . . . I don't know. But I can assure you that after tonight, I'm not going to try anymore. I'm going to drop Literature and just take it next semester," she tells me. Her arms are crossed in her lap, and the wind is blowing her hair behind her shoulders. I wonder if she's cold.

I don't want her to drop the class; it's the only regularly scheduled time I have with her. "Don't, please don't do that."

"Why would you care? You don't want to be forced to be around someone as pathetic as me, right?" I hear pain behind her words, but I don't know her well enough to judge if it's authentic. I wish I did. I wonder how many people actually know her, the real her. I'm talking about the one whose brows crinkle before she smiles, the one who maybe doesn't have her shit figured out the way her mum thinks she does.

"I didn't mean that . . . I'm the pathetic one." I sigh and lean back in my chair.

Her eyes pierce mine. "Well, I won't argue with that," she says, her lips pressed into a hard line. She reaches for the bottle, but I'm faster than her this time.

"So you're the only one who can get drunk?" She looks at me, her eyes focusing on the ring in my brow.

"I thought you were going to toss it again." I hand it to her. I don't like her drinking, but she's ready for a fight over it and I'm not. I just want her to stay here. I like how quiet it is when she's around.

She gags the moment she tastes the scotch. "How often do you drink? You implied before that it was never." She's grilling me.

"Before tonight it's been about six months." Six months down the drain. Way to fucking go, Hardin.

"Well, you shouldn't drink at all. It makes you an even worse person than usual," she says in a joking way, but I know she's serious.

"You think I'm a bad person?" I don't look up from the ground while I wait for her answer. She's going to say yes, just like everyone else would.

"Yes."

I'm not surprised by her answer, but I couldn't help but hope for her to say no.

"I'm not. Well, maybe I am. I want you to . . ." I begin. I'm not that bad of a person, am I? I could be better, for her, if she asked me to. I look at her, taking in the way her lips are trembling, waiting for me to finish my jumbled thought. I want to be good, I want her to think I'm good.

"You want me to what?" she asks impatiently. She pushes the bottle into my hands, and I sit it down on the table without taking a drink.

How do I answer that without sounding pathetic? I can stop drinking, I can be nicer to people, or just her.

"Nothing." I can't find the right words for her.

"I should go." She stands to her feet and rushes away from me. She's moving so fast, and I don't want her to leave. I'll try harder.

"Don't go." I follow her. When she stops, her face is so close to mine that I can taste the faint trace of scotch on her breath.

"Why not? Do you have more insults to throw in my face?" she shouts, her words hitting me harder than usual. She turns away from me again, and I reach for her. I wrap my hand around her arm and pull her back.

"Don't turn your back on me!" I yell at her. She doesn't get to come here and stir shit up and walk away. I'm fucking sick of people doing that shit to me.

"I should have turned my back on you a long time ago!" Tessa's hands push against my chest. "I don't know why I'm even here! I came all the way here the second Landon called me!" She's screaming at me now. Her face is red and her lips are moving so fast. Her tongue darts out to wet them so she can finish her angry rant. "I left my boyfriend—who, like you said, is the only one who can stand to be around me—to come here for you!"

Her words sink into me, one by one. She did leave her boyfriend to come here. She has no other reason to be here aside from me. Maybe I'm not as bad as I thought, and maybe she sees that in me.

"You know what? You're right, Hardin, I *am* pathetic. I'm pathetic for coming here, I'm pathetic for even trying—"

I close the space between us without another thought and press my mouth to hers. She pushes at my chest, fighting me, but I can feel her body relaxing in my arms.

"Kiss me, Tessa," I beg her. I need her.

"Please, just kiss me. I need you." I try once more, for the last time, to get her to kiss me. My tongue touches her closed lips, and they part. She gives in to me all at once, willingly and wholly. She leans into me, sighing against my breath, and I bring my hands to both of her cheeks, cupping her face, devouring the taste of her.

My tongue traces her bottom lip, and she shivers. I wrap my arms around her, anchoring myself to her steadiness. I hear a noise from the house, and Tessa pulls away. I don't kiss her again, but I keep my arms wrapped around her.

"Hardin, I really have to go. We can't keep doing this; it's not good for either of us," she says.

She's lying to herself. We can figure this out.

"Yes, we can keep going," I assure her. I don't know where this sudden bloom of hope has come from, but it feels nice here, settled in my chest.

"No, we can't. You hate me, and I don't want to be your punching bag anymore. You confuse me. One minute you're telling me how much you can't stand me or humiliating me after my most intimate experience . . ."

I did that. I fucked up—I need to explain what happened and that sometimes I fuck things up on purpose. I've always been like this. My gran once tried to have a birthday party for me when I was twelve. She sent out invitations and ordered a special cake. On the day of the party, I told everyone it was canceled and sulked in my room the entire day. I didn't touch that cake. I just fuck things up sometimes . . . but I can find a way to stop doing that. If it means I get to kiss Tessa, to feel her losing herself in me again, I'll do anything.

I try to interrupt her, but she stops me by pressing her index finger to my lips. If she didn't have a Band-Aid on it, I would be kissing her cut. "Then the next minute you're kissing me and telling me you need me. I don't like who I am when I'm with you, and I hate the way I feel after you say terrible things to me."

"Who are you when you're with me?" I ask her. I like who she is. She's a better person than most.

"Someone I don't want to be, someone who cheats on her boyfriend and cries constantly." Her voice cracks. She's ashamed of the person she becomes when she's around me. That makes me feel like shit. I want her to be happy about spending time with me. I want her to crave me the same irresistible way that I do her.

"You know who I think you are when you're with me?" I ask her. My thumb traces the line of her jaw, and her eyes flutter closed under my touch.

"Who?" she whispers, her lips barely moving. The air between us is calm now as she awaits my answer.

I answer truthfully. "Yourself. I think this is the real you and that you're just too busy caring what everyone else thinks about you to realize it.

"And I know what I did to you after I fingered you . . ." She cringes at my blunt word choice. "Sorry . . . after our experience. I know it was wrong. I felt terrible after you got out of my car."

"I doubt that." She rolls her eyes, dismissing me.

"It's true, I swear it. I know you think I'm a bad person . . . but you make me—" I can't finish. She's digging into me, deeper and deeper, and it's terrifying. "Never mind."

"Finish that sentence, Hardin, or I'm leaving right now." I can tell she means it. She waits, her hand on her hip and her eyes stone cold for me.

"You . . . you make me want to be good, for you . . . I want to be good for you, Tess," I breathe, and she gasps.

twenty

When she started pressuring him for labels and proofs of commitment, he panicked. He felt like a wild animal being cornered and trapped. His cage was honesty, and she threatened to lock him away without a key. He couldn't lose her, but with each day it grew harder to keep her. She turned the tables on him, questioning things he thought she would never catch on to. When she wanted more, she demanded it, taking nothing but yes for an answer, but when he wanted more, she pushed against it, excuse after excuse.

This could never work, Hardin—we're so different. First off, you don't date, remember?" she fires at me. She steps away from me, and I hope she doesn't try to leave my father's house. It feels like all we talk about anymore is the future. Marriage, living together, breaking up, not breaking up. Tessa feels pressure to plan her whole life, but I don't. At this point I think it's common knowledge that I don't handle this type of pressure well. Regardless, she keeps pushing for me to be better and better for her.

"We aren't that different—we like the same things; we both love books, for example," I tell her.

I always have to defend myself to her. "You don't date," she mocks me.

"I know, but we could . . . be friends?"

Friends? Really, Hardin?

Frustration glows in her eyes. "I thought you said we couldn't be friends? And I won't be friends with you—I know what you mean by that. You want all the benefits of being a boyfriend without actually having to commit."

I let go of her body and lose my footing. I quickly balance myself. "Why is that so bad? Why do you need the label?" I'm thankful for the space between us and the fresh, scotch-free air.

"Because, Hardin, even though I haven't really had a lot of restraint lately, I do have self-respect. I will not be your plaything, especially when it involves being treated like dirt." Exasperated, she throws her hands into the air. "And besides, I'm already taken, Hardin."

She's using that bloke as an excuse? Oh, come on! Who is she trying to kid here?

"And yet look where you are right now," I say dryly.

She's dangling her boyfriend over my head, taunting me with him and complaining when I do the same with Molly. She sees no double standard here, and the liquor is making it seem even worse tonight. I'm smart enough to know this, but dumb enough to stop myself from being a dick. I'm also liquored up enough to not give a fuck about much of anything. I shattered my father's dining room into tiny pieces.

Her mouth twists into a menacing frown, teeth bared and all. "I *love* him and he *loves* me."

Her words slice at my chest. The last ones hit the bone. I move away from her and knock into the chair. Fuck my lack of balance.

"Don't say that to me." I raise a hand as if it could guard me from her words.

She doesn't back down; she's full-fledged pissed the fuck off and fully intending to go straight for the throat here. "You're only saying this because you're drunk; tomorrow you'll go back to hating me."

Hating her? *Hating her?* As if I could possibly hate her?

I back away in frustration and try to focus on how green the trees are here because of all the rain. "I don't hate you," I finally say. "If you can look me in the eyes and tell me that you want me to leave you alone and never speak to you again, I will listen." I don't want to hear her say these words—they would kill me—but if she felt that way, if she wanted me to back off, I'd back off. "I swear, from this point on I will never come near you again. Just say the words."

I try to imagine my life if she left. She would take with her all the color I've worked on painting into my life.

Before she can answer, I continue: "Tell me, Tessa, tell me that you never want to see me again." I can't imagine it. I step even closer and reach out to run my fingers over her bare arms. Gooseflesh rises on her skin, and her lips part.

I lean closer and whisper, "Tell me you never want to feel my touch again." I press my fingers to her neck and gently drag the tips down the length of it, then along her collarbone. She's practically heaving now, unable to speak. I lean even closer, my face barely an inch away from hers. I can feel the electricity under her skin; the faint hum distracts us both. "That you never want me to kiss you again . . ." I lower my voice, and she trembles.

"Tell me, Theresa." I push for the words that I don't want to come from her lips.

I barely hear her when she says my name, but I feel her breath puff against my lips.

"You can't resist me, Tessa, just as I can't resist you." She looks hesitant but not appalled by this statement. "Stay with me tonight?" I ask her against her lips.

Tessa's eyes dart from mine to the house, and she pulls away. I turn to see what caused her to freak out. I don't see anything. She says she has to go.

No, she can't go. I'm not ready to be in this house alone yet. I can't believe I'm going to stay here.

"Fuck," I mumble, running my fingers over my hair. "Please,

please stay. Just stay with me tonight, and if you decide in the morning to tell me you don't want to see me anymore . . ." I don't want this to be an option, but sadly it is. "Just please stay. I am begging you, and I don't beg, Theresa."

I've never begged in my life. Is it the liquor or is it her that makes me so crazy? I can't tell.

Tessa nods, her eyes shining under the light. "And what will I tell Noah?" His name throws a wrench into my side, reminding me that she's only temporarily mine. I need more time with her. "He's waiting for me, and I have his car," she explains.

She left him back at her room? For me?

I don't know what to make of this. Did they break up? Does he know that she's here with me? I wonder if the boy even knows my name. It drives me fucking insane that I don't know how involved she is with me emotionally. Steph won't tell me shit, and Tessa gives even less away.

Does she really care so much about what her boyfriend thinks? I stare at the back of the house. The green vines are taking over the brick wall. The lights are so bright. I suspect that the reality of what she's been doing must be hitting her. "Just tell him that you have to stay because . . . I don't know. Don't tell him anything. What's the worst thing he can do?"

I'm curious as to why Noah seems to have so much control over her. She sighs; her bottom lip puffs out and she looks genuinely worried. What could be so bad . . . he would tell her mummy on her? She's eighteen now—doesn't she know that?

"He's probably asleep, anyway," I say. It's true; he's still on high school curfew.

Tessa shakes her head. I lean back against the ledge of the deck. "No, he has no way to get back to his hotel."

Hotel? This kid is staying at a fucking *hotel*? Is he even old enough to rent a room on his own? "Hotel? Wait—he doesn't stay with you?" I'm baffled.

"No, he has a hotel room close by." Tessa's eyes drop to the wooden deck floor and she shuffles her feet. She's uncomfortable.

"And you stay there with him?"

"No, he stays there," she quietly responds, looking embarrassed. She keeps her eyes on the ground and continues, "And I stay in my room."

No fucking way. Does he even like her? Does he like women at all? I mean, come on, look at her! "Is he *straight?*" I can't help but ask. There's no way he is. Unless he's cheating on her, which would be fucked up—but would help my case tremendously.

Not that she's not doing the same thing to him.

Tessa's mouth pops open in horror. "Of course he is!"

It's insane to me that she doesn't see anything weird about her boyfriend not wanting to stay with her. "Sorry, but something is not right there. If you were mine, I wouldn't be able to stay away from you. I would fuck you every chance I had." It's true. I would wake her up every morning with my face buried between her thighs. I would put her to bed every night by blowing her mind and making her scream my name.

A blanket of redness flushes down Tessa's face, and she looks away from my eyes. I love the way my words affect her. The darkness is giving me a headache. The trees are moving too much, their trunks twisting in unnatural ways. Also, I want to be inside, alone with her. Especially after the night I've had.

I turn to Tessa and can't keep my eyes off her parted lips. "Let's go inside. The trees are swaying back and forth. I think that's my cue that I've had way too much to drink."

Tessa looks at the house and back to me. "You're staying here?"

I nod and reach for her hand. She's staying here, too. I still can't believe I'm staying in Ken's house after the shit that man pulled. "Yeah, and so are you. Let's go." I take her hand before she can fight me again.

We walk into the house, and she tries to move her hand from mine by walking faster than me. I take a longer step as we pass through the kitchen.

Some of the mess is still there on the floor. Many of the shattered pieces of porcelain are now overflowing the bin, and most of the glass has been swept off the floor. Good, Landon can clean up this mess. He's getting my fucking dad, after all. Truth is, he already has him. Someone or something other than me has always had Ken Scott. The scotch, the bars, Karen, Landon, this big house. He spreads himself so thin, yet had no room for me in his life until the last year, and he thinks I'm just going to be okay with that shit? No fucking way.

I tighten my hold on Tessa's hand as we walk through the house and up the stairs. If I remember correctly, the room we're going to is the last one in the hallway upstairs. There are so many fucking doors up here. We wouldn't want to walk into Landon's room and find him wanking.

We finally reach the door at the end. Tessa has been quiet during the walk, and I'm okay with that. I don't want to push her too much, and I'm still trying to stop thinking about my sperm donor being a fuckup.

The room behind the door is dark. I struggle for the light switch.

"Hardin?" Tessa whispers in the darkness.

The curtain is open slightly, allowing a little bit of moonlight to come through. I let go of Tessa's hand and step farther inside. This damn light switch is impossible to find. I continue to run my hand over the smooth wall but find nothing.

What the fuck?

I can see the outline of a table, possibly a lamp, on the other side of the room, so I blindly move toward it. The toe of my boot catches on something solid, and I nearly fall to the ground. "Fuck!" I curse at the object. This room probably doesn't even have a goddamn light; Ken and Karen likely just wanted to fuck with me.

When I get to the table, my fingers feel for a lampshade. Bingo! "I'm right here," I tell Tessa as I pull on the chain. The bulb clicks on, and the startlingly strong light from such a small lamp blinds me. I blink a few times and look around the room. My room.

My room that I've never used. Ever.

The bedroom reminds me of some gaudy-ass hotel. The walls are painted a light gray, with crisp white trim along the ceiling and floorboard. The carpet even has those lines vacuumed into it. The bed against the back wall is disgustingly big, with a mountain of decorative pillows piled at the expansive cherrywood headboard. The only reason a bed this big would ever be necessary is if Tessa was lying naked in the center of the dark gray duvet. Unfortunately for me, she's not. She's standing next to a desk that matches the bed and holds a brand-new Mac desktop. Showy motherfuckers.

I rub my hand over the back of my neck. "This is my . . . room." I don't know what else to say about it.

Tessa pulls her bottom lip between her teeth and asks, "You have a room here?"

It doesn't feel like my room, not in the least bit, but technically it is. Ken has told me multiple times about the room here that's only for me. Like I'm supposed to be impressed by the four-poster bed or the giant computer monitor. "Yeah . . . I haven't ever actually slept in it . . . until tonight," I uncomfortably explain. I hope she doesn't ask any more questions, but I know she will.

There's a bulky storage bin at the end of the bed that I'm assuming has a single purpose: to hold the overabundance of pillows. I make it more useful by sitting down on it and taking my boots off. Tessa watches me, probably compiling a list of questions to ask, like the nosy little thing she is. I pull my socks off and tuck them into my boots. I have a few small cuts on my ankle. Some of the shards apparently got into my shoe. Fucking great.

Tessa must have finished her list. She takes a step closer and opens her mouth. "Oh. Why is that?"

I take a breath and decide to answer her instead of giving her shit about it. "Because I don't want to. I hate it here," I reply with honesty. I do hate it here. I hate that my bed at my mum's house in England had a stained mattress and the same sheet and duvet since I was a kid.

While Tessa processes my truthful answer and formulates her next question, I unbutton my pants and pull them down. Tessa's eyes go from distant to wide and alert within two seconds of me standing in my boxers in front of her.

"What are you doing?" she asks.

"Getting undressed?" I say, raising my pierced brow to her. I know she likes to ask questions, but why do so many of them have to be so unnecessary?

"I mean, why?" She stares at the crotch of my boxers. If she's trying to be subtle and pretend she isn't thinking about my cock right now, she's failing miserably.

My eyes meet hers. "Well, I'm not sleeping in skinny jeans and boots." My hair falls down my forehead and I push it back.

"Oh," Tessa quietly says.

I wait for her to say something further, but she doesn't. I watch her eyes as I pull my shirt over my head. Her stare moves from my neck down to my stomach, taking in every line of black ink. She focuses the longest on the tree tattooed there. I wonder if she likes it or if this part of me is unattractive to her. Her focus on me makes me uneasy. I don't know what to do while she's inspecting me for damage. Each inch of my skin that her eyes touch rises with gooseflesh. Instead of the burning I always read about, I feel the slow blowing of an icy breath.

Tessa is still staring, still focused only on my body. I surprise her by tossing my shirt at her. She's too entranced by me to catch it quick enough. I wonder what it would take to get her naked so I can inspect her body, with my eyes steady on her, taking in every inch, every blemish that she's insecure about but I won't see.

I wish I knew what she was thinking. I wish I knew her better. I find myself wishing that I could have known her in a different way. She could have been my neighbor who stops by and borrows things, and I could ask her as many questions as I want. I would ask her why she asks so many questions, why she always scrunches her eyebrows up when she's confused, or mad. I would ask her what she wants to do with her life. I would ask her how she'd feel if she didn't get to see me again. I would ask her if she could possibly find forgiveness and grant it to me.

But this is reality, and in reality, I'm still a stranger to her. She barely knows anything about me, and if she knew half of the fucked-up shit I've done, she wouldn't be so intrigued. My tattoos, or her reaction to them, would fade, and her response to my attitude would turn from sarcastic to venomous. I have to be careful with this, because if my mystery disappears, she will, too.

Fuck, all of this makes my head spin. My buzz is fading, and my head is starting to fuck me up. I need to lighten this shit up really quickly. "You can sleep in that." I smile at her. "I assume you won't want to sleep in just your underwear. But of course, I'm perfectly fine with it if you do."

"I'm fine sleeping in this," she says in the most unconvincing tone I've ever heard. She doesn't want to sleep in her bulky skirt and baggy shirt. I quite like her shirt; the light blue color goes well with her eyes. I've never had a thought like that before . . . *It goes well with her eyes?* What does that even mean?

She's messing me up more than the scotch tonight.

"Fine. Suit yourself; if you want to be uncomfortable, go ahead." I step closer to the bed and grab the first pillow I touch and throw it onto the floor.

Tessa looks offended by this. Or maybe she's offended that I'm half naked. I don't know. She walks to the foot of the bed and opens the ugly chest. "Oh, don't throw those on the floor. They go in here," she tells me, as if I didn't know that. Does she think I've never seen these types of pillows before? Does she think because I had a single mum that I don't know how to put overpriced bundles of cotton into a box?

No, Hardin, she's only trying to help . . . I try to talk myself down. My mind always goes straight for the worst possible interpretation, and I fucking hate it. My insecurities are eating me alive. I grab another, even frillier pillow and throw it onto the carpet. She groans, complaining while she bends down to pick it up.

While Tessa plays Molly Maid, I pull back the duvet and climb into the bed. It's never been slept in before, I can tell. It feels like lying on clouds. It's even better than a hotel. I watch Tessa watch me as I cross my arms behind my head. She's always watching me. I'm always watching her.

I cross my ankles as she shoves the last pillow into the chest and closes the top. Neat freak, she is.

Is she going to stand there all night? I would rather that she peel off her baggy clothes and climb into bed with me. "You're not going to whine about sleeping in the bed with me, are you?"

"No, the bed is big enough for both of us." Her smile shows no nerves, but her shaking hands picking at her nails do. She's being playful now. I love it.

"Now, that's the Tessa I love," I joke. Her eyes widen slightly, and I push the reason why away from my mind. Not today—not going anywhere near that thought today.

Awkwardly, Tessa climbs onto the bed after slipping off her shoes. She stays fully dressed, and she remains at the edge of the king-size bed, as far away from me as possible. She lies down, and I consider scooting closer to her, but I'm afraid she'll get spooked and fall off the bed. As I'm picturing her falling to the floor, I laugh, and she turns around to face me.

"What's so funny?" She's doing that thing with her eyebrows again. She's so fucking cute.

"Nothing," I lie. I don't think telling her that I was picturing her take a tumble will help my case tonight. Still, I can't help but laugh as she pouts.

"Tell me!" She looks up for a second and then deliberately pops out her bottom lip. Despite her fake pouting, or maybe because of it, her lips are so fuckable. I can't wait to feel them take a slow drag down the shaft of my cock. Thinking about her head bobbing up and down on me has me pulling my lip ring between my teeth. The metal is cold on my warm tongue.

I roll onto my side and face her while I ask, "You've never slept in a bed with a guy before, have you?" For that matter, I haven't slept in a bed with a girl before either. It wasn't my thing. I don't know if it is now, but so far so good.

I'm relieved when she answers, "No." I smile to show her how I feel about being the first guy she's slept in a bed with. I love that she has so much left of her to be claimed. In some ways, I have so much left of me to give her, too.

Tessa is facing me, lying only a few feet away from me. She's still dressed in her heavy clothing, and it's driving me insane. She lifts her hand between us and touches the dimple on my right cheek. It's such a simple, yet tender thing to do. No one, not even my mum, has touched me on the face in at least ten years. Even during sex, sometimes I kiss girls, but I don't let their fingers linger on my body.

I make eye contact with her and register her panic. She pulls away, but I grab her hand and put it back to my cheek. It feels good, having her touch me. Her touch is so gentle. I want her to touch me everywhere. "I don't know why no one has fucked you yet; all that planning you do must help you put up a really good resistance," I tease her. There has to be a reason she's so inexperienced. It's just not realistic that she would have absolutely no experience without a good reason for it.

"I've never really *had* to resist anyone," she says. I don't believe her words, but I believe her eyes. Still, it's just so hard to have faith.

"That's either a lie or you went to an all-blind high school." I look at her pretty mouth. "Your lips alone are enough to make me hard." It's true. She could easily reach down and feel the proof of my words. I almost tell her that, but I don't want to ruin the moment.

Tessa satisfies me by gasping at my filthy words. I laugh and think of all the ways I can drive her fucking wild. She's like driving a brand-new car, the excitement you feel when hearing the engine's low purr for the first time. I want to make her purr—I would make her *scream* if Landon wasn't here. I want to take this slow tonight, but I want to show her more than what I did at the stream. That was only one of my many tricks.

I lick my lips and take Tessa's hand in mine, bringing both of our hands to my mouth. She inhales a sharp breath, and I pull her hand along my wet lips. Her hands are shaking when I single out her index finger and gently bite down on the pad. She moans on instinct, and my cock twitches in my boxers. Tessa's hands are warm as I guide them down my neck. It feels so good to be touched, the level of high that I feel clouding my senses. The liquor has mostly worn off, and now I'm completely trashed off of a stubborn, sexy blonde. Tessa pulls her hand away, and I drop my own hand onto my lap. Her fingertips trace the ivy inked along the bottom of my neck. I can't concentrate on anything except for the cool, calm trail she's leaving behind on my skin.

After a few seconds of silence, I speak up. I'm curious and

horny, and I'm going to have fun with her. I bring my hand back to
hers. "You like the way I talk to you, don't you?"

I stare at her until her chest begins to rise faster and faster.
She breaks eye contact with me, and I continue: "I can see the
blush in your cheeks, and I can hear the way your breathing has
changed. Answer me, Tessa—put those full lips of yours to use."
I wish she would do this in more ways than one. She stays silent.
Man, I thought I was stubborn. I move closer to her and take her
wrist between my fingers. Tessa looks so flustered, pink taking
over skin. She's addicting.

Just when I think she's going to speak up about her attrac-
tion to me, she says, "Can you turn the fan on?" Really, Theresa?
She thinks I'm a sucker already? That I'm just going to climb out
of this comfortable bed where she's lying so close to me. I look
at her face, her gray eyes. "Please?" she whispers, still looking at
me. Before I realize what I'm doing, I'm climbing out of the bed.
Damn, she's good.

She looks pretty smug when I glance back to the bed. She
also looks ridiculously uncomfortable in those heavy clothes. Her
skirt is made up of as much material as the duvet. "If you're hot,
why don't you change out of those heavy clothes; that skirt looks
itchy, anyway."

Tessa smiles at me, rolling her eyes.

I'm serious, though . . . she dresses terribly. "You should dress
for your body, Tessa. These clothes you wear hide all of your
curves." I look at what I can see of her chest, which is barely anything. "If I hadn't seen you in your bra and panties, I'd never have
known how sexy and curvy your body actually is. That skirt literally looks like a potato sack."

She laughs at me. That went better than expected. "What do
you suggest I wear? Fishnets and tube tops?" She raises her brow
and waits for an answer.

Tessa in a tube top and short denim shorts flashes in my mind. "No, well, I might love to see that, but no. You can still cover yourself, but wear clothes your size. That shirt hides your chest, too, and your tits are nothing you should be hiding."

"Will you stop using those words!" She shakes her head, and I laugh as I climb back into bed with her. I don't know how close to lie, so I slowly inch nearer until I'm practically touching her. She sits up and gets out of the bed. My chest burns.

"Where are you going?" I ask, hoping I didn't piss her off enough to leave.

She walks across the room in quick steps. "To change." She bends down and picks up my dirty T-shirt from the floor. I smile, happy that she likes to wear it as much as I like for her to.

"Now, turn around and don't peek," she says as if I'm a child. She knows damn well I'm going to look.

"No." I shrug and she glares at me.

"What do you mean, 'no'?" she asks, frustrated.

I'm honest when I tell her, "I won't turn around. I want to see you."

She agrees but then betrays me by flicking off the light. What a tease! I groan, loving the flirty game she's playing. I whine loudly, to let her know that I'm not going to play fair if she isn't. I hear heavy fabric fall to the floor—the skirt. I pull the chain for the light, and Tessa jumps at the brightness. She gasps my name like it's a curse word: "Hardin!"

I continue to stare at her, from her legs to her eyes and back down again. She takes a deep breath and raises her arms to put my shirt on. Tessa's bra is plain white cotton with very little padding. Not that she needs any. Her panties match; the cut covers nearly her entire ass. Her ass is perfect. Round and perky . . . I would love to take her there, too.

"Come here," I whisper. I can't wait another second to touch her body. Tessa's walking toward the bed, turning the room into a goddamn burlesque show, and I fucking love it. I need a better view. I move up to the headboard and rest my back flat against it. Tessa flushes under the heat of my stare, and it makes my pleasure all the greater.

When she reaches me, she puts her small hand into mine and I pull her to me. She straddles my body, her knees resting at my sides. I love having her like this. My imagination is going fucking wild. Tessa holds herself up, keeping her body from touching mine. *I don't think so.* I gently grip her hips and guide her down onto my body. She bites down on her lip, and her eyes meet mine. I look away first because I can feel the boner coming from a mile away. Tessa's legs are so soft and the way my shirt is lifted up to her hips is so sexy.

I smile at her, admiring how good she feels and looks. "Much better." I wait for her to smile back, but she doesn't.

"What's wrong?" I gently stroke at her cheek, making her smile. Her eyes close, and I wonder if this is breaking the rules of the Bet somehow. I think I'm beyond that at this point.

"Nothing . . . I just don't know what to do," Tessa says. When she won't meet my eyes, I know she feels embarrassed.

I don't want there to be a lot of pressure on her. Any way that she touches me is going to be enjoyable. I don't know how to explain any of this without actually showing her. "Do whatever you want to do, Tess. Don't overthink it."

Tessa raises her hand and seems to be about to touch my bare chest. When she doesn't touch me, I look up at her. She looks into my eyes for permission to touch me. No one has done that before, either. I nod, nervous but excited, and watch her. Her index finger slowly drags down my stomach to the waist of my boxers. I try to stay still even though I want to grab her wrist, flip her over, and fuck her into the mattress. I close my eyes and feel her finger trace over my tattoos. I like when she does this.

When she pulls her hand away, I open my eyes. I need more. I'm an addict.

"Can I . . . um . . . touch you?" Tessa is hesitant as she stares at the bulge in my boxers.

Fuck yes! I want to shout at her. Instead, I stay as calm as possible. Nodding, I beg, "Please."

Tessa looks nervous as she lowers her hand to my crotch. She hovers over my growing length before barely touching it. She lowers her hand a little more and continues to feel it out. Her fingers are gentle as she drags them up and down my cock, making me grow for her.

"Do you want me to show you what to do?" I suggest. I want her to be comfortable.

When Tessa nods her head, I gently place my hand over hers. My hands are so much larger than hers that her fingertips barely pass my knuckles. I bring both of our hands down my body and stop over my boxers. I help her grip my cock in her hand. She gently squeezes, and I moan and let go of her hand. She's got this. The look on her face when she realizes she has complete control is so filthy but trying to play innocent. Her pupils are blown out, her lips are parted, and her cheeks are rosy.

"Fuck, Tessa, don't do that," I mutter. I'm going to explode if she gets that expression on her face again.

Tessa, taking me at my word, stills her hand. Fuck, I forgot how literal she can be.

"No, no, not that. Keep doing *that*—I mean don't look at me that way," I clarify.

Tessa bats her lashes in the most naive way. "What way?"

"That innocent way—that look that makes me want to do so many dirty things to you." So, so many things, Theresa.

She's nervous as she moves her hand on me. Her grip isn't as tight as it could be, but I don't want to point that out. She'll get the hang of it on her own. I'll sure as hell help her figure it out. She's chewing on her lip as her slow strokes make me moan her name under my breath. If I could have one thing forever, this would be it.

"Fuck, Tess, your hand feels so good wrapped around me," I moan. My words encourage her, but maybe a little too much. She squeezes me, and a soft rush of pain shoots through me. "Not that hard, baby." I gently guide her, careful not to embarrass her.

She kisses me and continues in slow strokes. "Sorry," she whispers against my neck as she touches her lips to my skin. She moves her tongue up my neck to the base of my ear. *Fuckkkk*, that feels so fucking good. I need to touch her; I'm not going to last long.

My hands find her chest, and her bra feels like a wall between her body and me.

"Can I. Take. Off. Your . . . bra?" I beg. I want to feel her sexy body. Reaching under her shirt, I can feel her perfect breasts: round and full. Tessa nods, breathless. My hands shake as I quickly unclasp the hooks and let her breasts fall. I pull the straps off her shoulders and down her arms. It requires a lot of control for me not to rip her bra off. Tessa takes her hands from me so I can remove her bra completely. I toss it onto the floor, move my hands back to her breasts, and cover her mouth with mine. I gently pinch her hardened nipples, and she moans into my kiss. I like the way she kisses, soft but frenzied. She wraps her small hand around my length and moves her hand up and down, up and down. Tessa is bringing me pleasure, in my bed, wearing my clothes.

"Oh, Tessa, I'm going to come," I breathe. My body is out of my control. Tessa has become the puppet master, gathering and pulling every sensation out of me like the strings of a marionette. I'm on fire and in an ocean of ice at once, and I can barely keep my mouth from shouting her name. I concentrate on kissing her, massaging her sweet tongue with mine. My hands are still rubbing her chest. Her moans let me know how much she likes it. I drop my hands from her tits as I climax. The warmth of my come spreading through my boxers feels like the relief of letting out a thousand breaths.

When the rush starts to diminish, I drop my head back and close my eyes. Tessa stays sitting on my thighs. I'm glad. Despite popular belief, I've died and gone to heaven, I'm sure of it. I feel Tessa getting anxious, so I open my eyes and look at her. I'm a little nervous about how well I'm catching on to her little quirks. She smiles at me, and my nerves are calmed. I smile back and lean in to kiss her on her forehead. She sighs and I like the sound.

"I've never come like that before," I share with her. I like that she's giving me new experiences.

"It was that bad?" she asks, horrified and jumping to conclusions.

"What? No, you were that good. It usually takes more than someone just grabbing me through my boxers."

She stares into space and doesn't respond. Something is off. I try to repeat the last thirty seconds in my head to see if I offended her. I don't think I did. I decide to ask, "What are you thinking?"

She doesn't answer. She accuses me of being uncommunicative, but she herself is that way with me.

"Oh, come on, Tessa, just tell me," I complain. She always tries to keep things from me but expects me to give her thorough explanations all the time. So I decide to tickle her. The old sitcoms I watched as a kid taught me that tickling is an easy way to get women to talk, plus it adds flirty points. And I need as many of those cute, little flirty things as I can get.

"Okay . . . okay! I'll tell you!" Tessa shrieks, her legs kicking like a horse's. She looks silly with her face scrunched up, teeth bared, kicking at me to stop tickling her. My stomach is in a knot from laughing.

"Good choice," I say, feeling the wetness in my boxers. "But hold that thought. I need to take a quick shower and put on clean boxers."

I didn't bring a change of clothes, and I only have shirts in my car trunk right now. As I stand up, I look around the room for an option. The dresser is full of clothes; Karen told me it was. I've fought the idea—it's creepy, really, that she filled up a dresser of clothes for someone who doesn't want anything to do with her.

Fuck it. I don't have any other options, and Karen really isn't that bad. I broke her entire dining room into pieces; I guess I can make her happy by wearing her charity donations. I hope for the best when I open the drawer. My hope is crushed when my eyes meet a sea of plaid underwear. Blue and white, red and white, green and red, red and blue, white and green. It's endless. I want to slam the drawer shut, but I'm desperate here. I grab the least offensive one, a blue-and-white pair, and hold it between my thumb and index finger as if it's contaminated.

"What?" Tessa asks. She lifts up, rests on her elbows, and looks at me. I'm entertaining her; she's having fun here. I can see it in her eyes. Each minute I spend with her, I know her better.

"These boxers are hideous," I groan. Plaid? Cotton? Size XL? Who is she shopping for?

"They aren't so bad," she lies. I hold the blue-and-white-plaid monstrosity in the air and shake my head.

"Well, beggars can't be choosers. Back in a minute." I grab the ugly-ass boxers and leave the room without looking back at Tessa in the bed. On my way to the bathroom I pass Landon's room. I touch my ear to the door. I'm not surprised when I hear some character in a movie say something about elves. I knock lightly to be sure Tessa doesn't hear me. I listen for him to answer, but it's late, so he probably fell asleep watching *Twilight*. I knock again, and the door opens. His face is relaxed at first, until he realizes that it's me. I step toward him, and he holds his hands up in front of him in defense.

"I'm not here to start shit," I whisper. He's an asshole for assuming that I was.

I can tell he doesn't believe me—not one fucking bit.

"Then what is it that you want?" he questions in a dubious-sounding way.

I wave my hand in the air. "May I?" I ask him, gesturing toward the room. I look inside his dark room and notice the size of the TV on his wall. It has to be at least sixty inches. Of course it is. There's also a wall of signed jerseys hanging in shiny frames, probably handmade by some sweet lady at the craft store. She likely glued them together with her sweat, just for Landon. He seems to get whatever he wants. He stands only about two inches shorter than me and he's got a lot of muscle on me. Where my body is tall and lean, his is shorter and more fit. He almost looks like a younger, nerdy version of David Beckham. He's dressed in a WCU T-shirt and flannel trousers. There's no hope for him.

He looks me up and down and raises his eyebrow at my boxers.

"Fuck off—your mum is the one who bought them," I snap at him.

He raises his hand to cover his mouth so he can pretend he's not laughing. "I know, that's why it's funny." He laughs to himself at my expense, and I'm reminded how annoying he is.

"Never mind." I push past him and head toward the bathroom. I should have known better than to try to talk to him.

He raises his hands. "Wait, I'm sorry. I just thought it was funny because my mom still buys me those, even though I keep telling her they're terrible."

I don't laugh along with him, but the idea *is* a little funny. "I wanted to talk to you about Tessa."

He gets defensive. I watch as he stands a little taller and his lips press together. "What about her?"

I push my hair back from my face. "I wanted to make sure you know she's . . ."

He raises his hands again, this time to shut me up. "Tessa knows what she's doing; she doesn't need me acting like she can't take care of herself," he says. His tone is stern, but there's no malice in it.

I have no idea what to say to that. I figured he would be the douchebag, protective friend who would tell her to run as far as she can from me.

"Well . . ." I hesitate in the hallway. "I'm gonna go to bed now." I look back at him as he's closing his door and see a smile on his face. Well, that was awkward—but went better than I expected.

After showering, I go back to my room and find Tessa in the bed, curled up like a kitten. Her eyes dart straight to the boxers I'm wearing. Ugly things.

"I like them," she lies.

These things are fucking horrendous. You can't even see how big my cock is. I shoot a dirty look at her before I tug on the lamp chain and grab the remote. I'm surprised the fancy Mr. Scott didn't install a fucking holographic television in here. I turn it to a random channel for background noise and lower the volume close to silent. I climb into the bed and lie next to Tessa, facing her.

"So, what were you going to tell me?" I ask her. She pulls her lip between her teeth. "Don't be shy now—you've just made me come in my boxers." I laugh at the irony of her embarrassment. I wrap my arms around her and pull her close to me.

I wait for Tessa's dramatic performance to end. I love how carefree she is sometimes. I seem to pull that from her, and I'm proud of it. When my dramatic friend returns to normalcy, her hair is a mess. Loose waves fall down around her face. Without thinking, I touch her hair and push it behind her ear. She has the tiniest little earrings on. They remind me of when I went through a phase of wanting to gauge my ears until my friend Mark's got infected. They were disgusting, and the most horrid odor came from them.

I need to think about something else.

I kiss her softly on the lips, and she takes over my entire mind.

"Are you still drunk?" Her question is yet another example of her being nosy and pushy.

"No, I think our little screaming match in the yard sobered me up."

"Oh, well, at least something good came out of it."

I don't know what to do with my arm. I should put it on her back? I'm not sure. I face her and touch it to her back. "Yeah, I guess so." I rest my arm now, focusing on the way her head is lying on my chest. She moves with each of my breaths like she's already gotten used to the position. I like that.

She's smiling, a bright smile, for me. "I think I actually like drunk Hardin better," she says.

Drunk Hardin . . .

I can almost hear my mum's voice shouting through our small house. *"You're nothing but a drunk, Ken!"*

I distract myself from the memories threatening to break through and ruin this time with her.

She was probably teasing, anyway. I need to try to learn how to think before I speak. Being around Tessa is very good practice. "Is that so?"

"Maybe." She pouts. If she thinks this foolishness is going to make me forget that I want an answer from her, she's dead wrong.

Bringing the conversation back to the subject at hand, I say, "You're terrible at distractions; now tell me."

"Well, I was just thinking of all the girls you've . . . you know, done things with . . ." The moment she finishes, she digs her head into my chest to hide.

That's what she's thinking about right now? All I can think about is how I love the way her fluffy hair keeps tickling my nose and that she smells like she rolled in vanilla perfume before she came over. "Why were you thinking about that?"

She sighs as if I should catch on to what she's talking about.

I have no idea. "I don't know . . . because I have literally no experience and you have a lot. Steph included." The bitterness in
her voice is beyond evident. I imagine I would be the same if she
were to fuck Zed. The thought is brief, but it comes with a sharp-
ness that I didn't expect.

I throw that out of my mind for now. Zed has no place in this
bed with her. I do wish he could see the way she's looking up at
me, though, eager for my attention.

I can't tell if she's upset or jealous or curious. Sometimes I
can read her like a book, and other times the book is shut.

So, since I can't figure it out, I decide to just ask her. "Are you
jealous, Tess?"

I hope like hell she is.

"No, of course not."

She's lying through her goddamn teeth.

I'm going to play with her. She practically asked for it. Her
body is so warm against mine. I've never lain like this in a bed before, cuddling with a girl after coming in my boxers. I've never
done that before, and I've also never been that connected to
someone during any type of sexual activity, and I sure as hell
haven't ever slept in bed with anyone before. "So you don't mind
if I tell you a few details, then?"

She's so quick to shriek, "No! Please don't!" I tighten my arm
around her and laugh a little. I like that the idea bothers her. I
would rather drill holes into my eardrums than hear about her
fucking someone else. I stare at the ceiling and try to remember if I ever even thought about what it would be like to spend
my nights with someone else in my bed. Outside of a possible drunken thought or two, I haven't. Tessa is quiet, too quiet.
I think she may have fallen asleep. I reach for my phone on the
table and check the time. It's barely midnight.

"You're not going to sleep, are you? It's still early," I tease.

"Is it?" Tessa's voice is thick with sleep. She really was going to pass out on me. Honestly, I could use the sleep, but I want to spend more time with her. She yawns and I roll my eyes.

I almost lie and tell her that it's only ten. "Yeah, it's only midnight."

I bet she sleeps the doctor-recommended eight hours every night. That's why she's always so smiley and happy and shit.

"That isn't early." Her yawn is even cuter the second time.

She's usually easily persuaded, so I'll see what I can do. "To me it is. Plus, I want to return the favor."

Tessa tenses in my arms. I can imagine the flush of her cheeks. Her mind is probably racing, imagining how a warm, wet tongue will feel sliding up and down her pussy or drawing small circles over her clit.

"You want me to, don't you?" I ask in my lowest voice. She shivers next to me, and that's my signal. She looks up at me, her lips turned up into a smile. I wrap my other arm around her and softly turn her body and mine so I'm on top of her. In my mind, her mouth is open in ecstasy. Her fingers are tugging at my hair, and her sweetness touches my tongue. In reality, Tessa wraps one leg around my back and pulls me closer. My fingers graze over her thigh and up to her knee.

She feels so good under me. Her body is so tempting. I'm convinced that she was sent here just to torture me, to test every bit of my self-control. A small, soft voice in my head reminds me that maybe, just maybe, she was sent here for the opposite reason. Maybe I'm meant to be with her, to show her a new perspective on life? It's probably complete rubbish, but maybe she's not here to punish me—maybe she's here to *save* me.

"So soft . . ." I move my hand up and down her luscious legs again. The reminder of what's at the end of those legs is thick in my mind and my boxers. She shivers again, her skin rising into small bumps. I love the consistent way her body reacts to me. Her lust never seems to falter; her body responds to my every touch. I wet my lips and press them to the inside of her knee. Her skin is so soft and tastes of vanilla. I could devour her entire body within seconds. *Self-control . . . self-control . . .*

"I want to taste you, Tessa." I watch her eyes, waiting for her to react. She has no idea of the level of pleasure I can bring her. My tongue will drive her crazy—she'll never want me to stop.

Tessa's full lips part, and she leans into me, waiting for me to kiss her mouth. Her inexperience is both refreshing and frustrating.

"No. Down *here*." I tap her pussy over her panties, and she sucks in a harsh breath. Her chest moves up and down, and it seems like I can feel her hormones raging through her body. With gentle strokes, I tease her, and the wetness on her panties grows under my fingertips.

She's already soaked, and I tell her so. She's so beautiful, and her beauty is even more radiant when she's like this, swollen and wet for me. "Talk to me, Tessa. Tell me how badly you want it," I urge her. It's an obsession, to hear her beg for me.

My fingers keep rubbing at her, focusing on her clit.

"I didn't want you to stop." She's whimpering. I love it.

"You didn't say anything," I reply. "I didn't know if you were enjoying it."

"Couldn't you tell?"

I pull my body up to sit on top of her thighs. I can't keep my hands off her. My fingers trace the smooth skin on her thighs, making her body jerk under me.

"Say it," I push her. "No nodding—just tell me what you want, baby," I encourage her. I love hearing her tell me how much she wants me.

"I want you to . . ." She inches her body toward mine. I try to keep my hands to myself and let her come to me and tell me what she wants.

I raise my brow. "Want me to what, Theresa?" I ask her.

"You know . . . to kiss me."

I kiss her on her lips twice. She frowns.

"Is that what you wanted?" I tease her. She playfully slaps my arm. I want to hear her beg for my tongue.

"Kiss me . . . there." Just as I move to obey her, Tessa covers her face and shakes her head. I can't help but laugh as I reach for her hands, lowering them. Her scowl is deep. "You're embarrassing me on purpose." She's actually upset. When did this happen?

She rolls her eyes when I try to explain to her that I can't help it, I just wanted to hear her say the words. "Never mind, Hardin." She pulls the blanket over her body to hide from me. Damn it. She's lying the other way now, staring at the wall.

I hate that I made anything sexual a bad experience for her. In bed with me is supposed to be her haven, the place where she can shut off all thoughts and let everything go except for the pleasure I'm bringing her. I fucked up, and now this experience is going to piss her off every time she thinks about it. I shouldn't have pushed her this hard. She's so new to all of this and I'm a goddamn fool.

"Hey, I'm sorry," I say into her hair. I hate fighting with her. I was only teasing her; I just didn't know when to stop. I'm an idiot sometimes, in case she hadn't noticed.

"Good night, Hardin." Her voice is tough. She's not in the mood to play games with me, so I use every bit of strength I have to let her be. The last thing I should do is push her even further.

See, I'm learning, I want to say.

"Fine, you stubborn ass," I grumble back. I watch her breathing slow, then wrap my arm around her and try to fall asleep. She sighs a few times, mumbling incoherent thoughts. When she falls asleep, I sit up and watch her for a while, wondering how long she's going to be mad at me and if I'm ever going to be able to figure out how to be a good boyfriend.

twenty-one

Everything was changing so quickly in his life, he barely had time to keep up. He was happy . . . he'd finally learned what the word meant. Every day was passing too quickly for him to realize what was happening. When she opened herself to him, he climbed right in, making a home inside of her. She willingly gave him the deepest part of her innocence and he took it knowing it wasn't his to take, but he would be lying if he said he didn't wish she would never find this out. He was loving her and using her, and he wasn't sure how he could reconcile the two. He loved her, and he knew this wasn't an excuse for all the mistakes he was making, one after another, but he hoped that he could enjoy the time he did have with her and possibly convince her that he was worth forgiveness.

I'm pulling into Tessa's dorm parking lot and wondering what the fuck my plan is. I had a clear idea when I left my place. I was going to come to her room, tell her everything, and beg for her forgiveness. It wasn't a completely solid plan, but it's all I had. The guilt is eating away at me, gnawing at my insides, begging for release. I'm terrified what will happen when I tell her, but she deserves to know. She has to know.

I only had a little to drink. Just a few gulps to take the edge off.

I can't deceive her with my kiss or distract her with my touch for another hour. The parking spaces for Building B are never completely taken, and I park in the spot closest to the sidewalk. Her dorm reminds me of an old apartment building with a lot of windows, but the dark red brick gives it a creepy institution-like feel. It has the least amount of supervision by the staff of the university. I would know—I've been chased both from Buildings A and D.

I type a quick text to Steph to tell her to stay the fuck away from the room if she's out. She doesn't respond within a minute, so I climb out of the car and hope she'll be gone. There's a text from Tessa below that, telling me good night. I should have responded. Why am I such a dick?

The hallway is empty, and I nervously stand in front of room B20 instead of B22 without noticing for at least five minutes. I can't decide if I should I knock on the door. She's not exactly expecting me, but I'm sure she's here. No, I shouldn't knock. There's no reason to. My hands are shaking when I turn the knob. As the wooden door creaks open, I walk straight in, hoping I'm not met with a shoe to the head or a dick in Steph's mouth.

My eyes adjust to the dark room just as the lamp clicks on.

"What are you doing?" Tessa asks. She's sitting upright, her eyes squinting in the harsh light.

I pass Steph's bed and stop a few feet away from Tessa's. "I came here to see you," I say, and now that I'm seeing her, something inside me shifts, calms. She turns to lie on her side and rests one hand on her hip. When she sits up, her bare feet hang over the edge of the mattress and her blond hair is wavy, covering most of her back. The cotton T-shirt she's wearing looks so soft. I want to reach out and touch the soft fabric that clings to her skin. I crave being able to run my thumb along her forehead and brush the loose hair away from her face. I need to touch the pout on her lips.

She frowns, her eyebrows push down her forehead, and she looks like an angry kitten. "Why?" Her voice is high and very whiny.

Not knowing what to do with myself, I sit down in the chair at her tidy wooden desk. After a moment's hesitation, I answer truthfully.

"Because I missed you."

Disbelief and anger are crystal-clear as she rolls her eyes. Has she missed me?

Do I comfort her in her sleep like she does for me, or do I haunt her dreams? I have no fucking clue.

She sighs and her shoulders slump. "Then why did you leave?" Her words are soft. I take a moment to look around Tessa's dorm. Her bed is unkempt for once; the duvet is bunched up at the end of the bed, and one of the pillows is hanging off the small mattress. Steph's side of the room is messy, as usual, and I have to bite back a chuckle when I think about how much that must drive Tess crazy. I'm surprised she doesn't clean her room while she's alone in here. For all I know, she does.

I shrug, and she crosses her arms in front of her chest. *I have a lot to say, Tessa, please be quiet for once . . .* "Because you were annoying me."

She huffs and kicks her feet like a primary-school student. "Okay, I'm going back to sleep; you're drunk and you're obviously going to be mean again." She shakes her head, and her eyes fall closed. My chest burns from her anger, and my fists burn from mine.

I try to convince her I'm not being mean, that I'm only a lit-tle drunk, and that I wanted to see her. I desperately try to stop myself from sitting on her bed with her. I want her to lie back on the bed and let me touch her. I keep up my sweet talk and try to make her smile.

She's not buying it. "You should just go," she says. She lies down with her back toward me, turning to face the wall. Stub-born little child, she is. It's half infuriating and half cute.

If she wants to act like a child, I will treat her like one. "Aww, baby, don't be mad at me." Her shoulders tense, and I wish I could see her face. Though it was meant to annoy her, the word *baby* feels so nice when attached to her. "Do you really want me to go? You know what happens when I sleep without you." I hope that my vulnerability will touch something in her.

She sighs dramatically, and I hold my breath. I don't want to leave. I don't want her to want me to.

"Fine. You can stay, but I'm going back to sleep." She doesn't turn around. I wonder how hard she would slap me if I were to lie down behind her or grab her shoulder and turn her to face me.

I don't mind her sleeping, but I would rather be able to enjoy her company. I had half of a plan when I showed up here, and now that's completely out of the question. She's already annoyed; she'll be beyond talking to if I drop this shit on her right now. "Why? You don't want to hang out with me?" I ask her.

Once again she tells me that I'm mean and drunk. I tell her I'm neither, and that she's just acting like a child.

"That's sort of mean to say to someone. Especially when all I did was ask you about your job," she says.

My head spins; she doesn't stop going in circles. "Oh God, not this again. Come on, Tessa, just drop it. I don't want to talk about that right now."

It dawns on me that if I just come clean, the majority of our problems would go away. The problem is, she would go with them.

"Why did you drink tonight?" Tessa questions me.

It seemed like a good idea. I was tense and miserable, and when I tried to come up with a clear thought, I failed. Liquor on my breath makes my confessions less important, less offensive. I can utter drunk ramblings, and if she's appalled, I can deny the words tomorrow.

Fuck, I can't stop lying.

"I . . . I don't know . . . I just felt like having a drink . . . well, *drinks*. Can you please stop being mad at me? I love you." I do love her and I need to be close to her. I hate when she's mad at me, but in a sick way, the fact that she worries about me gives me comfort.

Her anger is softening with every second that passes. "I'm not mad at you. I just don't want to backtrack in our relationship. I don't like when you turn on me for no reason, then just leave. If you're mad about something, I want you to talk to me about it."

What is this, Dr. Phil? It takes me a moment to realize she's talking to me as if we have a standard dating arrangement. Which we are the furthest thing from. She's rambling on about communication, when all she does is roll over on the bed and give me the silent treatment. I've been busting my ass for this girl, and she still isn't pleased. I'm trying to be reasonable, to not let my anger flare, but it's so hard with someone like Tessa, who pulls every trigger I have.

"You just don't like not having control over everything," I fire back. I still can't believe she's trying to give me advice on how to handle shit. As if she knows everything, the way she thinks she does.

"Excuse me?" Her voice cracks. She leans up, resting her elbows on her knees.

I tell her she's a control freak. She denies it.

She asks me if I have anything else to insult her with, and I ask her to move in with me. She looks as stunned as I thought she would. I'm right with her, surprised that my mouth chose this exact moment to bring this subject up. She studies my face intently, as if she's memorizing what I tell her about the place. She's excited, I can tell. But she's also unsure, and not good at hiding it. I'll show her that she has nothing to be afraid of. I can continue to be better for her and make her happy. I know that I can. The energy between us has shifted drastically and she's biting into her bottom lip and teasing me and I can't wait to move in with her.

The hurricane of truths is floating above us, swirling and building, ready to rain down any minute. I pretend we're in a novel and that she'll forgive me as Elizabeth forgave Darcy. If we were words on a page, she would find herself in my arms again, no matter the depth of my mistake, just like Catherine. She would crave the adventure that I bring to her life and find it impossible to stay away, just like Daisy. The disaster can't touch us if we're safe in our own world, our own apartment, our own novel.

This place will be a fortress, not a prison, I silently promise her. The words die on my tongue, and I turn to her again. She's staring, glossy eyes full of controlled excitement.

"So you'll move in with me?"

Say yes, Tess. Please say yes.

She rolls her shoulders, and a hint of a pink bra strap shows. I was under the impression she only owned white-and-black cotton lingerie. I keep my eyes on her shoulder, waiting for another peek.

"Jesus, let's take this one step at a time. I'll stop being mad at you for now," she says, doing her version of compromising. "Now come to bed with me." She lies down on the bed and pats a spot for me. Suddenly I'm a yappy little dog whose owner let them into the bed. I unbutton my jeans, pull them down my legs, and toss them on top of a stack of textbooks near Steph's bed. I look at Tessa, and she's focused on my shirt, silently suggesting that I take it off. The thin cotton T-shirt she has on is sexy enough, but there's nothing like her wearing my shirts. I absolutely love when she wears them to bed.

When I take it off and lay it in front of her, her face breaks into a beautiful smile and she lifts up her own shirt. Her smooth skin is so sexy, the way her stomach curves into soft breasts. My eyes nearly pop from my head onto the floor at the sight of her lacy ensemble. I'm used to a soft cotton, no-form bra holding her tits up, not a structured push-up bra with lace lining the fabric.

"*Fuck,*" I can't help but say. "What are you wearing?" This girl is so goddamn sexy and doesn't even have a fucking clue. Her cheeks are a wild, deep red.

Her voice isn't much over a whisper. "I . . . I got some new underwear today." She's embarrassed even though she looks like a goddess, with her long blond hair, her smooth legs, and her pouty lips just begging for my cock to push through them . . .

I immediately wonder what else she got today, and how hard it would be to convince her to try it all on for me in a private little show.

I've never been this turned on by a woman in my entire life. She's so fucking sexual without even trying to be, and she has no idea how many women would kill to be her, to have her sexy curvy body. "I see that . . . Fuck."

Tessa shakes her head. "You already said that." She loves hearing it, though. Tessa blooms under my compliments, and it's highly, highly satisfying. It amazes me every day that she doesn't see herself for who she is. I repeat how beautiful she looks, and she smiles more. I can't possibly look away from her tits, pushing up toward her, and I can't possibly stop my cock from pulsing under my boxers. Tessa's eyes are focused there, on my swollen cock straining against the black cotton of my boxer briefs.

Tessa's eyes are hungry as she flicks her tongue over her top lip, gently sinking her teeth into it. She says something to me, but I couldn't repeat it if my life depended on it.

"Mmm . . ." I agree with whatever it is that she's saying. I can't think of anything else except the way her body calls to me; it's like she was made for me. Using my knee, I support my body weight over hers and press my mouth against her full, wet lips. Her tongue is velvet and scotch, soft and sharp as it swipes over mine, cutting through me and healing me at once.

This is a dangerous game I'm playing, I'm walking along the most fragile line, but I've developed a talent for balancing. If she moves in with me, she'll see how ready I am to be better for her.

She'll see that one mistake counts for very little compared to how much I love her, compared to what I can become for her.

Her mouth is hungry on mine. She's an expert at this; her tongue moves with mine, and with every sound of hers I swallow, I become more infatuated. I push my hand through her soft hair, desperately trying to get closer to her somehow. I press my body against her, needing some friction on my cock before I combust. The relief rushing through my body when I rub against her is frightening to me. She controls my mind and my body, and I don't know what she'll do with them.

I lean up on my elbow, taking in her beauty. Her mouth is dark pink now, and inside my mind I'm running through an entire book of things I crave to do to her. My other hand traces the soft pink lace across her chest; the thin fabric is barely holding her in.

Patiently and ever so gently, I trace my fingers over the cup, under the strap, and I push my fingers inside the fabric and feel the hard pebbles of her nipples. She's fucking heaven. "I can't decide if I want this to stay on . . ." I could spend every hour of every day with her lying here, waiting for my touch. I apply a pinch of pressure to her nipples, and she moans in surprise.

I want her breasts bare in my hands. "Off it goes," I groan. I'm horny and impatient, and when she arches her back as I unclasp the small hooks, I nearly come in my boxers. I palm her fleshy tits, pushing them up and then down just to watch the perfect way they move. Her tits are perfect—she's my living fetish. "What do you want to do, Tess?"

I want to do every fucking thing with her. I want to do things I've never done, and experience things from my past in a new way. "I already told you before," she whines, pushing her chest against my hand. Such a horny little freak she is.

Are we ready? Is she ready? I think she's ready. She's panting, and I can see the crotch of her panties glistening under the light of the lamp.

I run my hand down her stomach and to the hem of her lacy panties. I try to control myself, but she moans and I need to hear more of my favorite sounds. Fuck me, she's got me wrapped around her finger.

My fingers move to her pussy, and I tap gently over the swollen mound, feeling how much she soaked her panties. Her sweet scent fills the air, and I want to taste her. I push my fingers into her, pumping into her to the knuckle. She cries out, and her sounds seep into me as she wraps her arms around me to steady her jerking body. She's tight around my two fingers, and she gasps each time they enter her pussy.

Tessa's hands are frantic as she finds my thickness, palming and squeezing and stroking me through my boxers.

"You're sure?" I ask her. I need her to be absolutely positive about this. I need this to be as perfect for her as it will be for me.

It takes a breath for Tessa to realize that I'm speaking to her. Her mouth is open, eyes wide. "Yes, I'm sure. Stop overthinking it."

I lean my head down and chuckle against her neck. The irony of this is killing me. She's the one usually overthinking everything, but I'm the one who is now. I'm so close to finally having her, and it's tainted by the stupid Bet. The guilt I've been holding on to since I grew to love her is flowing through me. I'm battling within myself: the good boy who loves the good girl and the bad boy who's too broken to love anyone are fighting with swords. Each one wants something different from the princess. The boy in black gets knocked to the ground.

"I love you. You know that, don't you?" I say into her mouth. Can she taste my panic?

If she can, she doesn't show it. "Yes . . ." She kisses me, slowly and softly. "I love you, Hardin."

Tessa's legs are gently kicking out as if her body can barely handle the pleasure of my fingers sinking in and out of her tightness. She's a whimpering mess for me as images flicker through my mind of her body writhing beneath mine while I break her skin and claim her body. Not until she makes the first move . . . I set up a boundary to keep. My mouth moves to her neck to claim her in a different way. I suck at the soft skin there, feeling the heat of blood rushing beneath the surface. She's mine.

"Hardin . . . I'm . . ." she whimpers when I leave her empty. She's so ripe, so ready to be fucking devoured. Suddenly I'm a starving man. I need my mouth on her. I scoot back on the bed and pull off her panties and spread her thighs. The smell is so sweet, so intoxicating, I've never experienced anything close to this hunger roaring inside of me. My lips peck a tender trail down her stomach. She's soaked. I can't help but blow on it and delight in the way she moans, lifting her ass off the bed. I dive in.

Her taste fills my senses as my tongue swipes wide licks up and down her. With each moan, my tongue licks harder, more precisely, and she fists her white sheets to keep from screaming.

"Tell me how good it feels," I say, making sure to blow a breath against her with each word.

She chokes out, "So . . ."

I suck at her and lick her into a shaking, whimpering state.

I want to give her all the encouragement she needs. "That's it, baby, come for me, I need to feel it on my tongue." She obeys. I'm high with her as she orgasms for me. I'm no longer drunk with liquor; now I'm drunk with power.

I climb up her body, my cock probing at her stomach, and kiss her. She snaps out of her sated state and kisses me hard. She's already ready for more. I'm impressed. "Are you . . ." I ask her, to be sure.

She nods frantically, lifting her lips to mine. "Shh . . . Yes, I'm sure," Tess begs. The sharp ends of her fingernails dig into my back as she takes my mouth again. Her lips suck at mine, her tongue pushes through my lips, and I'm high again. Her hands push my briefs down my ass and legs, and the sensation of being bare and so fucking hard against her skin has me manic.

I need to be inside of her—I have to make her body mine.

This is going to change everything. Neither of us will ever be the same again. She will no longer be an innocent girl; she will be a woman with a sex life. She will have to check the sexually active box at the doctor's office. She will get married one day and have to tell the guy that she fucked me. Any talk of her past sexual experiences will be filled with me. I feel immense guilt but extreme satisfaction. It's a liberating but frightening experience.

"Tessa, I . . ." I have to tell her. My body is ripping itself into two pieces.

"Shh . . ." she whispers. She has no idea what she's saying.

I feel the weight of my body on hers, such a perfect fit. I look over her face, trying to save this moment forever. "But, Tessa, I need to tell you something . . ."

"Shh. Hardin, please stop talking." She's begging me now. Her eyes are full of love and excitement. My life is changing, and right now, I'm going to change everything. She takes control before I can get a word out and presses her lips to mine. Her hand wraps around my hard cock, and she jerks me, tempting and hushing me. I inhale a sharp breath when her thumb swipes over the bead of precome on the tip.

"I'm going to come if you do that again," I whine. I want to feel her delicate fingertips tracing over the head of my cock, teasing me, making me beg for more.

More than anything, I need to bury myself inside of her. Now.

I assume she doesn't have any condoms and only feel slight shame that I always carry one out of habit. I have few rules when it comes to sex, but using a condom is a complete must for me.

Tessa is watching me from the bed as I gather my jeans off the floor and dig through the pockets. I feel like a pervert, carrying a condom around in my wallet in anticipation of fucking.

One look into Tessa's eager eyes banishes that thought, and I climb back onto the bed, condom in hand. I wait a second for her to take the condom from my hand, but she doesn't. No shit, Sherlock, she's probably never seen one outside of Sex Ed.

"Are . . ." I don't know how to ask her if she wants to try to put it on me. Some women like to, some don't.

She raises her voice. "If you ask if I am sure, I will kill you."

I believe her.

So I decide to go with option two, which is to cherish this moment while I have her. I shake my head and wave the condom in front of her. "I was going to say, are you going to help me put this on, or should I do it?" I would be quicker, I'm sure.

Tessa looks nervous as she chews on her lip. My cock is aching for her. I'm tempted to just fuck her without a condom.

I have to remind myself that that's a stupid fucking idea.

"Oh. I want to . . . but you have to show me how." She's so shy and so damn sexy. Her tits, so heavy and round, are distracting me. I need to speed up this process.

"Okay," I agree. Tessa scoots closer to me and crosses her legs. I'm happy to show her, but I'm only halfway in reality. Mostly I'm already on top of her, pushing into her. She's moaning and clawing at my back and my arms. She's begging for more, she's coming and I'm claiming her.

"THAT WASN'T SO BAD for a virgin and a drunk," Tessa teases when the deed is done and the condom is on. I remind her that I'm not drunk and explain that her sassy mouth has caused me to sober up.

"Now what?" she asks, genuinely wondering.

I guide her hand to grasp my cock. "Eager?" I ask her.

She nods her head.

"Me, too," I say. I *am* eager, I've never wanted anything more.

She's still jerking me; my hardness is wrapped in her palm. I move between her legs and part them with my knee.

Once again, her pussy is glistening for me. "You're soaking wet, so that will make it easier." I can smell her again. She's so responsive, and it drives me fucking mad. I kiss her mouth, dotting my lips against the corners of her soft lips, her nose, her mouth again. Tessa's arms wrap around me, and I inhale as she presses me closer. I brush against her wetness and nearly explode. She's impatient, pulling me closer.

I warn her. "Slow, baby, we need to go slow." I kiss her temple. I don't want to hurt her. I wouldn't if I didn't have to. "It's going to hurt at first, so just tell me if you want me to stop. I mean it, okay?" I stare down at her. Her pupils are blown out, her cheeks flared, and her hair a wild mess across the pillow.

"Okay." She swallows nervously. I stare at her, silently reminding her how much I love her, need her, cherish her. With a deep breath, I find her opening and push gently inside. Her tightness clings to every inch that I push through, and I stop when her eyes screw shut.

"You okay?" I ask, breathless. She's nodding, her lips in a hard line. She's so warm, so tight for me.

"Fuck," I moan when she groans, tightening again.

"Can I move?" Fuck, I need to move. I knew she would feel like heaven, but I had no idea how fucking extravagant heaven would be.

She takes a few breaths before answering. "Yeah," she agrees. I go slow, not wanting to hurt her. I can feel her easing up her grip on my arms with each kiss I give her. Her neck, her pretty mouth, her nose. I love every inch of her body. Every inch of *my* body.

I repeat to her how much I love her as I slowly draw in and out of her. Her eyes are still closed, but she's not showing any unusual signs of discomfort. When twenty seconds pass and she hasn't responded, I stop. "Do you . . . fuck . . . do you want me to stop?"

She shakes her head and I close my eyes again. I can picture every inch of her under me. Her smooth skin, her body molding to mine. She's mine now and forever, even after we leave this bed. I maintain my pace, and she keeps her arms wrapped around me. I can feel my heart in my chest, pumping and coming alive as I climb closer to the edge. I've never felt anything during sex.

I feel alive and brilliant, and when I look down at my love, she's looking back at me with radiant admiration, and I know now that somehow, everything will be okay.

Tessa's strength surprises me again as a silent tear rolls down her cheek. I kiss it away and give her the praise she deserves. "Fuck, Tess, you're doing so good, baby. I love you so much." I push my fingers into her hair and suck at the sweat-coated skin of her neck.

"I love you, Hardin," Tessa declares. That's all it takes and I'm there.

I kiss at her mouth, licking at her lips and tongue with a feverish hunger. "Oh, baby, I'm going to come. Okay?" My spine is on fire, her skin is shining with sweat, we are wild.

Tessa nods, encouraging me to spill into her. In this moment, I have a hatred for the barrier between us. I want to fill her—I want to make her mine in every way. Her lips suck at my neck and I tense, my body giving in to the pleasure, and I spit her name through clenched teeth as I reach my climax. I lie on her chest, catching my breath, and she lazily caresses my skin.

Everything has changed now. I've changed everything between us. I comfort her and ignore the pushing and pushing of the truth, which is threatening to burn me alive. As I comfort her, I pray to whoever is listening that my world doesn't turn to ashes.

twenty-two

Everything began to unravel for him, and the flimsy little house of cards he built was becoming shakier and shakier with each passing day. At each mention of his lies, he would panic, scrambling to come up with a plan. He was convinced he had been cursed as a child . . . there was no other explanation for the suffering he had been dealt. He was beginning to question whether Tessa was his saving grace or his biggest curse. He had her, every part of her, yet she was slipping away with every passing second.

Tessa is at her internship when I go by her room a few days later. Molly has been telling me Steph is going off the deep end. She's dropping hints that Steph may be losing her fucking mind, and I need to talk to her before she does.

When I get to the room, Steph is lying across the bed, her red hair a thick mess. Chunks of curls are stuck with pins on her head. Her makeup is dark; smoky gray shadows her lids, making her look like a haunted version of a Valley girl. Her skin is white and her lips are a dark red.

"She's not here," Steph announces, and shuts the screen on Tessa's laptop. What's that doing here? "I'm only watching movies. Relax, psycho."

I grab the laptop from her bed and slip it under my arm. "I know she isn't. I wanted to talk to you," I tell her. She raises herself up on her elbow, and her boobs push against her tight dress, revealing more than an eyeful.

"Talk to me about what?" Her eyes are cold as she waits for my answer. I've always known something is loose inside her mind, but I can never tell just how dangerous it is. Everyone has a screw or two loose, but in Steph's case, it feels like something more sometimes. I used to think she was a cool girl, but she ended up more like the redheaded version of Amy Dunne's crazy ass.

"You know what." I sit down on Tessa's bed and turn my body to face Steph.

"Molly called you," she answers, connecting the dots. "She's becoming such an annoying little cunt. Isn't she?" Steph rolls her head back and sits up. "I'm not going to say anything to Tessa. I know that the only reason you're here is to beg me not to say shit to her. I'm not going to."

"And I'm supposed to believe that?" I question her, and she rolls her tongue against her teeth.

"Believe me or not. I got my fun from it. I'm bored with it now, and I'm starting to feel a little bad for her." To be honest, this completely surprises me.

"You are?" I scoot to the edge of Tessa's mattress and rest my elbows on my knees.

She begins to laugh—a feral, high-pitched laugh—and I sigh. I should have known. "No, of course not. I *am* bored with it, though." I watch as she tugs at her dress to show me more of her chest. I look away.

This is for Tessa. I need to not make a scene.

"You're almost done with her by now anyway, I'm sure."

Almost done with her? Has she lost her fucking mind?

"Aren't you? You fucked her—now you're done with her. That's how it goes with you."

The weirdest thing about this is that Steph isn't giving me

shit, she's just making a statement. Given my history, her assessment would be accurate, except I've spent much longer working on Tessa than I did on any of the others.

Tessa made me fight for her because she was fucking worth it. Too bad I ruined everything.

"No . . ." I clear my throat. "I'm not done with her."

Steph's eyes roll and she licks her lips. "I knew you weren't. How many times have you fucked her now? Is she *actually* still tight? I mean, with the way you ruin things."

My eyes must be ready to pop out of my head when she looks at me, because she moves farther away from me.

"*Is* she?" Steph repeats. "I'm sure she's nice and used up for you. Now you can move on, and she can go away. I see her enough as it is."

"You really don't like her." I rub the back of my neck. Tessa thinks Steph is her friend, and I don't want to get in the middle of that unless I have to. If Steph ever tries to pull anything on Tessa, though, I would take care of it.

"No, I don't really like her. Let's move on. Just dump her and go back to getting BJs from Molly every other day."

"I'm going to still be seeing Tessa." I don't know how to say this to her. I don't want her to have more power over me than she does, but I also don't want her to be under the impression that Tessa isn't a permanent fixture in my life.

She isn't a permanent fixture, but I'm still praying to find a way for this to work.

But that's not Steph's business. Fuck, this is a mess. A huge fucking mess.

"Why did you come here, Hardin? I know it wasn't just to check on my big mouth." She licks her lips again and pushes her elbows against the sides of her chest in the least subtle way possible.

My temper flares momentarily, and I stand to my feet. "You've lost your fucking mind if you think I would touch you!"

"Tessa's nothing special. I don't know why you and Zed are both so fucking obsessed with her."

"Zed is not relevant in this conversation." My hands are shaking, and I can see that Steph's growing more and more pleased with herself and the reaction her mention of Zed is getting out of me.

Don't let her get to you, Hardin.

She's antagonizing me purposely, and I'm letting her. What is that thing my gran used to say?

Shit, I don't remember.

"Zed *is* a pretty relevant—"

"Enough." I press my hands together and bring them to my face. I pinch the bridge of my nose and breathe in, breathe out.

I came here to talk to her about Molly's worries, to make sure that Tessa wouldn't be torn from me by any crazy or vicious action on Steph's part, but now I'm here and Steph is being an exceptionally terrible human being, and honestly, I just feel like being a dick. Steph acting like Queen of the Assholes makes me feel like I'm not any different than I was before Tessa. I thought I was better than her and the others somehow, but here I am. I'm going to be sitting right next to her in hell.

I can't help but push her. I thrive on making her feel as shitty as I do. I look at Steph and put my biggest grin on my face. "Maybe you should worry about your own boyfriend and the way he always stares at Molly. I've seen them alone a few times . . ." I say some other things about them—I don't even know what, really—and by the time I finish my lie, her eyes are watering, shining red in my triumph.

"You're lying." She's trying to hold in her tears. *Gotcha.*

"Nope, too bad for you," I tell her. I put Tessa's laptop in the top drawer of her dresser. I need to get her out of this dorm, and soon.

Before Steph can get another word in, I leave the room. When I get into my car and common sense starts kicking in, I realize that I made another dumb fucking move. Steph isn't like most girls. She won't sit on her anger and wait for the right moment to strike. She's irrational, and I can see her spilling every detail of the Bet to Tessa, exaggerations included. I should just tell her—I should tell Tessa every disgusting truth before she finds out. This is eating me alive.

I climb back out of the car and walk back to the dorm room to try another route with Steph.

But I hear Tessa's voice as soon as I reach the door. *Fuck.*

I lean against it, listening to the girls' conversation. "I don't think Tristan would go for her; I see the way he looks at you. He really cares about you. I think you should call him and talk it out," I hear Tessa say. I press my ear harder against the door and hope that no one walks by.

"What if he's with her?" Steph asks.

She actually believed that shit?

"He's not," Tessa comforts her roommate.

"How do you know? Sometimes you think you know people, but you don't," Steph begins.

Fuck this. Steph's going to tell her. She's going to tell her right fucking *now*.

"H—"

I open the door.

"Hey . . ." I say when I step into the room. They seem to be bonding; an outsider would be fooled. "Um . . . should I come back?"

"No, I'm going to go find Tristan and try to apologize." Steph stands up. "Thank you, Tessa." She hugs Tessa and stares at me, letting me know that she's not done here.

Distraction—I need a distraction. "You hungry?" I ask Tess as Steph gets ready to leave.

"Yeah, actually I am," she says, rubbing her hand over her stomach. She's distracted now and doesn't seem to notice the awkward hate stare Steph is firing at me.

twenty-three

His paranoia took hold of him, dragging him further and further away from her. He tried to grasp on to the tiny sliver of hope that he could have the life he wanted to have with her. He tried to come up with plan after plan to save the only good thing that had ever happened to him. He begged his enemies, pleaded with his friends, for their silence. None of his plans would work, none of them could hide what he did to her, and he knew it was all going to blow up in his face.

I take Tessa to the mall, where my shitty luck continues as we sit in the food court before deciding which stores to go to. Paranoia seems to be haunting me, stalking me wherever I go. I can't stop thinking about everything Steph could have told her. Does she know everything I've been hiding from her? Will she finally see me as I am, not worthy of her?

I pick at my meal, lost in my head, while Tessa eats slowly, watching me the entire time. What is she looking for? Signs of my lies coming to the surface?

"We can find your outfit first, I guess?" I say. I still can't believe I agreed to go to the wedding. It's going to be so fucking awkward for me, and my only plan at this point is to focus on Tessa and not remember a damn thing that happened earlier than three months ago.

"Well, you have the luxury of looking beautiful regardless of what you wear."

Her cheeks light up at my flattery. "That's not true; you're the one who definitely pulls off that 'I don't give a crap how I look but I look flawless' look." She's laughing, and my chest aches a little less at the sight.

"I do, don't I?" I smile at her. But she carries that look off, too. Much more than I do, and she doesn't even try.

Tessa's phone vibrates on the table. She's acting pretty normal for someone who knows they are being toyed with this way. Maybe she's acting normal on purpose to distract me until she can play me and get her revenge.

Or maybe she really doesn't know?

"It's Landon," she says as I read his name on the screen. My chest stops pounding out of control. She answers the phone and I watch her mouth as she speaks. She sucks on her lower lip for a few seconds and looks me up and down.

I have to come up with a way to prevent her from ever being alone with Steph. I need to keep her closer from now on. I've been too casual about this whole thing. I should have her by my side at all times.

"Okay, well, I'll do my best to get him in a tie," she says into the phone, and it's obvious who she means by "him."

She presses her hand to her cheek and rests her elbow on the table. She looks adorably pushy. But a tie? Good luck with that.

Tessa starts saying something else to Landon, but my attention goes to the middle of the food court, where Zed, Jace, and Logan are standing. They're all dressed in different ways, each trying to make a statement about who they are by means of their wardrobe. Logan is the preppy, kind of punk kid with a baby face, and is less badass than the other two. Zed, the tall and dark one, looks like he's modeling leather even though he's in a middle-class mall. He looks out of place. Jace looks like the delinquent, the one all the teenage girls should stay away from.

"I'll be right back." I stand up from the table, leaving my food.

Thank God she's on the phone, so she won't follow. Not immediately.

Logan's rubbing a small tube of ChapStick over his lips when I reach them. Jace is looking awfully fucking smug, and Zed's looking pretty stressed out. "Nice to see you, too," Logan says, and taps his foot against the linoleum while Jace laughs a breathy, stoner-y laugh. The three of them have dilated pupils and thin red veins mapping their eyes. They smell of pot and stale cigarettes. If Zed and Tessa kissed, would she like the taste of tobacco on his tongue?

"What are you guys doing here?" I ask, checking on Tessa out of the corner of my eye.

"Where? At the public mall?" Jace asks.

I take a breath, silently threatening him. If he fucks this up today, I'll have no problem hurting him.

"We were just in the area," Logan explains. He shrugs his shoulders and looks at me with some sort of understanding. He knows what I'm worried about, and somehow he's telling me that's not why they're here. "Really." He pushes this, and I slightly relax.

"Where's your little pet?" Jace flicks his tongue out in a disgusting way. Zed cringes, and Logan ignores all of us and stares at the cracked screen of his iPhone.

"Oh, she's over there!" Jace's voice rises, and I nearly jump him. He's the nastiest type of guy, much like my old friend Mark, who played with people like toys and had no remorse about his shitty actions. *I guess I'm the same way, though*, I think, regarding the Bet, and at the end of the game the group of us played, I was the one who held the winning piece.

"Cut the shit," I say, stepping forward, and Jace smiles a wicked smile. He loves how agitated he can make me. He's pressing buttons on me as we speak. He knows it, I know it, and soon Tessa will know it, too.

"She's coming over here." Logan is still staring at his phone, but he's warning us of Tessa's arrival. My palms are soaking, and the skin on my knuckles is straining each time my nails dig into my palm. They're going to ruin my life right now, here in this mall in some shitty town in America.

"Hey, Tessa, how are you?" Zed moves toward Tessa, and I take a step forward. He wraps his arms around her, and I could easily rip them from his body at the sight.

"Hardin, aren't you going to introduce your friend?" Jace stares at me, humor dancing in his bloodshot eyes.

"Um, yeah." I wave my hand between the two of them, counting the seconds we've been letting this drag on. "This is my friend Tessa; Tessa, this is Jace."

Tessa's brows bunch together in anger, and I look around, confused. Why is she mad? I study her face and wait for her to look at me. She doesn't.

"Do you go to WCU?" she asks Jace. Why does she always have to make polite small talk with people? It's obvious that she hasn't had a lot of social experience; she seems to have zero sense of etiquette.

"Hell, no. I don't do the college thing." He laughs, and Tessa relaxes a bit. "But if all the girls there looked like you, I would be happy to reconsider."

Tessa looks a little frightened, and I'm mentally counting the shades of blue I can turn Jace's face via strangulation.

"We're going to the docks tonight; you two should make an appearance," Zed says.

An appearance? Fuck you, Zed.

"We can't. Maybe next time," I say, ending the conversation.

"Why not?" Jace asks, clearly challenging me in front of Tessa and Zed.

"Tessa has to work tomorrow. I suppose I can drop by later. Alone." I make it clear to all of them. They won't be in the place, ever again. It's going to be hard, but I'm foolish enough to think I can possibly pull this off. I won the Bet, she's mine, and Zed can fucking rot, for all I care.

"That's too bad." Jace smiles at Tessa, and I struggle to keep my shit together. He's taunting me. He's dangling this devil's game I agreed to play over my head like I'm a little rat and he's got a nice piece of cheese for me.

"Yeah, I'll hit you up later when I'm on my way," I lie to him.

I have to think of what the fuck I'm going to do about him. He's itching to find a time to tell Tessa about the Bet . . . he's a fucker like that. But I know if I bring it up to him, it will only encourage him to open his big mouth or plant the idea of telling if he hadn't thought of it yet on his own.

The three of them walk away, and Tessa stares daggers into their backs. I stay silent and follow Tessa's temper tantrum through Macy's. She walks faster in a childish, petulant way to prove a point and throw a fit.

"What's wrong?" I ask. Something always seems to be wrong with her. I'm saying something, doing something, someone's cat looked at her the wrong way . . . it's always something.

"Oh, I don't know, Hardin!"

"Me either! You're the one who just hugged Zed!" I yell at her. Her arms around Zed is the only thing I can think of right now, and she's starting shit with me?

"Are you embarrassed to be with me or something? I mean, I get it, I'm not exactly the cool girl, but I thought—"

I don't understand what she's getting at here. She thinks I'm embarrassed about being with her? Why does she always go to this?

"What? No! Of course I'm not embarrassed about you. Are you crazy?"

She *is* crazy, though. We both are.

"Why did you introduce me as your friend? You keep talking

about living together, and then you tell them we're friends?" Tessa's voice is growing louder with each word. "What are you going to do, hide me? I won't be anyone's secret. If I'm not good enough for your friends to know that we're together, then I don't want to live with you."

How can I call her more than a friend? She's going to hate me more than an enemy when my time runs out with her. She's so much more than a secret to me. I'm not trying to hide her. I don't want to keep her hidden any fucking more. I want to show her off proudly and let every motherfucker know that she's mine. Only mine. But I'm too stupid to be able to make things work between us, which is why I have to hide the most beautiful thing, the only treasure, in my entire life. I have to hide her instead of letting her bloom in the sunshine, and it's eating me alive from the inside out.

"Tessa! Damn it . . ." I trail off, and she glances toward the dressing room in the women's clothing section of the store. "I'll follow you," I warn her. I mean it, too. I'd like to follow her inside that dressing room and fuck her against the full-length mirror.

She raises her eyebrows and purses her lips. She knows damn well I will follow her. I'd follow her to the deepest pits of hell if she merely asked me to. "Take me home. Now," she demands of me. Take her home? All because of a stupid fight? Tessa makes her point by walking way ahead of me out of the store and back to my car. Once outside, I try to open the door for her, but she won't have it.

"Are you done throwing a fit?"

"A fit? You aren't serious!" She's gone to shrieking now.

"I don't know why it's such a big deal to you that I called you my friend; that's not what I meant. I was just caught off-guard." A half-truth.

"If you're embarrassed about being seen with me, then I don't want to see you anymore." Her voice is shaky. She's trying to stop herself from crying. I'm familiar enough with her ways by now to know that she's digging her fingernails into her thighs and her gray eyes are filling with tears. More tears that I caused her to shed.

"Don't say that to me." I run my hand over my oily hair, wanting to yank it out piece by piece. "Tessa, why do you assume I'm embarrassed about you? That's just fucking ridiculous." I don't have any reason to be embarrassed about her; if anything, it's the other way around. To my friends, she's now a joke; every fucking moment I've shared with this girl has now been diminished to nothing. I turned everything into nothing and she's going to find out soon and there's nothing I can do to stop this freight train from tearing into my life once again. I had just begun to build it up, and now I've gone and fucked everything up.

"Have fun at your party tonight," she says with a pout from the passenger seat.

"Please, I'm not going to the docks with them. I just said that so Jace would lay off." Which is true. I don't want to go to a stupid party. I want to be buried between Tessa's thighs all night.

"If you aren't embarrassed of me, then take me to the party."

I should have known she would throw in this one. Everything is always a game to her, everything.

I'm one to fucking talk.

"Absolutely fucking not," I say.

OF COURSE WE WENT to that fucking party, because, once again, Theresa Young got her way.

As the days go by, I'm more comfortable in my own lie than I care to admit. I pretend that everything isn't slowly crumbling, that tiny pieces of everything that holds us together aren't chipping away with each minute that passes that I don't tell her. I can't tell her. I can't open that can of worms and let them destroy us. The truth will drown us; there's no way around that. It's inevitable, the same way my love for Tessa is inevitable.

"Well . . . welcome home?" I call through the apartment when the real-estate agent leaves us alone, finally. I thought he would never fucking leave. Tessa laughs, covering her mouth with the back of her hand, and steps toward me. I wrap my arms around her, thanking whoever gave her to me for letting her stay a little while longer before she's ripped from my life. I deserve a shred of happiness while it lasts, don't I?

"I can't believe we live here now. It still doesn't seem real." Her wild eyes are curious, excited and alive in a way they haven't been since I met her. I've given her freedom in such a large gesture. I've given her a beautiful apartment where she can be herself, the version of her that no one can judge or demand things from. Her mum isn't here to tell her to brush her hair, and Steph isn't here to think of manipulative ways to hurt us.

"If someone had told me I would be dating you—let alone living with you—two months ago, I'd have either laughed in their face or punched them . . . either one." I laugh and bring her face between my hands. She's so warm, her cheeks alight with excitement.

"Well, aren't you sweet?" She rests her hands on my hips and leans into me. Her head is heavy on my chest, my anchor. My life is perfect for the first time since I can remember. I'm completely ignoring the catastrophe that's coming my way, but for now my life is perfect. "It's a relief, though, to have our own space. No more parties, no more roommates and community showers," Tessa adds. My chest pounds against her cheek, and I wonder if she can sense my growing paranoia.

"Our own bed." I mask the feeling with humor. "We'll need to get a few things—dishes and such." The more things she has here, the harder it will be when it's time to leave. Fuck, I'm trapped in this lie and tying the ropes around her as we speak. This beautiful girl will never forgive me, she won't.

I'll think about it later. I'll figure something out.

She brings her hand to my forehead and lightly applies pressure. "Are you feeling okay?" She grins. "You're being awfully cooperative today." Her sarcastic humor makes me care for her even more.

I bring her hand to my lips, peppering the back of it with kisses. "I just want to make sure you're pleased with everything here. I want you to feel at home . . . with me." And I do. I've never felt like I had a home until Tessa signed along those dotted lines to move in with me. Waking up to her annoying alarm clock every day has grown into something I need, something I was missing and didn't know it.

"And what about you? Do you feel at home here?" Her voice is full of hope. It's tenuous hope, though . . . she's waiting and expecting me to deliver a ruthless opinion about our living situation. I can see it in her eyes; she's hopeful, but she expects the worst from me because that's what she always gets.

"Surprisingly enough, yes." I answer her honestly while trying to make my voice sound as convincing as possible. I really do love it here, with her.

"We should go get my stuff," she suggests, then tells me about the books and clothing I've already taken care of.

"Already done." I smile.

She tilts her head in confusion. "What?"

"I brought all of your belongings from your room; they're in your trunk." I just couldn't wait. I wanted her to see the place and never leave. I need her to never leave here, so I needed to make her as comfortable as I could.

"How did you know I'd sign the lease? What if I hated the apartment?" She turns her cheeks up at me, curiosity and a challenge filling them.

"Because if you hadn't liked this one, I'd have found one that you did like," I tell her.

She nods, acknowledging that I'm completely serious. "Okay . . . Well, what about your stuff?" she asks me.

"We can get it tomorrow. I have clothes in my trunk."

"What is with that, anyway?"

"I don't know, really. I guess you just never know when you'll need clothes." She's nosy, so nosy. I keep clothes in the trunk of my car for many reasons; most of them she surely wouldn't like to know. "Let's go to the store and get all the shit we need for the kitchen and some food," I suggest.

Tessa turns to me when we step into the lobby. "Okay. Can I drive your car again?"

"I don't know . . ." I tease her. But of course she can drive it.

part three
AFTER

He was finally becoming the man he'd never known he could be. His rage was channeled into his writing, and he was becoming proud of the person he was. She was the only reason his life turned out this way, and he would fall at her knees and thank her every second if he could. She stayed by him until it was no longer good for either of them, and then she gave him time to sort his life out on his own. She supported his choices month in and month out and never failed to make him strive for more.

During that time, each month he was sober, he would get a card in the mail, the old-fashioned way, with her name and a heart. He knew her well enough to be sure that the two years they spent apart weren't easy for her. It was hell for her, eternal purgatory for him.

When the handwritten words from his binder became lines on a printed page, she didn't call for a week. He knew she read the book, and he was sure she spent the entire week pacing around the small apartment she shared with his brother. He had moved into a new place by then, adjusting to a windy city with tall buildings and an overabundance of hot dogs and baseball. It didn't feel like home there, though she visited him more times than he deserved. His days went on like this, working, waiting for her to call or email, planning for the next time he'd be able to see her. As he became more and more worthy of her, he started to like the man he saw in the mirror each morning.

When that week was over and she finally did call, her voice cracked on her first word, and he couldn't find the right thing to tell her. He wanted her to understand that no two people were more right for one another. She congratulated him on his book, but with a cool distance. He grew tired, wondering if this would be his life, alone in a high-rise apartment eating takeout while watching reruns of *Friends.*

Weeks later, he couldn't stop his heart from racing when she called to tell him about her visit to his city, how there was a wedding she needed a date for. She danced with him the entire night and lay beneath him in his bed for three days . . .

Until she left, taking his heart with her.

He visited her next, in chaotic New York City, and was impressed with her new life. But he missed his place in it. She had a good thing going there: friends and family. He had an imaginary life with her, and he was waiting for her to come around and make it a reality. Seeing it as his only hope for a good life, he continued to show her that he was a better person than he used to be. Much better. More alive.

At some point, his development as a human being, and the ways it showed in his behavior with other people, started to make him feel valuable, and with that came heavier responsibilities. His brother suffered a heartbreak, and he made sure he was available to talk and help him through it. In different ways, big and small, he found himself feeling of use to his family.

He was the best man at his brother's wedding. She was there, glowing with her love for him, and somehow they both realized, mercifully, that their separation had run its course. They were both grown now, more equipped to handle the world together. He had stopped being selfish; she had figured out who she was. The time apart had done them good, but they were ready to begin their lives together.

Together, they suffered heartache—greater than any they had caused each other in their early years—and sometimes they didn't know if they could go on. On the loneliest day of all, when he packed up the room of their lost child, he wondered if he was being punished, if his past sins were the reasons why they had to deal with such a loss.

The day his first child was born, so was he. Reborn, alive again.

He had come such a long way, and he had changed. Reaching both a deeper and a higher level of love and understanding became possible for him. The little girl's fingers were small, but she had wrapped them around his heart. He watched the girl he had loved for years turn into a woman, and then a mother to *his* child. There was nothing more beautiful than that . . .

Until she became a mum a second time, to their little boy.

As their children grew older, this new man and his woman . . . they somehow felt younger, falling in love all over again each day.

He felt so lucky, so gifted, so tremendously proud of the life they built together; he couldn't believe what a lucky bastard he was.

Zed

Every novel has its own take on the romantic hero. Most novels use that classic trope that we've all grown tired of: the Love Triangle. Wickham lied about Darcy's father to gain Elizabeth's affections. Jay Gatsby wined and dined Daisy Buchanan, offering her a life her husband, Tom, couldn't. Linton was the safe choice of my favorite heroine, Catherine Earnshaw, who chose him over a life of destructive passion with Heathcliff. Even a tan and buff werewolf boy tried to win the ever-so-witty Bella Swan's heart over that sparkly ancient vampire lover dude.

It's been done over and over again, and since he'd lived this through story after story, he thought it laughable when he found himself in his own real, actual love triangle. In his own story, the bad-boy-turned-wannabe-saint with daddy issues tries to keep the stubborn innocent virgin away from the trendy and emotional boy who wants to save the flowers and the planet all in a day's work. The classics end with most of the aforementioned characters' deaths, or the birth of half-vampire babies, but they all have a common theme: one of the two men never stands a chance, and when it came to his relationship with her, he didn't know if how much she cared for him would mean he would win out in the end.

Still, they deserve props, the other guys who get back out into the game after losing to the obvious suitor.

Another party. Another overcrowded party where everyone does the same shit on a different day. Drinks are poured into red cups, and the music blasts from room after room. Every person I pass as I walk down the hallway looks even more bored than the last, so I find it odd that this year's kickoff party is much more crowded than last year's. Where do all the people come from? Has everyone become so bored with themselves that they cling to a large group of other people pretending to have amazing social lives? I'm beginning to see that's all college is. Washington is very different from where I grew up in Florida, but colleges seem to be the same everywhere you go.

"I need to piss," I complain to the air as I lean against the wall next to the bathroom door. A few moments later, a petite girl with blond shoulder-length hair steps out of the bathroom. Her gaze turns down toward the floor when she walks past me. She's wearing a long-sleeved shirt that extends down to hug the curves of her hips perfectly despite her loose, even baggy jeans.

"Excuse me," she says, and smiles at the carpeted floor as she maneuvers past me and down the hall.

I step into the bathroom and close the door. The small space smells like artificial vanilla spray. It's quite disorienting, so I piss quickly, wash my hands, and open the door . . . and step into a crowd of girls. One of them looks me up and down, her eyes widening as she takes in my features. I can almost read her mind. She opens her mouth to speak, but when I look over her head, the blond girl with the killer hips is standing at the top of the stairs. I watch as she goes to grab something from her back pocket, but coming up empty, she licks her lips and rolls her eyes. I can feel her attitude from here. I had made it a point not to look for anyone for a while after the Tessa thing, but I find myself moving down the hallway toward the blonde. I'm not looking for anything serious, but I could use a decent conversation at this point.

As I near the top of the staircase, her small hand wraps around the metal post in a very delicate manner. I take a few steps closer to look at her, and she descends the stairs slowly and cautiously even though she's wearing sneakers. Her hair is thick, covering half of her back. I watch as her eyes scan the crowd. She's aware of her surroundings—I can tell by the way she rests her eyes on every face she sees. Is she looking for someone? I watch her teeth pull in her top lip and decide to approach her. Her jeans are rolled at the bottom, and I can make out the shape of a star near her ankle.

"Are you looking for someone?" I ask her.

When she turns to face me, her brown eyes are big, nearly too big for her face, which makes her seem slightly terrified. "I was looking for my friends, but I think they left." She frowns.

"Oh. Do you want me to help you find them?" I offer.

Continuing to look around the room, she reaches past my face and lifts a baseball cap off of a passing guy. He grumbles and she smiles, only slightly embarrassed and somewhat desperate seeming.

I look at her, wondering why she did that. "My friend John is wearing a cap, too," she explains. I can't tell if she's timid or aggressive yet, but I want to find out.

"Can't you call them?" I ask.

"No, my phone is in my friend's purse," she says with a sigh. "I didn't want to have to bring one. I knew I shouldn't have come here. Parties aren't my thing." Her voice grows louder, and she begins to gesture with her hands. "And yet Macy begged and begged. It will be fun, she said—we'll only stay for an hour, she said."

With a little huff her nose crinkles up, and I bite down on my bottom lip to keep from laughing.

She flushes, embarrassed. "What?"

"Nothing," I lie. She's pretty damn cute. "Do you want a drink or something?"

"I don't drink often," she says softly.

"Often or at all?"

"Sometimes, but definitely not at crowded parties with a bunch of strangers."

"Well, I guess that makes sense." I smile, letting her know that I find it kind of cool that she's not feeling the need to get wasted like the rest of the girls here. Or the boys, for that matter.

"It's not like I can't have fun without being trashed."

"Okay." I nod, finding her more attractive by the second. "Well, I can get you some water or pop and you can hang out with me and my friends until you find yours?"

"Um, I'm not sure." She looks around the living-room-ful of strangers. "I don't know anyone, and parties like this are usually pretty shady." Her gaze moves to two drunk guys circling a group of freshman girls in small dresses.

She's got a point.

Nate waves at me from across the room, and I look at this intriguing girl once more.

"Well, if you decide you don't want to stand here alone, you're more than welcome to join us over there." I point toward the group and watch her eyes widen as she takes in the hundred or so tattoos among the lot of us.

"They're nicer than they look," I tease. When she smiles uncertainly, I add, "Well, some of them, anyway."

She surprises me by barking out a little laugh and then following me over to my group of friends. Tristan stands up, allowing her to sit on the couch, and she politely thanks him. I haven't seen him too much lately, but I'm glad he's back from Louisiana, single and officially done with Steph's bullshit.

"Here's to the last year of this college bullshit." He raises his cup and taps Logan's. Molly joins in and adjusts herself on his lap.

"Ugh, not for me—I still have two more," Nate complains. The girl he's been seeing—Briana, I think—rolls her eyes, mutters what I think is a playful "Drama queen," and grabs his cup to take a drink.

"I should have gone to a trade school." He tilts his head back, and the girl watches him in amusement. "College fucking blows."

"I told you you should have taken that apprenticeship at the tattoo shop," she scolds him. He rolls his eyes and tugs at the tiny strap holding her shirt on one of her shoulders; half of her deep brown skin is showing, but I sure as hell don't mind.

"I'm still thinking about it," he tells her. Honestly, it sounds like a decent play, since he's having such a hard time finishing college.

"Anyway, enough of this boring career-planning shit. Who's this?" Molly points to the girl I met in the hallway.

"This is . . ." I look at her for help. I forgot to ask her damn name.

"Therise," she says, and I get a tiny hint of an accent I hadn't noticed before.

Damn.

"You've gotta be shitting me." Molly laughs, leaning against Logan.

"Nice name." Jace smirks, licking along the edges of the rolling paper in his hands.

"Wanna play a game, Therise?" Molly says with a tone I know. "Truth or Dare?" She looks to me, and I shake my head.

"No, no one wants to play that shit," I say, glaring at Molly. Therise is clueless and looks anxious and slightly uncomfortable.

"Oh, come on. I *bet* it would be fun," Jace says.

Molly nods along. "Yeah, from the looks of her, maybe you could win—"

Logan reaches up and covers his girlfriend's mouth. I still can't believe these two are together.

"Cut it out," he says to her.

She rolls her eyes but stays quiet once his hand moves from her big mouth.

"I'm not having any part in a repeat of last year. That was too much drama." Logan kisses Molly's bare shoulder, and she smiles, for real this time, looking far less evil while doing so.

Therise looks at me with a wrinkled brow, then at everyone else and their suddenly weird energy. "What was last year?" she asks.

"Nothing," I proclaim, and look at my friends, hoping they'll keep their mouths closed. I just met this girl—it's too early for her to be bombarded with this crap.

"This guy named Hard—" Molly just can't keep her mouth closed.

"We aren't going to talk about Hessa anymore!" Logan groans. "They're like that reality-show couple that no one was supposed to mention."

"What the fuck is a Hessa?" Nate's girl asks.

Molly proudly raises her hand. "I came up with it!" she practically shouts. "I get full credit for that shit. I named those crazy fucks, and I expect an invite to their wedding." She laughs. Her hair is a washed-out pink; it's faded a lot, and she hasn't dyed it in a while. It's mostly blond now and in an elvin haircut.

"They aren't getting married," I snap at her.

I'm so tired of hearing about those two. I'm tired of seeing Tessa's posts on Facebook. She's so happy in New York; Hardin's so happy; everyone is so damn happy.

Yay for them.

"Not right now, but I would bet money on that shit." She smiles. "And *I*? I would *win*." She's drawn circles around her eyes with black pencil, and when she winks at me, she looks like a cat.

Logan adds salt to my wound by nodding sagely to this. Like it's so obvious to *everyone*.

Molly waves her hand for silence among the group. "Anyway, before you all came, we were reliving the grand tale of Zed's ex-girlfriend."

"*Wasn't* my girlfriend," I say through gritted teeth.

"*Damn*," someone says. Jace, maybe?

"Well . . ." Therise stands to her feet and awkwardly cracks her knuckles. "This is when I leave." She smiles hesitantly and walks away.

I must have a pained or annoyed or angry expression—I felt all of those things—because Logan pipes up, "You may as well let her go; you're only going to gain another enemy. She probably has a boyfriend who'll slash the tires on your truck."

Apparently my friends have all decided they'll give me shit all week about my history of expensive mistakes.

This expectation that my dating life will always be one disaster after another deflates my anger a little bit. I don't have the energy to be mad, really, when it's always the same. "I didn't know that chick was engaged, and I'm pretty sure it was her, not her fiancé, that did that shit," I say, and cringe when I remember what Jonah Soto did to my car. That dude should not be able to hold a professor position here. Total nutcase.

Nate shrugs, taking a swig of his drink. "Stop sleeping with random chicks, then."

"That was over a year ago, and how was I supposed to know that her fiancé was going to be a professor here?"

That whole weekend was a disaster. If I'd known the chick was at the club for her own bachelorette party, I wouldn't have gone home with her. I mean, there's a reason tradition dictates they wear those tacky feather boas and fake tiaras and that sash that reads BACHELORETTE or something. It's like a fair-warning label so that guys don't do something stupid—or she doesn't do something stupid. The sash is like the first thing you'd have to take off, so it being there is a big reminder to her that, oh yeah, she's getting married. In this case—the very next day.

It was just my luck that the only time in my life I had a one-night stand, this was the result. (I may have led my friends to believe a generally exaggerated version of my sex life, but they don't need to know that.) The guy was cool, cooler than I would have been, until he tried to get me removed from the science program and fought to keep Hardin from being expelled. No one seemed to question why a young professor would take the side of a troublemaker he doesn't even know. That was bullshit, but at the end of the day, I'm glad Hardin wasn't expelled.

"Who are you all talking shit to, anyway"—I wave an arm at the group—"because Molly here has fucked half of you."

"Watch it," Logan warns, and everyone tenses.

But instead of arguing with him, I choose to follow after the new girl.

I don't know her, but she seems chill and she's drop-dead gorgeous. Yes, she reminds me of Tessa, and yes, it's taken a long time for me to get over that one, and maybe this is a bad idea—but aren't most things?

With all that swirling through my mind, I get up to find her.

I didn't mean for the situation with Tessa to become what it did. I cared about her, yes, but I got caught up in my stupid jealousy and petty need for some type of revenge against Hardin for his having sex with Samantha. I did like Tessa a lot, but my feelings for her were nothing close to the way Hardin felt about her.

Samantha was amazing; she was fun and a few years older than me. That was a turn-on, but she was wild. Since this thing with Tessa ended, I've often thought her relationship with Hardin was equivalent to what I had with Samantha. But Samantha slept with Hardin, and didn't see much of a problem with it. She acted like it was a normal thing to do, to sleep with my friend. He didn't care either, of course.

I cared. I was devastated and pissed, and I let it fester inside of me, waiting for the right time to strike back at him. Tessa trusted me, even after my involvement with the Bet in the beginning. I was the one who told her the details about it, and she always came to me when she needed me. That was the problem, though: she only came to me when he tossed her to the side, and I'm not about that kind of thing. I don't want to always be second choice. And besides, it was too much drama, and after the initial win of getting under Hardin's skin, it became exhausting to keep running to her rescue and keep up with their childish relationship.

I should have left her alone after her psycho boyfriend hit me the first time. But no, his anger only spurred me to keep going and win. Why should *he* get to sleep with Samantha, then participate in the Bet, and then get to decide when everything's okay and settled and the game's over and I have to stop caring?

It was all so childish. I can see that now. I shouldn't have tried to come on to her that night at her mom's house, and I shouldn't have said half the shit that I did. My stupidity has kept me single since then, and I haven't heard from Tessa in over a year. The sad thing is that I miss talking with her.

I've been told she moved to New York City with her friend Landon, but I know it won't be long until Hardin follows her there. As much as I hate to admit it, they have something special between them. As dysfunctional as they are, I've never seen two people fight for each other the way those two do. Hardin sure as hell doesn't deserve her, but it's not my place to interfere, not anymore.

I step outside and scan the yard for Therise, then spy her perched on top of the broken stone wall, bringing another memory to mind. She's picking at the chipped stone, and when I approach her, she moves to jump down.

"Wait." I hold up my hand and wave it in a gesture of peace. "I can help you find your friends or find someone to give you a ride home."

"I don't know." She eyes me carefully, watching for hints of a serial killer, maybe.

"It's only a ride home. My friends are loudmouths, but none of them will hurt you. I'll come along if you wish. I've been drinking, so I can't take you."

I raise a brow to her; she shakes her head. "Wow, so the cute punk boy does have some common sense." She smiles, mocking me in a sweet way.

"Sometimes," I admit with a shrug. I reach out to shake her hand. "I'm Zed."

She hesitates for a moment before reaching for my hand.

"It's nice to meet you, Z-ed." She says my name like she's afraid to swallow it.

"Nice to meet you, too, Therise."

Landon

He hated the perfect boy before he even met him. When his dad told him he was getting a new brother, it was like he was expected to be happy about it. He was supposed to suddenly care about things like family and dinners and baked goods so he could keep up with his father's new son.

When he met this other child, his hatred only grew. He knew he didn't have a reason beyond pure jealousy to hate him, but still he did. He couldn't name athletes or keep up with sports like his father's new son could, and he couldn't charm the table at a dinner party. He knew he couldn't compete with the boy, but as he changed his life, he realized he'd never really had to. He fought so hard—too hard—to keep his distance from the Golden Boy who in the end would become his closest friend.

The first three thoughts that go through my mind each day are:

It's less crowded here than I thought.

I hope Tessa is off work today so we can hang out.

I miss my mom.

Yes, I'm a sophomore at New York University, but my mom is one of my best friends.

I miss home a lot. It helps to have Tessa around; she's the closest thing to family I have out here.

I know college students do this all the time; they leave home and can't wait to be away from their hometowns, but not me. I happened to like mine, even if it's not where I grew up. I had a plan at the time I applied to NYU; it just didn't work out the way it was supposed to. I was supposed to move here and start my future with Dakota, my long-term girlfriend from high school. I had no idea that she would decide she wanted to spend her first year at college single.

I was devastated. I still am, but I want her to be happy, even if it's not with me.

The city's chilly in September, but there's barely any rain compared to Washington. So that's something, at least.

As I walk to work, I check my phone, like I do about fifty times a day. My mom's pregnant with my little sister, and I want to be sure that if anything happens I can get on a plane and be there for her quickly. So far the only messages from her have been pictures of the amazing things she whips up in the kitchen.

Not emergencies, but, man, I miss her cooking.

The streets are crowded as I make my way through them. I'm waiting at the crosswalk with a crowd of people, mostly tourists with heavy cameras around their necks. I laugh to myself when a teenage boy holds up a giant iPad to take a selfie.

I will never understand this impulse.

When the light turns yellow and the crosswalk sign starts flashing, I turn up the volume on my headphones.

Out here I pretty much wear headphones all day. The city is so much louder than I had anticipated, and I find it helpful to have something that blocks some of it out and at least colors those sounds that get in with something I like.

Today it's Hozier.

I even wear the headphones while working—in one ear at least, so I can still hear the coffee orders shouted to me. I'm a little distracted today by two men, both dressed in pirate outfits and screaming at each other, and as I walk into the shop, I bump into Aiden, my least favorite coworker.

He's tall, much taller than me, and he has this white-blond hair that makes him look like Draco Malfoy, so he kind of creeps me out. On top of his Draco resemblance, he happens to be a little rude sometimes. He's nice to me, but I see the way he looks at the college girls who come into Grind. He acts like the coffee shop is named after a club rather than coffee grounds.

As he smiles down at them, flirting and making them squirm under his "handsome" gaze, I find it all pretty off-putting. He's not that handsome, actually; maybe if he was nicer, I could see it.

"Watch it, man," Aiden mumbles, slapping my shoulder like we're crossing a football field together in matching jerseys.

He's making record time in annoying me today . . .

But brushing it off, I head into the back and tie my yellow apron around my waist and check my phone. After I clock in, I find Posey, a girl who I'm supposed to be training for a couple of weeks. She's nice. Quiet, but she's a hard worker, and I like that she always takes the free cookie we offer her every training day as an incentive to be a little happier during the shift. Most trainees decline it, but she's eaten one every single day this week, sampling the variety: chocolate, chocolate macadamia, sugar, and some mystery greenish flavor that I think is some gluten-free all-natural localvore thing.

"Hey," I say, smiling at her where she leans against the ice machine. Her hair is tucked behind her ears, and she's reading the back of one of the bags of ground coffee. When she looks up at me, she smiles a quick greeting, then returns her eyes to the bag.

"It still makes no sense that they charge fifteen dollars for a thing of coffee this small," she says, tossing the bag to me.

I barely catch it and then it nearly slips from my hands, but I grab it tightly.

"*We.*" I correct her with a laugh, and sit the bag down on the break table where it came from. "We charge that."

"I haven't worked here long enough to be included in the 'we,'" she teases, and grabs a hair band off her wrist and lifts her curly reddish-brown hair into the air behind her. It's a lot of hair, and she ties it up neatly, then nods her signal that she's ready to work.

Posey follows me out to the floor and waits by the cash register. She's mastering taking customers' orders this week, and will likely be making the drinks next. I like taking orders the most, because I would rather talk to people than burn my fingers on that espresso machine, like I do every shift.

I'm putting everything in order at my station when the bell attached to the door sounds. I look over to Posey to see if she's ready, and sure enough, she's already perked up, all set to greet the morning's caffeine addicts. Two girls approach the counter chatting loudly. One of the voices strikes me, and I look over at them to see Dakota there. She's dressed in a sports bra, loose shorts, and bright sneakers. She must have just finished a run; if she were leaving for a dance class, she'd be dressed slightly differently. She'd be wearing a one-piece and tighter shorts. And she would look just as good. She always does.

Dakota hasn't been in here in a few weeks; I'm surprised to see her now. It makes me nervous; my hands are shaking, and I find myself poking at the computer screen for absolutely no reason. Her friend Maggy sees me first. She taps Dakota on her shoulder, and Dakota turns to me, a big smile on her face. Her body is coated in a light layer of sweat, and her black curls are wild in a bun on her head.

"I was hoping you'd be working." She waves to me and then to Posey.

She was? I don't know what to make of this. I know that we agreed to be friends, but I can't tell if this is just friendly chatting, or something more.

"Hey, Landon." Maggy waves, too. I smile at both of them and ask them what they'd like to drink.

"Iced coffee, extra cream," the duo says at once. They're dressed nearly identically, but Maggy is easily overshadowed by Dakota's glowing caramel skin and bright brown eyes.

I go into automatic mode, grabbing two plastic cups and shoving them into the ice bin with a smooth scooping motion, then pulling up the pitcher of premade coffee and pouring it into the cups. Dakota is watching me. I can sense her eyes on me. For some reason, this is making me feel quite awkward, so when I notice that Posey is watching me, too, I realize I could—*should*, probably—explain to her what the heck I'm doing.

"You just pour this over ice; the evening shift makes it the night before so it can get cold and not melt the ice," I say.

It's really basic, what I'm telling her, and I almost feel foolish saying it in front of Dakota. We aren't on bad terms at all—we just aren't hanging out and talking like we used to. I completely understood when she ended our three-year relationship. She was in New York City with new friends and new surroundings. I didn't want to hold her back, so I kept my promise and stayed friends with her. I've known her for years and will always care about her. She was my second girlfriend but the first real relationship I've had up to now. I've been hanging out with So, a woman who's three years older than me, though really we're only friends. She's been great to Tessa, too, helping her get a job at the restaurant she works at.

"Dakota?" Aiden's voice overpowers mine as I start to ask them if they want me to add whipped cream, something I do to my own drinks.

Confused, I watch as Aiden reaches over the counter and grabs Dakota's hand. He lifts their hands into the air, and with a big smile she twirls in front of him.

Then, taking a glance at me, she inches away just a bit and says more neutrally, "I didn't know you worked here."

I look at Posey to distract myself from eavesdropping on their conversation, then pretend like I'm looking at the schedule on the wall behind her. It's really none of my business who she has friendships with.

"I thought I mentioned it last night," Aiden says, and I cough to distract everyone from the noise I just made.

Fortunately no one seems to notice except Posey, who tries her best to hide her smile.

I don't look at Dakota even though I can sense she's uncomfortable; in reply to Aiden, she laughs the laugh she gave my grandma upon opening her Christmas gift last year. That cute noise . . . Dakota made my grandma so happy when she laughed at the cheesy singing fish plastered to a fake wooden plank. When she laughs again, I know she's *really* uncomfortable now. Wanting to make this whole situation less awkward, I hand her the two coffees with a smile and tell her I hope to see her soon.

Before she can answer, I smile once more and walk to the back room, turning the sound up on my headphones.

I wait for the bell to ring again, signaling Dakota and Maggy's exit, and realize that I probably won't hear it over yesterday's hockey game playing in my ear. Even with only one bud in, the cheering crowd and slaps of sticks would overpower an old brass bell. I go back out to the floor and find Posey rolling her eyes at Aiden as he shows off his milk-steaming skills to her. He looks weird with a cloud of steam in front of his white-blond hair.

"He said they're in school together, at that dance academy he goes to," Posey whispers when I approach.

I freeze and look toward Aiden, who is oblivious, lost in his own apparently glorious world. "You asked him?" I say, impressed and a little worried about what his answers would be to other questions involving Dakota.

Posey nods, grabbing a metal cup to rinse. I follow her to the sink, and she turns on the hose. "I saw the way you acted when he held her hand, so I thought I'd just ask what was going on with them." She shrugs, and her big mass of curly hair moves.

Her freckles are lighter than most I've seen and are scattered across the top of her cheeks and the bridge of her nose. Her lips are big—they pout a tad—and she's nearly my height. These were things I noticed on her third day of training, when I suppose my interest flared up for a moment.

"I dated her for a while," I admit to my new friend, and hand her a towel to dry the cup with.

"Oh, I don't think they're dating. She would be insane to date a Slytherin." When Posey smiles, my cheeks flare and I laugh along with her.

"You noticed it, too?" I ask.

Reaching between us, I grab a pistachio mint cookie and offer it to her.

She smiles, taking the cookie from my hand and eating half of it before I even manage to get the lid back on the bin.

Christian

The connections we have with family are supposed to be soul binding. We're supposed to love our parents and siblings and the rest simply because we are born with the same blood running through our veins. As a young child, he would question this. Was he supposed to love the stumbling man whose loud voice regularly woke him up on school nights? The man whom he would walk out into the living room and see there, leaning against the fireplace mantel in a struggle to take his boots off? The little boy would keep his body hidden behind the wall as he watched the man struggle and fall to the floor. Then he would hurry back to his room as the man's boot hit the wall near his head.

He hated those nights and he would count the days until his mummy's friend who laughed a lot would come over. He would wish that his mum's friend was his dad. Maybe this other man would take him places, he used to think. He remembered the man always carrying a book tucked under his arm. He talked about the books with the boy, telling him their plots, their themes, making him feel smart and grown-up.

The first book the man gifted him he will always remember. That book quickly became the boy's first real friend, and as he grew older and his mum's friend came around less and less, he remembered missing him and missing the books during the long periods between visits. Still, even into the boy's rebellious teenage years, when the man arrived, he always had books with him. The boy knew his mum loved her friend, but he had no idea just how much of his life was a lie because of that fact.

The house is silent. I glance over at Kim, asleep on the couch with Karina lying on her stomach; the girl's little hands are gripping her mum's sweater. Kim fell asleep talking to her about me and my accent, telling our little girl that she will have the most adorable voice, a mixture of Mummy's sweet tones and Daddy's devilish accent. "Devilish," she called it. As if the woman can afford to talk. She's the most stubborn, devilish woman on this earth, and I love the hell out of her.

Kimberly has gone from being my secretary to my business partner, and she has quite an eye for potential. Perhaps that's why she married me. Or maybe she just really, really likes my son, Smith. It would be pretty hard not to.

A pile of pages sits before me on the counter: a contract for the New York restaurant we'll be opening in the next year. As exciting as it is, it's nothing compared to my newborn. I've now expanded my investments in restaurants from Washington to New York to Los Angeles, but it's nothing compared to the joy of getting to see this girl grow up before my eyes, something I've not been fortunate enough to have done with my other children.

I glance over at my wife again; snoring louder than usual. So I do the sweet, loving thing and pull out my phone to record her. The contract can wait until tomorrow. I miss my wife. I watch her as she takes breath; the noise is horrendous.

I press record and quietly walk over to the couch. Within five seconds, she opens her eyes, immediately glaring at the phone in my hand, and instantly I feel like an arse for disrupting her sleep when she gets so little of it anymore.

"Aren't you supposed to be working?" my love whispers, her voice soft and sleepy as she stretches her arm above her head, keeping her eyes on Karina.

"Yes, my dear, but fucking with you is much more fun." I laugh, and she kicks her foot out at me. Karina stirs on her chest, opening her little beady eyes to look up at her obnoxious parents.

"Now you've done it," Kimberly scolds me with a smile. She sits up and lifts Karina at the same time, and when I reach for my daughter, she gently places the soft bundle in my arms.

"My beautiful little girl," I quietly say to Karina, nudging her chubby little cheek with my nose. She yawns, and I see so much of my smile in her face. Smith and Hardin both have that same dimpled smile.

I remember Anne and Ken discussing names for the little boy one night when we were all standing around in their kitchen. Trish's belly had been so swollen that she couldn't tie her shoes.

"I like the name Nicholas or Harold," Ken had suggested.

Harold? No.

Nicholas. Double no.

Trish had smiled softly, rubbing her hand on her bump. "Harold—I kind of like that."

Admittedly, I didn't *hate* the name—it just didn't feel right. That boy was tough on Trish's body, kicking her all night and growing so quickly that he stretched her skin to incredible lengths. He was a fighter, that kid . . . the name Harold—*Harry*—it was too sweet of a name, too calm.

"It's too common," I'd interjected before Ken could say anything. "How about the name Hardin?"

It was a name I had picked out for my first child while I was only a teen. As a little boy in Hampstead, I used to think I was going to write a great novel one day and the main character would be named Hardin. Not typical, but very convincing-sounding for old England.

Trish sounded it out to see how it felt on her tongue. "Hardin. I'm not sure . . ."

But when she looked to her husband—who I was so jealous of in that instant—he'd just shrugged, uninterested but trying to be courteous.

"It sounds fine," he said quietly.

His shoulders did another shrug, and Trish smiled a weak smile. "Hardin? . . . Hardin."

"There we have it, then," Ken declared, looking very relieved.

Trish didn't seem surprised or even bothered by his mild reaction to the choosing of their first son's name. I cared, though, and I knew Trish really did as well.

I would like to think that Ken would normally have cared, but he was in college and always busy, I had reasoned at the time. He studied so much, and rumors flew that he'd started snorting the devil's candy while studying for his law exams. His pupils were usually dilated, but he had to study a lot, and I got that. I wasn't anyone to judge him, but I knew he had been slipping on the facade of being a perfect dad to the little guy, trying it on uncertainly, long before the tyke was even here yet. That bothered me more than it should have, given the situation I'd gotten myself into.

Two decades ago . . .

The sun is hot, blazing for Hampstead in April. Trish lies beside me on the grass, the wind whipping her thick brown hair across my face, which she found to be the most entertaining moment of her entire sixteen years in this world. Most of the time she's mature for her age, going on and on about her theories about the world and its leaders, but in this moment she's choosing to be the eleven-year-old version of herself.

I push her hair away from my face for the tenth time.

"Weren't you supposed to be cutting that gargantuan mane?" I ask cheekily as I scoot my body a few inches away from hers. Last week she claimed that she was planning to cut all of her hair off to prove some point, but I forget what the point actually was.

Hampstead Towne Park is nearly empty today, so Trish's laugh echoes off the trees enclosing us in the grass. We come here often, but most of the time Ken misses our meetings because he's so busy.

"I was considering it, but this is too much fun," she replies. Trish rolls her body closer to mine and throws her brown hair across my face once more. It smells like flowers and a little bit like mint. It's a scent that always pulls me in. Her body is pressed to my side, and she kicks her leg up over mine.

I should move it, but I don't. It feels too nice there.

"What if babies were born with long hair?"

Her question is random, but not one bit surprising. Trish Powell is known for her questions. *What if this? What if that?* It's her thing, and I find it equal parts weird and cool. She's so different from all the girls at my school—even the girls at the local university aren't like her. Her wild hair was the first thing I noticed when I met her, and now it's become the biggest problem in my Tuesday afternoon.

"Did we really skip class to talk about babies coming out of their mums' bodies with rocker hair?" I ask.

I open my eyes and roll onto my stomach to get a good look at her. She has so many freckles. I want to connect them with my fingertips and watch her eyes flutter closed in delight.

"No, I suppose not." She giggles, and I follow her eyes to the shadow approaching us. Ken sits down on the grass, and I watch his eyes change from the moon to the sun as he studies Trish's face.

She smiles back at him, and Ken looks like he's won the lottery as he makes his way through the tall grass. I can't tell if she notices the way he looks at her. I've always noticed it—and gotten used to pretending it doesn't burn like acid through my veins.

It's common knowledge that of the two of us, he's the better man.

The sun is becoming too hot on my skin, and I stand, shading my eyes with one hand. "I'm going to head out—I have a date,"

I say, and wipe my hands on my jean shorts. Seeing their brown hue against the faded denim, I again marvel how I've gotten quite the tan over the summer. Trish mentions it almost daily. It must be from hanging out with her so much.

Trish rolls her eyes and mouths something rather dirty to both of us. Ken flushes just a little in the apples that are his cheeks. His hair is growing long, looking ratty where it starts to cover the back of his neck. There are dark bags under his brown eyes from studying like a madman to prepare for his entry exam into law school. Ken Scott is the most stable student in Trish's and my entire level; I have no idea how someone like him ended up becoming our best friend. I suppose Trish is a tad more stable than me. She's firecrackers and sunshine, but she's also cool stone and steady waves. She knows when to cut loose and when to be cautious and smart. I've always loved that about her.

"Can I talk to you for a minute?" Ken says when I stand. He comes a little closer to me; he's taller than me by a few inches. I nod, waiting for him to begin, but then seeing his eyes focus on Trish, I catch on that he means alone and gesture for him to lead the way. I follow him for about twenty meters, at which point he stops next to an old metal bench. He sits first and pats the empty space next to him.

He's acting so serious—should I be worried? A young couple walks past us, their hands linked together. Ken waits for them to pass and my worry to rise before he finally speaks.

"I wanted to talk to you about something," he says. His brows draw down, making him look much older than seventeen.

"You're not dying, are ye?" I push my shoulder into his, and he relaxes a fraction.

He shakes his head. "No, no. It's not that." The noise he makes is half laugh, half nervous titter.

What could he be so tense about? I wish he would just spit it out.

"I-want-to-ask-Trish-to-be-mine," he breathes out in one long syllable.

Now I wish I could cram the words back inside his anxious face, or that maybe he *was* dying. Okay, not something so harsh, but something else. Anything else.

"To be your . . . what?" I struggle to keep my composure.

Ken's eyes roll. "My girl, you twat."

I want to tell him that he can't have her, that it isn't fair that he's the one who gets to ask her first. *Give her a choice*, I want to tell him. *She was always supposed to be mine*, I want to argue.

"Why are you telling me?" comes out instead.

My friend sits back against the bench and rests his palms against his knees. "I just wanted to make sure . . ." he starts, but the words are trapped behind his tongue.

And in that sudden silence I realize I'm caught between being honest with my best friend and making him happy. It's impossible to do both.

I break into a smile, choosing his happiness over mine.

I'm not surprised when Trish accepts Ken's offer, but I would be lying if I said I didn't hold on to some fraction of hope that maybe she loves me, too. She loves stability more, though, and so for the next year, I avoid every thought of Trish being anything other than my best mate's girlfriend. Sometimes when they kiss in front of me, I catch her looking at me for approval after they've pulled away from each other. I keep that little morsel of hope alive, and it makes my year a very rough one. When I fuck, I think of her. When I kiss, I taste her.

I have to stop.

It's an easy task at first. I stop comparing all the girls I date to her. She stops slipping her hand through mine when we're talking. I begin to see the world differently now that I no longer think of her as a tether to home. She's no longer keeping me here. Nothing is.

I've outgrown Hampstead. I know it. Trish knows it. Even the local bakery has grown suspicious of my recent behavior and the fact that my weekly trips to buy sweets there have tapered down to nothing.

Suddenly I crave more of this world than living in this town. I want to move to the States, away from the daft minds of my mates who have no plans for their futures—and even farther away from my two favorite lovers. I've quickly become a fifth wheel with Ken and Max and their ladies. I want to learn more about the world, about people in general, and I can't settle down here. Everyone around me has their roots firmly planted here already. They've opened up bank accounts and chosen a local university. I can already foresee their ambition short-circuiting when they take their first job doing what one of their parents did. They settle into these roles and never audition for any others.

Trish has become one of them. She's gone from being an excited liberal arts major to barely attending her classes. She and Ken moved into a small apartment across from the campus of his school to save travel time. He's a mess lately, working so much. Every time I see him he's behind a stack of textbooks. Trish is less of a lover and more of a mother to him now. She sets his alarm clock every evening. She makes sure his clothes are clean and laid out on their bed in the morning. She makes his coffee, his breakfast, packs his lunch. She waits for him to get home, she feeds him a hot meal and is ignored in favor of his books, and then the next day the same tedious cycle repeats all over again. She's no longer the vibrant risk-taking flower child she once was. She's the overworked and underslept waiting woman. Because of her efforts, their apartment is as clean as it is small, and she's managed to charm up the place. Trish has even taken in a stray kitten and named it Gat after one of my favorite characters. I suspect Ken doesn't care for the creature, or the name she chose.

Her what-if games that I enjoyed on the hill become less and

less frequent every day, and more and more of what she expresses
can be called free-floating anxiety. She no longer indulges in
flights of fancy that entertain us both; instead she worries about
minute things, and I'm no longer a playmate in a grassy field, but
someone who has to reassure her, even though I'm not the first in
her heart.

Even through this, though, she still keeps her humor—and
I pray to God each night that she won't lose it completely. The
more often I stop by, the brighter she seems to burn. I make it a
point to stop by weekly, then twice a week, as she asks me to do.
The hours Ken's gone become longer, leaving their home emptier.
She shares with me her worries and whispers her darkest questions into the dark room. I pretend to have all the answers, and
like a good friend to them both, I encourage her to share her fears
with her lover.

Quickly, I regret this decision. One night, a rare night when
Ken is at home and not studying, we're all sitting around the
kitchen table, each of us with a glass of whiskey in hand. During
a lull in the awkward conversation in which we try to catch up
with one another's recent life, Ken refills his glass. He doesn't
bother to look for ice—he never does anymore.

Trish sighs loudly and gets up, only to go into their small living room and sit on the arm of their couch. "What if the whole
world exists in a glass case inside some alien child's bedroom, like
an ant farm of sorts?" I swear Trish's accent grows deeper each
time she drinks.

"What a fucked-up question," I snort, the whiskey burning in
my nostrils. Ken doesn't break a smile; his lips don't even make
the slightest upturn. I get up to stretch, to not be the only one sitting at the table with him.

"Fine. What if the world ends tomorrow, proving that we all
are wasting our time working so hard and sleeping so little?" Her

eyes are light in the dim room. Gat climbs up onto her lap, and she runs her fingers through his burnt-orange fur.

I begin to think through her question. If I died tomorrow, would she know how much I ache for her? How much I love her?

Ken finally laughs, but his comment is not what I expected. "*Working hard?* As if you know anything about that."

He's smiling now, head tilting back in a sinister way as he leans over the table. Gat seems to sense the threat as Trish takes in a deep breath. I've never seen them fight, but if they do, my money is on Trish. The cat jumps down and prances off into the hallway. I should follow it—I should leave and stay out of this—but I can't.

Ken lifts his glass to his lips and gulps down the remainder of the brown liquor in his tumbler.

"I'm sorry, I couldn't possibly have heard that correctly," Trish says through her teeth.

I ignore the way my hands shake under the table when he stands up and starts raising his voice. I ignore my instinct to tackle him and shake him until he wakes up from this sleep-walking state he's been slipping into lately, a state in which he starts yelling at her, calling her terrible names, and saying terrible things about her. I ignore the way my stomach feels like surging lava when she slaps him across the face. I ignore the way her tears burn through the flesh of my arms as I hold her on the couch, after he's been gone for thirty minutes, drunk as a fish and out driving somewhere even though he's incapable of walking straight—but after the way he stormed out of here, not bothering to turn around when I called after him, I'm glad he's gone.

"What if he doesn't come back?" Trish's lips tremble as she finally starts to calm down, her head on my chest.

"And what if he does?" I ask her.

She sighs and squeezes my hand between hers. I look down

at her face, and my heart aches. She's so beautiful, even when her lips are red from chewing at them, and her eyes are swollen from wetting them with her tears. She's calm now, her eyes stuck on my lips.

"What if I'm losing sight of the man I thought I knew?" Trish's question comes out quickly, her next even more so. "What if I would rather have attention than a stable life?"

She seems frantic now, pushing her fingers through her thick brown hair. She faces me, squaring off her shoulders. "What if I confused friendship with love? Do you think Ken and I did that?"

She looks down at my hands, which are reaching for her without my having realized it.

"I don't know," I say, pulling my hands back to run them over my hair and then sitting back against the couch. I confused friendship and love when I chose friendship over my feelings for Trish, but now my best friends have made a life together. The problem they face isn't a lack of love, it's a lack of time. That's all. He loves her, and if she loved me rather than him, she would have told me long before now.

She moves onto her knees on the couch, just to reach me. Her hand moves to my hair, and she pushes it back for me. "What if it's not that simple?"

Can she sense how I feel for her? Is that why she's moving closer and closer with every rise of her chest?

When her face is only an inch from mine, she looks me straight in the eyes. "Do you ever think of me?"

The whiskey on both of our breaths hangs in the air even though both of us had far less to drink than Ken. There I go mentioning Ken again; it's like his presence is everywhere in this apartment. He marked Trish's body as his; he lies with her every night. He gets to feel her breasts under his palms. He gets to touch the pale skin on her stomach, her thighs. Her lips touch him. He tastes her . . .

And I never will.

"I shouldn't . . ." I say.

But I would be a fool not to think of her slender hips and perfect skin. I watched her grow up, and fantasizing about her was a daily, constant thing.

Trish is pleased by my answer. I can see it in the way she licks her lips while staring at mine, the way her mouth is slightly open. Does this mean she's been having . . . well, having thoughts about me? Why else would she ask?

When her eyes flicker to my eyes, then back to my mouth, common sense and self-restraint are no longer in my vocabulary, and I wrap my hand in her hair and pull her mouth to mine. I take her mouth slowly, claiming every bit of her tongue, her lips. She's mine in this moment, and we're both taking full advantage of it. Quickly she grows eager, aggressive in her movements, and shoves me to the floor and climbs onto my torso. The look on her face is one of deep relief as she slips her tongue back inside my mouth. I groan, lifting my hips to meet hers. I'm hard for her, and I want her to feel it.

Her fingers lace through mine, and she guides them between her legs. She's excited to show me how wet she is; she's ready to confess her need for me. I'm ready, too, and I show her when I grind my hips up into her; she curses, begging me to take this to the next level.

Can we—

"What if we get caught?" she asks, pulling back only a fraction.

I don't know if I care as much as I always thought I would.

"What if we don't?" she then says to herself and silences any further questions either of us may have with her tongue between my lips and her hands unbuttoning my trousers. Her hand slips inside, gripping me, and I melt into her. My fears of being caught by an angry Ken, my knowledge that she is not mine for the taking, the anxiety I'm filled with when I think of leaving here—all of it melts. The only thing I can think of is being buried in her, needing every part of her.

I tug at my trousers, pulling them down along with my boxers. Her mouth is tasting me, tongue probing, licking the swollen vein down my center. She closes her eyes, relishing the way her wet mouth takes me all the way into her throat, then back up. She's becoming less cautious as she devours me, quickly yet efficiently. She's pleasing me as if she won't ever taste me again. It's true that she won't.

"Lie down, facing up, legs spread wide. I want to look at you," I tell her. I have to look at her while I finally have what I want beneath me. Trish moves toward the center of the carpet, dragging the dark cherry coffee table to one side. She quickly undresses, and I don't mind, because watching her is something else. Her long cotton dress is falling to her feet, and her arms are already lifting the straps of her simple white bra. My eyes follow the curve of her body; her nipples are tight little pebbles as my gaze passes them. Her stomach is tight; the muscles on her torso curve down to her hipbones.

I'm throbbing and heavy in my hand when I reach her. She's lying down on the carpet, her legs spread wide for me. My cock hangs heavy between us, and I can smell the wetness of her pussy. I swear I can feel how tight she'll be. I inch closer, pushing against her until I slowly fill her. She feels like a damn glove as I thrust in and out of her. I don't think I can stop this, ever. I already need more of her. Trish's eyes have rolled up into her head, and I know I'm not going to be able to hold on much longer. I rock my hips, and she wraps her thighs around my waist. She's coming, she says, "so hard," she whimpers, clawing into my arms as I fuck harder.

I spill into her, wishing this wasn't the first and only time I'll be able to enjoy her body in this way. She's breathing hard into my

shoulder, and I'm kissing the wet marks on her neck from my pre-
vious licks.

Minutes later, we've returned to reality with a crash of sore
arms and legs, of sweat and exhausted breaths. Trish is sitting on
the floor, legs crossed, and I'm on the couch, keeping as much
distance between us as possible.

"What if we can't stop?" she says, looking at me, then toward
the kitchen table.

I'm not sure what to do. Not sure what I want, what she
wants. Not sure what's possible. "We have to," I say dumbly. "I'm
leaving next month."

Even though she's heard me say this—even though she
helped me book my flight—she turns her head to me suddenly,
looking as if she's hearing the news for the first time.

Then, without a word, she nods her head, both of us feeling a storm of guilt and relief and loss for something we truly
never had.

The wondrous present . . .

Ken was my friend—my closest friend, I would say—and I was
obsessively mad about his wife. I loved the crazy woman and the
fire that burned along with her presence. She was challenging and
brilliant—my weakness. It was unacceptable what we were doing,
and she knew that. She knew it, but neither of us could help it.
We were stuck, victims of bad timing and worse choices. It wasn't
our fault, I would convince myself each time I collapsed, spent
and panting, onto her naked body. We simply couldn't help it; it
wasn't our fault. It was the universe, it was the circumstances of
our situation.

I was raised that way. I was taught as a young boy that nothing was my fault. My dad was always right, even when he wasn't,

and he taught his eldest son to think the same way. I was a spoiled child, but not by money. During the times I got to spend with my father, I was taught his arrogance. My father never owned up to any of his mistakes; he never had to. I learned that in life there was always someone else to blame. I tried to be a different father than he was, a better one.

Kimberly says I'm doing a great job at that. She praises me much more than I deserve, but I'll take it. She can dish it out, too—her mouth is worse than my university mates' after a twelve-pack of cheap piss-water beer.

"Put Karina to bed and I'll be waiting for you." Kimberly kisses me on the cheek and gently slaps my bum, winking and grinning as she prances into our bedroom.

I love that woman.

Karina makes a little burping sound in her sleep, and I gently rub at her back. One of her tiny hands rises up and grasps mine.

I still can't believe I'm a dad again. I'm old now. Patches of gray hair keep popping up here and there.

After Rose passed and it was just Smith and me, I never expected to have another child. Or to discover that I had already had another child. Still less than that, particularly given the way things started, I never expected to have a twenty-one-year-old son in my life as a friend and man. Hardin went from being my biggest regret to my greatest joy. I used to fear for his future, so much so that I hired him at Vance just to make sure he had a job.

What I didn't expect was for him to turn out to be a goddamn genius. He was struggling so hard during his teens that I thought he was going to ruin or end his life before it really ever began. He was so pissed off all the time, and the little shit that he was gave his poor mum hell.

I watched Hardin go from being a troubled and lonely young boy to a bestselling author and advocate for troubled youth. He's become everything I could have dreamed for him to be. Smith looks up to Hardin in every way, with the glaring exception of his tattoos, which they both love to argue over. Smith finds them tacky, and Hardin loves to show Smith each new tattoo he manages to somehow squeeze onto his already covered skin.

I look down at the sleeping beauty in her crib and switch on the night-light on the dresser while I silently promise this sweet, precious girl that I'll be the best father I can possibly be.

Smith

As a young man, he didn't know how to be a role model. He had absolutely no fucking idea why anyone would want to be like him, but the little boy did. The little dimpled boy followed him around every time he visited, and as the boy grew, so did he. The boy would end up being one of his closest friends, and by the time the boy was as tall as him, he was truly his brother.

Hardin is coming over again today, and I'm more excited than usual because he hasn't been here in a few months. I thought maybe he wasn't going to come back. When he moved, he promised he would make sure to visit every once in a while, as much as he could, he said. I like that he's kept his promise so far.

These past few days, my dad keeps making me do stuff to distract me, things like my math homework, unloading the dishwasher, and taking Kim's dog out to pee. I like taking the dog, Teddy—he's nice and really small, so I can carry him when he gets too lazy to walk. But still, I'm really distracted that Hardin's coming.

Today was long: school, piano lessons, and now homework time. Kimberly is singing in the other room. Man, she's so loud. Sometimes I think she thinks she sounds good, so I won't tell her that she doesn't. Her high-pitched notes sometimes scare her little dog.

Each time Hardin comes to my house, he brings me a book. I always read them, and then we talk or text a little about them later. Sometimes he gives me hard books that have language I can't understand, or books that my dad takes away because he thinks I'm too young to read them. With those, he always swats Hardin on the head with the book before putting it away for me for "someday."

I think it's funny when Hardin cusses at my dad. Which usually accompanies those thumps to the head.

Tessa told me once that Hardin used to teach me curse words when I was younger, but I don't remember that. Tessa always tells me things about when I was younger. She talks more than anyone else, except Kim—no one talks as much, or as loudly, as Kim. Tessa is pretty close, though.

As I pass the front door, the alarm system beeps a few times, and I look over to see a small screen pop up on the living room TV. Hardin's face, with his big nose, covers the little box screen. His neck is there now, his tattoos making it look like he scribbled on the screen. I laugh and press the speaker button.

"Did your dad change the code again?" Hardin asks, which is funny because his lips move faster on the screen than his voice goes through the speaker.

His voice is the same as my dad's almost, but slower. My grandma and grandpa talk like them, too, because they all were born in England. My dad says I've been there four times, but the only time I remember is last year, when we went to his friend's wedding.

My dad got hurt on that trip—I remember his leg looked like cow meat that someone ground up to cook and eat. It reminded me of *The Walking Dead* (but don't tell him I found a way to see some episodes). I helped Kim change his bandages, and they were so gross but they left some cool scars. Kim had to push him around in a wheelchair for a month; she said she did it because she loves him. If I was ever hurt and needed to be wheeled around, I'm sure she would push me, too.

I buzz Hardin in and walk to the kitchen as I hear his shoes stomping through the living room.

"Smith, honey," Kim says when she comes into the kitchen. "Do you want something to eat?" Today her hair is curled up around her face; she kind of looks like her dog, Teddy, whose hair is everywhere. I shake my head, and Hardin joins us.

"I do," Hardin says. "I'm hungry,"

"I didn't ask you, I asked Smith," she says, and wipes her hands on her blue dress.

Hardin laughs, a loud noise. Shaking his head, he looks at me. "Do you see how she treats me? She's terrible."

I laugh, too. Kim says Hardin picks on *her*. They're both too funny.

Kim opens the fridge and takes out a pitcher of juice. "You're one to talk."

Hardin laughs again and sits down on the chair next to me. In his hands are two small packages wrapped in white paper. No bows, no writing on the outside. I know they're mine, but I don't want to be impolite.

I stare at them and try to read the title of the books through the paper, but it's no use. I turn to the window and pretend to be looking outside so I don't seem too rude.

Hardin sets the packages down on the counter, and Kim hands me a cup of juice, then goes to the cabinet for some chips. My dad always tells Kim not to let me eat a lot of them, but she doesn't listen. My dad says she never does.

I grab for the bag, but Hardin swipes it and holds it over my head for a minute.

He smiles down at me. "Thought you weren't hungry."

The hole under his lip looks like someone drew a dot on his

face. He used to have a piercing, I remember. I always tell him to put it back. He tells me to stop listening to Tessa.

"I am now." I jump up and grab the bag back from him, and it makes a loud crinkling sound in my hands. Hardin shrugs, and he looks happy. He thinks I'm funny. He tells me all the time.

Once I've unclipped the bag, he takes a handful of chips and shoves them into his big mouth. "Are you going to open your gifts before you shove your face full of crisps?" Crumbs of food fly out while he talks, and Kim makes a grossed-out face.

"Christian!" she yells for my dad.

I laugh, and Hardin pretends to be scared.

I scoot the bag of chips away. "Well, since you asked, I want to open the books first."

Hardin picks up both packages and holds them to his chest. "Books, huh? What makes you think I brought you books?"

"Because you always do." I reach for the thickest one, and he slides it across the counter.

"Touché," he says—whatever that means.

Forgetting my manners a little bit, I tear at the paper until a colorful cover is revealed. It shows a boy with a wizard hat.

"*The Chamber of Secrets*," I read the title out loud. I'm happy about this book. I just finished the one before it.

When I look up at Hardin, he pushes his hair away from his face. I agree with my dad—he should get a haircut. His hair is as long as Kim's now.

He points to the book. "It's from Landon again. He likes that tiny wizard."

My dad comes into the kitchen and cusses at Hardin. Hardin slaps him on the shoulder, and Kim calls them children. I act more like a grown-up than they do, she says.

"Well, that's nice of him," my dad says. "Smith, make sure you say thank you to Tessa's friend."

Hardin scoffs. "Tessa's friend? He's *my* brother." He smiles and scratches the tattoos on his arms. I want tattoos like him when I'm older. My dad says no, but Kim told me that once I'm out of the house he really can't stop me.

I can get whatever I want when I'm a grown-up.

"He's not your *real* brother," I tell him. My dad explained that Landon isn't his real brother.

Hardin's smile goes away, and he nods. "Sure. But he's my brother, still."

While I ponder what he means by this, Kim asks my dad if he's hungry, and Hardin looks around the kitchen. He seems a little sad for some reason all of a sudden.

"Your dad is my dad. So is Landon's mom your mom?" I ask.

Hardin shakes his head no, and my dad kisses Kim on her shoulder, which, of course, makes her smile. He always seems to make her smile.

"Sometimes people can be family without sharing parents."

Hardin stares at my face like I'm supposed to say something back. Really, I don't know what he means, but if he wants Landon to be his brother, too, that's okay with me. Landon is really nice. He lives in New York, so I don't see him very much. Tessa is out there, too. My dad has an office there; it's shiny and smells like a hospital.

Hardin touches my hand, and I look at him. "Just because Landon is my brother doesn't mean you aren't, too. You know that, don't ya?"

I'm embarrassed a little because Kim is making a face like she's going to cry and my dad looks scared.

"I know," I tell him, and look at the Harry Potter book. "Landon can be my brother, too."

Hardin looks happy when he smiles, and I look up to see Kim is making that face again.

"Yeah, he sure can." He looks at Kim and says, "Stop it already, lady! You would think someone died, with the way she's acting."

My dad calls Hardin a bad name, and Kim jumps out of the way when Hardin throws an apple at his chest. He looks like a baseball player, the way he snags it out of the air . . . and takes a bite, which makes us all laugh.

Hardin slides the other book across the counter, and I grab it. The paper is harder to tear on this one, and I get a small cut from one of the corners. I wince a little but hope nobody else notices. If I tell anyone, Kim will make me wash it right now and put a bandage on, but I really just want to see what this one is.

As the last piece is torn away, I see a big cross on the cover of the book.

"Dra cula?" I sound out the word. I've heard of this before. It's a vampire book.

My dad moves away from Kim and walks around the counter. "Dracula? You've got to be kidding me. He's not even ten!" He holds his hand out for the book.

I look at Kim for help. She pushes her lips together and gives Hardin a mean look.

"Usually I'll take your side," she says. Hardin calls her a liar, but she keeps talking. "But Dracula? Out of all things? Harry Potter and Dracula—what a mix."

My dad nods and stands still like he's some big statue, the way he always does when he wants to show he's right.

After a moment, Hardin rolls his eyes and tugs at the collar of his black T-shirt. "Sorry, man, your dad's being a tool. You can read the *Chamber* book now, and when I come next time, I'll bring you another—"

"One with no violence," my dad interrupts.

Hardin sighs. "Sure, sure. No violence," he says in a funny voice.

I laugh again. My dad smiles, and Kim is hugging him.

I wonder how long it will be until I see Hardin again.

"When will you be back?" I ask.

Hardin scratches his chin. "Hmm, I'm not sure. A month, maybe?"

A month feels really long, but I suppose the Harry Potter book *is* pretty long . . .

Hardin leans a little closer to me. "I will come back, though, and bring a book every time," he whispers.

"Like my dad did for you?" I ask him, and his eyes look at my dad. Our dad. Hardin doesn't call him dad, though. He calls him Vance, which is our last name. Not Hardin's; his is Scott. He got it from his fake dad.

When I tried to call my dad Vance, he told me I would be grounded until I turned thirty if I said it again. I don't want to be grounded that long, so I call him Dad.

Hardin shifts his body in the chair. "Yeah, like he did for me."

He seems sad again, but I can't tell for sure. Hardin is sad, then mad, then laughing, all the time.

He's really weird.

"How did you know about that, Smith?" my dad asks.

Hardin's face turns red, and he mouths, *Don't tell him.*

I lift my hands up and reach for more chips. "Hardin says not to tell."

Hardin slaps his forehead, then mine, and Kim smiles at us both. She smiles so much, all the time. I like when she laughs, too; it sounds nice.

My dad walks closer to us.

"Well, Hardin doesn't make the rules, remember?" My dad puts his hands on my shoulders and rubs. It feels good when he does that. "Tell me what Hardin said, and I'll take you for ice cream and buy you a new track for your train."

My train is my favorite toy. My dad always buys me new

tracks to add, and last month Kim helped me move the whole thing to an empty room, so now I have a whole room just for my trains.

Hardin looks like he's sweating. But he doesn't look mad, so I decide I can tell my dad.

Plus, there's the new train stuff I'll get.

"He said you brought him books like this." I hold up the heavy books. "And that it made him happy when he was a little boy like me."

Hardin turns his head, and my dad looks surprised by what I said. His eyes are shiny now, and he's staring at me.

"Did he, now?" My dad's voice is weird.

"Yeah, he did," I say, nodding.

Hardin stays quiet, but he looks back at me. His face is red, and his eyes are shiny like my dad's. I look at Kim, and she has her hand over her mouth.

"Did I say something bad?" I ask them.

My dad and Hardin say "No, no" at the same time.

"You didn't say anything wrong, little man." My dad puts one of his hands on my back and one on Hardin's.

Usually when he tries this, Hardin moves away.

Today he doesn't.

Hessa

New York is having one of its hottest summers when Tessa has Auden. It's Tuesday, release day for my newest novel, and Tessa and I are lying on the carpet, staring up at the ceiling fan we installed just last week.

We keep redecorating our small apartment, for some insane reason. We know we won't end up staying here, yet we keep putting money into this place. Our very impulsive decision to completely redo our son's nursery when he was only eight weeks old has ended up being much more of a task than we expected. The renovation has Auden's crib in our room, centered at the end of our bed. I find it stuffy and cramped, like we're refugees in a tiny boat, ones who decided to give their five-year-old, our daughter, Emery, the main cabin while we took the escape raft.

Tess loves it.

Some nights she falls asleep with her feet facing the headboard and holds his hand while they both sleep. Half of the time I wake her to right her position by nibbling at her ear, rubbing her tense shoulders. The other half, I wrap my arms around her legs and just sleep that way. I have to touch her in some way. She always ends up next to me by the morning, nibbling on *my* ear or rubbing *my* lower back.

I already feel like an old man; my back aches from my shitty excuse for a writing posture: sitting slouched on the couch or cross-legged on the floor with my laptop on my actual lap.

Tessa points up to the fan. "It's crooked. We should repaint."

Currently, the nursery is painted a soft, Easter yellow to go along with a gender-neutral room. We wanted to keep the space light, having learned firsthand what a mistake—and subsequent pain—it was to assume one's daughter wanted cotton-candy-pink walls. Those we painted before she was born. But as soon as Emery learned that she didn't really like pink, it took us three afternoons and three coats of green to cover that damn color. We learned our lesson from that, and Tessa learned a few new swear words from me. So, insisting that a muted pastel yellow was all the rage, we went with that; we all know how I just *have* to keep up with the Joneses and please my lady. That, or the fact that it'll be a really easy color to paint over when Auden starts expressing preferences.

The nursery contains several different shades of yellow. I didn't realize there were shades of yellow, or that they could clash so much. Each has come from Tessa's stops at IKEA and Pottery Barn, which I swear occur at least three times a week. She finds all sorts of things she loves and hugs them to her chest, exclaiming things like "This decorative pillow will look soooo good!" and "This toy is so cute I could eat it up!" And then she tucks said item under a sofa cushion or into a random cubbyhole in the nursery that she hadn't filled yet.

The room has ended up being a big ball of undulating sunshine that Tessa can't be in for longer than ten minutes without getting nauseous. She made me promise her that I would never again let her decorate a room—especially not a nursery. And now she wants me to repaint it all again.

The things I do for this woman.

And I'd do more. I do all I can.

One thing I could do for her is, by some magical means, make it so she can leave more of her work at her office. She's been so tired lately, and it's driving me fucking mad. She won't slow down, but I know how much she loves her job. Her career is her third baby. She works so incredibly hard to produce the most beautiful weddings imaginable. She's new, brand-new in the industry, but she's fucking amazing at this.

Tessa was terrified when she'd brought up her potential career change with me. She was pacing back and forth in our small kitchen. I had just loaded the dishwasher and "finished" painting Emery's nails. I thought I was doing fine with the role reversal, but Emery made Tess fire me when I claimed that the mess I was making on her tiny hands was okay, that the red polish just looked like she had killed something.

I hadn't realized any child of mine could have such a weak stomach and sour sense of humor.

"So, I want to turn down the promotion at Vance and go back to school," Tessa said casually from the kitchen table. Or what I took as casually. Emery sat quietly, having no idea of the impact such adult choices have on people's lives.

"Really?" I rubbed a towel over a wet plate to dry it.

Tessa tucked her bottom lip between her teeth, and her eyes went wide. "I've been thinking about it so much lately, and if I don't do it, I'll go insane."

She didn't have to explain that to me. Everyone needs a change sometimes. Even I got bored between books, and Tessa came up with the idea of me substitute teaching two or three days a month at Valsar, Emery's elementary school, where Landon happens to work. Granted, I quit after three days, but it was an entertaining experiment and earned me brownie points with my girl.

As always, I encouraged Tessa to do what she wanted. I wanted her to be happy, and it's not like we needed the money. I'd just signed my next contract with Vance, my third in the last two years. The money from *After* went straight into an account for the kids. Well, after I bought Tessa a "please forgive me for being a fucking idiot repeatedly" gift. It was simple: a charm bracelet made of metal to replace her old one, which was made of yarn.

Over the years, the yarn tore apart, but Tessa kept the charms and she was overly excited that the new bracelet had the option of adding, changing the charms as often as you like. It seems like a pretty stupid concept to me, but she loved it.

The next morning, Tessa sat down with Vance and politely declined the promotion, then cried for an hour when she got home. I knew she would feel guilty for leaving her job, but she won't be upset long. I knew Kim and Vance would reassure her every day until her two weeks' notice was over.

When she got her first wedding-planning client, she squealed and I watched her come alive in a way I hadn't seen before. I still didn't know why this insane woman stayed with me after all the stupid shit I did when I was young, but I was pretty fucking happy that she did, if only to see her as excited as she now was.

Of course, Tessa nailed that first wedding and got recommendation after recommendation, enabling her to hire two employees after a only a few short months. I was proud of her, and she was proud of herself. Looking back, it seemed silly that she had ever worried about failing. Tessa's one of those annoying people who touch a pile of shit and it turns to gold.

That's pretty much what happened with me.

She worked and worked, and she was overworking herself again after we had Auden.

I nudge her. "You need a night off. You're practically falling asleep on the floor while staring at the ceiling fan."

A playful elbow is pressed into my hip. "I'm fine. You're the one who barely sleeps at night," she whispers into my neck.

I know she's right, but I have deadlines and no time to award myself with sleep. Besides, when I'm stuck on a passage I'm writing, it stays glued to me and I can't sleep. Still, I hate the idea of her noticing my lack of sleep, since she'll always worry about me much more than I will myself.

"I mean it. You need to take a break. You're still recovering from that little monster tearing you open," I say, and slide my hand up her shirt and rub her stomach.

She flinches. "Don't," she groans, trying to push my hands off her soft skin. I hate how insecure she's become since having our son. Auden's birth did more damage to her body than Emery's, but to me she's sexier than ever. I hate that the touch of my hand makes her uncomfortable like this.

"Baby . . ." I move my hand away, but only so I can lean up on my elbow. Looking down at her, I shake my head.

Pressing two warm fingers to my lips, she smiles. "I know this part of the novel. This is where you give me the heroic husbandly speech about how I earned my scars and I'm much more beautiful for having done so," Tessa says, giving the words at the end a dramatic flare.

She's always been such a smartass.

"No, Tess, this is where I *show* you how I feel when I look at you."

I move my hand to her breast and squeeze just hard enough to ignite her, letting her body warm up to me. I catch her moan before she does, and she whimpers when I find her hard nipple and pinch it beneath her clothing.

She's done for. I know it; she knows it. She accepts it openly, and I react as fast as I can.

My hands quickly find the leg of her shorts and slide under the fabric there. Sure enough, there's a damp spot at the front of her panties. I love the feel of her wetness and crave the taste of it on my tongue. I take my fingers away and lift them to my lips. Tessa moans and pulls my index and middle fingers to her mouth and sucks their tips.

Goddamn, this woman ruins me.

Her eyes are glued to mine as her teeth nip my fingertips. I push my body against hers, letting her feel how hard my cock is from her little tease-fest. I pull at the waistband of her cotton shorts and push them down her thighs and to her feet. She kicks them furiously when her panties get stuck there. She wants it now, needs me now. I suck at the skin on her neck and feel her hand grip my cock. She's as frantic as I am as she undresses me. By the time she climbs on top of me, she has me down to my socks. Tessa's insecurities seem to disappear as she lowers her body down on mine and brings her wet lips to my hard skin. Her warm tongue swipes across the tip, earning her a drop of me on her tongue. She keeps her mouth moving at a steady pace, taking more and more of me as I moan her name.

I lay my head back against the floor and reach up to grip her chest. Her tits are still inflated from the breastfeeding—one body change she *loves*, and I'm sure as hell not complaining about having even more of her to play with.

"Fuck, I love your tits," I say as she slides her mouth down my length.

Tessa's mouth draws harder on me, hugging me as I feel the tension building up my back. Just as I weave my hands through her hair, she pulls back, licking her lips while her eyes stay on mine. She lifts herself up on her elbows and brings her chest to my groin. I pant like a dog waiting for his owner to pet him after a day alone in a cage. Tessa pushes her beautiful tits together and slides my cock between them. With three of her movements, I come on her skin. As I catch my breath, Tessa's tongue darts out between her lips and she gives me a shy smile, her cheeks flushed from the way her body responds to pleasing me.

She lifts herself to her feet, then, looking down at her chest, says, "I'm going to need a shower."

Still panting, I grab my black T-shirt from the floor and lift it to her chest. She pushes her hand out, making a face at me, and moves toward the door. Over the years she has become less and less fond of me cleaning up any bodily fluids with my T-shirts. It's apparently inappropriate and that's what towels are for, she warns each time.

I follow her into the bathroom, ticking off in my mind all the ways I'm going to repay her in the shower.

Her chest looks amazing pushed up against the glass. The mirror on the wall there has to be one of the best things in this apartment.

Hessa

Easter

Hardin, Auden is up." Tessa's voice breaks through my cloud of
sleep. "We need to wake Emery up and let them find their
Easter baskets."

She shakes my shoulder, begging me to wake up.

"Hardin, come on." Her voice is low, but excitement rings
through her barely contained whispers.

If this is how I'm woken up for the rest of my life, I'll be a
lucky bastard.

I groan, barely opening my eyes as I pull her to my chest.
"What's the ruckus?" I ask, pressing my lips against her temple.
Her hair sticks to my face, and I brush the strands away. She's
topless, her soft breasts pressed against my side.

She sighs, wrapping a stubbly leg through mine. I flinch away
in jest, and she playfully nudges me. "The kids need to find their
baskets and I want to start breakfast, so you need to get up."

And like that, like she's not totally turning me on, she wiggles
her body free of mine and rolls over to climb out of bed.

"Come on, baby," I complain, missing the warmness of her
body.

As she opens the dresser, I glance over at her naked chest. A
whine leaves my throat, and I wish I'd woken up earlier to keep
her in the bed with me. I would be inside of her right now, buried
deep inside her warm, wet . . .

A pillow smacks me in the face. "Get out of bed! We have a busy day today, you know."

Sighing, I roll out of our king-size bed and toss a shirt over my head before she throws something else my way. She spent months redecorating the place only a little bit ago; I'm sure she doesn't want to damage any of the precious decorations she picked out with the insane decorator she convinced me we needed. The guy was a loon, painting the living room a salmon color, then repainting it a week later with a slightly less nauseating shade.

"I know, darling. Baskets, bunnies, eggs, and shit." I catch my reflection in the mirror hanging on the wall and run my fingers over my hair. Using the band on my wrist, I pull my hair up and look over at a glaring Tessa. The corners of her mouth are attempting to stay straight, but I can see the struggle.

"Yes, and shit." She laughs finally and reaches for her hairbrush. "We have to be at Landon's at two. Karen and Ken have flown in, and I haven't even made the potato salad we're supposed to bring."

After finishing with her long hair, she goes to hand me the brush with a smirk.

I shake my head. I don't need to brush it; my fingers do the trick.

"I'll make the potatoes while you get ready," I offer. "Now let's go watch the kids find their baskets."

She makes a face, judging my ability to make the potatoes for her an iffy proposition at best. I'm fully capable of this . . . except maybe last Christmas, when I burned the chicken.

Tessa is dressed in white cotton pants and a navy-blue T-shirt; her skin has a hint of a tan from spending time out on the patio tending to her small garden. She loves our small yard here in Brooklyn; it's her favorite part of the new town house I bought her to celebrate my newest book deal.

In the hallway she stops by Emery's room. "Wake her up and meet me in the living room." She kisses my cheek and yells for our son. I slap her ass as she walks away, and she rolls her eyes at me—the usual.

When I go into Emery's room, she's lying sprawled out on the bed, her long legs hanging over the edge of her small Disney-themed bedspread.

"Em." I gently shake her arm.

She stirs but keeps her eyes shut.

When I do it again, she whines "Nooo" and turns onto her stomach and buries her face in the pillow.

Dramatic little one, she is.

"Baby, you have to get up. Auden is going to take all your Easter candy if you don't . . ."

And just like that she's hopping out of bed, her blond hair a wild mess. Her hair is wavy like mine and thick like her mum's.

"He *better not!*" she declares as she pushes her feet into her slippers and bolts from the room.

When I catch up, she's pulling open every cabinet in the kitchen.

"*Where is mine?*" she shrieks.

Tessa laughs, and Auden messily unwraps a chocolate egg with his chubby little fingers before shoving the entire thing into his mouth. He chews for a moment, then opens his mouth wide.

Tessa leans over to him and pulls a piece of aluminum wrapping from his tongue, and he smiles, chocolate covering his crooked teeth. He lost his front tooth last week, and it's absolutely fucking adorable. I give him shit about his lisp, because that's a perk of being a parent: I get to tease them when I please. It's a rite of passage.

"Mom!" Emery complains from the hallway closet. "Dad hid mine—didn't he? That's why I can't find it!"

I laugh at her dramatics. "Yes. Yes, I did."

She's a sweet girl, just full of sass and opinions at the young age of eleven. It's why she doesn't have many friends.

Emery continues rummaging through the town house as Auden devours half his basket of candy, tossing little strings of fake grass onto the floor.

"There's a drum in there, too," I tell him. He nods, mouth still full of candy, not seeming to be too interested in anything that isn't made of chocolate.

"Daddy." Emery walks into the kitchen with empty hands. "Can you please tell me where you hid my basket? This is too hard. Harder than last year." She stands next to where I sit on the barstool and wraps her arms around my waist. She's so tall for her age, and she's trying to play me for a fool.

"Pleeeeeeease," she begs.

"You aren't fooling me, my dear. I'll give you a hint, but a hug and a sweet voice won't work to bribe me. You have to work for things, remember?"

She purses her lips and hugs me tighter. "I know, Daddy," she says into my chest.

I smirk at this new tactic and look over to find Tessa watching Emery with suspicious eyes.

"It's somewhere you never, ever go. It's where your clothes are that you refuse to help us fold." I rub my hand over her back, and she unlatches her arms from my neck.

"The washer machine!" Auden shouts, and Emery squeals. She rushes over to her brother and touches the top of his head. He smiles, looking awfully like a little puppy as he gets praised by his big sister.

Within a minute, Emery is running into the kitchen with her basket. Tiny chocolate Easter eggs fall onto the floor. Ignoring them, she continues to dig at the full basket. Tessa stands up to help her clean up the mess Emery herself doesn't seem interested in cleaning at all.

Emery sits down on the floor. Her basket rests on her crossed legs, and she's scarfing down a handful of colorful jelly beans. I turn toward Tessa and Auden. He's in her arms with his arms wrapped around her neck. In her arms he looks almost as big as his mum. I have no fucking idea where the time has gone or how I—a fucked-up rebellious little shit—produced such empathetic and calm children.

I mean, Emery has had her share of tantrums, sure. Like when she threw a plant into a wall. But that wasn't hard to deal with: I took her door off the hinges. I don't fucking play that spoiled-child anger bullshit. She doesn't have anything to be angry about at eleven, not the way I did. She has two parents who love her and are always here.

Really, they are both great kids.

Tessa and I are always here for both of our kids. They've never gone without a hug, kiss, and at least two mushy *I love you*s before the end of each day. Emery gets some of the trendy stuff that circulates as social currency among the popular kids at school. I never want my kids to be like I was, the kid with the holes in his shoes. I want them to know how it feels to want things like toys and then teach them a way to earn them, by doing simple things like hugs and kisses on the cheek and encouragement, which are never going to be scarce around here. We decided that the moment they were born. I wasn't going to be like my father, either one of them. I was going to raise children who knew they were loved, never having to guess or assume that they were alone in the world. The world is too big to be alone in, especially for two little Scotts.

I stopped the pattern of piss-poor dads right in its tracks before I could ruin two little lives.

Within an hour, Emery is passed out, one leg sticking straight up on the back of the couch and one arm dangling over the side. Auden is on his favorite couch that, while supposedly "miniature," takes up too much space but that Tessa brought home over my protestations anyway. The couch came complete with a nice overpriced ottoman, which also takes up too much space for a Brooklyn living room. I was overruled in the furniture discussion, so here I am staring at my six-year-old, who's sprawled out in a candy coma with traces of chocolate still smeared on his square little chin. He's got more of me than his mum in him.

"Look how sweet they are," Tessa says from behind me. When I face her, she looks exhausted; her eyes are cloudy and her skin is slightly pale.

I touch my lips to her cheeks, hoping to kiss some of the color back into them. She sighs, and I feel her hands rest on my stomach.

"What do you plan on doing during this nap time?" I ask her. She always manages to use every valuable minute of the kids' nap time—which has been getting shorter and shorter—for productive things. She's too busy, that woman, but she doesn't listen to shit I say, so there's nothing to be done here.

I watch as she mentally checks items off her list. "Well," she says slowly, then begins spouting off things like "call Fee about the cake" and "get Posey to double-check those bouquets" and something else I don't hear when I bring my hand to the front of her loose pants. She eyes me carefully as I tug at the drawstring and dip my fingers into her panties.

"Don't distract me," she complains, but pushes her body toward me, making me apply more pressure.

"You're working too much," I tell her for the thirtieth time this week. She rolls her eyes for the thirty-first.

She grabs my free wrist and lifts my hand to her chest. "Says the man who doesn't sleep for days when he has a deadline."

She's open to being distracted by me today, a little different than usual, but I'll sure as hell take it. I palm her roughly and watch as her tits push up to her neck and back down. She whines, whimpering for more of me. I'll give it to her.

Grabbing her hand, I lead her down the hallway. She walks quickly, anxious to get to our room. The moment we step through the doorway, Tessa slams the heavy thing, nearly knocking loose a giant framed painting of the kids from the wall. When she'd first proposed getting it done, I found it creepy, but Tessa loved the idea of having an image of them the size of a damn billboard in here. The only part of this I had a say in was that it be placed on the opposite side of the room from our bed. No way am I staring at an abstract neon-painted version of my children while fucking my wife. No fucking way.

"Come here," I tell her, beckoning her to my lap. I'm sitting on the edge of our king-size bed. We shared a bed with both of our children sporadically over the last few months. Auden went through a nightmare phase, one where I kept myself awake at night wondering if this was something he had inherited from me. Emery followed suit, being jealous of her younger brother, and came asking in whispers for protection from her "bad dreams," which I knew wasn't true. She was wiping her eyes like she was six again and everything.

Both of them lay between us.

It was awesome, let me tell you.

"Hardin?" Tessa's voice is soft, raspy, and her eyes are on mine. "What are you thinking about?" she asks. Her fingers trail up and down my stomach, her nails gently scratching at my skin.

"The kids and when they used to sleep in our bed." I shrug, smiling at her.

"That's awkward," she says with a shake of her head. But a smile peeps through her lip.

"It's only awkward because it's me who's distracted instead of you this time, my darling."

I tease her hardened nipples, and she moans. I lift her shirt over her head. It drops to the floor, and she shakes her hair back, making her look wild, red cheeks and pink lips. Wild blond hair and hungry eyes. I reach out, tracing my finger over the lining of her black lace bra. This woman wears the sexiest lace bras. I dip under the material and tug at her nipples. "Lie down, baby," I instruct. She drops her pants and panties, kicking them to the floor, and lies back on the bed. She reaches for a pillow and tucks it under her head. Her eyes tell me exactly what she wants: she wants me to go down on her. It's her favorite lately.

She's tired, worn down, and her feet hurt, so she simply wants to be pampered. This will be reciprocated, of course— my woman returns the favor, taking my cock down her throat on mornings when the kids let us sleep past 7 a.m. Tessa lifts her legs up, bends them, and opens her thighs wide directly in front of me. I bite down on my lip, trying to squash a groan before it falls from my lips.

She's soaking, glistening under the light, and I have no self-control when it comes to her. I nearly lunge forward, pressing my open mouth against her soft, wet skin. My tongue moves in a single harsh line down her, sucking gently as I go.

Her hips shift, pushing her body against me. I hook my arms around her thighs and roughly pull her to the edge of the bed. She yelps, an adorable little sound of surprise mixed with her excitement. My hands are gripping her ass and my mouth is devouring her as she moans my name mixed in with *yes* and *oh my* and a thousand other dirty things.

I love her little exclamations of encouragement. They cause me to make her legs shake, to make her hands clutch the sheets. Now she's gripping my hair, an entire handful. I fucking love it.

"Har-din . . ." Her voice breaks, and I bring a finger to her pussy, sliding it in, driving her mad. I circle her clit with my tongue, humming and circling, humming and circling. I taste her as she comes, the sweetest flavor.

I come up for air and lift myself up to lay my head on her stomach as she catches her breath. She tugs at my hair, dragging me up her body. I'm still hard, and lying on top of her naked leaves little room for anything except sex in my list of wants and needs. Tessa knows this, which is why she's lifting up off the bed again, rubbing herself against me.

"You want me to fuck you? You haven't had enough?" I ask her, pressing my hardness against her wetness.

"I'll never have enough . . ." she whines, and I whimper as she wraps her hand around my cock and guides it inside her. I make one long drag inside her and watch in awe as her eyes roll back in her head. Her tits are pressed up against my chest, her thighs wrapped around my waist.

"More," she begs, wanting me to move inside of her. I oblige, thrusting quickly. One of her hands is in my hair, and the other is digging into the skin of my back.

I won't last long.

At all.

I feel her legs tightening around me, and I reach my high at the same time, riding out my last few pumps as her body turns to gel with mine. She keeps her eyes closed, and I collapse next to her.

As my breathing slows, I glance over at Tessa. Her blue-gray eyes are closed, her lips are parted, and she's just as beautiful as she was the day I met her.

I can barely remember the kid I was when I met her, but every detail of our lives together since runs through me like a song.

This stubborn woman still refuses to legally marry me, but she's my wife in every way that matters, and she's the mother of my beautiful children. We want to have at least one more, when her work slows down.

I'm anxious about bringing another child into the world. I get a little worried each time.

The responsibility to raise decent human beings weighs heavily on me, but Tessa carries half of the weight and reassures me that we are great parents. I'm not like my father was. I'm my own man. Certainly, I've made my share of mistakes. But I served my penance and came out forgiven. I'm not a particularly religious man, but I know there has to be something bigger than Tess and me at play here. My world went from nothing to everything, and I feel pride in who I am now. I see my own light in my children's eyes, and I hear my happiness in their laughter.

I'm proud of the difference I make in local teenagers' lives with my fund-raisers for the community center. I've met thousands of people whose lives were affected by my words on pages. I fought for so long to keep everything in, but once I let go, my heart opened up. It would have been selfish for me not to share my experiences, not to help teens who suffer from addiction and mental-health disorders. Through the years, I learned not to focus on the past, but only look toward the future. I'm aware of how cliché and just flat-out fucking sappy my thoughts sound, but it's my truth.

I lived in darkness for so long; I want to help bring light to others.

I'm blessed with a family that I couldn't have dreamed of, and I'm raising kids who will be better than I ever was.

Tessa's head falls to the side, and I brush her hair away from her sleeping face. She's been my calm, my fire, my breath, my pain, and no matter what we've gone through, every second was worth getting to the life we have now.

I dragged Tess and myself through hell and back, but here we are—After everything, we made it to our own version of heaven.

Acknowledgments

I feel like all of my acknowledgements for this book are exactly the same as the last, but the same wonderful people helped me with them—so thank you all!

Adam Wilson: Once again, I thank you for working so hard with me. I learn so much from you and your patience with me. We've had five books (that are really the length of ten) in one year, and that's just fucking nuts. I can't wait for the next three ☺.

Kristin Dwyer: You're the bomb, dude. You keep me organized (as much as possible, since I just started to actually save dates in my calendar). Thanks for everything!

Wattpad: Thank you for still being my home base and staying organic and giving millions of people a place to do what they love.

Ursula Uriarte: It's so crazy to think that you came into my life as a blogger who happened to like my books and now you're one of my closest friends. Even though I still can't spell your name, you are so, *so* important to me and to Hardin and Tessa. You love them like I do, and that means a lot to them. (They told me!)

Vilma and RK: I love you both and appreciate your friendship so much. You talked me through the stages of writing this book and listened to my freak-outs. I love you both.

Ashleigh Gardner: Thank you for being the best agency friend I could have!

Thanks to the copyeditors and production staff, who worked very hard under such tight deadlines.

A huge thank-you to all of my foreign publishers, from the editors to the publicists and everyone in between. You all work so hard to translate and market my books across the globe, and it means so much to me and the readers. I've had the best time visiting so many places and meeting so many readers all over the world.

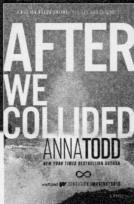